right where
we belong

Also by Brenda Novak

brenda novak

right where we belong

mira

mira

ISBN-13: 978-0-7783-3108-7

Right Where We Belong

For questions and comments about the quality of this book, please contact us at CustomerService@Harlequin.com.

MIRABooks.com

BookClubbish.com

Printed in U.S.A.

Dear Reader,

Many of my Silver Springs books are based on men who faced extreme difficulty while growing up and were sent to a boys ranch called New Horizons for reformation. Aiyana Turner, who started New Horizons, has dedicated her life to making the ranch's students whole, and the love she offers has succeeded in many instances.

This story is about Gavin, one of the boys she adopted when he was first sent to her. Gavin's unique in that he's been able to overcome his tragic childhood better than the others in the Turner family. Not only is he functional, but his background has made him sensitive to the needs of those around him. He knows how to help and is willing to do so. That makes him a special hero, which is lucky for the heroine of this story. Savanna Gray is in a world of hurt, and Gavin's just the man to make life a little easier.

I've often been curious about those women who—to their utter shock—find out that their husband is a rapist or a murderer. All the press is dedicated to the crime and the perpetrator. We never get to hear how their families quietly picked up the pieces and moved on— if they were able to do that. This is a romance but also a story about overcoming such a terrible blow.

I spend a lot of time on Facebook interacting with my readers. If you're on Facebook, too, definitely like my page at www.Facebook.com/brendanovakauthor. Also join my online book group. It consists of eight thousand of the most fabulous bookworms, and we have so many fun things going on (group T-shirts, personalized and autographed bookmarks, monthly "professional reader boxes," a birthday program, an annual in-person event, a commemorative pin for anyone who's read more than fifty Novak novels, and more)! You can find the link to join and learn all about it on my website at www.brendanovak.com.

Here's hoping you love Gavin and Savanna's story...

Brenda Novak

right where we belong

To Debra Watson Duncan,
a member of my online book group
and one of my favorite readers. Thanks for
all the love and support you give me, Debra!

CHAPTER ONE

"You knew! You *had* to have known!"

The vitriol in those words caused the hair on the back of Savanna Gray's neck to stand on end. She was just trying to pick up a gallon of milk at the supermarket with her kids, had never dreamed she might be accosted—although since her husband's arrest, it felt like everyone in town was staring daggers at her. The crimes Gordon committed had shaken the small, insular town of Nephi, Utah, to the core.

"Don't you dare run off!" someone said behind her. "I know you heard me."

Savanna froze. She *had* been about to flee. Her emotions were so raw she could barely make herself leave the house these days. She wished she could hole away with the curtains drawn and never face her neighbors again. But she had two children who were depending on her, and she was all they had left. Those children now looked up at her expectantly, and her son, Branson, who was eight, said, "Mommy, I think that lady's talking to you."

Gripping her shopping cart that much tighter, Savanna swung it around. She was determined to do a better job of defending herself against this type of thing than she'd done in the past. But then she recognized Meredith Caine.

A videotape of Meredith—clothes torn, mascara smeared and lip bleeding while her sister, who was with her now, tried to comfort her—had played on the news several times while police searched for the man who'd attacked her as she carried a load of laundry down to the basement of her apartment building. That man was Savanna's husband. Since his arrest, Savanna's house had been egged—twice. Someone had driven onto her lawn and peeled out, leaving deep ruts. And someone else had thrown a bottle at her parked car that'd broken all over the driveway. But she'd never been directly confronted by one of Gordon's victims, only their friends or family or others in the community who were outraged by the assaults.

Facing Meredith wasn't easy. Savanna wished she could melt into the floor and disappear—do anything to avoid this encounter. Meredith didn't understand. Savanna had watched her on TV with the same compassion and fear all the other women in the area felt. She'd had no idea she was *living* with the culprit, *sleeping* with him—and enabling him to operate without suspicion because of the illusion she helped create that he was a good family man. She'd thought he *was* a good family man, or she wouldn't have married him!

"Meredith, don't do this. Let's go." Her sister tried to drag her off, but Meredith remained rooted to the spot, eyes shining with outrage.

"Where *were* you, huh?" she cried. "How could you have missed that your husband was out stalking women at night?"

Gordon had been a mining equipment field service technician for the last seven years of their nine-year marriage, which meant he drove long distances to reach various mines and worked irregular hours. Savanna had believed he was on the road or repairing equipment, like he said. She'd had no idea he was out prowling around. Despite what Meredith and everyone else seemed to believe—that simply by virtue of being close to him she should've been able to spot such a large defect in his character—he'd never done anything to give himself away.

"I thought… I thought he was doing his job," she said.

"You believed he was *working* all those hours?" Meredith scoffed.

"I did." She hadn't been checking up on him. She'd been trying to manage the kids, the house and her own job working nine to five for a local insurance agent. Besides, Gordon always had a ready excuse for when he came home later than expected, a *believable* excuse. Another piece of equipment had failed and he'd had to drive back to his last location. His van wouldn't start, and he'd had to stay over to get a new battery. The weather was too terrible to begin the long trek home.

Were those excuses something a wife *should* have been leery of?

"Maybe you should've paid a little more attention to what he was doing," Meredith snapped.

Savanna began to tremble. "I wish I had. Look, I'd be happy to talk to you—to explain my side so that maybe you could understand. But please, let's not do this here, in front of my children."

Meredith didn't even glance at Branson and Alia. She was too angry, too eager to inflict some of the pain she'd suffered on Savanna. "Your husband didn't care about *my* children when he put his hands around my neck and nearly choked the life out of me. Thanks to him, I haven't been able to have sex with my own husband since!"

"Meredith!" Her sister gasped, obviously more aware of the children and, likely, the attention this confrontation was drawing.

Alia, Savanna's six-year-old daughter, pulled on Savanna's sleeve. "Mommy, why did Daddy choke her?" she whispered loudly, her big blue eyes filling with tears.

"Your father..." Savanna's throat had tightened until she could scarcely breathe, let alone talk. "He made some poor choices, honey. Like we talked about when he went away, remember?"

"Choices?" Meredith jumped on that immediately. "That man is pure evil. But keep lying—to them and yourself."

At that point, Meredith's sister managed to pull her away. They left Savanna standing in front of the cooler that held the milk and cheese, feeling as if she'd been slugged in the stomach.

"Show's over," she mumbled to those who'd stopped to watch the drama unfold.

"The kids at school say Daddy grabbed three women and ripped off their clothes," Branson said, his voice small as his gaze followed Meredith and her sister to the checkout register at the opposite end of the aisle. "That's true, isn't it."

He wasn't asking. He was just now realizing that Gordon wasn't innocent as they'd all stubbornly hoped. That her son would have to accept such a terrible truth, especially at his tender age, would've broken Savanna's heart—if it hadn't already been shattered into a million pieces. "They've been talking about your father at school?"

For the most part since Gordon's arrest, Branson had clammed up when it came to discussing his father, pretended as if nothing had changed. Almost every day, Savanna would ask him how things were going at school, and he'd insist everything was fine.

This proved otherwise, which made her feel even worse.

Head bowed, he scuffed one sneaker against the other. "Yeah."

"Mommy?" Alia's lower lip quivered as she gazed up, looking for reassurance.

Savanna knelt to pull them both into her arms. "Don't worry. Everything's going to be okay. You aren't responsible for what your father did." She wanted to believe *she* wasn't, either, but part of her feared that maybe she had more culpability than she cared to admit. Had she been too gullible, too trusting, as everyone implied?

She must've been, or she wouldn't be in this situation. And standing by Gordon even after the police searched the house had only made public opinion worse. She'd wanted so desperately to trust her husband above others, to protect her family, so that was what she'd done—until the mounting evidence grew to be too much. But that process of utter shock, denial, crushing pain and, finally, numb acceptance wasn't anything others had witnessed her go through. They merely saw her as being tied to him, as loving and supporting the monster who'd raped three women, and since he was no longer walking around town, *she'd* become the target of everyone's resentment.

"Boys aren't supposed to hurt girls," a bewildered Branson said.

"You're absolutely right, honey," she told him. "You shouldn't hurt anyone."

"So…why would Daddy choke that lady?"

Tears burned behind Savanna's eyes as she hugged them both tighter. "I don't know." That was a question she asked herself at least once a day, but she had no answers—for any of the terrible things he'd done. It wasn't as though she'd ever denied her husband physical intimacy. Other than a few oddities she'd chalked up to personal quirks, she'd thought they had a normal sex life. Since this whole thing had come out, however, she couldn't help wondering if she could've been more alluring or adventurous or exciting to him. Maybe if *she'd* been satisfying, he wouldn't have gone searching for something else and none of this would've happened…

Straightening, she shoved her cart to the side, left the few incidental groceries they'd gathered and took hold of her children's hands.

"Where are we going?" Branson asked when she circled around to the far side of the store to avoid Meredith as she led them out.

"Home," she replied.

"What about the milk?"

"We'll get it later." She couldn't stay in the store another second.

After helping her children get buckled up, she slid behind the wheel of her little Honda, which, fortunately, hadn't been impounded by the police like the van Gordon had driven to work.

"Are you sad, Mommy?" Alia asked.

"No, honey," she replied. *Sad* could never cover it. The nightmare that had started when the police showed up with that search warrant only got worse and worse. She kept telling herself that she'd survive and find solid ground again, be able to stabilize her life, but she'd been far too idealistic. It'd be two more months before the trial even started. Then who knew how long the legal proceedings would take. Gordon and his crimes were all people could talk about—all they would be talking about—for the foreseeable future.

Given the evidence, he'd likely be convicted, but even if he wasn't, Savanna wouldn't stay with him. She hoped she'd never have to lay eyes on him again. She no longer felt safe in his presence, no longer felt as if her children would be safe. She'd already filed for divorce, but she knew that wouldn't remove him from her life for good. He was the father of her children. The repercussions of his actions would ripple through the next decade or two, maybe longer.

Once they got home, she fed Branson and Alia and helped with homework, but her mind wasn't fully engaged. She went through the motions like an automaton, trying to persevere until they were in bed and she could call her younger brother.

At nine-thirty, she tucked them in, poured herself a glass of wine and carried it into her bedroom, where she shut and locked the door and dialed Reese's cell.

"Hey, sis. I'm out with a friend," he said as soon as he answered. "Can you make it quick?"

She blinked against the tears she'd been battling for several hours. Quick? Gordon's emergence as a suspect, the gathering of evidence, the search of the house, the arrest…it seemed like the longest, most invasive process she'd ever endured—as well as one of the most painful. "I can't stay here, Reese."

"What do you mean?" he responded. "In that house? Or in Nephi?"

"In Nephi. In Utah. I have to get out of here, leave the whole area. I never want to see any of these people again."

"But we talked about this. You said it would be better to keep the kids in the same school rather than rip them away from their friends and teachers. They've already lost their father."

"I felt that way at the time, but I've changed my mind. I don't think it's good for them to stay here, to try to bear up beneath all the negative energy. And I *know* it's not good for me. We need a fresh start."

There was a slight pause. Then he said, "Why the sudden change of heart?"

"I told you. I can't handle the anger and the blame. It feels as if almost every person I meet hates me. And I doubt that'll go away anytime soon."

"What do you mean? Why would they hate *you*? You're not the one who raped those women. They don't think you helped Gordon in any way…"

"No one has launched that accusation, thank God. Right now, they're only blaming me for missing whatever signs I should've seen." She stared glumly into her glass. "And maybe they have the right. I can't say anymore what I should or shouldn't have done. Would some other woman have noticed that he was too secretive? Would she have called his work to verify his hours and location? Would she have searched his stuff and found that 'rape kit' hidden in the shed out back?"

"We've been through this. There was nothing to make you doubt him. You even had a regular sex life—or that was what you told me."

"We did, for the most part. But how would *I* know? I was twenty when I married him, and he's the only man I've ever been with. Who am I to say what's normal between two people? I can only judge from my own experience. Maybe *you* should tell *me*."

"*I've* never been married. So far, my longest relationship has lasted two months."

Still, he had more sexual experience than she did, but when he chuckled about that, she wondered, as she often did, why he hadn't ever made a commitment to anyone.

She figured he would eventually—he was only twenty-four. Regardless, that was a question best left for another time. Tonight, she was too bogged down by thoughts of Gordon and what he'd done. "They found blood from one of the women in our van. Did I tell you that? He had his family riding around in a vehicle that still had the blood of a woman he'd attacked."

"You told me. That was when we both decided we could no longer maintain our faith in him, remember?"

She raked her fingers through her hair as she studied herself in the mirror above the dresser. She no longer even looked like the woman she used to be. She hadn't taken the time to get her hair trimmed—hadn't wanted to visit the salon she normally frequented while everyone there was whispering about her— so it had grown out of the bob she'd been wearing before her world collapsed. All she could do was pull the thick, auburn mass into a ponytail or let it go wild and curly. She'd always liked the gray blue of her eyes, but they looked empty now— hollow, shell-shocked. Who was this person staring back at her with a face so pale she could almost trace the blue veins underneath? "Maybe I should've noticed the blood."

"You have children. They scrape their knees and elbows now and then, don't they? And Gordon fixed mining equipment, which meant he had to have injured himself occasionally. Why would you assume—from a few drops of blood—that he was out harming women?"

She turned away from the mirror, couldn't bear to look at herself any longer. "I don't know. It's just that so many people think I should've spotted *something*. I'm beginning to doubt myself. The morning after he raped Meredith, he had scratches on his arm. I asked how he got hurt. He said he backed into a ditch he didn't see at a mine site and got scraped up by blackberry bushes while trying to get a two-by-four under his rear tire. Maybe that seems like a lame excuse now that the police have pointed out the *pattern* of those scratches. It did look like four fingernails had gouged his arm, but... I honestly thought nothing of it at the time."

"It's only been a month since they locked Gordon up, Savanna. Surely things will get easier."

She detected a hint of impatience. He'd heard so much about her problems of late. As sympathetic and supportive as he'd tried to be, she'd been falling apart for too long, ever since she'd learned that her husband was the primary suspect in the string of violent sexual assaults that'd sent the good people of Nephi into a panic. Understandably, Reese was eager to get back to his regular life. He was her younger brother, after all, wasn't used to having to support her so much. *She'd* been the one to carry them both through the loss of their elder brother and both parents a little over a year ago.

He'd had enough sorrow for one fourteen-month period. She felt like an idiot for not realizing before now that she'd exhausted his reserve of compassion, that this was the point where she'd need to soldier on alone.

"I'll let you go," she said abruptly.

After a brief silence, he said, "I'll call you later, okay?"

He probably felt guilty for revealing that hint of impatience. But he was with someone. He'd said that. Anyway, if he was capable of moving on after losing, all at once, three members of their immediate family and was beginning to feel good again, she wouldn't continue to drag him down. "There's no need," she said. "I'm fine. I just wanted to let you know that I'll be moving as soon as I can arrange it."

"That takes time. You've got to sell the house, don't you?"

"No."

"You're going to walk away from it?"

"Why not? There's no equity. Gordon took out a second mortgage almost as soon as he inherited it from his grandmother. With the market the way it is...we've been upside down on this place for two years or more."

"What about your credit?"

"The house is in his name. He never put me on the loan or the title. If his mother wants to save this place, she can move in and make the payments. I'll leave all of his stuff behind—" she'd already boxed them up and stacked them in the garage, anyway "—and put the keys under the mat."

"But where will you go? Back to Long Beach?"

"No." They'd sold the beautiful five-bedroom, four-bath home their parents had owned in Los Angeles, where they'd been raised, and split the proceeds. Reese had paid off his student loans and was using what he had left for graduate school. He was planning to be a doctor. She'd spent a portion of her inheritance on Gordon's defense—which she now considered to be a waste of money.

"Then where?" he asked.

The only place she could go. "The farmhouse in Silver Springs." It was all she had left.

"Savanna, no. That place needs too much work. Dad was barely getting started with it when he...when they had the boating accident. How will you *live* there?"

"I'll renovate it myself." And why not? They had to do *something* with it. And neither one of them had wanted to put it up for sale. That home hadn't been just another real estate purchase to their father, although he'd done a lot with real estate over the course of his life. This was the ranch his grandparents had once owned. He'd had fond memories of the place, was so excited to be able to bring it back into the family where he'd said it belonged.

"With what money?" Reese asked.

"The money I have left from the LA house."

"That won't carry you very far, not when you'll be using it for the repairs as well as your monthly overhead."

"Without a mortgage or rent, I should be able to manage a basic renovation and survive for a year, if I'm careful."

"And what will you do once the renovation is complete?"

"I don't know, Reese. Worst case, I'll have to sell and move on, figure out what comes next for me. Best case, I'll be able to get a loan against the property, give you your share and rebuild my life in Silver Springs."

He cursed.

"What? You don't like the idea?"

"I don't like what you're having to deal with. It's not fair. First, we lose Mom, Dad and Rand—and then, as if that wasn't tragic enough, Gordon starts *raping* women? How does all of that even happen to one person?"

She didn't answer his question. Her mind had shot off on a tangent. "Maybe that was why I missed it."

"Missed what?" he said, sounding confused.

"What Gordon was doing. I was so torn up I wasn't paying as much attention to him as I should have been. I was barely holding myself together, trying to get through it."

"But he only raped one woman last summer. The other two he attacked six months ago—almost back-to-back. Why the big gap if it was your bereavement over Mom, Dad and Rand that set him off?"

"There might not be a gap. The police believe he victimized

other women. They're looking at unsolved cases that might be similar in the cities and towns near the mines where he worked."

"Shit..."

"You're missing the point. I'm saying my grief—the fact that I was wrapped up in my own problems—is what might've started him down that road."

"I understand, but that's hardly an excuse. My God, you were mourning the loss of more than half your family. He should've been trying to support *you* for a change."

She took a sip of wine. Gordon had never been particularly supportive, not in an emotional sense. He'd worked and contributed his paycheck to the upkeep of the family, same as she did, but he wasn't all that engaged. He'd been gone too much and tired and remote when he was home.

Still, she'd thought they had a *decent* marriage, one that she could make work. Her parents had been together for thirty-two years when they were killed. She'd wanted that kind of life—one devoted to her family—and had been determined to stick it out for the long haul, even if Gordon wasn't perfect. "You're right. I don't know what started it. I just keep guessing."

"There's something wrong with him. That's what started it."

She leaned against the headboard and covered her feet with a blanket. "I wish I could go back to using Dad's last name."

"Why can't you?"

"Because then I'll be a Pearce and my kids will be Grays."

"So change theirs, too."

"I will eventually. But not now. I can't deal with that on top of everything else."

"No one in California will tie you to the rapist in Nephi, Utah, anyway."

"Thank God I won't have everyone staring at me when I go to a gas station or a store." She heard a woman talking to him in the background. "I'll let you go. Have a nice night."

"Savanna?"

She pulled the phone back to her ear. "Yeah?"

"Call me when you're ready to move. I'll come help you pack and drive the van."

He was in graduate school at the University of Oregon in Eugene, which wasn't close. And it was the third week in April, so he had finals coming up. She didn't plan to wait until he could help. "There's no need, little brother. I got it."

Taking a deep breath, she hung up, finished her wine and somehow resisted the urge to pour another glass. She had to be careful, couldn't allow herself to fall into a bottle. Gordon's mother had been an abusive alcoholic—it was why his father had left them so long ago. Savanna would never forget some of the upsetting stories he'd told her—of coming home to find his mother passed out on the couch, soaked in her own urine; of his mother nearly dying of smoke inhalation after falling asleep with a lit cigarette; of his mother screaming and cursing and throwing objects at him when he was a small boy. Maybe Dorothy was the reason he'd turned out so bad. The detective investigating his case had said that rape was more about power and control—and venting anger—than sexual gratification. But it wasn't as if Gordon's victims had resembled his mother in any way. And he'd grown close to Dorothy in recent years. They seemed to adore each other...

There were no easy answers, she decided, and got up to start packing. Part of her felt she should stay until the end of the school year. Although it went longer than Reese's semester in college, it was still only six weeks away. But now that she'd made the decision to move, she couldn't wait even that long.

CHAPTER TWO

Two months ago, Gavin Turner had given up his studio apartment over the thrift store in Silver Springs, California, an artsy town of five thousand not far from Santa Barbara, and purchased a home—a converted bunkhouse from the 1920s that sat on a whole acre about ten minutes outside of town. After living in such a small space, surrounded by buildings, he almost didn't know what to do with all the extra room. His friends jokingly referred to his remote location as the "boondocks," but he enjoyed being out in the open and even closer to the Topatopa Mountains, where he often went hiking or mountain biking. He'd always been drawn to the outdoors. The beauty and solitude brought him peace. He was pretty sure he wouldn't have been able to navigate his unusual and difficult childhood if not for his love of nature. And music, of course. He strummed on his guitar almost every night, had started singing at various bars in the area and along Highway 101, which ran along California's coast. He hadn't landed any notable gigs yet, just performed in various coastal or farming communities, mostly up north. He wanted to break into the music scene, but the competition was so fierce he felt he'd have to move to Nashville, where there was so much happening in the music industry these days, to get where he was hoping to go, and he couldn't commit to that quite yet. Not while his mother—or, rather, the woman he called his mother—needed him. For now, he enjoyed singing at a different hole-in-the-wall each week. The money he earned augmented what he made working at New Horizons Boys Ranch, the boarding school for troubled boys his adoptive mother had started over twenty years ago and where he'd gone to high school himself.

Tonight the weather was warm and the cicadas were loud as he sat out on the porch in a simple T-shirt and worn jeans, writing a new song. He'd just sat back to take a break and was wondering whether he should get a puppy—he was leaning toward yes, since he hadn't been able to have a pet in town—when a large moving van came rumbling down his road.

He rarely had visitors, but no one else lived on this road, so he set his guitar to the side and stood.

The truck didn't stop, however. The woman driving—he was fairly certain it was a woman, but he was judging on size alone, since it was difficult to see in the dark—barely glanced his way. Focused on what was right in front of her, she barreled forward as if she'd had a hard journey and would finish it, this uneven surface be damned.

Who was that? And where was she going? The only other house nearby was the ranch house to which his own converted bunkhouse had once belonged. And it had sat empty for the past three years or longer. According to what Gavin had been told, it wasn't even for sale—not that he could've afforded the bigger property, anyway.

He shoved his hands in his pockets as he watched the truck bounce and sway past him. Although the road was supposed to be privately maintained, it hadn't been maintained at all, not in a number of years, which made the potholes deep and difficult to miss—and she seemed to be hitting most of them.

Did this mean he had a new neighbor? If so, how would she get through to her house? The bridge over the creek that ran between the two properties had washed out in the last heavy rain.

She didn't seem to be aware of that, though. At least, she wasn't slowing down…

He took off running to warn her before she could wind up in the water. Banging on the truck as he came alongside, he attempted to get her attention before she could crush him against one of the trees that gave him so little room as it was. "Whoa! Hey! Stop!"

She seemed reluctant to let him waylay her. Either that, or she was afraid of what encountering a strange man out here in the middle of nowhere could mean. Because even after she hit the brakes, she barely cracked the window so that they could hear each other speak. "Something wrong?"

He edged around a thorny bush in order to get close enough to see her. About his age, with a riot of thick, copper-colored hair and light-colored eyes, she studied him with more caution than he'd ever seen before. Two children—a boy and a younger girl—leaned forward to peer around what he could only assume was their mother.

"You can't go down that way," he explained, gesturing at the road ahead. "The bridge is washed out."

"What bridge?" she asked.

He blinked in surprise. "The bridge that goes over the creek."

She scowled. "You mean *before* you reach the house?"

He swatted a mosquito. It'd been a wet year, and now that spring had arrived, the vicious little monsters were coming out in force. That was the one downside to living in the country. "Haven't you ever been here before?"

"No."

He wiped some blood from a scratch on his forearm. That darn bush had gouged him before he could avoid it. "You've got all your belongings with you, right? You *are* moving in."

She finished rolling down the window. "Yes, but I've only ever seen the pictures my father sent."

"So he's the one who owns the house."

"Not anymore. He passed away in a boating accident a little over a year ago. The property belongs to me and my younger brother now."

"I see. I'm sorry for your loss."

She frowned. "Not as sorry as I am."

Gavin's gaze shifted to the children. "Where you all from?"

"I was born and raised in LA—Long Beach. But I've been living in Utah since I left for college. That's where both my children were born."

"In Nephi," the boy piped up, seemingly proud that he could add this bit of information.

"Nephi, huh?" Gavin said. "Never heard of it."

"It's small but not too far from the Salt Lake Valley, if you're familiar with that," the woman said. "About two hours south."

Gavin whistled. "Sounds like a long drive from there to here, especially in a moving van."

She blew a strand of curly hair out of her face. "You have no idea. We left at four this morning and have been on the road ever since. According to MapQuest, it was only ten hours, but it took nearly twice as long traveling with two children in a vehicle that can't go faster than fifty-five." She peered through the front windshield again. "So...how do I get in? Do I go around? Is there another road or—"

"'Fraid not," he said. "This is it."

Her eyebrows shot up. "You mean I can't reach the house?"

"Not tonight. Someone will have to repair the bridge before you can cross, especially driving this beast." He tapped the side of the heavy truck.

She looked crestfallen. "You've got to be kidding me."

"I hate to be the bearer of bad news, but...no." She was obviously disappointed, but there was no way he could change reality.

She picked up her phone, then tossed it back in the seat and cursed under her breath.

Her little girl's eyes widened. "Did you say a swear word, Mommy?"

"I said 'shoot,'" she grumbled.

"No, you didn't," her boy insisted.

Gavin tried not to smile at the exchange. "What's wrong?"

"The battery on my phone is dead. I haven't been able to charge it. The cigarette lighter in this truck doesn't work. Neither does the air-conditioning, probably why they gave me such a good deal."

They'd been without air-conditioning on a day like this? That had to be another reason they appeared slightly frayed at the edges. "If you need to make a call, you can use mine." He pulled his cell out of his pocket and put in the passcode before offering it to her. "Is someone planning to meet you and help you unload?"

She waved off his phone. "No, it's only me and the kids. I wasn't planning to make a call. I was going to look for a motel. But maybe you know of one I should try."

"The Mission Inn is nice and reasonable."

"Is it far? How do I get there?"

"Wait! We're not staying?" her son broke in. "You said we were home. That we'd be able to get out!"

"I have to go potty," her daughter added in a whine.

"I wasn't expecting to run into a washed-out bridge, okay? Let me… Let me figure out where we can spend the night. It shouldn't take much longer," she told them, sounding exhausted.

Gavin wiped the scratch on his arm again. "Look, why don't you come in for a few minutes? I've got some soda—or juice if you prefer—for the kids. They can go to the bathroom and have a drink while we use my laptop to book you a room."

Her son opened the door as if he'd only been waiting for the invitation, but she grabbed hold of his arm. "Stay right where you are."

With a groan, he obeyed. "*Why?* He said we could have a soda."

She turned back to Gavin. "Thanks for the offer. I appreciate it. But we'll just... We'll be on our way."

How? he wondered. Turning that truck around wouldn't be easy, not on this narrow road. She couldn't use his driveway, not with such a tall van. The electrical wires were strung too low. She'd have to back up all the way to where she made the turn to begin with. "Are you sure?" he asked. "Because I don't mind." He lifted his hands to show that he was harmless. "I realize we're strangers at the moment, but I *am* your new neighbor, so we'll be getting acquainted soon."

When she hesitated, he got the impression she wanted to trust him but didn't dare.

"Backing down this road will be tricky," he added. "Especially in the dark. I mean...maybe you drive semis for a living and are especially good at that sort of thing, but—"

"No," she broke in with enough exasperation to reveal what he'd already suspected: it'd been a challenge just to get them all to California without an incident. "I had to sell my car to avoid making this any more difficult by trying to tow it behind me."

"Then why risk wrecking into a fence or a ditch? I'd wait for morning, unless you're determined to go tonight. I'll get a flashlight and try to guide you out, if that's the case."

She rested her forehead on the large steering wheel.

"I *really* want a soda, Mommy," her little girl said. "And I have to go potty!"

"Come on," Gavin coaxed. "Once we find you a room, I'll drive you to town. You can leave the van here until morning, when you can get someone out to help you cross."

"Do you know of someone who could do that?" she asked.

He gazed toward the creek in question even though he

couldn't see it for the dark and the trees. "I'm pretty good at temporary fixes. I'm sure, with the proper supplies, I could create something that will work." Tomorrow would be Saturday, after all, so he didn't have to go to New Horizons. He didn't have set plans until evening, when he had a gig in Santa Barbara.

"How much will it cost?"

"Nothing for my labor. I don't mind helping out. So...whatever the lumber and other supplies will be. You'll need to get an actual building contractor for the permanent structure, though."

She sighed.

He dipped his head to get her to look at him again. "I'm Gavin Turner, by the way."

"I'm Savanna. This is Branson and Alia."

She didn't offer a last name, but he didn't press her. "Happy to meet you. I've lived here for fifteen years and have never hurt a soul. You have no reason to be afraid of me." He didn't mention what he'd done before that. Some things were better left unsaid.

"I'm not sure you'd tell me if you were an ax murderer, but... okay," she said, and her kids scrambled out before she could change her mind.

Savanna watched Gavin carefully. He wasn't overly large or imposing. Maybe five-eleven to six feet tall, he had broad shoulders and big hands but a thin frame and wore his dark hair in a man bun with a closely trimmed beard and mustache. To her, he looked like an artist or a musician—or maybe just a vegetarian (not that she'd known many of those in Nephi). Gordon had *hated* men who looked like Gavin, had made fun of their "hippie lifestyle," especially if they had tattoos, and Gavin had plenty of those. Ink covered one whole arm—a big saxophone, a guitar and musical notes as well as the detailed face of some singer.

Savanna knew if the man she'd married could be dangerous, anyone could. But Gavin's face was so delicately sculpted, and he had such kind eyes—big and brown with a thick fringe of lashes—that it was difficult to be afraid of him. Even if he hadn't given her the impression that he was a pacifist, his gentle manner would've put her at ease. He'd been teasing the kids since they came in. The way he interacted with them reminded her of her father, which made her think she was being paranoid to be so cautious of him.

Evil people weren't funny, were they?

Not in her experience. Gordon had never had much of a sense of humor...

"Sprite—or Pepsi?" Gavin turned his attention to her after he finally let Alia wrangle her soda out of his grasp.

Savanna shook her head. "Neither, thanks." Her stomach had been churning all day. It was anxiety and not true illness, but she didn't see any point in exacerbating the problem by drinking loads of sugar and carbon dioxide.

"What about a beer?"

"No."

"Some water, then?"

"That'd be nice."

He poured a glass from a chilled pitcher in the fridge. When he brought it over, she couldn't help thinking—once again—about how quickly Gordon would've judged her new neighbor based solely on his looks. And yet it was all-American, wrestling-champion Gordon with the stocky build, lantern jaw, green eyes and short blond hair who'd been a danger to society. She'd seen the crime scene photos—the way he'd battered his victims before and during each sexual assault. The detective had shown them to her, trying to upset her and shake her faith so that she'd talk more freely about him.

Gavin popped open a beer and took a long pull. "So...what brings you to California?"

When he glanced at her left hand, she realized he was checking for a wedding ring. Because she'd shown up out of the blue, and hadn't given him much of an explanation, he was trying to figure out who she was and what she was doing in Silver Springs alone with two children, trying to move into an old, dilapidated house. "I'm no longer married," she said, even though it wasn't the answer to the question he'd voiced.

He didn't act surprised that she'd correctly interpreted his thoughts. "Is that new?"

"Yes." The divorce wasn't final, but she didn't care to go into the details. She didn't consider herself married anymore; that was the salient part. Gordon had refused to sign the papers, was trying to convince her that he still loved her and was wrongly accused, but her attorney insisted that once he was convicted, especially of such heinous crimes, he wouldn't be able to waylay the process any longer. The law would then be entirely on her side. "I'm starting over."

"Do you plan on living next door for any length of time?"

"At least a year. I'm a half owner, remember? I figure I might as well take advantage of that. Why pay rent?"

He looked pained when he said, "I see the logic. But how much did your father tell you about the condition of the place?"

"I know it's not in *good* shape. Fixer-uppers rarely are."

"I doubt this one's even livable."

"That's okay. I'm here to *make* it livable."

"Then you have some experience with renovating?"

She took a drink of water. "No, but there's a tutorial for everything on YouTube these days."

When he laughed, she couldn't help smiling. She liked that he immediately knew she was joking. Gordon would've freaked out and set her straight on how difficult restoring a house would be. He'd always taken everything so literally. "Maybe there's a video on how to back a twenty-foot trailer down a narrow country road in the dark," he said, and opened his laptop. "Should we check?"

"Why not? Might save you the trip into town," she replied, but she could tell he wasn't serious, either.

"I don't mind dropping you off." He called up his browser and typed in "The Mission Inn, Silver Springs, CA."

"What'd you do for a living in Utah?" he asked while a list of links began to appear.

"I was an administrative assistant in an insurance office." She considered adding what Gordon had done to contribute—no way could they have survived on her income alone—but bit her tongue. The less she said about him, the better.

"Oh, an administrative assistant. I should've guessed," he said.

"Guessed?" she echoed.

"Office work. Contracting. It's the same thing."

It was her turn to laugh. "What about you? What do you do for a living?" She gestured toward the guitar he'd carried in when he let them into his house. "Or does this give it away?"

"I write and sing, gig now and then. But I also have a day job."

"Doing…"

After he clicked on the website for the Mission Inn, he keyed the phone number into his cell. "Maintenance and repair at New Horizons Boys Ranch."

"You don't mean 'ranch' as in 'ranch,' right? You're talking about one of those boarding schools for teenage boys who act out?"

"Yeah. We take in troubled kids. Quite a few have been through some traumatic—" he seemed about to say "shit" but substituted as he glanced at her children "—stuff. Others are just angry. Or narcissistic. Or both."

"They have boys ranches in Utah, too. My husband—my *ex*-husband now—was shipped off to one for a year." She lowered her voice so that Branson and Alia, who were trading sips of their sodas, wouldn't be likely to catch what she said. "I should've taken that as the warning sign it was and stayed away from him."

Her neighbor's smile disappeared. "I graduated from New Horizons."

She felt her face begin to burn. Why had she said that? She'd decided *not* to talk about Gordon, not to drag all that negativity to this new location with her. "I'm sorry," she said. "I didn't mean... Well, everyone's different. No two stories are the same."

"It's okay," he said, but from that moment on he was all business. He helped her get a room for a hundred dollars per night and delivered her, Branson and Alia to town.

"Thanks for your help," she said as they got out of his truck.

"No problem."

She wished there was something she could say to cover for her earlier gaffe. She'd been tired and frustrated that she couldn't get through to the house after making such a long drive, or she would've been more careful with her words. But he'd indicated he worked at New Horizons. She'd assumed he'd understand how conflicted, even dangerous, some of the boys who went to those places could be. She'd *never* expected him to say he'd been on the other side, as well.

She thought about offering him another apology but figured it was better to let it go. "'Night."

CHAPTER THREE

As long as the day had been, and as exhausted as she was from driving so far while trying to keep her kids happy and entertained, Savanna lay awake. Alia slept beside her and Branson slept alone in the other double, since he'd recently started wetting the bed. Fortunately, what Gavin had told her turned out to be true. The Mission Inn was a decent motel, as good or better than any in Nephi. So she wasn't uncomfortable, just filled with restless anxiety. Relocating had been such a big decision. She'd taken her children away from everything and everyone they'd known so far. Now that she was back in California, she could only hope she'd made the right decision—for all of them.

The fact that she hadn't even known she'd have to cross a bridge to get to the house where they'd be living told her there would be other surprises. Would she be able to handle them?

She hoped so, but Gordon's betrayal had left her shaken. She'd never felt *this* unsure of the future. He'd essentially burned down her whole life.

One day at a time. She had to live in the moment.

But this moment would lead to the next moment, which

meant the sun would soon rise, and she wasn't prepared for the day. Her new neighbor hadn't made any specific plans with her when he dropped her off, hadn't given her a set time when he'd pick her up. He'd simply said, "See you tomorrow." Had she offended him when she made that boys ranch comment? Would Gavin really come back? Or would she have to find someone else to help her cross the creek so that she could move in?

She needed to get some sleep or she wouldn't be able to cope. But the glowing numerals on the alarm clock between the beds mocked her reluctance to see the minutes pass. She turned the clock away and accidentally knocked her phone to the floor.

As she checked to make sure it was still charging—she didn't want to go another day without the conveniences it provided—she saw that her mother-in-law had sent her another hateful text, which must've come in while her phone was dead.

How can you fire Gordon's attorneys? Do you know what kind of defense he'll get from a public defender? NO defense! Are you TRYING to send him to prison for the rest of his life?

Supposedly, Dorothy was no longer drinking. But even if that were true, Gordon's mother had cleaned up her act so late in life that she had no net worth. She eked out a living by working at a large discount store, but, as usual, she had nothing to give her son. She expected Savanna to use what she had left from her parents' estate to provide Gordon with the best attorneys possible.

Frowning, Savanna scrolled up and read several of the other texts her mother-in-law had sent over the past several weeks. She hadn't answered any of them, nor had she picked up Dorothy's calls. She knew Gordon's mother was trying to use guilt to manipulate her. But it never ceased to amaze Savanna that Dorothy could think *she* was the one to let Gordon down. He'd let *her* down, in the worst possible way, but only after his own mother had screwed up his childhood.

You've filed for divorce? Gordon hasn't even been in jail a week. I should beat your no-good ass. If this is all the faith you have in him, he's better off without you.

Savanna wasn't sure he was better off without her, but she was convinced of the opposite.

Why won't you pick up? How is avoiding me going to help the situation? You have my grandkids, for God's sake! I have a right to see them.

Except she'd never shown any interest in Branson and Alia before. She'd brought them a bag of candy occasionally when she'd come for dinner, but that had been the extent of her involvement in their lives. Savanna would never forget how upset Branson had been when his grandmother told him she'd attend his school play and then stood them up, calling two days later with some lame excuse that didn't even make sense.

How can you pretend to be a loving wife when you abandon Gordon so easily? He's always worshipped the ground you walk on, been a good husband and father, and you do this?

Was he being a good husband and father when he was out stalking women—attacking and raping them? How could Dorothy make such a ludicrous statement?

But that was Dorothy. She never troubled herself much with reality.

He would never have abandoned you in your hour of need. He would've believed in you and fought for you until the end— and you should be doing the same for him.

The police had found Theresa Spinnaker's blood in their van! Was Dorothy *completely* delusional?

You coward! You won't be able to avoid me forever.

Dorothy had driven down from Salt Lake after that message, but Savanna had refused to let her in. When she'd started cursing and kicking the door, Savanna had called the police, who'd escorted Dorothy off the property. That was the night Savanna had received the worst text of all.

Gordon's going to kill you when he gets out.

Savanna always shivered when she read those words. The only thing that made them bearable was the fact that she didn't think Dorothy meant them literally.

Forcing herself to put down her phone, she slid Alia over—Savanna could barely move, was already feeling claustrophobic simply by circumstance—and tried, once again, to go to sleep.

The motel had a free breakfast, so Savanna was able to feed her kids the following morning, but she still wasn't sure Gavin would show up. At ten, she hadn't heard from him. He hadn't even asked for her cell number last night.

Was she on her own?

She could only assume she was. She was trying to figure out the best way to hire some help and get back to her new place—would a Craigslist ad work in such a small town?—when the phone in her room rang.

She thought it might be the motel manager. She'd asked for a late checkout in case she needed the extra time, but the caller turned out to be Gavin.

"You had breakfast yet?" he asked.

"We have," she replied.

"Then are you ready to go?"

She breathed a sigh of relief. "We are."

"Great. I bought the lumber for the bridge and brushed up on a few how-to videos. We should be all set."

So *that* was why he hadn't come sooner. He'd been shopping. She could tell he was joking about the YouTube stuff. But she was so happy to hear from him she had no comeback, just sincere gratitude. "Wow. That's nice of you. I was afraid... I was afraid maybe you'd changed your mind about being so neighborly."

"I wouldn't leave you stranded. I would've called earlier, but since I had to go to Santa Barbara to get the wood, I thought I'd let you sleep."

"Kids at this age don't sleep late." Most of them didn't wet the bed, either, but poor Branson had had another accident last night. Fortunately, she'd put a plastic tablecloth under the sheets so she wouldn't have to worry that he might ruin the mattress. But she felt bad for him. She knew he was embarrassed and hated that her son was struggling so much as a result of his life being turned upside down. "Still, thank you. I appreciate the thought."

"No problem. I'm outside, so whenever you're ready."

She disconnected, called the front desk to let them know they could have the room and gathered the few items she'd brought with them, which she shoved into the school backpack she'd borrowed from Branson. "Gavin's here. Let's go," she told the kids, and ushered them out the first-floor motel room to find their new neighbor sitting in the lot with the engine idling.

"I didn't know your truck was *blue!*" Branson said as he got in the back seat. "It looked black last night."

"Of course it's blue," Gavin said. "Is there any better color?"

Branson beamed as he scooted over to make room for his sister. "No."

"Do you have some more soda?" Alia asked.

He smiled at her in the review mirror. "At the house I do."

Savanna eyed the lumber that filled the bed of Gavin's truck while putting the backpack between her kids. "That's a lot of wood," she said as she climbed in front.

"A big part of the old bridge is lying around on the property, but it's so rotted there's really nothing we can salvage from it, so… I think we're going to need to start from scratch."

"Of course," she muttered with a sigh. Nothing could be easy, although now that she could see the town in full daylight, she was encouraged. Nephi looked sad and depressed by comparison. In Silver Springs she could easily find evidence of the wealth and affluence that was so prevalent in parts of LA. Tasteful murals covered several of the buildings downtown. There were no empty or run-down businesses—and something else was different. It took her a moment to realize what, but after they drove a few blocks, she said, "There are no chains here!"

"*Chains?*" Gavin echoed.

"You know, businesses. McDonald's. Best Western."

"Oh, right. Chain stores aren't allowed. The town promotes small business."

"I've never heard of a town taking such a stand."

He grinned. "Welcome to California."

The cost of living would be greater here if she couldn't run to a box store every time she needed groceries or school supplies for the kids, but she thought it was a sacrifice worth making. She was looking forward to coming back and exploring, to walking into a store without fear of being recognized and reviled…

She studied a secondhand store that appeared to be particularly well run. Maybe she could find a few things for the house there to help her get by… "This place has a strong Southwest flavor," she said.

"There's a lot of Spanish Revival architecture," Gavin agreed.

"Like the motel where we stayed—with its white walls, red tile roof and bell tower."

"Is that a positive thing or a negative thing, in your mind?" he asked.

"I like it. It's clean and well maintained—not nearly as run-down as parts of Nephi."

"Look! There're ducks in that park!" Branson exclaimed, pointing out the window.

Savanna craned her neck to see. "I'll have to take you there sometime."

"Me, too!" Alia chimed in.

"Of course. I'll take you both." She gestured to the right. "What's the name of the mountains that surround us?" The valley was so narrow, barely four or five miles across.

"The Topatopa Mountains. They're part of the Los Padres National Forest."

"Does it snow here, Mommy?" Alia asked.

Savanna looked to Gavin. She hadn't even thought to check.

"Not in town. The temperature's pretty mild year-round, but you will see some white caps on the highest mountain peaks in winter."

The buildings gave way to citrus orchards and small farms as they drove down the valley. After about ten minutes, he turned onto the narrow road leading to where she and her children would soon live—the road she'd had such difficulty finding in the dark last night without the GPS on her phone.

"Now I'll get to lay eyes on this creek I've been hearing about," she said.

Gavin had backed her moving van into a wide spot in the road near the turnoff so they'd be able to get past it. As soon as he parked, they all piled out. The kids began to run and play while she remained at Gavin's side.

The creek, only about twenty feet from where she'd stopped last night, was much wider than Savanna had anticipated. "Wow. Lucky for me you were sitting outside when I arrived."

"You didn't seem to be slowing down," he admitted.

"I would've barreled right into this." The current wasn't strong enough to carry off a truck. Nor was the water high enough that they would've risked drowning. But they would've gotten stuck in the mud. And she had no idea how she would've pulled the U-Haul out, especially late on a Friday evening, in the country. No doubt the right kind of tow—and any damage she caused the van—would've cost a small fortune.

"I guess you owe me," he teased.

She froze in surprise. Owed him *what*? Was he flirting with her?

Her eyes flew to his face. She didn't want to be unfair, didn't want him to go to a lot of work thinking she might be willing to get involved with him. "I'll pay you," she said.

He gave her a funny look. "For saving you from driving into the creek?"

"For your time today." She checked her kids to make sure they weren't wandering too far. They were getting muddy, but they were having such a great time searching for tadpoles she didn't call them back. They deserved some carefree fun after the upset of the past few months. "I don't expect anyone to work for free."

He shrugged. "I don't mind helping out a neighbor."

She tried to let the subject go but couldn't stop herself from speaking up again. "Would you be helping me this much if I were a man?"

He responded without hesitation. "A man with two kids, who was recently divorced and moving in next door? Of course."

She breathed a sigh of relief. Maybe he *hadn't* been flirting with her. Maybe he was what he seemed to be—a really nice neighbor. It'd been so long since she'd been single and in a situation where a man might hit on her, she could have misinterpreted his behavior. "Okay, but... I need to let you know that I've been through something extremely difficult, and...and I'm still not over it. I don't know if I'll ever get over it. So don't do anything for me because...because you might be...you know, looking for female companionship. I'm not an option."

He looked surprised. "Whoa. Where did that come from?"

Branson and Alia had taken off their shoes and socks and were wading ankle-deep in the shallow, slow-moving creek. They weren't paying attention to the conversation, but she lowered her voice all the same. "I'm sorry. I'd hate for you to think I'm being rude, but I'd feel worse if you were ever to believe that I tried to take advantage of your kindness. I'd rather be clear on where I stand from the beginning. You need to charge me—for the wood, which I'll reimburse you for before you leave today, *and* the labor. I'll pay you a fair price for everything, even the ride last night."

He went to his truck and got a pair of leather gloves from under the seat. "I appreciate your honesty, but I'm not going to let you pay me for the ride, and I have a few hours I can contribute to helping so that you can move in today. You won't owe me anything beyond what I spent this morning."

"Are you *sure*?"

He looked slightly confused as he pulled on those gloves. "Will you answer one question for me?"

"What is it?"

"Does this immediate stiff-arm have anything to do with my boys ranch history? Because we've barely met, and yet you're already telling me you don't want to get involved. I admit I find you attractive. *Really* attractive—"

"I have two kids," she broke in, as if that should've been a deal breaker.

"I've met them," he said with a wink. "I like kids. They don't have to be mine. But I feel like you might be lumping me into the same category as your ex-husband simply because we both ran into a spot of trouble in our teenage years."

He was far more up front than anyone she'd ever encountered. Taken aback by his frank honesty, she struggled to find an appropriate response and wound up focusing on what concerned her most. That "spot of trouble" he'd mentioned might not be a small thing. Gordon's behavioral difficulties from the same period—his truancy, lying, stealing and general belligerence—had revealed that something was wrong, and it was never fixed, or he would not have done what he'd done later in life. He'd merely learned how to hide his worst self so that he could meld into society.

Still, she didn't know Gavin, didn't know if his behavior had been worse or better than Gordon's when they were young, and owed him the benefit of the doubt. Not every boy who attended a boys ranch turned out to be a violent criminal. "I appreciate the compliment. I do. After what I've been through, any kind word feels good. And I'm sorry about what I said regarding the boys ranch last night. Your past has nothing to do with anything."

"Then you're just not into me."

He said that with a twinkle in his eye, as if he was man enough to take no, if that was her answer. This had to be the most emotionally brave individual she'd ever met. She couldn't help admiring his self-confidence. Gordon would never have risked his ego that way. "It's not you *specifically*. I'm done with men. *All* men. I wish I'd never gotten involved with the one I married."

He peered at her closer. "Certainly you've had other males in your life, besides your ex, who haven't been that bad."

"If you count my father and brothers. But that's about the limit of my experience. I never had a steady boyfriend before Gordon. I met him my first day of college and got pregnant eighteen months later, at which point we both dropped out of school to get married."

"And the marriage lasted..."

"Until two months ago." She hadn't officially filed at that time, but that was when she'd first begun to doubt Gordon's innocence, which was the point of the *real* rift.

"Which makes you...what? Twenty-nine?"

"In two weeks." She assumed they were similar in age. From his appearance, he couldn't be much older.

"That's young to be so jaded."

"I can't help it."

"I'm sorry," he said.

"For..."

"Whatever he did."

Apparently her kids had given up trying to find tadpoles. They were now scrounging around for rocks they could try to skip across the water. "So am I, especially for Branson and Alia."

He moved to the back of the truck and lowered the tailgate. "I understand that you've been burned recently, but swearing off men *completely* seems a bit extreme. Surely you'll recover at some point."

"No. Never," she insisted.

He started to slide out the two-by-twelves. "Never's a long time. Won't you get lonely?"

"Probably."

"What will you do then?"

She drew a deep breath as she considered the question. It wasn't realistic to think she wouldn't crave some kind of companionship in the future. "Maybe I'll become a lesbian."

A grin tugged at his lips. She could tell he didn't know whether to take her seriously. "Is that a joke?"

"No," she said. Although this wasn't an option she'd ever considered before, it did seem to solve the problem. She'd never heard of a woman raping anyone. Sure, that had probably happened somewhere in the world at one time or another, but the odds of encountering such an anomaly had to be small.

"You can't judge all men by the actions of one," he said.

He'd made that point before, but she was too traumatized to be so fair. "No, but I can take precautions."

"Like changing your sexuality."

"Yes."

"That's a pretty big deal. Please tell me you're bi at least."

"Not yet. But I'm hoping I'll be able to change. I'm willing to try. I mean, I've already got kids, so I don't need a man in order to have a family. And settling down with a sweet, harmless woman who will be happy to help me cook and clean and raise children—what could be better than that?"

As he carried two of the boards to a staging area near the moorings of the old bridge, she tried not to admire him in those jeans. He had one heck of a nice butt. She had to admit that much, despite her plans for a man-less future.

"I see your point," he said when he returned. "A sweet, harmless woman who cooks and cleans has her merits. But not all women are harmless."

She moved to get a two-by-twelve herself. But he was the one with the gloves. He waved her back, out of the way. "I got this."

"The woman I find will be so passive and supportive she'll barely say a word," she told him. "I might even include that in my dating profile. 'Seeking mild-mannered lesbian who loves children and books and abhors any kind of violence.'"

He laughed outright.

"What?"

"Why don't you just advertise for a roommate? That might turn out to be a better fit."

"No. Roommates come and go. I think I'll stick with a same-sex relationship, so there's a commitment involved, but add a line to my dating profile that says something like, 'low libido a must,' since I'm not sure I can please a woman in that way—or sleep with her in the first place."

He laughed even harder. "Sounds like you've got it all figured out."

"Not until this moment." She tapped her temple with one finger. "But it's becoming clear."

He returned to the truck for another load. "Won't you miss having a man in your bed?"

At this moment, it didn't seem like it. She shuddered whenever she thought of Gordon's hands on her body. Knowing she'd been intimate with someone like that, someone so cruel, angry, selfish and deceitful, turned her stomach. And, in retrospect, some of the things he did—the way he liked to put his hands around her neck when they were making love—freaked her out. Had he been thinking about strangling her when he was moaning above her? Had such dark fantasies increased his pleasure?

Probably, given the type of person he'd turned out to be.

On the other hand, it was a man's body that excited her. She'd never been aroused by any woman...

When she didn't answer, Gavin looked up at her. "You're thinking about it..."

"I'm thinking about passion."

"Passion," he repeated.

"Yes. The kind they portray in the movies. If that were real, men would be much harder to give up. But..."

"Wait—you've never felt that kind of desire? Not even when your relationship with your ex was new?"

"Maybe," she admitted. But those feelings had faded fast. Toward the end, sex was more of a chore, something she simply tried to get through. Maybe that was why she felt she might be partially responsible for what Gordon did. She'd tried to hide her apathy, to summon some enthusiasm, but the possibility existed that she hadn't done a very good job of faking it. "Right now that seems so long ago. Even if it was that way once, it didn't last."

He whistled. "Your husband must've sucked in bed."

Gordon had sucked at being a good husband in other ways— maybe that was why she'd lost interest in the first place. It seemed as though she'd always been trying to ignore some frustration or inadequacy when he hit her up for sex. She'd never turned him down, but maybe acquiescence wasn't enough. "I wouldn't know about that. I don't have anything to compare him against."

"Then you're giving up too soon."

"Better safe than sorry," she grumbled.

"Even if you're missing out?"

She checked her kids again. Still happily occupied. "Lesbians have dildos and stuff. I'm sure I'll be fine."

He lifted another load of lumber. "Okay, but if you get tired of pretending, feel free to give me a call. I like it soft and gentle, and I won't get in the way of your search for a lesbian partner."

Savanna's jaw dropped, but when he winked at her and carried the last couple of two-by-twelves to his staging area, she was pretty sure he was just trying to shock her.

CHAPTER FOUR

Gavin had no idea what Savanna had been through. He thought she might open up, talk about it as the day wore on, but she didn't. She hadn't even given him her last name. The only thing he knew was that whatever trauma she'd suffered had left a deep scar. He'd never had a woman tell him she was hoping to change her sexuality so that she'd never have to deal, on an intimate basis, with another man. He was fairly certain she hadn't been entirely serious, but still. Even the kids didn't mention their father, and yet Savanna had admitted the missing member of their family had been part of it until quite recently.

What had gone so terribly wrong?

He wondered the whole time he was building the makeshift bridge. Fortunately, since the structure wasn't intended to be permanent, it didn't take him long.

He laid the two-by-twelves across the water, created a support on each side so they wouldn't slip and lashed them together to keep them stable. Then he drove the van over to the house to be sure it was safe, and stayed to help unload the furniture and boxes.

Together with the kids, he and Savanna made several trips

before he managed to convince her to let him finish up so that
she could go in and start cleaning. He'd recently moved. He
knew how difficult it was to get organized—and he'd had only
himself to worry about.

Branson and Alia helped if he found something small they
could carry. When he put the last box on the worn and ripped
carpet of the living room, he stood back to survey the scene.
"So, what do you think of the house?"

Savanna had started in the kitchen—was cleaning out the
drawers and cupboards. Too bad the place wasn't in better shape.
She had to be overwhelmed by the enormity of the task ahead.

"I'll make it work," she said, but her smile seemed forced.
They'd discovered earlier that someone had broken in and stolen a few things, so she didn't even have a stove.

"You can use my kitchen until you get yours up and running," he told her. "I'm not home during the week, so it's not
as if you'll be in my way."

She'd been kneeling on the floor. She stood, wearing rubber
gloves and holding a wet rag, and used her forearm to move a
piece of hair out of her face. "I appreciate that. I'm sure things
will come together here quicker than it seems, though."

He had to admire her stubborn optimism, but the land was
worth more than the house. Part of him wondered if she wouldn't
be smarter to tear it down and start over. "On the bridge…"

"What about it?" She'd already given him cash for the wood.

"What I built will only get you through the next few days,
so don't wait too long before replacing it. I know a guy—James
Glenn—who'd be ideal for that sort of thing." He found a pen-
cil and a business card on the counter, left by the Realtor who'd
sold the property, and jotted down James's number using the
contact record in his phone. "He'll give you a fair price, and
he works fast."

"I'll give him a call."

"Great. I'm going to take off."

She caught him before he could leave. "Why not stay a little longer? I was thinking of ordering pizza. I'm sure you've got to be hungry, too. You've been helping me for hours."

"Stay!" Branson cried.

Gavin mussed his hair. "I can't. But thanks."

"I feel like I have to do *something* for you," Savanna said. "You've done so much for me."

He arched an eyebrow at her. "We've already discussed this."

"We're talking a few slices of pizza…"

"Another time. I've got plans tonight."

"Oh." She seemed embarrassed to have pushed it. "No problem."

He couldn't tell if she was disappointed he couldn't stay, but he sort of wanted her to be. As he'd told her at the creek, he found her attractive. And it wasn't just her looks. There was something about her he liked, and he'd felt it from the first moment he'd chased her down before she could run into the creek.

He went back and added his phone number under James Glenn's on that card. "Call me if you need anything. I can make a run to the dump, when you're ready. You'll need some way to dispose of all the trash and other junk that's accumulated."

"That's really nice of you."

"I'm a nice guy," he said with a grin.

When she met his eyes, she blushed and glanced away.

"When do you have to return the van?" he asked.

"I was hoping to take it back today, but I have to drop it off in LA, where I also need to buy a car, and it's getting too late for that. So… I'll pay for another day and take it tomorrow."

"That's a good idea. What kind of car do you plan to get?"

Not a van. Anything except a van. "An SUV would be ideal— if I can only find one I can afford."

"Good luck with that."

She walked him to the door. "Thanks again. I don't know what I would've done without your help."

"We all need a hand now and then."

He had to grab a sandwich, take a shower, pack up his gear and make the twenty-minute drive to the bar where he'd be playing, but when he got home, he made the sandwich and went to his computer instead. If what Savanna and her children had been through was traumatic enough to make her believe she'd never want to be with another man, he thought it might be serious enough to be reported in the news, especially because she'd made an odd comment when describing her ideal lesbian partner—something about wanting a woman who abhors violence.

A search for Nephi, Utah, brought up a link with some general information on the town. Essentially an all-white population (ninety-seven percent). Mostly married (over sixty percent). First settled by Mormons. Only 3,600 people, so even smaller than Silver Springs. Not a lot of industry. Everything of any real interest seemed to be located in the Provo/Orem area about an hour north, or even farther in Salt Lake City.

He clicked off that page and typed in "Nephi, UT, crime," and learned that the overall crime rate was one percent higher than the national average. From what he could tell, that was mostly due to drug busts and burglaries. Nothing too serious. At least, that was what he assumed until he stumbled across an article in the *Times-News* that reported a couple of rapes.

Two women had been attacked in Nephi—one who was walking to a waitressing job in the early morning, and one who was carrying her laundry down to the basement of her apartment building late at night a week later. Both victims claimed their attacker had worn a mask and wielded a knife, that he'd cursed and screamed the whole time not to look at him. And, like many rapists, he'd threatened to come back and kill them if they went to the police.

The investigation had been exhaustive, but the police kept coming up empty-handed—until DNA testing confirmed that the crimes were linked to a third incident in Springville, near Provo. Then the detectives knew the rapist was working in a much bigger area and cast a wider net.

Gavin searched for other articles on the same crimes and found one that indicated a woman in Provo had reported some guy lurking about her Mormon church one night after choir practice. He left without approaching her, but he spooked her enough that she jotted down his license plate number. That was what had focused the investigation on one particular suspect.

Yet another article indicated that someone had finally been arrested for those assaults: Gordon Gray, a thirty-year-old white male who was a husband and father.

There it was. The perpetrator had a wife and children. That fit. The suspect had operated in and around Nephi. That fit, too. And Savanna had mentioned that her ex-husband's name was Gordon, which wasn't all that common. *Everything* fit. She'd been married to a man who'd assaulted three women. The victims were complete strangers to Gordon Gray and to each other, which was what had made it so difficult to catch him, but police had plenty of evidence and were now working to see if they could link Gray to more unsolved cases.

Gavin rocked back. *Holy shit.* No wonder Savanna wanted to become a lesbian. She'd been living with—and had children with—a man who was a violent criminal. Had Gordon mistreated her, too?

Gavin wanted to read more about the situation from which his new neighbor had apparently fled, but if he didn't get showered, he'd be late for No Good Pete's. Then he might not be able to get *any* gigs.

"A *rapist*," he murmured, still shocked as he pulled off his shirt. How had the beautiful woman moving in next door gotten involved with a guy like that? And had she realized, at some point, that there was something wrong with him—or had it all come as a surprise?

★ ★ ★

Reese called after the kids were in bed. "Hey, you never let me know when you got in last night."

Savanna had forgotten to notify him. She'd had so much on her mind. That she'd have to keep the moving van another day before she could get to LA to return it and buy a car, which would stretch her budget when she was trying to cut every corner. That, after what Gavin had said about the condition of the house, it might be worse than she was expecting, which had turned out to be the case. That her neighbor might not return to help her cross the creek after what she'd said about students of a boys ranch. That her mother-in-law's threats might turn into more than a turn of phrase if Gordon didn't get convicted. And then, of course, underneath it all, the big question—the question of whether she was doing the right thing in the first place.

"Sorry," she said. "It's been crazy."

"In what way? You're there, aren't you? And the kids are okay?"

She was working from the floor again. She'd cleaned out the cupboards and unpacked her silverware and dishes. Now she was organizing and putting away her pots and pans. "Yeah, we're here and everyone's fine."

"Well? Was it what you were expecting?"

"Not entirely." She was so tired she could hardly move, but she intended to finish the kitchen so she could go to bed feeling she'd made a strong start. "Silver Springs is amazing, though. I can't believe it hasn't been voted one of America's top places to live. Or…maybe it has. I never check those things."

"What makes it so great?"

"It's nestled in this pretty valley only an hour or so from the sea. It's clean and stylish and feels far more friendly than Nephi—although I've only met two people, so as far as friendly goes I don't really know," she added with a laugh.

"You used to like Nephi."

She hadn't hated it in the beginning. That was where Gordon's grandmother had lived and, disappointed in her only daughter, she'd left Gordon the equity in her house when she passed. Given that his job required him to be in central Utah, and living in Nephi saved him significant time on the road, they'd stayed instead of trying to sell so they could remain in Midvale, a suburb of Salt Lake, where they'd lived for the first part of their marriage. "Not at the end."

"I hope this place will treat you better."

"I have an exceptionally nice neighbor, so that's a start." She remembered Gavin saying he found her attractive and couldn't help smiling. Hearing those words come from such a handsome and charismatic man felt good. But that was only because it'd been so long since she'd been seen as anything other than a tired wife and mother, she told herself. She was flattered, not truly *excited*, even though she had to admit that she found him attractive, too.

"I was under the impression from the way Dad talked and the pictures he sent that the ranch house was out in the country," Reese said.

It required some effort to draw her mind back to the conversation. For a change, she was preoccupied by something other than Gordon's crimes. That was a relief in and of itself. "It *is*. I'm pretty sure Gavin's place used to be part of the original ranch and was recently split off and converted from something else—a barn or tackle house. It's not big, but it's cool. Fits him in that way."

"Meaning *Gavin's* cool?"

Reese pounced on her last sentence right away, making her wish she hadn't included that information. But Gavin *was* cool— even a little exotic from her perspective. Given the homogenous sector of people she'd circulated among in Utah for so long, he stood out. Not only were the people of Nephi mostly white, they were mostly the same religion and political persuasion, which was different from the diversity she'd known growing up in California. She'd never lived in Silver Springs before, and yet she felt a strong sense of having come home. "Yeah."

"How old is your neighbor?"

"Didn't ask, but I would guess he's about my age."

"I take it he's single…"

"I got that impression." She *hoped* Gavin wasn't the kind of douchebag who would say what he did if he had a girlfriend…

Her brother took a few seconds to consider her answer before responding. "Is he attractive?"

She wished she'd never mentioned him. She hadn't meant to send her brother into full alert. "In his own way. I mean…he's not the athletic type—like you and Gordon. Not what *I* go for. He's more…the rock star type."

"That's interesting."

She felt her face heat as if she'd given something away, which was a ridiculous reaction. What was there to give away? Gavin had told her he found her attractive—*really* attractive (she couldn't help recalling the emphasis he'd placed on that word), but she hadn't encouraged him. She was just embarrassed because the conversation she'd had with Gavin at the creek hadn't been a normal conversation for two people who were nearly strangers.

"Not as interesting as you seem to think," she said in an attempt to back away from the subject. "I'm grateful he's been so nice. That's all. If he hadn't helped me get over the creek, I could still be at the motel where I had to stay last night. That's the other person I met. The motel manager. He was middle-aged and balding." Not nearly as appealing as Gavin, but then she'd never met another man who'd interested her quite so quickly.

"You had to cross a creek?" Reese said.

"Not a very big one, but you can't drive a moving van through it. The bridge was gone, washed out in the last big rain."

"That must not have come as a pleasant surprise."

"Could've been worse." She shuddered to think how the night

would've ended had Gavin not scraped himself up in order to save her from getting stuck.

"What about the house? Will you be able to stay there?"

She shifted so that she could get off her knees and sit cross-legged as she surveyed the kitchen. She'd been trying not to let the condition of the place get her down. It didn't matter what it looked like now, she'd put everything in order, make it comfortable. But since her father had sent those pictures, several of the windows had been broken, the back door had been kicked in, someone had shot a rifle or some other kind of gun at several of the lighting fixtures, which had also put holes in the walls, and the stove and dishwasher had been stolen. Replacing those items on top of renovating the house would eat up even more of her budget. As far as appliances went, she'd brought only her washer and dryer from Nephi, since her refrigerator had needed to be replaced, anyway. Thank goodness Gavin had had a dolly with which to unload them. The entire drive, she'd been stressed about how she was going to get the heavier items into the house. She'd only been able to get them on the truck in the first place because she'd recruited help from her neighbor in Nephi. "I have my work cut out for me. No way to sugarcoat that. And you should see the mess that's been left behind. There're cigarette butts and beer cans everywhere, not to mention evidence of animals."

"That won't take too long to clean up. Do you have heat?"

"No."

"You didn't call ahead and get the utilities turned on?"

"I did. There's something wrong with the heater. Fortunately, it's warm enough this time of year—in this area—that we'll be okay during the day, and when it chills off at night—" like it was now "—I can pile blankets on the kids."

"You need to get that fixed."

"I'll have someone take a look at it." She hoped it was only a blown fuse. Replacing the whole unit would be expensive.

"Is the town big enough to have the goods and services you'll need?"

"They'll have some things. For others, I'll have to go to Santa Barbara or LA. Anyway, getting the heater checked is *way* down my list. First, I have to buy a refrigerator and a stove, so I can cook."

"You don't have a stove?"

"Someone stole it."

"What about a microwave?"

"There was one, but that's gone, too."

"Damn it, Savanna. You should've waited until I could come with you."

"I had to leave right away," she said. "I was getting so defensive in Nephi I couldn't function."

He sighed into the phone. "I know, but now you're even farther from me than you were before—"

"No, it's almost the exact same distance. I checked." She'd been nervous about putting more miles between them.

"Still, it sounds like you're in a big mess, and I've got finals and can't do anything to help."

"We'll be okay." At least she wouldn't have to worry about running into one of her husband's victims, or having her ex-mother-in-law show up to start another argument. Here she was on her own, but she was no different than anyone else, would have a chance to heal in an emotionally safe environment.

Reese lowered his voice. "I know Branson, especially, is struggling with everything that's happened. Do you think he'll be able to adjust?"

She thought of the bed-wetting they'd been dealing with since Gordon was arrested. "I do."

"Maybe you should get him some therapy."

"I should get us *all* therapy, but there's no money for that."

"Have you heard from Gordon?"

Like his mother, her ex had tried calling her many times, as many times as he could use the phone in jail. But after the first few days, when her faith had completely given way and she'd broken down and screamed her rage and anger at him as he begged her to ignore the proof she'd been shown—which she *couldn't*—she'd stopped accepting his calls, too. That was when he'd started writing her long, rambling letters pledging his love and pleading his innocence. The last one had insisted that he'd found God, that he was attending daily Bible study and was praying that she'd be able to see that the police had the wrong man.

She hadn't bothered to write back. She felt too conflicted when she communicated with him, hadn't even told him—or his mother—that she was taking the kids and moving to California. She'd simply packed up and left as soon as possible. She planned to get a new phone number, too—to cut every tie that still attached her to Gordon. But all of that took time and attention to detail, and right now she was buried in far more basic tasks. "Not in the last couple of days," she said.

"What about Dorothy?"

"Of course. She texted me again yesterday."

"What'd she want this time?"

"More of the same. She's desperate to get me to pay for his attorneys."

"How can she still believe he's innocent?"

"I'm not sure she cares if he's innocent. His victims don't matter to her. She wants to save her baby."

"After all the shit she put him through in the past, it's shocking she's so defensive now."

Savanna saw a spider crawling across the floor and jumped up. She hated spiders. "Ironic, isn't it? And yet she claims *I'm* ruining his life. She got to him long before I did."

"What about his father? Do you think he'll step in and try to help?"

With a shudder of revulsion, she swept the spider into her dustpan and hurried to take it outside. "No. Gordon's never gotten along with Ken. Once he left Dorothy, he never looked back." What happened to Gordon when he was a child wasn't fair. Both of his parents had let him down—and now he'd passed on the favor. "I feel bad for him when I think of his past, but that doesn't change the present. I have to do what I can to save my sanity so that I can support our kids."

"Branson and Alia are great. They're going to make it through this and so will you."

That spider had unsettled her, made her more cognizant of the dirt and all she had to accomplish to make this place into a home. "I hope that's true, given we don't have any choice."

"Will you return to Utah for the trial?"

"No. I don't want to go back for anything."

"I thought there was some question about whether you'd testify."

"Detective Sullivan once asked me if I'd be willing to take the stand and talk about how secretive Gordon was—and how much he was gone. Sullivan wanted me to confirm that Gordon wasn't at home when the attacks took place, but they have my sworn statement, which lays it all out, and the forensic evidence is far more damning than anything *I'd* have to say. I suppose they could contact me if they feel the trial isn't going well and ask me to come, but right now it doesn't appear they need me."

"Will you be able to do it if they ask?"

"I don't know, to be honest. I'd rather not be involved."

"I don't blame you."

After that, they talked about having him come visit once the semester ended so he could help fix a few things. But he also worked as a bartender and couldn't jeopardize his job, wasn't sure how many days he'd be able to get off.

"I'll see what I can do and let you know," he promised before ending the call.

Once they'd disconnected, Savanna finished unpacking the kitchen. Then she walked down to the end of the drive to see if her neighbor had come home. Why she was curious enough to make the effort when she was so tired, she couldn't say. She just couldn't quit thinking about him. She supposed she was romanticizing him a little bit, since it was much more fun to think about this new person in her life than all the dark things she'd been thinking about for the past couple of months. Occasionally, she even caught herself wondering what it would be like to kiss a man who had facial hair. Gordon had hated beards and mustaches—even goatees—so he'd never worn one.

Would she feel the hair on Gavin's face or only his full, soft-looking lips? And what would a man who had long hair and tattoos be like in bed?

I like it soft and gentle, and I won't get in the way of your search for a lesbian partner.

That she felt a tingle when she remembered the way he'd said those words told her she'd be hopeless as a lesbian. She hadn't been serious in the first place.

Still, she wasn't interested in another relationship. She'd been burned too badly. He just gave her something to daydream about that wasn't upsetting, and she couldn't see any harm in fantasizing if it made getting through the day easier. It wasn't as though she'd ever act on those fantasies.

The stars were out. She hadn't noticed them in ages. She stopped to gaze up at the sky and to feel the cool wind ripple through her clothes. She was glad she'd come to California. She felt she could breathe for the first time since the nightmare with Gordon started. She didn't have to worry about the police dropping by to ask her any more questions, didn't have to fear that every car she heard was someone coming to vent their anger, didn't have to worry about what someone might say to her children or dread another visit from her mother-in-law. She'd unshackled herself. And even though that freedom would come at the price of living in a tumbledown old ranch house for a while, she was willing. For the first time since she

said "I do" nine years ago, she realized that even her marriage
had been confining. She'd accepted that being Mrs. Gray was
her "forever" lot in life, would never have considered leaving
Gordon, if only for the sake of her children. But now that he'd
made the decision for her, perhaps one day she'd be glad that
she'd been given the chance to reinvent herself.

That was an interesting thought, one she hadn't considered
in all the misery of the foregoing weeks, but one that seemed
to hang in the air tonight as a tantalizing promise. The future
could be what she made it...

Hauling in a deep, cleansing breath, she smiled as she continued to the creek.

She couldn't see Gavin's place from there, so she crossed over
and peered through the trees.

There were no lights on at his house, and his truck was still
gone.

It was after midnight. This late, he had to be with a woman,
didn't he?

Probably. Maybe he was even staying the night...

She told herself he had the right to do whatever he wanted; it
made no difference to her. But she didn't feel quite so relieved
and happy as she turned and walked back to the broken-down
house that awaited her attention in the morning.

CHAPTER FIVE

Gavin was exhausted when he turned down the narrow road leading to his house. No Good Pete's had been rowdy, and the crowd hadn't left until the bar closed. Normally, he liked playing for a packed house. All musicians dreamed of being well received. But his mind hadn't been on his music tonight. He'd been thinking about his new neighbor—about how pretty she was and about the fact that she'd been married to a rapist. How did something like that happen to a woman like her? And how had it affected her and her children?

He'd also been making a mental list of all the things she would need over the next few weeks in order to make her house a home, and he was so preoccupied with what he could do to help that he didn't notice until he was ready to pull into his own drive that there was a Toyota Pathfinder in the way.

He recognized that SUV instantly. It belonged to Heather Fox, his on-again, off-again girlfriend for the past few years, who was now with Scott Mullins, a guy Gavin had known almost since he moved to Silver Springs at fourteen.

"*There* you are," she said as he got out. "Your gig must've gone late."

Her statement struck him as odd. "You knew I had a gig?"

"Yeah, I saw it on your website. I like what you've done there, by the way—how people can book online."

He'd forgotten about the website. "It's been convenient. I still go over all requests to make sure they're not too far away and negotiate if they want longer hours or more than one show, but it handles a lot of the initial inquiries, since people can see my rates and whether I'm off on certain days or already booked."

"It's cool that your music career is taking off. You deserve it. You're so talented."

She'd always encouraged him when it came to his music. She'd been flattering in other ways, too. That was probably why he fell back into a relationship with her every once in a while even though he wasn't in love. "Thank you."

"So you were in Santa Barbara tonight?"

She must've gotten that from the website, too, because he hadn't talked to her since seeing her at the Blue Suede Shoe three weeks ago, when she'd been with Scott. "Yeah. No Good Pete's."

"Oh. I've never seen you play there. I'll have to go next time."

With or without her current boyfriend? he wondered, but didn't ask. "They're having me come back next Saturday."

"Perfect. Santa Barbara's not that far. But…why are you home so late? Don't most bars close at two?"

He could hear the jealousy in her voice. She suspected he'd been with someone. She hadn't been happy the last time he—yet again—broke it off. "This bar did, too, but it took me a while to pack up." He grabbed his guitar from the back seat. "What are you doing here? Did I miss a text?"

"No." She gave him an enticing smile as she came toward him. "I thought I'd surprise you."

Why? "It's late. *Really* late."

"Is that a problem? I figured you might be lonely all the way out here. The last time we were together, you were still in your apartment, remember?"

This was generally how things started with Heather. She'd hit him up and he'd succumb simply because he *was* a little lonely, she was comfortable, he missed the physical intimacy and it was hard to tell her no. He didn't like disappointing her, and after he'd had some space, he tended to remember only the good things about her, which then made him wonder if he shouldn't give the relationship another shot. She'd been fixated on him for so long he wished he could return her love. But wishing never seemed to make it possible.

He stopped before she could walk into his arms. "Does Scott know you're here, Heather? Because the last I remember, you two were seeing each other." And Scott wouldn't be happy to learn she'd shown up at her old boyfriend's place. He was threatened by Gavin—as evidenced by the dirty looks Gavin received whenever they happened across each other in town.

A sheepish expression claimed her face. "It's none of his business."

"Because…"

"We broke up tonight."

"I'm sorry to hear that. I thought it might be serious for you two."

"Oh, come on," she said. "You know my heart has never really belonged to him. You're the only man I've ever truly loved."

Gavin began to feel a little uncomfortable. He didn't want this to go the way it usually did, where he wound up in a relationship he was eager to get out of. "Heather, I hope *I'm* not the reason you broke up."

"Of course you're the reason! I don't know what to say. I can't get over you."

Shit. She'd seemed happy. Having Scott in the picture had taken so much pressure off him. "I care about you," he said. "I hope you know that. But… I don't want to get back together."

He hated having to be so blunt, but he didn't want her to ruin her relationship with Scott, with whom he'd thought she finally had something, because of false hope.

Instead of the hurt and anger he expected, a tentative smile curved her lips. "Come on. I treat you right, don't I? Have I ever said no to you?"

She hadn't. That was part of the problem. He lived in a small town, which meant as a single person he went long stretches without sex. By the time she cycled back to hit him up, the physical intimacy she offered usually tempted him beyond his ability to refuse.

But he wasn't going to succumb tonight. He'd met someone else, someone he thought he might *really* be interested in. He knew getting to know Savanna, in order to make sure, wouldn't be easy. She'd been through a lot, and it was all so recent. But he'd felt an honest attraction when he was with her—one he didn't have to force—and he wasn't going to ruin his chances by sleeping with an old flame he couldn't seem to get rid of. "I've never said you didn't treat me right."

"Good! Because after what you experienced as a child—"

He lifted a hand to stop her. He didn't want to go into that. But she waved him off.

"I know you won't talk about the past. You've told me next to nothing. But the whole town knows you were left at a park when you were a kid. It isn't a secret. I'm only saying that you've been on your own for a long time. Aren't you ready to have someone to love?"

He raked his fingers through his hair. He *was* ready. But he had to find the right person, and he knew it wasn't Heather. He'd tried with her—several times. "It'll happen when it happens."

She grabbed his arm. "How do you know that? Maybe you have to *act*."

"Heather—"

"Wait. Before you say anything else, I—I need to tell you something."

He didn't see how he could refuse to listen. She had tears in her eyes. "Go on…"

"I'm pregnant, Gavin."

His heart began to pound against his chest.

"I found out a week ago," she added.

He swallowed against a tight, dry throat. "You're not saying… I mean, we haven't been together in…in a while. Two months at least. So…this must be Scott's child, right?"

She wiped away the tears that were starting to fall.

"Right?" he repeated when she didn't answer.

"I don't know." Her words came out a frightened whisper.

Gavin closed his eyes. This couldn't be happening. "Is that why you and Scott broke up?" he asked when he looked at her again. "You told him about the baby, and he thinks you might be pregnant with *my* child?"

"Yes. I believe it *is* yours. In any case, I hope it is, because you're the one I love."

When Gavin's knees threatened to give out on him, he set his guitar down and reached for the door frame. "You were on the pill," he said, keeping his voice measured and calm despite his panic.

She wrung her hands. "I was. But my doctor told me that certain medications can make the pill ineffective. And I was on antibiotics our last week together."

Gavin let his head fall against the door frame above his hand.

"You're not going to say anything?" she asked when he didn't respond.

"I don't know what to say." He knew how religious her family was. Although she didn't buy in completely, an abortion would be out of the question. He wasn't sure he'd suggest terminating a pregnancy in the first place. So…what other options did they have?

"When can we find out?" he asked. No doubt Scott wanted to learn the child's paternity as badly as he did…

"Not until the baby's born."

He straightened in surprise. "That's nine months!"

"Seven months," she corrected. "I'm about nine weeks along—or that's what we think. I've never been good at keeping track of my cycle."

"Seven months is an eternity. Surely, there's got to be a way to find out sooner."

"We could do a prenatal paternity test, but it'd be safer—better for the baby—to wait. My doctor told me he wouldn't recommend it."

He felt sick. She was right. He had begun to want a family, but not with her. With someone he could truly love.

"Gavin? Are you okay?"

He struggled to voice a few words. "Yeah. I'm fine."

"You're just standing there, looking dazed."

He was screaming inside, but he didn't want to make this any harder on her. The fact that she was crying told him she hadn't planned the pregnancy. "What can I do to help?" he managed to say.

"There's nothing anyone can do at this point. But I'm hoping you'll be open to giving us another chance. For the sake of the baby. I mean…maybe the universe is trying to tell us something."

Gavin didn't believe the universe had anything to do with it. As far as he was concerned, it was plain bad luck. "It'll be okay," he said, but that was a lie. At least, it was for him. "We'll get through it somehow."

She gave him a funny look. Could she tell he was only going through the motions? That his heart wasn't in those words?

"Is that a yes?" she asked. "You're willing to try again?"

Apparently, his response hadn't been entirely appropriate. Or it wasn't what she'd been looking for. But he was picking up only about every other word. With effort, he focused harder. "I'm sorry. What'd you say?"

"*Will you give me another chance? I* think we're good together. You couldn't find anyone who would love you more."

He squeezed his forehead. "Let me think about it, okay? This is... This is a bit of a shock."

She sniffed as she attempted a watery smile. "Okay. Yeah, of course."

"Thank you," he said politely, and went inside, where he set his guitar carefully to one side and slid down the door.

In elementary school, Gavin had been fascinated by the story of *Hansel and Gretel*. His first theft—at seven years old—had been a worn copy of it he'd stolen from the school library and hidden under his bed. He'd loved the happy ending—even though it made him sad, given his own situation—but hated the book, because he couldn't understand how the father could miss the evil in Hansel and Gretel's stepmother. None of the other kids who read the book or were told the story seemed to hold the father responsible, but Gavin knew the woodcutter *had* to have seen some sign of the stepmother's unkindness, just as *his* father had witnessed the way Gavin's stepmother, Diana, had mistreated him. Diana had claimed he was a behavioral problem, had complained about him constantly—and he had been a rambunctious boy—but he hadn't been seriously delinquent until well after she was out of his life. That was when he'd acted out in earnest.

He should've been able to depend on his father to look out for him. Since his birth mother died of a heart defect when he was two, he'd had only his father to act as his protector. Had Miles cared enough, Gavin's stepmother would never have been able to leave him at that park.

Gavin had been only six when she drove off, but he'd never forget coming out of the bathroom to find her gone. The sickening almost instant knowledge that she hadn't left him by accident. The gut-ripping fear when the hours dragged on and she didn't return. Or the whispering of the stranger who came across him and called the authorities.

Letting his head fall back on the door with a thud, Gavin cursed under his breath. He was still on the floor, hadn't moved since Heather left, and it'd been almost an hour. The news she'd delivered had decimated him, opened him up to his past in a way nothing else could—probably because he was terrified of being responsible for someone else's happiness, terrified of failing the way his father had failed with him. It required all his focus and energy just to stave off the memories that were assaulting him like machine-gun fire.

Squeezing his eyes closed, he hugged his knees to his chest and brought his head forward again. *Don't remember. That was another life, someone else's decision. You're an adult now, in charge of your own fate and your own happiness.* That was what Aiyana had taught him. He'd been *much* happier after she'd come into his life. He'd quit stealing, quit getting in trouble with the law, and had eventually found an inner peace that had always eluded him before. He managed that by refusing to give a mental audience to anything that'd happened to him before the age of fourteen, which was when he started at New Horizons and was adopted a few months later by Aiyana. But now that he was finally hearing from his old man every once in a while, it was more difficult to keep those old memories bottled up. Just the sound of Miles's voice—or that name on his caller ID—dredged up the pain.

The fact that he might be having a baby seemed to be doing the same thing. Heather seemed fairly convinced he was the father. Was she right? Or was she simply feeling as though she finally had something with which to force him to commit?

Gavin pulled the tie from his hair and let it fall. They wouldn't know the baby's paternity for *seven months.*

How would he ever wait that long?

Finally, he stopped fighting the urge and called Aiyana. He

hadn't wanted to wake her. It wasn't the thoughtful thing to do. And he considered himself too old to need her, hadn't had to make a call like this in years. But he knew, from experience, that she wouldn't mind. She would do anything for him. Maybe that was why her love had had the power to redeem him, to pull him out of the darkness. "Mom?" he said as soon as he heard her sleepy hello.

"*Gavin?*" she replied, her voice instantly filling with fear. "What's going on? Are you okay?"

"I'm fine. I mean... I'm not hurt."

There was a slight pause, after which she sounded more lucid. "So what is it? Did something happen in Santa Barbara? Do you need me to come get you?"

"No. I'm at home. Safe."

"Then...you're drunk?"

"No." He'd never had a drinking problem, but he had enjoyed some wild nights, especially when he was younger. Apparently, getting a call like this had triggered Aiyana's memory of those days. "Haven't had a drop."

"Then what?"

"I shouldn't have called, I guess. I'll talk to you in the morning."

"Wait," she said. "I'm here whenever you need me. You know that."

"I do. But now that I'm actually talking to you, I'm not sure I want to tell you what's on my mind, so it's a little crazy that I woke you up."

"Say it, anyway," she insisted. "We'll work through it together, the way we always have."

He couldn't help smiling at how fast she came rushing to his rescue. She was an amazing woman, had saved so many lost boys. And he was extra lucky because he was one of the eight New Horizons students she'd officially adopted. "You remember Heather Fox?"

"Of course. You've brought her to many a Sunday dinner over here. But you told me she was with someone else now."

"Scott Mullins."

"That's right. Is that what this is about? You haven't been in a fight with him, have you? You told me you were *glad* Heather had moved on, that you were hoping she'd marry Scott. You—"

"I haven't been in a fight." He broke in to stop her before she could go any further down that road. "And I wasn't lying when I said I was glad she'd moved on. That's part of the problem."

"So you're not sad?"

"No."

"Whew! Then what's the rest of the problem?"

He didn't see any way to break the news gently, so he blurted it out. "She's pregnant."

Silence. Then his mother said, "I see. But…what does that mean for *you*? Are you upset that she's having a child with Scott?"

He could tell it was a leading statement. Aiyana was beginning to catch on to what this call was all about. "I'm upset that she might be having *my* child."

"She *told* you it was yours?"

"She told me it might be. She doesn't know for sure."

"She slept with you both *that* close together?"

"She probably went straight to his house after I broke up with her. That next week, she tried hard to make me regret my decision, to evoke some jealousy. I saw them everywhere together."

"I see. So…when will you be able to find out?"

He stared up at the ceiling. "Not until after she has the baby."

Aiyana sighed deeply.

"It's been a long time since I've run up against something that threatens my peace of mind like this," he said, putting her sigh into words.

"You didn't use any birth control?"

He could hear the disapproval in that statement. "Of course we used birth control, Mom. It didn't work." He didn't mention why. He wasn't going to blame Heather for what'd happened. He was fairly certain she'd believed they were safe.

"So what are you going to do? Is she still with Scott?"

"No. They broke up tonight. I can't imagine he was happy to hear that she might be pregnant with my child."

"I can't, either."

"Now she wants to get back together with me."

"She told you that?"

"Yes. She was waiting for me here at the house when I got home from my gig tonight."

"How do *you* feel about the idea?"

"Between you and me? I'm not excited about it."

"Did you tell her that?"

"Of course not."

She sighed again. "It's going to be a long nine months."

"Seven—she's at two months already. Not knowing will be terrible. I keep hoping that all of this panic and concern will be for nothing. But if the baby *is* mine, I could use seven months— and then some—to prepare for such a big responsibility."

"You'll be a good father," she said.

He drew a deep breath. Maybe that was what he'd needed to hear. Maybe that was why he'd called her. "I can't believe this is happening."

"You know your brother and Cora have been trying to have a baby, how excited and hopeful we've been for them."

He did. But Elijah was married to the love of his life. Gavin's situation would be entirely different.

"Damn it." He'd thought he had his life all figured out. Sure, he battled a few demons late at night, especially if he drank too much, which was why he usually didn't. But anyone who'd been left at a park at six and then raised by a family who'd only taken him in for the stipend they received from the state would have a few scars. If only he hadn't gone back to Heather that last time, he would've escaped cleanly...

"Gavin…"

"What?"

"If it *is* your baby, you're going to love him or her with all your heart. This isn't the end of the world."

"Right." Just the world as he knew it. "Thanks, Mom," he said. "I'll talk to you tomorrow."

"Gavin…"

He could tell she was reluctant to let him go. "I'm fine. Just tired." As he disconnected, he forced himself to get up. He needed sleep. But as he walked to his room, pulling off his clothes as he went, he thought of his new neighbor. He'd been excited to get to know her. Not only did he find her attractive, she seemed different from any of the other women he'd dated. Unusually pure-hearted. Wise for her age.

Tragedy had a way of tempering people. Maybe that was why he liked her. They'd both faced unusual challenges.

But with what was going on in his life now, he knew he'd be crazy to pursue her. She'd be *much* better off if he just left her alone.

CHAPTER SIX

Elijah, the oldest of the eight ranch students adopted by Aiyana, woke Gavin the following morning by barging into his bedroom and letting the door bang against the inside wall. "Hey, you! It's past noon. Are you *ever* getting out of bed?"

Gavin rolled over to gaze up at his brother. He never bothered to lock his house, not when he was home, so it wasn't any wonder that Eli had been able to get in. It was much more of a surprise that he'd show up out of the blue—and alone. These days he was usually with Cora, his wife. "What're you doing? You never drive all the way out here."

"Why would I? We see each other all the time."

They both worked at the ranch, and Eli lived there, too. It used to be that they also met in town quite a bit. But that didn't happen much anymore. Since Eli had gotten married, Gavin was left at loose ends on the evenings they would've spent together. Fortunately, he'd started gigging, which helped to fill that hole. But the fact that he hadn't yet found anyone he enjoyed hanging out with as much as his brother made him think that maybe it was time for him to settle down, too. He'd actually been feeling that way for a while.

Maybe having a baby with Heather would force his hand. She wasn't a *bad* person. Surely, he could come to love her—now that he knew he might not have any choice. Then everything would end well.

"You haven't answered my question," Gavin said. "What are you doing here?"

"I came out because my calls kept going straight to your voice mail."

Gavin covered a yawn. "Did it ever occur to you that I might've turned off my phone for a reason?"

"It did. That reason is why I skipped going to LA with Cora to visit her folks and came over here instead."

He groaned. "Oh. I get it. You're worried. Mom told you about Heather."

"Was it a secret?"

"I'd rather not have the news spread all over town." But Gavin had a sneaking suspicion that he wouldn't be able to avoid it, and he knew Aiyana and Elijah wouldn't be the ones responsible for doing the talking. No doubt Scott would have plenty to say— every time he was asked why he and Heather had broken up, he'd probably blame Gavin, make it sound as though she'd been cheating with her ex while she was with him, which wasn't true.

"Mom's concerned about you. And let's be honest. She assumed you'd tell me eventually," Eli added with a grin.

"I'm sure I would have." Although Gavin struggled to get along with a couple of his brothers—not too shocking given that they all came from such difficult backgrounds and some were more damaged than others—he was totally devoted to Elijah. They couldn't be closer if they were related by blood.

"So?" Eli said. "How do you feel about the news?"

Gavin felt sick about the pregnancy—and then he felt guilty for reacting so negatively. Despair wasn't what Heather needed, and it wasn't fair to the baby, who wasn't to blame for Gavin knocking up a woman he liked but couldn't seem to love. "Do I need to spell it out for you?" he asked with a wince.

"There must be something about Heather. You keep going back to her."

Gavin shot him a look. "You *know* it was finally over for me."

Eli frowned as he sat on the foot of the bed. "Yeah. It did feel pretty permanent this time."

"That's what makes this so ironic." He shoved a few pillows behind his back.

"She's been with Scott Mullins for a while. Are you sure it's not *his* baby?"

Gavin wanted to reach for the hope that possibility evoked but didn't dare. "I'm *not* sure, but...she doesn't think so."

"She could be wrong."

"She would know better than we would."

Eli scratched his neck. "She's always had a thing for you. Could saying the baby is yours be nothing more than wishful thinking?"

Gavin had considered that. He didn't think she'd get pregnant on purpose. Or that she'd tell an outright *lie*. But he could see her using a bit of doubt to get him to reconsider their relationship. "I honestly don't know."

"What does that mean? Are you going to give her another chance, or wait until—"

"I'm going to support her through the pregnancy and then decide about anything more permanent. If the baby's mine, I'll marry her."

"You will."

"Yes."

Resting his elbows on his knees, Eli stared at the rug covering the hardwood floor. "What if you two get close over the next several months and it turns out that the baby *isn't* yours?" he asked when he spoke again.

Gavin immediately thought of his new neighbor and the

opportunity that would provide but pushed Savanna from his mind. Even if he wasn't facing this problem, she'd made it clear that she wasn't interested in pursuing a romantic relationship. So he wasn't losing anything, even though it felt like he was.

"If I could fall in love with her, that would be a good thing."

"Regardless."

"Isn't that what commitment's all about?"

"You're saying you'd love Scott's baby. Help raise it."

"Of course."

Eli got up and began to pace. "Okay. Playing devil's advocate here...what if you two can't make it work, and she goes back to him?"

Gavin kicked off the covers. "I hope that doesn't happen. Scott already resents me. No doubt this will make him hate me all the more."

"No man likes living in the shadow of a former lover."

"I get that. But I didn't put him there. I've always been honest with Heather, told her my feelings aren't as strong as hers."

"You couldn't tell by the way you treat her. Maybe that's the problem."

"I'm supposed to treat her badly?"

"I'm not suggesting that. It's just... I don't know. Frustrating for me to feel as though you're being railroaded. If only she could love Scott half as much as she loves you, you'd be off the hook."

"No. I don't want her to go back to him *now*, don't want my child to be raised by a stepparent. Not after what I went through. Especially when we're talking about this particular situation. The last time I was at the Blue Suede Shoe, Scott and Heather were there, too. Heather couldn't take her eyes off me. Every time I looked up, there she was, and Scott didn't miss it. They got into an argument before the night was over. Then Scott insisted they leave."

"I see your point. Given her history with you, he'd always be jealous." Elijah scrubbed a hand over his face. "I'm sorry, bro. She's really got you cornered."

"She didn't do it on purpose."

Eli stopped moving and propped his hands on his hips. "I hope not!"

"She didn't! At least, I can't imagine why she would. She's got to be as panic-stricken as I am. A kid makes life real, you know? Anyway, we'll figure it out." Although, at this point, Gavin had no clue *how*. He'd never been able to force his heart, wasn't sure anyone could.

A knock sounded at the front door.

"For living in a remote place, you're getting a lot of visitors this morning," Eli said.

Gavin barely refrained from grimacing. "That's got to be her." When he'd asked for some time to think, he'd been hoping for several days. But maybe she couldn't give him that. She had to be upset and eager to reach a resolution…

"Should I get it?" Eli asked. "I could say you're in the shower or something to buy you more time to come to terms with this."

"No. I might as well reassure her that I won't leave her holding the bag." He got out of bed, pulled on his jeans without bothering to button them and went out to talk to her. But it wasn't Heather. Branson stood at the door. Savanna was in the moving van with Alia, letting it idle in front of the house while her son ran up to the door.

Feeling a twinge of guilt for not getting up earlier and taking over some milk and cereal or eggs, Gavin quickly buttoned his pants. "Hey, little buddy. What's going on?"

"We found a fridge for sale in Santa… Santa Something," Branson said. "But not Claus."

Gavin chuckled. "Santa Barbara?"

"That's it. We're going to pick it up while we have the truck. My mom was wondering if you'd help us unload when we get back."

"Sure, I'll be here. My brother's visiting, too, so he can help."

"I'll tell her." Branson spoke over his shoulder as he ran back and opened the truck door to convey the message.

"Who was that?" Eli asked, but before Gavin could respond, Savanna called out a thank-you.

Although Gavin felt slightly self-conscious that he hadn't yet combed his hair, and he didn't have on a shirt, he strode out to have a word with her. "You don't need me to go with you and help you load it in the first place, do you?"

"No," she replied. "The guy I'm buying it from said he has friends who can help. I was just worried about how I'd get it off the truck once I returned, wanted to make sure you'd still be home and wouldn't mind lending a hand."

"I don't mind at all," he assured her.

Her gaze lowered to his bare torso before shifting to a spot behind him, and he turned to see that Elijah had followed him out. "This is my brother Eli. Eli, Savanna, my new neighbor."

"Did you say *neighbor*? Out here?" Eli gestured at the wide expanse of raw land.

"I'm currently moving into the ranch house—or what's left of it—next door," she said. "But I never would've made it across the creek yesterday if not for your brother."

Eli gave Gavin a playful shove. "I guess that means he's good for something, huh?"

Her smile broadened. "He's pretty handy to have around."

Gavin felt the pull of attraction. He wasn't sure he'd ever been more taken with a woman, not so quickly.

"He's a real pain in the, um, neck," Eli said, choosing his words carefully in deference to the children. "Don't let him fool you."

She leaned forward in an attempt to get a better look at Eli's face. "I hope you don't mind, but he signed you up to help me move a fridge."

Eli shrugged. "Might as well make myself useful."

"What about a stove?" Gavin asked. "You'll need one of those, too."

"That'll be tougher to find. I'm not even sure if I should get gas or electric. I thought you might know."

He nearly laughed. How she was going to go about remodeling the ranch house, he had no idea, but he sort of liked that she needed him. "Gas."

"Got it. I'll grab a microwave so we can get by in the meantime and hope to come across a gas stove. I appreciate the help." She put the transmission in Drive. "If all goes well, and the fridge looks as good in real life as it does in the pictures I saw, I'll be back in an hour and a half."

"We'll be here," Gavin said.

As soon as she drove off, Eli nudged him. "Wow!"

Savanna's smile had left Gavin a little dazed. "What?"

"The color of her hair is sort of unusual, but she's striking."

Gavin watched the moving van until it reached the highway. "Yeah. She's pretty, all right."

"So what's going on? She married?"

"Divorced." He thought of what her ex had done but chose not to reveal that information. Although he could trust Eli not to tell anyone else—except maybe Aiyana—opening his mouth felt disloyal somehow.

"Then why haven't you mentioned her?"

"She's just got here yesterday."

"The same day you learned that Heather is pregnant."

He let his breath seep out in a long, dejected sigh. "Yeah. Can you believe it?"

"Did you see all of Gavin's tattoos?" Branson asked, his voice full of awe as they gathered as much speed as they could muster, given the limitations of the van.

Since Gavin had come out of the house without a shirt, Savanna couldn't have missed his tattoos—or his bare chest. But she didn't mind having seen that. She *liked* the way he looked. A lot. His brother was probably more classically handsome. With such dark hair and blue eyes, he reminded her of Elvis Presley, but she found Gavin's less conventional looks more attractive. "I saw them," she said.

"They went clear up to here!" Branson indicated his shoulder.

Alia, who was busy playing a game on Savanna's phone, made no comment.

Curious to see what her son would say, Savanna glanced over at him. "Do you like tattoos?"

He seemed stumped by the question. His father had railed about the kind of "trash" that would mark up his or her body, so she knew Branson had to be remembering that. He also had to be thinking that maybe he no longer cared what his father thought about something as benign as tattoos, that maybe he'd venture to form his own opinion. "Do *you*?" he asked uncertainly.

Since she'd met Gavin, she did. He had to be the sexiest man she'd ever come across, tattoos and all, which was odd because if someone had asked her only a few days ago to describe the perfect man, she would not have described anyone who looked remotely like him. "I do," she admitted. "Especially his. They suit him." Gordon would've been shocked to hear those words come out of her mouth, but until now she'd never had strong enough feelings on the subject to contradict him when he criticized ink.

Gordon's cutting remarks suddenly seemed highly ironic, though, considering what *he'd* done.

"So can *I* get one when I'm old enough?" Branson ventured.

She veered to the right, hugging the shoulder so that a car that'd become impatient with following her could get past. "As long as you're at least eighteen. Then you'll be an adult and can decide for yourself. You can't get one any sooner than that."

"Why not?" he asked. "You said you liked them."

"I do, depending on how they're done and where they're at on a person's body. There's an art to it. Anyway, tattoos are permanent. You need to know yourself well before you make that commitment, be certain of what you're doing."

"Oh."

She could tell he was deep in thought. Was he considering easygoing Gavin as a new role model? And was he wondering if maybe he'd rather be like Gavin than the kind of large and in-charge person his father had always been?

She'd been worried about Branson. She'd read enough online to know that bed-wetting wasn't a good sign, but she hoped her son could recover from the blows they'd recently sustained. If not, she was going to do what she could to seek help.

"*I* like Gavin's tattoos," Alia piped up, smiling in a way that let Savanna know she also found him appealing. Alia had been so engrossed in her game Savanna had thought she wasn't paying attention. But this proved that the whole family was a little smitten with their neighbor.

Was it only because he was new—something different? Even before Gordon had been accused of rape, Savanna had let her life fall to routine, had merely been going through the motions. She didn't think that automatically happened in a marriage, but somehow it'd happened in hers. So what had come first? Had *she* neglected Gordon in some way—maybe while she was grieving the loss of her mother, father and older brother—so he'd turned to getting his thrills elsewhere? Or had he turned to getting his thrills elsewhere, thus showing less interest in her, and *then* she'd started focusing strictly on the kids to avoid feeling any dissatisfaction with her marriage?

Someday, maybe she'd get him to tell her why he'd done what he'd done. What led up to that type of thing? What made him hurt people—people who had little chance of fighting back? After living with him and feeling as if she knew him better than anyone, she wanted to understand *why* above all else. But whenever she tried to get him to level with her, he did the exact opposite—swore up and down that he was wrongly accused. That he'd play the martyr when there were women who'd suffered serious injury at his hands made her as angry as anything.

Even if she never got the answers she craved, she'd be better off if he'd just leave her alone, she decided.

Too bad she had little hope of that happening. Now that he was in jail, she was about all he had. He wasn't likely to let her go easily.

Her phone rang. She didn't have Bluetooth in the van, so she couldn't have answered even if she wanted to—not while she was driving—but when she glanced down and spotted caller ID, she didn't *want* to. It was Dorothy. She opened her mouth to tell Alia not to pick up, but Alia had the phone and pressed Talk before Savanna could even get the words out.

"Hi, Grandma!"

Tensing, Savanna pulled off the highway onto a side road and put the truck in Park. She was terrified that Dorothy might say something terrible to Alia, something that would come as too much of a shock to a child of six. Savanna hadn't mentioned to her children that she and their father's mother were still feuding, was trying to keep them from being caught in the middle.

"What'd you say?" Alia's smile slid from her face. "You have *Daddy* on the line?"

"Let me talk to them," Savanna whispered, but Alia wouldn't relinquish the phone.

"Daddy wants to talk to *me*," she said.

Apparently, Dorothy had Gordon on a three-way. *Damn it!* If not for Alia, this call would've transferred to voice mail like all the others.

Savanna curled her fingernails into her palms as she tried to decide whether to insist on taking the phone. Would it be better for her daughter to hear from Gordon—or not?

She supposed that would depend on what he had to say,

whether he'd be angry and use Alia to pass whatever accusations he might launch along to Savanna, or try to comfort Alia after all she'd been through.

Alia deserved some reassurance.

Please let him give her that...

Savanna held her breath and waited.

"Hi, Daddy... Okay... I love you, too... Because we don't live there anymore... Far, far away... Yeah, in a big truck! And someone stole our fridge!... No, this morning we had to eat the peanut butter sandwiches Mom brought for the drive, and they were all smashed..." She wrinkled her nose to show how unappealing they'd been. "Miss you, too... I don't know..." She glanced up when she said that so Savanna knew Gordon's question had something to do with her. "Do you want to talk to her?"

Branson, who was also watching Alia, had a dark expression on his face. As long as Gordon was being nice, Savanna hoped he'd ask to speak to his son—in case it might soothe Branson's hurt to some degree.

"Just a minute..." Alia held the phone out to her brother. "Daddy wants to say hi."

Savanna breathed a sigh of relief. But Branson didn't move.

Alia tugged on his shirt. "Branson, it's Daddy!"

Branson looked up at Savanna. "Did he really hurt those women?"

He knew the answer to that question; he just needed confirmation. It wasn't easy to shake a child's faith, not when that child had once believed his father to be totally reliable.

Savanna nodded. She couldn't lie. The kids had a right to know the truth.

"Then I don't want to talk to him," he muttered, and turned to the window.

Alia didn't seem to know how to react.

Steeling herself for what would likely be another emotional episode, Savanna took the phone. "Hello?"

"Branson won't talk to me?" Gordon said. "You've turned him against me already?"

"I haven't turned anyone against you. *You* did this."

"My mother told me she went to the house to see the kids, and it's empty."

Savanna knew Dorothy hadn't traveled to Nephi to "see the kids." She'd come to "talk some sense" into Savanna, was still hoping to get Savanna to use the last of her money to pay for a fancy lawyer. "We've moved," she admitted.

"Where?" he demanded.

"Stay right here," she told the kids, and got out of the truck so she could talk without an audience. She had no doubt that this conversation would be unpleasant—all of her conversations with Gordon had been unpleasant since he'd been arrested—and she preferred their children not hear another argument. "I'd rather not say."

"You won't tell me where you've gone? When have I ever been any threat to *you*?"

"Until the police came knocking on our door, I never realized you were a threat to *anyone*. Since then I've decided that I never really knew you, or I knew only a small part of you, the part you were willing to show me. So you tell me, Gordon. Was it freak luck that I turned out to be your cover while those other women turned out to be your victims?"

"That's crazy! Listen to yourself! You're overreacting, babe. I'm still the same man you married. The same man you said you loved." He lowered his voice. "The same man you slept with at night."

He meant that to sound alluring; she could tell. But she couldn't help wincing. She didn't care to remember their more intimate moments. "What you did changes everything, Gordon."

"I didn't do it!"

Balling her free hand into a fist in an attempt to control her own simmering rage, she hissed, "Stop lying! They have proof!"

"Doesn't matter what they have. I'm innocent!"

She wished she could believe him. Or maybe it was better if she didn't. Wouldn't it be worse to think her children's father had been wrongly imprisoned, especially when she could do so little to help? "Please, stop. Things are difficult enough. There's no point in fighting. It won't change anything."

He seemed to make an effort to speak calmly. "I'm not trying to upset you."

"Just hearing from you upsets me!" She turned her back on the truck because both children had their noses pressed to the glass.

"So what am I supposed to do? Give up my family as well as my freedom when I haven't done anything wrong?"

She squeezed her eyes closed. It was so hard to hear that over and over. His protestations tempted her to scream at him, to *make* him take responsibility and quit lying. She had let loose once, but doing so hadn't made her feel any better. She'd promised herself she wouldn't do it again, wouldn't be reduced to that. "Please, let me forget you and move on. *Let us go.* After hurting those women, the least you can do is take the punishment you deserve without dragging us all down with you."

"Easy for you to say," he cried. "You're not the one who'll be rotting in prison for fifteen or more years!"

"You're to blame for where you're at, not us."

"I can't believe this," he muttered to himself. "You don't care if I *ever* see my kids again."

Dorothy cut into the conversation, which came as a bit of a shock. She'd remained silent for so long Savanna had almost forgotten she was there. "Told you," she said to her son. "What kind of wife abandons her husband at the first sign of trouble? She's not the person we thought she was!"

Savanna had had enough of her mother-in-law. "This isn't

just *trouble*, Dorothy. It's serial *rape*, one of the most heinous crimes there is."

"Except he didn't do it!" Dorothy responded.

"Mom, I got this," Gordon broke in. "Let me talk to her, okay?"

A brief silence ensued during which Dorothy restrained her desire to take over the conversation. When Gordon spoke again, he did so with a renewed attempt at being cordial. "I haven't hurt anyone, Savanna. Somehow, I need you to believe that."

"How?" she said. "They found Theresa Spinnaker's blood in our van!"

"Because I gave her a ride once!"

"*What?*" This was the first Savanna had ever heard of that. "*When?*"

"Just after Christmas. That's why I've been so desperate to reach you. She's admitted it. You can call my defense lawyer if you don't believe me. He'll tell you it's true."

"You gave her a ride," she said skeptically.

"Yes. To that restaurant where she worked."

Savanna covered her left ear so she could hear above the engine of a semi that rumbled past. "Because..."

"It was snowing out! I saw a woman trudging through the storm in her little waitressing uniform with barely a sweater on and felt sorry for her. So I pulled over and gave her a lift."

"Then why didn't you say that from the beginning? You told me the police planted the evidence. Now you're saying she was in our van but for something completely innocent?"

"It took me a while to remember that I *had* seen her before. She was so bruised in the pictures the cops showed me I didn't recognize her. We'd only crossed paths once, and for such a brief time. I couldn't place where. You know I've picked up a lot of hitchhikers over the years. Doing so helped relieve the boredom of all the driving I had to do."

She *was* aware of that. They'd talked about it before. Savanna remembered warning him of the danger involved in picking up strangers.

"But once my confusion and panic subsided, and I could think clearly, I realized she was the same woman," he went on. "So I told my attorney, and after he reminded her, she remembered it, too."

"Was she *bleeding* when you did that?"

"Not that I could tell, but I didn't check her for injuries. The drops of blood the police found were so small, who knows how they got there? You could barely see them with the naked eye. For all I know, they were planted, like I said before."

She pivoted to check on the kids, who were still peering out at her. "That's not the only evidence tying you to these crimes, Gordon."

"It's the most compelling. DNA evidence always is."

"The things you kept in our storage shed tell their own story."

"What are you talking about? Those things were part of a Halloween costume! I thought it would be cool to dress up as a murderer, in a scary sort of way. You know I like the macabre. But then I realized it would be going too far and never did anything with it."

"Since when were you ever interested in dressing up for Halloween, Gordon?"

"It's been a while. I don't even remember when I assembled that. I mean, come on, babe. Have some faith. I miss my family. I miss *you*."

Babe. The endearment made Savanna feel…odd, sad, guilty (of what, she didn't know), repulsed and confused, all at once. Now that she could look back on their marriage from the vantage point of a new perspective, she was beginning to believe it had been like a piece of fruit left to rot on a tree. It'd hung on for a long time, had looked fine on the outside, but once it fell to the ground and broke open, it was easy to see it'd been rotting for quite a while.

Branson opened the van door and leaned out. "Mom, it's getting hot in here. You coming?"

She lifted a hand to signal that she'd only be another moment. "I can't talk anymore," she told Gordon—and Dorothy, who was, of course, listening in.

"Wait! Before you go, promise me that you'll at least accept my calls from now on, let me talk to you and the kids once in a while. I'm going crazy in here. I think about you all the time."

Did she *have* to remain in contact? Did she owe it to him by virtue of the fact that they'd once meant so much to each other? And what was fair when it came to their children?

Turning, Savanna saw her kids staring back at her. God, this was difficult. She had no idea how best to protect them—except to make a clean break from their father. "I hope I'm not misjudging you, Gordon. I really do. And I'm sorry if that's the case. But... I don't want any contact."

"Wait. *What?* Why not? I've been nice, haven't I? I didn't say anything to upset Alia when I had her on the phone. You can trust me."

"No, I can't. It's all smoke and mirrors, and I don't like the feeling that you're constantly trying to prey on my humanity." She hit the end button. She couldn't allow him to mess with her head, couldn't allow him to undermine her confidence in the decisions she'd made.

Branson and Alia both watched her solemnly as she climbed back behind the wheel.

"What'd he say?" Branson asked.

"Nothing that changes anything," she replied.

"Are we going to see him?" Alia asked. "He says we can visit him if we want."

Savanna gazed into her little girl's earnest face. "No, we're not going to see him."

Alia's eyes filled with tears. "Maybe later?"

With a sad smile, Savanna pushed her daughter's hair back

and started the truck. "Yeah, maybe later," she mumbled. It was a lie, and she felt bad for telling it. But she was hanging on by such a thin thread she couldn't withstand Alia's tears right now. She was too busy choking back her own.

CHAPTER SEVEN

The fridge wasn't the best Gavin had ever seen, but it wasn't too bad. He and Eli helped unload it and get it plugged in. Then, looking hot and miserable, since the day was so warm and the truck didn't have air-conditioning, Savanna took her children and headed to LA. Gavin told her it'd be late by the time she got there, what with traffic. Even on a Sunday, gridlock could be a problem in Southern California. But she wouldn't postpone the trip. She said the car lots would be open until nine—and would likely stay open later if she was in negotiations on a purchase. She wanted to get that over with so she could return the van.

Gavin watched them drive off while standing in her driveway, drinking a cold beer with Eli. He'd brought drinks for everyone from his place before Savanna and her kids had left.

Once they were out of sight, Eli gestured toward the ramshackle structure behind them. "They're really going to live *here*?"

Gavin frowned. "Can you believe it?"

"No. It's a dump. She can't even lock the back door."

"She'll replace that—and a lot of other things."

Eli lifted his beer for emphasis. "Renovations take time. Helps if you have money. That can speed up the process a lot. But considering what she chose for a fridge, I'm not getting the impression she's sitting on a fortune."

Apparently, Gordon hadn't left his wife with much extra when he went to jail. She'd told Gavin she'd worked as an administrative assistant for an insurance agent, which meant she couldn't have been making a lot more than minimum wage. And, according to the articles Gavin had read, Gordon had fixed mining equipment. His job had given him the freedom to roam but couldn't have paid a great deal. "I can help her with basic fixes," he said. "That'll bring the costs down."

Eli shot him a look. "That's how you'd like to spend your off-hours—doing more maintenance and repair?"

"I don't mind," he said. "It's what I'm good at."

"And you don't think Heather will have a problem with you hanging out at your gorgeous neighbor's all the time?"

"I have no idea what's going to happen with Heather..." Every time he saw Savanna, his future plans with Heather went a little out of focus.

Silence fell, but neither one of them moved.

"Savanna likes you, too," Eli said at length. "You realize that."

Finished with his beer, Gavin crushed the can. "No, she doesn't."

"The chemistry between you is unmistakable. I caught her looking at you so many times while we were moving that refrigerator—and when she'd see that I was watching, she'd blush and glance away."

Part of Gavin really wanted to hear what Eli had just told him, and yet he tried to shrug it off. After the way she'd been betrayed, it would take forever and a day for her to recover. And now he had his own problems to deal with. "We barely know each other."

Eli wiped the sweat from his forehead onto his pants. "You

both live way the hell out in the boondocks—and it's just the two of you."

"So? A lot of people who live in the country have only one or two neighbors."

"I'm saying it looks like you're going to have plenty of time together."

And Gavin was supposed to be falling for someone else, someone who might be the mother of his child. He hadn't missed Eli's point; he didn't want to acknowledge that it could become a problem. He was tempted to believe he'd dreamed up Heather's visit last night. But then a car turned down the street, coming toward them, and he knew he hadn't. "Maybe I'm seeing Savanna as an escape from what I have going on in my own life," he said, and gestured to draw Eli's attention to the Camaro.

The second Eli glanced up, he lowered his beer. "Shit. That's Scott, isn't it?"

"No question."

"You don't think this will come to blows..."

"I have no idea. He's not happy. He glares daggers at me, even follows me sometimes when he sees me in town like he wants to start something."

Eli straightened. "Jealousy is a dangerous emotion."

"I'm well aware of that."

Scott pulled into Gavin's drive, got out and waited for Gavin to walk over, which he did with Eli at his elbow.

"Can I have a minute?" Scott asked, glancing from Gavin to Eli and back again.

"Sure." Gavin tossed his crushed can into the small recycle bin he kept by his chair on the front porch.

Although Eli had been planning to leave—he'd said something earlier about wanting to get a few things done around the house before his wife returned—Gavin guessed he wouldn't go anywhere right now. As protective as Eli was, of his whole family, he'd stay to make sure he wasn't needed to break up a fight.

"It's hot out today," Gavin said to Scott. "Why don't you come in?"

When they moved toward the door, Eli didn't follow, so Gavin turned to see what he was planning to do.

"Don't worry about me." He tilted his beer in a salute. "I'll stay here and relax for a few minutes, finish this."

Close, but not *too* close...

Gavin wasn't afraid of Scott, but he wasn't eager to get in a fight, either. That wouldn't solve anything.

Knowing Eli's presence would discourage that sort of thing, Gavin shot his brother a grateful look. "Can I get you a drink?" he asked Scott as they went inside.

Scott shook his head. He seemed upset, which, of course, came as no surprise. Gavin was upset, too—only in a different way. He was angry with himself for going back to Heather the last time.

"Would you like to sit down?" Gavin indicated the couch.

Scott's chest lifted as he drew a deep breath. "No, I'll make this brief."

"If you're here to tell me about the baby, I know. Heather came by last night."

His eyes widened. "She did? *When?*"

Should he not have revealed that? The last thing he wanted was to make Scott angrier. "She was waiting for me when I got back from a gig in Santa Barbara."

"Had to have been late."

"It was," he admitted.

Scott shook his head in apparent disgust. "She must've come straight over here from my place."

"She's not in a good situation—"

"None of us are!" he broke in.

Gavin attempted to modulate his voice so that he wouldn't ignite what was already a potentially volatile meeting. Truth be told, he felt sorry for Scott. But what could he do? He hadn't planned on getting Heather pregnant. "True, but she's the one who has to carry and deliver the baby. So I think we can agree that she has the worst of it. She was upset and…and looking for some support."

"From *you*."

Remembering what she'd said about hoping to get back with him, Gavin cleared his throat. "You two had just broken up. I'm assuming she didn't feel comfortable trying to get it from you."

"We didn't break up. We had an argument. That's all. She was with me all night before she said a word about the baby. And then, right when I wanted to make love…*wham*, she told me she was pregnant with someone else's child. You'd be pissed, too!"

"She told me she wasn't sure the baby is mine," Gavin said, purposely skirting the rest of it.

Scott's hands curled into fists. "That it's even a possibility makes me want to tear your head off."

Gavin lifted his hands. "With the childhood I had, you wouldn't want to fight me." Gavin had gone to juvie for fighting. It wasn't as if he didn't know how.

"I'm not scared of you! You've got to be thirty pounds lighter than me!"

"That'd be my guess, too. But trust me. I've done a lot more fighting in my day than you have. Nothing good ever comes of it."

Scott looked a little less set on violence when he shoved his hands in his pockets. "I'm doing my best to remain calm, but… I don't know what to do."

"Fair enough. Let's start here, then. The last time I was with Heather was before she started seeing you."

"For the second time."

Scott had been trying to get with Heather for a while. "Still, even if it was the third or fourth time, it's not as if she was cheating on you, if that's what's causing you so much pain. You weren't together at the time. That's the point I'm trying to make." Gavin knew that wasn't really the root of the problem. Scott was upset by the fact that Gavin could get Heather back in a heartbeat if he wanted to, and now that she could be having his baby, he'd have reason.

"It's not that simple! I'm in love with her. I was planning to marry her. And now she wants *you*—right when I thought we were finally past all that!"

"I'm sorry," Gavin said. "I don't know what else to say. Is that why you're here? You're looking for some sort of an apology?"

"I guess I'm hoping to hear you say you won't take her back."

When Gavin hesitated, Scott's eyes narrowed.

"You don't love her..."

That was true. But Gavin couldn't make the admission. It could mean giving up easy access to his child. He didn't trust Scott to allow him to coparent, felt certain Scott's jealousy would get in the way—and might cause Scott to be unkind to the baby. After what Gavin had been through with his own stepmother, he wasn't about to give someone as emotionally immature as Scott that much power over an innocent child, especially *his*. "Why don't we...try to keep things open for now."

"*Open?*" he echoed.

"Until the baby's born. We'll see whose child it is and go from there."

"You expect me to hang in limbo, go on feeling this way for seven months, while you decide whether you really want her?"

"I didn't say that. A bit of time would give us the chance to calm down before making a decision that could impact the rest of our lives, as well as that of an innocent child. That's all."

"To hell with waiting," he cried. "I say she gets an abortion. She's *my* girlfriend now, and I don't want your filthy bastard growing up in my house."

For the first time since Scott had arrived, Gavin felt like throwing a punch. After a statement like that, he might've done so, returned to the troublemaker he used to be. But Scott had already turned and was stalking toward the door.

Gavin followed him, catching the screen before it slammed. "I would never let you raise my child," he called after him from the stoop.

Halfway to his car, Scott whirled around. "Yeah, well, we'll see who winds up with Heather in the end. At least I'm willing to step up and marry her!" he said, and flipped Gavin the bird.

Eli pushed off Gavin's truck, where he'd been waiting, and watched as Scott peeled out of the drive. "That seems to have gone well," he said sarcastically.

"He's a dick. There's no way I'll give him any influence over my child."

"So what will you do?"

"Pray it isn't mine."

"And short of that?"

He frowned. "Marry Heather myself. Surely, I'd make a better husband than he would."

Concern darkened Eli's face. "Even if you don't love her?"

Gavin didn't have an answer for that.

It was almost midnight when Savanna drove her "new" 2016 Ford Fusion, a $14,500 purchase with forty-seven thousand miles on it, past Gavin's house. She wanted to show him her car, but she was exhausted, and the kids were asleep in the back. She hesitated to wake them. Hearing Gavin's voice might get them excited, which could make it hard for them to go back to sleep. So she continued across the temporary bridge and parked, even though she saw a light on at his house.

After she woke Branson, who stumbled sleepily inside, she carried Alia in, which wasn't easy. Her daughter was getting big—she took after her father—and Savanna was only five-four.

The moment she stepped inside the house, she knew something was different. *Better.* Her house was warm. If she listened carefully, she could hear the hum of the heater, which meant her HVAC system was working. How, she had no clue, but she felt a huge wave of relief. What with all the additional fees and taxes involved in buying a car, she'd realized that her money wasn't going to last as long as she'd initially thought.

It wasn't until she took Alia potty and tucked her in, and checked on Branson to kiss him good-night, that she noticed there were other changes. The broken windows had been boarded up, and her back door was fixed. It now locked! She could see the square piece of plywood that had been used to re-inforce the broken part. It wasn't beautiful, but it made the door functional, which was the most important thing. She felt safer already. Not only that, but there were two boxes of cold cereal sitting on the counter, and when she looked in the refrigerator, she found a gallon of milk.

Gavin. He had to have fixed the heater and done all the rest. Maybe Eli had helped him...

There were no flowers, no Welcome to Your New Home card or treats, like a woman might think to add. His contribution had been entirely practical. But as far as she was concerned, no one had ever done anything nicer.

As she sagged to the floor, she felt tears of gratitude well up. What would she have done without her neighbor? He'd gotten them to a motel when they first arrived and made it possible to drive the moving van across the creek so they could unload the next day. He'd helped her empty the van of furniture and boxes, even put the beds together. Then he'd unloaded the heavy fridge, which she couldn't have budged on her own. And while she was gone today, he'd done enough around the house to make her feel as if she had a warm, safe place for herself and her children.

Blinking away her tears, she used the counter to help her back to her feet. She told herself she'd have him over for dinner sometime to thank him, but she didn't want him to have to wait that long to receive the acknowledgment he deserved.

So she went into the bathroom to fix up a little, pulled on her best pair of jeans and a V-neck T-shirt and walked over to see if his light was still on.

Sure enough, it was.

She felt oddly nervous as she approached his front porch and knocked. Was it too late to bother him? Should she hold off until tomorrow, after all?

When he didn't answer immediately, she turned to go. But the door opened before she could travel more than ten steps, and she could tell by the way he was still messing with his shirt that she'd once again caught him half-dressed—only this time he'd hurried to put on something.

"Hey," he said. "You're back."

"Yeah." She tucked her hair behind her ears as she returned to the stoop. "Sorry to bother you so late. I wanted to thank you for...for fixing the heater and the windows and all the other stuff you did. I can't tell you what a surprise that was."

"You're welcome."

She loved his smile. "I hope you don't come to regret that I moved in next to you. Now that I have the basics, I'll try not to be such a nuisance."

"Don't worry about it," he said. "I fix stuff for a living, so it wasn't hard."

"I saw the cereal and milk, too. That'll make tomorrow easier. I meant to pick up a few groceries, but then the kids fell asleep in the car and I forgot."

"No problem. Did you get an SUV?"

"Those in my price range had too many miles on them. But I got a car." She gestured toward her house. "Would you like to see it?"

"Sure. Let me grab my flip-flops."

Since he left the door standing open, Savanna couldn't help peering into his living room while he was gone. She'd seen it before, when she was there with the kids while he booked her that motel room, but now that she knew him better, she was a little more interested in taking note of the details. His place was clean, manly and decorated in neutral colors. She remembered that. What she hadn't paid much attention to before was the fabulous art hanging on the walls.

When he returned, she gestured toward a big canvas depicting a forest of redwoods centered above his couch. "That's a cool painting. Where'd you get it?"

"My brother's the artist."

"Eli?"

"No, Eli helps our mother run New Horizons. It's my other brother Seth."

"How many siblings do you have?"

He hesitated as if there was a story behind that question. But he must've opted not to tell it to her because when he answered, he didn't elaborate. "Seven brothers."

"Wow! That's a lot. Does Seth live here in town?"

"No, he's in San Francisco."

"He's talented!"

"Seriously. I used to buy a lot of his stuff. His work really speaks to me. But it's getting pricey these days."

"He doesn't give you a family discount?" she teased.

"He gives me a free piece here and there—for my birthday or Christmas. But he has some…issues that sometimes come between us. They come between him and everyone actually. He tends to wall himself off."

"I'm sorry, especially because you're obviously one of his biggest fans."

"It didn't help that he got married several months ago and lost his wife only weeks after."

"To…"

"Sepsis. She got bit by a stray cat she was trying to help, went into the hospital and never came out."

"How tragic."

"Especially for someone like Seth. He doesn't open his heart very often."

She studied him. "You seem to do the opposite."

"As far as I'm concerned, life only gets harder when you insist on going it alone."

"You'd rather open yourself up to loss?"

"Loss is part of life. There's no way to avoid it."

She'd never met anyone like Gavin, she decided. He wasn't arrogant. Didn't act as though he was always right or that his opinion mattered more than everyone else's. He seemed calm, forgiving, patient—and wise beyond his years. So what had he done as a teenager to be sent to a boys ranch? "I hope I can be as brave as you someday."

Their eyes met—and something spine-tingling passed between them, something Savanna hadn't felt in a long, long time. Her heart began to race, and she grew a little short on breath by the time she looked away.

"You're going to be fine," he said.

That seemed to be true, now that she had him as a neighbor. He'd already made a huge difference in her life. "Thanks for being there for me, even though I'm new and you don't know me very well."

"That's what friends are for. Let's go see your car."

CHAPTER EIGHT

Gavin tried to keep his attention on Savanna's vehicle, but it wasn't easy. What had happened back at his house? The way her gaze had fallen to his lips had almost tempted him to move in for a kiss.

"Gets decent gas mileage, too," she was telling him, still listing the features of the Fusion as he slowly circled the sedan.

"What'd you drive before?"

"An old Honda that had a big dent in the back. So even though this could hardly be considered a luxury car, it's several years newer and it's not wrecked. That's a step up."

Her phone went off. Surprised that she'd get a call so late, Gavin saw her look down at it and watched as the excitement and enthusiasm she'd exhibited a moment before dimmed.

"Everything okay?" he asked.

After first acting as though she'd shrug off the interruption, she seemed to reconsider her answer. "No. But there's nothing I can do about it, so…it is what it is."

Although "it" was none of his business, he could tell that call troubled her even if she didn't care to admit it. "Was that Gordon?"

Confusion drew her eyebrows together. "How do you know my ex-husband's name? Have I mentioned him to you?"

"Once, the day you moved in. You didn't provide a last name, but his first name was enough."

She blinked at him. "For what?"

"To be able to figure out why you moved to California alone with the kids."

She didn't seem pleased that he knew. "His first name was all it took to give away my recent past?"

Gavin came around the front of the car. "You mentioned a little more than that. A simple Google search did the rest."

Folding her arms, she leaned against the driver's-side door. "I should've made up a name for him and a whole new background for myself, but...that's not as easy as it sounds, especially when you've got kids who know the truth and will correct anything you say," she added ruefully.

"It's too hard to be anything other than yourself, anyway." He tilted his head to get her to look up at him again. "Don't you think?"

"I think it's better than carrying Gordon's legacy along with me."

He leaned against the driver's side, too, next to her but not touching. "Why do you care if people know? Are you afraid they'll gossip about you? That you'll be put on the spot and have to explain?"

"I don't want to be connected to something so horrible and embarrassing. And I don't want to have to justify what I did or didn't know like I had to do in Nephi. That's why I moved. I'm tired of people assuming I must be stupid, or as bad as Gordon, simply because I was married to him."

She seemed so beleaguered he couldn't help feeling sorry for her. "You won't be treated like that here. Silver Springs is far enough from the victims and their families that no one is emotionally invested in the situation. That'll make a big difference. Anyway, *I'm* not going to tell anyone."

She slanted him a glance. "You didn't tell Eli?"

She was testing him; he could hear it in her voice. "No." Now he was glad he could say that.

"I guess it doesn't matter either way. There's no avoiding the fact that I was married to a serial rapist." She kicked a pebble across the drive. "I'll never be able to escape it."

"How'd you get a divorce so fast?" He was under the impression their breakup had been as recent as Gordon's arrest, only a month ago.

"The divorce isn't technically final," she admitted. "But I've filed. The marriage is over. We'll never be together again. And if Gordon gets convicted, he won't be able to contest it. The paperwork will go fast from there."

"What if he *doesn't* get convicted?"

"I can't even think of that right now."

Gavin could understand why. As hard as it would be to have a husband who'd raped three women and been sentenced to prison, it would be harder still to have a husband who'd raped three women and gotten away with it. Then Gordon would be around to fight the divorce and/or pursue custody or visitation. And how could she let her children go with him on the weekends if there was even a small chance it wasn't safe? "But is it a possibility?" Gavin persisted. "Even a remote one? Or is the case too strong?"

She leaned back to stare up at the sky. "Anything's possible, I guess. The police seem to believe they have an open-and-shut case. But the lawyer I hired to defend Gordon—some expensive bigwig by the name of Howard Detmer—told me it was winnable."

"Is that what you wanted to hear?"

"At the time. I thought he was innocent."

"And now?"

She rubbed her forehead. "I've changed my mind."

Gavin told himself to ease off with the nosy questions. This was obviously a difficult subject. But she didn't sound *completely* convinced of where she stood, which surprised him. "I take it he hasn't confessed."

"No. That would make things easier, of course. But when I look back, I see certain warning signs despite what he has to say." She rubbed her palms on her thighs. "Maybe that's why the past month has been so hard. I let everyone down, especially the women he attacked, by not knowing what those warning signs indicated."

Gavin slid a little closer. "What warning signs are you talking about?"

"He'd get mad if I ever got into his things. Was *super* private. And he'd clam up, would hardly talk to me for days. I thought he was just moody, you know? He had a difficult childhood and has struggled to make peace with his mother's alcoholism and neglect. So I tried to give him the space to cope." Her voice hardened. "Little did I know what he was doing with all of that space…"

Images Gavin didn't care to see rose in his mind. "He didn't ever get violent with you or the kids, did he?"

"No. Then maybe I would've had a real clue, something to prepare me for the shock of what he was doing when he was supposedly at work."

Gavin breathed a little easier. "Did he ever talk about bondage or that sort of thing?"

"Never. If he had violent fantasies, rape fantasies, he didn't say a word. He knew how horrified I'd be, which is probably why." She toyed with the ends of her hair. "But…"

Her words trailed off, so he prompted her to continue. "But?"

"In order for him to get aroused enough to…to climax during sex, he had to—" She stopped as if she didn't generally discuss such intimate details with anyone, let alone a new neighbor. "Never mind."

Gavin nudged her with his elbow. "You might as well finish. We've talked about dildos, remember?"

She laughed in spite of the seriousness of the subject. "I *still* can't believe I made that comment. I've never said anything like that to anyone else."

"You can always speak your mind with me."

She studied him as if she was trying to decide whether it was really safe to be that open and trusting. "Fine," she said. "He'd put his hands around my throat like this while we were making love."

As she stepped in front of him and her cool, small hands slid around his throat, Gavin couldn't help feeling defensive of her. "Did he ever squeeze too tight?"

Her hands dropped away and she stepped back. "There was only one time when I had to tell him I couldn't breathe."

"What'd he do then?"

"He came before letting go. But it happened right away. And I believed he loved me, that he'd hung on a pinch too long because he was so close to orgasm and wasn't thinking clearly. Besides, he apologized."

"How'd you feel about that kind of sex play?"

"I hated it. Believe me, there are plenty of other places I'd rather have a man's hands, places that feel a lot better."

All the blood in Gavin's body rushed to his groin. Her ex hadn't treated her right, and he couldn't help craving the opportunity to rectify that. "But no one wants to be accused of being a bad sex partner, someone who refuses to be a little adventurous, so you tolerated it."

"Everything in a marriage comes down to compromise," she said.

Still battling an onslaught of testosterone, he tucked the hair that'd come out of the tie holding the rest back behind his ears. "Surely, not all marriages are difficult."

"I would hope not, but why take the risk?"

"A good marriage must be as wonderful as a bad marriage is terrible, I guess."

She glanced over at him again. "You've never been married?"

"No."

"And you're…what? Twenty-eight? Twenty-nine?"

"Twenty-nine."

She moved the dirt on her driveway around with one toe. "Since you've been asking me some pretty tough questions, I have one for you."

The wind was growing stronger. Gavin pulled the tie out of his hair, gathered it all back and secured it more tightly. "Shoot."

"Have you had *any* long-lasting relationships?"

"I was with someone named Winn for a couple of years, but we were barely out of high school, too young to even consider marriage." He thought of Heather, who'd come much later. He wondered if he was being fair to leave her out, but they'd never been together for more than a few months at a time, and she'd never been anyone he'd considered marrying—until now.

"Where's Winn these days?" Savanna asked.

"Living in LA, building a family with someone else."

"Do you ever regret the breakup?"

"Not really. We're still friends, and that's enough for me."

"You keep in contact with her?"

"I keep in contact with most of the women I've dated."

"That's kind of odd, isn't it?"

"Why would it be? I care about them, as friends."

"Is Winn happy in her marriage?"

He crossed his legs at the ankles. "I don't think she's terribly *un*happy. She echoes what you said—marriage is a compromise."

"I'll never marry again, never be willing to put up with so much or try so hard to make the best out of something bad. But

I always wanted a family, so once I made that commitment, I figured I needed to be happy with what I had."

Gavin grinned to lighten the mood. "And now that you have the kids, you no longer need a man. You're free to become a lesbian."

She stared over at him. "You're *so* different—like a pretty rock that you almost step over because you assume it's the same as all the others. But then you pick it up and realize how lucky you are to have found it."

As a child, he'd been a rock *no one* wanted. Even his father hadn't cared enough to fight his stepmother to keep him. And because of Savanna's word choice, which was what he got from people who didn't approve of his long hair or tattoos, he wasn't sure she meant it entirely as a compliment. "A *pretty* rock?"

He thought she might back away from that statement, now that he'd questioned her word choice, but she didn't. She seemed completely unapologetic in her opinion. "Yeah," she said. "You're the prettiest man I've ever seen. And it has nothing to do with your long hair. Everything works together just...perfectly."

Gavin was tempted to pull her to him. She was shivering, and he wanted to warm her. He wanted to stand behind her and shore her up in other ways, too. Working at the ranch, he'd had a lot of practice patching up broken hearts. Like his adoptive mother, fixing things, fixing *people*, came second nature to him. If not for that, he was fairly certain he wouldn't have been able to patch himself up after what he'd been through. So many of his brothers struggled worse, especially Seth.

His tendency to gravitate toward broken things made him wonder, though. Was part of his attraction to Savanna due to the fact that she needed someone so badly? He felt that was a suggestion Aiyana would've made, and his mother was usually right. She could read people so well. But if Heather was pregnant, she needed him, too, and yet he had far less desire to be with her.

"Are you still paying that expensive lawyer to defend Gordon?" Gavin asked.

"No. After I lost confidence in Gordon's innocence, I fired Detmer and asked for the balance of my retainer."

She was rubbing her arms for warmth as she replied, so he shoved off the car. "You're cold. I'll let you go inside. Thanks for showing me your new ride."

After a brief hesitation, she caught his arm. "Why don't you come in with me? I can't offer you anything except a glass of milk—and that's only because you got it in the first place—but it feels nice to talk to someone. You have such a...a measured way of looking at problems."

He knew he shouldn't accept the invitation. Maybe *she* thought she was only looking for someone to talk to, but she hadn't let go of him, and he could feel desire curling through his veins.

He opened his mouth to tell her they'd have to talk later. But then she added, "Just for a few minutes?" and he couldn't bring himself to refuse.

"Sure," he replied. "I have a bottle of wine. I could grab it if you'd like a glass."

She nodded. "That'd be nice."

Again, he told himself he should bail out. But he didn't. "I'll be over in a minute."

CHAPTER NINE

Savanna could feel her heart beating all the way out to her fingertips. Why was she nervous? So she'd invited her neighbor over to talk for a few minutes. That wasn't a big deal!

Except…it really was a big deal. Because she wanted to do a lot more than talk. And after the past two months, she felt she owed herself whatever this night might bring. She'd done everything she could to be a good wife, and yet she'd ended up in the worst possible situation. Why not forget all that restraint and do exactly what she wanted for a change? Especially because she couldn't see how one night with Gavin could hurt. He made her feel like the person she used to be years ago, before her world lost most of its color. For the first time since before her children were born, she felt free, and that made her hungry for the fulfillment she'd been missing as an individual.

But she barely knew him. And he was her neighbor, which meant she'd definitely have to face him after tonight. She couldn't let recklessness overcome her better judgment, could she?

Although the woman she'd been since she'd married Gordon said no, the sudden resurgence of physical desire was proving to be a powerful force. And Gavin seemed so mellow. He was friends with most of his ex-girlfriends, so if *anyone* could take a one-night stand in stride, it would be him.

She looked in at her kids to be sure they were settled. Only this time she shut each door as she went out. She didn't want to consider why she felt compelled to do that...

Gavin knocked softly before letting himself in. "Are you sure you're not too tired for a little conversation?" he asked.

She wasn't tired anymore at all; she was completely wired. But she understood that wasn't really the question. He was giving her a chance to back out before anything could happen. She'd seen the way he looked at her, knew he was interested, too. "I'm fine if you are."

He didn't answer. He popped the cork on the wine he'd brought over, and she pulled out two stemmed glasses that she'd unpacked and washed when she organized the kitchen. "My new fridge looks nice filling that gaping hole. Thank you for helping to get it there."

He clicked his glass against hers. "You've made nice progress in here."

"Only the kitchen. But I'll get to the rest. I didn't bring that much stuff with me, so it shouldn't be too hard." Anything that hadn't fit in the truck, she'd left behind for Gordon to deal with—or Gordon's mother, since he probably wouldn't get out of prison for some time. "I'll buy a microwave tomorrow and use my slow cooker for dinners until I can find an affordable stove."

Gavin put his glass to one side so he could pull himself up onto the counter. She loved that he made his visit as comfortable as possible. He didn't crowd her or come on too strong even though he had to know what she was contemplating.

"You'll want some new carpet for the living room soon," he said. "Would you like me to look for a nice remnant? I could probably lay it for you, which would save you some money."

She lifted herself up onto the opposite counter. Since they

were about five feet apart and facing each other, she had a great vantage point, given how much she liked looking at him. "Are you this nice to everyone?" she asked.

A crooked smile claimed his lips. "Well, I don't offer to lay carpet for everyone," he admitted.

When Savanna had to remind herself to breathe, she knew she was getting too caught up in Gavin. He hadn't even brushed against her when he came in, hadn't made contact at all, but the memory of his warm neck beneath her hands while they stood in the driveway made her long to feel his skin again. "I think I might be in trouble when it comes to you," she said softly.

The way he studied her let her know he understood exactly what she meant. "You don't have to worry. We're only having a drink. This doesn't have to go anywhere."

She swallowed against a dry throat. "What if I want it to?"

Obviously taken aback by the candidness of her response, he said, "Then I might be in trouble, too, because there's no way I'm going to say no. But we don't have to decide anything right now. Let's just…talk."

She rolled her eyes. "You don't want to talk to me."

"Why would you say that?"

"Because after what I've been through, and how recent it was, it's all I can talk about." She lifted her glass. "And who wants to hear about *that*?"

"I do," he said simply.

Feeling a bit jittery inside, which couldn't have anything to do with the wine after only a couple of sips, she pulled her gaze away from him. Maybe she *should* talk about Gordon. Maybe focusing on the recent destruction of her former life would quell the arousal she was feeling. "There are moments when I still can't believe it was *my* husband who assaulted those women."

Gavin sipped his wine. "It said in the paper that his victims were strangers. But Nephi's such a small town. You didn't know *any* of them?"

"Not personally." The change in subject seemed to be help-ing—as long as she didn't look at him for too long. "But I ran into Meredith Caine, the woman who was attacked while car-rying her laundry to the basement of her apartment complex, only a week before I moved. And that was...hard."

"She recognized you?"

"She did. By then, everyone in town knew who I was. She said I *had* to have known what Gordon was doing."

"But you didn't."

"Of course not." She leaned over to set an abandoned plate one of the kids had left on the counter in the sink. "Do you think I should've checked up on him? Is that what most wives do?"

"Your other friends would probably be better equipped to answer that question. What do they say? Do they check up on their husbands?"

"I haven't had anyone to ask."

"You don't have any married friends?"

"I don't have a lot of friends, period. I was so focused on other things that I drifted away from the kids I was closest to in high school. I spent most of my time with Gordon that first year of college, didn't meet many other people. Then we dropped out. And once we were married, we moved to a town where we didn't know anyone. I thought we were fitting in and making friends, but after he was arrested, I realized that the people I'd met in Nephi were nothing more than polite acquaintances." She savored a sip of her wine. "Maybe if we'd attended the Mor-mon church, like his grandmother used to and like most every-one else in town, the members would've rallied around me. As things stood, I felt completely isolated."

"You told me you worked. You didn't meet any friends through that? Or the kids' school?"

"I worked for a single agent in an old house that had been converted into a commercial property on the main drag. He was much older, also married, with grandkids, and it was only the two of us there each day—well, when he was in. At the end, I was pretty much running the office myself. He'd spend only a few afternoons a week at his desk. Even when he came to the office, we didn't talk about anything besides work and the weather."

"And the kids' school?"

"I met various staff and some of the parents when I volunteered in the classroom, and as the mom of a boy who played in a soccer league. But those are the people who turned out to be far less committed to me than I expected." She stared into her glass, remembering how quickly they'd begun to eye her with suspicion and doubt. "You have to understand, it's different when you're married. My family was my whole life. Working and taking care of Branson and Alia, especially since Gordon was gone so much, didn't leave me a lot of time for hanging out with friends. Besides, Gordon had me convinced that he was working so hard. I felt guilty if I ever went anywhere without him, especially because getting a babysitter cost money."

Gavin poured himself a splash more. "Would he have minded if you'd spent the money, gone out and had a good time now and then?"

"*Without him?* Oh, definitely. That would cause a fight, so I did what he expected of me." She set her empty glass to one side. "That was why, after he was first accused, I stood by him, tried to defend him. It's not like I turned on him immediately. That didn't happen until the police told me about the items they discovered in our shed, and even then it took time for it all to sink in and destroy my loyalty."

"You're talking about the rape kit."

The last thing she wanted was for one of the kids to wake up and hear this conversation, so she spoke quietly. "Yes. They found a mask, a knife, zip ties and a flashlight in an old duffel bag in our shed, shoved down behind where we kept the Christmas tree."

Gavin slid off the counter to pour her some more wine. "What I don't understand is why Gordon would keep that on the property," he said as he returned to his place. "Wasn't he afraid you might stumble across it?"

She started on her second glass. "No. I never went out to the shed. It was full of camping gear, which we hardly ever used, holiday stuff—and spiders. I *hate* spiders." She eyed, with more than a little trepidation, all the cobwebs she had yet to clear away here in her new house. "If I needed anything, I asked Gordon to get it. And he kept a lock on the shed. Said he didn't want any of the neighborhood kids getting into our storage and making a mess."

"He probably took that duffel bag with him when he was gone, anyway."

"Some of the time, I'm sure."

"I can only imagine how you must've felt when the police found that."

She closed her eyes as she recalled Detective Sullivan marching into the kitchen, brandishing the duffel bag he'd retrieved and opening it so that she could have a look. That was the moment she'd had to accept that she'd never really known her own husband. "It was horrible," she admitted.

Gavin didn't speak again until she looked up at him. "What did Gordon have to say when they found that?"

"He told me the detective had to have planted the evidence in order to get a conviction."

"Is that when they took him into custody?"

"No. They waited a few days, until they had proof that he'd had contact with one of the victims."

She'd never forget lying beside Gordon during those long nights, trying to convince herself that she wasn't sleeping next to a rapist. He'd been so angry with Sullivan, so full of accusations of police misconduct. She'd wanted to believe he was telling her the truth, that it was Sullivan who was being dishonest. But it was in the wee hours of those sleepless nights that she'd begun to think about all the little things she'd discounted through the years—how difficult it was for Gordon to climax during regular sex, how standoffish and moody he could get, that he hadn't been home on any of the three nights those women were attacked.

"Did he say why he went to that Mormon church in Provo if he wasn't a member?" Gavin asked.

"He insisted he did it because he was missing his grandmother, and she was so devout. He felt closer to her there."

"Is that something he'd be likely to do?"

"Sounded a little off to me. But, like I said, he was troubled and struggled with his past. His grandmother helped care for him when he was young, so…maybe."

He turned his glass around with two fingers. "That's why his presence at the church didn't mean much to you."

"To be honest, even the items in the shed didn't *completely* destroy my faith. The police had been so antagonistic with us. Apparently, they thought that was the best way to go about the investigation—by threatening and intimidating us. Because of how the detective had behaved, I could believe he *might* try to falsify evidence." She picked a piece of lint off her jeans. "He didn't do himself any favors by treating me the way he did. I probably would've come around sooner without that."

"But then they found forensic evidence on the knife or something?"

"They're still testing it. Real labs aren't like the ones in the movies. That type of thing takes a long time, since there's usually a backlog. They did rush the DNA test on the blood in the van because they needed to arrest him before he could hurt anyone else, but we have to wait for the rest."

"Do you get the impression Gordon is nervous about what they might find?"

"No. He insists they won't find anything, but I'm hoping they will. Otherwise, he'll keep denying it. And I want him to stop lying, you know? I *really* just want him to tell the truth—at last—so I don't have to go on second-guessing every move I make."

"What does he say when you ask him for the truth?"

"He swears up and down he's innocent. I told you he said the police must've planted the knife and those other things? Well, that was only at first. Now he's saying that he pulled those items together for a Halloween costume—even though I've never seen him dress up once in all the years I've known him. If he was home, he usually watched the slasher kind of horror movies I hate while I took the kids trick-or-treating."

"He wouldn't go with you?" Gavin sounded surprised.

"Wasn't interested. But his love of all things 'dark' makes his costume excuse *somewhat* plausible." She shook her head. "Or maybe not." The more she drank, the less certain she became. Everything seemed to be running together in her mind. "He said he thought it would be a cool costume, but once he assembled it, he decided it'd be too creepy."

"Some people dress up as Freddy Krueger…"

"True, but being a character from a movie is one thing. Pretending you're an actual murderer is a little different. Don't you think? I admit I wouldn't have liked it."

"So why didn't he put it away? Why keep it all in a handy duffel?"

She could hear Gavin's skepticism. It was one thing to draw a conclusion as an unbiased person and quite another to have to condemn the father of your children. "He claims he didn't take the time. That he wasn't concerned about it, since he saw it as harmless fun."

Gavin gripped the edge of the countertop with both hands. "I can see where you could get confused, but an article I read indicated that investigators found the blood of one of the victims in Gordon's van."

"They did." She'd thrown up when the detective told her about the blood. She still felt squeamish when she thought about how many times she and the kids had ridden in the vehicle her husband had supposedly used for his crimes. "It was Theresa Spinnaker's."

"There's no getting around DNA evidence," Gavin said, making that point again.

For the past several weeks, Savanna had been almost as certain as he was. But after talking to Gordon this morning...

Was there any chance he could be telling the truth? She hated the way he made her doubt what seemed clear to everyone else. Just when she thought she had it all straight, he'd get hold of her and infuse a little doubt. That was one of the hardest things about what she was going through. One minute, she was certain he was guilty and felt he deserved to lose his family and spend the rest of his life in prison. The next, she was asking herself, "What if?" Could Gordon be *that* good at concealing his true character? He wasn't an easy man to live with, but was he really a sadist?

"It was only a few spots," she explained. "And Gordon told me this morning that he once gave Theresa a ride to work— picked her up on the side of the road because he felt bad that she was walking in the middle of a snowstorm."

"Doesn't that prove he knew her?" Gavin asked. "Maybe that's what drew his attention to her in the first place."

"Could be. But it also establishes a legitimate reason for her DNA to be inside the van."

"We're talking blood, not just DNA."

"She could've had a small cut or something."

"She can refute that she was ever there, can't she?"

Savanna drained her glass. "She could. Then it would be his word against hers. But Gordon told me that she *admits* getting in with him. Supposedly, once his lawyer brought that encounter to her attention, she remembered it."

The chime of Savanna's phone interrupted. She knew who'd

be calling, and yet she couldn't stop herself from lifting her cell to check.

Sure enough, it was Dorothy. Dorothy had been leaving threatening messages all day. In one, she'd said she'd follow Savanna to the ends of the earth, if necessary, to get the money Gordon needed.

With a grimace, Savanna silenced her ringtone and slid her phone away. Gordon knew her parents had left her a house in Silver Springs, and Silver Springs wasn't that big a place. But surely Dorothy wouldn't come to California...

Gavin tipped his glass in the direction of her phone. "The jail allows Gordon to make calls this late?"

"It's not Gordon," she explained. "It's his mother. She calls me all the time."

"In the middle of the night?"

"Whenever."

"What does she want? I can't imagine she's hoping to talk to the kids if it's well after their bedtime."

"She doesn't have much of a relationship with the kids. She didn't have much of a relationship with Gordon, either, until she got older and sobered up. Anyway, to answer your question, she wants me to continue paying for Gordon's defense. But I can't help him. I have two kids to worry about. If I invest the last of the money I inherited from my folks in lawyers, how will I take care of them?"

"I think you're doing the right thing," he said.

She didn't reply. As much as she'd tried not to dwell on what Gordon had said when she'd been standing on the side of the road outside the moving van, bits and pieces of that conversation had been coming back to her all day.

"After nine years together, it must've been a hard decision to withdraw your support," Gavin said, breaking into her thoughts.

It had been *agonizing*. If Gordon was guilty, she couldn't help him get off. The police insisted he'd only hurt more women if she did. But if there was some way that he could be telling the truth, she didn't want to see the father of her children spend a huge chunk of his life behind bars.

Maybe that was why she was drinking more than she should tonight.

No. She knew Gordon wasn't the reason. It was Gavin. She wanted something from him she wasn't sure she dared take, and drinking eased that anxiety.

She slid off the counter. She should send him home. Remove the temptation. But with her mother-in-law saying such terrible things, Savanna didn't want to be alone. It didn't matter that she could now lock the back door. Her sense of security had been shattered.

So she let Gavin top off her glass before emptying the bottle into his own. "Nothing about what's happened has been easy," she said.

Gavin gestured toward the hall. "Do the kids know what their father has done?"

She tried to keep her mind on the question, but the wine was hitting her hard, and she couldn't help admiring the shape of Gavin's lips. Besides her kids, and how much she loved them, he seemed to be the one bright spot in everything that'd happened the past two months. She liked him. She wanted him in a way she hadn't wanted anyone else. She'd never seen better lips…

"Savanna?"

She blinked and lifted her gaze to his chocolate-colored eyes. "What?"

"Do the kids know what their father has done?"

"They do, but they don't fully understand it," she replied. "They've heard what people have said, that there were naked women involved and choking. In other words, they know their father has done something terrible, which was why Branson wouldn't talk to Gordon when he happened to get through to me this morning." She motioned for Gavin to follow her. But she didn't turn toward the door. She turned toward the living room. "Let's go in here. It'll be more comfortable on the couch."

She held her own glass while Gavin carried his, and they left the empty bottle. "You said Gordon 'happened' to get hold of you," Gavin said as he trailed behind her. "You didn't know it was him?"

Savanna explained as, crossing her legs underneath her, she sat on the couch, which was more the size of a love seat. She hadn't brought the big couch. She hadn't had room for it in the van. "So I had to take the phone from Alia," she said as she finished the story. "I wish I'd hung up, though. All he wanted to do was mess with my mind."

Had a chair been available, Gavin might've taken it. But there were boxes everywhere. Only the couch had been cleared off. "I'm sorry," he said as he sat next to her. "For everything."

She studied his handsome face—the closely trimmed beard, the thick hair, the kind eyes with long lashes. He didn't seem to be in any hurry to see if this was leading anywhere. She got the impression he believed she'd let him know if and when she was ready, and that was more enticing than anything else he could've done. "Your lips are amazing," she said.

"My lips?" he repeated with a sexy half smile.

"All of you."

"I'm flattered. But you've been through a lot. I don't want to make that any worse."

She ignored his response. "I'm glad I came to Silver Springs," she said as she gazed around the room. "This house may not look like much, but it's the escape I needed. Thank God for my parents. They were so good to me. I wish they were still around."

"You've lost them *both*?"

"My mother and older brother were killed in the same accident that took my father's life fourteen months ago. My younger brother, Reese, who's in college to become a doctor in Oregon, is all I have left. And the kids, of course."

"It's been a rough year for you."

She finished the last of her wine. "It's been a rough *nine* years. That's the weird thing. I didn't even realize I wasn't particularly happy. I just kept pushing forward, trying to make the most of the decisions I'd made. But now that Gordon is incarcerated, and the truth has come out, I'm wrecked but sort of relieved at the same time, if that makes any sense."

"You've been released from a marriage that didn't fulfill you."

That was it. That explained the element of relief that occasionally surfaced despite everything—like when she'd seen the stars last night and experienced a sense of rebirth. "And now I'm wondering why anyone ever gets married."

"Most people do it for love," he pointed out.

"Love is what got me into trouble in the first place," she grumbled. "As far as I'm concerned, love is overrated. Never again will I give a man that much power over my life. Not now that I understand you can never really know someone."

"You'll learn to love again," he said gently.

"Not for a long time. Maybe never."

"Your lesbian partner, when you find her, might take issue with that," he teased.

She set her empty glass on a nearby box. "I've come to the conclusion that changing my sexual preference isn't really an option."

"That didn't take long," he joked.

"Thanks to you."

He said nothing.

"You made me an offer at the creek," she said. "Have you changed your mind?"

"No. I want what you want, Savanna. I'm just trying to be cautious. Relationships can get complicated."

"I'm not asking for a relationship. That's not what I need from you. I just need you to hold me, to help me forget my regular life for a little while."

She could see his chest rising and falling rapidly, felt her own breathing grow short. "But I live next door. That pretty much means we'll have *some* type of relationship. And I think you might need a friend more than a lover."

This was why he remained friends with the women he dated, she realized. He put that first. "We'll be fine. You'll see."

He chuckled at her bold pronouncement. "You're not helping me walk out of here."

"Because I don't want you to walk out. I'm too curious."

"About…"

She lowered her voice until it was barely audible. "What you'd feel like inside me…"

His nostrils flared as his gaze moved over her. "And tomorrow?"

"We won't owe each other anything."

"You won't be embarrassed or reluctant to see me…"

"Not at all. We'll be friends and neighbors again. This is for one night and one night only. A simple and quick escape." She'd never dreamed she'd consider something like this, ever *want* something like this. But she'd never dreamed she'd find herself in her current situation, either.

"Aren't you worried about your kids waking up?" he asked. "Should we go to my place?"

"I can't leave them—even to go next door. We'll lock the door and be quiet. *Really* quiet."

He stood and offered her a sexy smile along with his hand. "Then you'd better not scream too loud when I make you come."

CHAPTER TEN

Gavin sat on Savanna's bed, which he'd put together when he helped her move in. "Take off your clothes," he said.

A sudden wave of self-consciousness caused Savanna to hesitate. "This is how you'd like to start?" she asked nervously.

"Why not? I want to watch."

Even after three glasses of wine, she wasn't sure she had the nerve to strip down on her own. She preferred *he* do the honors—and that it happen in the dark, so she wouldn't feel quite so exposed. She started across the floor, but he got up to intercept her. "What are you doing?"

"Turning off the light."

"Because…"

"Because I have some imperfections I don't want you to see." Like the stretch mark that'd appeared on her lower right abdomen when she was pregnant with Alia…

"I'm not worried about your imperfections," he whispered. "That's not what I'm looking for. If we have only one night, I want to remember every detail. That's all. Let me see you. Let go of your fear and inhibition and just…act on what you feel."

It was unusual that she felt *anything*. She was grateful if only

for that. With Gordon, sex had become as monotonous as vac-
uuming the floor. But it was the exact opposite with Gavin.
She was so excited she could barely breathe. "I know it sounds
strange, since I've been married for nine years, but... I'm not
used to having a man look at me the way you're looking at me
right now," she told him. "I mean...it feels like you actually *see*
me. And that leaves me nowhere to hide."

He caught her face between his hands. "I *do* see you. And I
like what I see. You don't need to hide from me. So come on,
Savanna, show me more."

Closing her eyes, she tried to let go of her worries, to embrace
the buzz the wine had given her as well as the pleasure of de-
siring a man who desired her in return. Even if Gavin wasn't as
impressed with her body as she wanted him to be—which was
partly what was hanging her up; no one had seen her after she'd
had her children except Gordon—what did it matter? This was
only for one night. And then it would be over. She had nothing to worry about. She'd cared so much about everything for
so long. Now she was exhausted in a way she couldn't even describe and refused to care about anything except getting lost in
this moment.

"There you go," he murmured as she pulled her shirt over
her head, revealing the sheer black bra underneath.

When he backed up to look at her, and she saw the effect she
had on him—the highly focused expression and proof of his
arousal farther down—she grew confident enough to smile as
she unhooked her bra.

"That's the sweetest smile I've ever seen." His gaze shifted to
what she'd revealed, and he added, "*Damn*, you're gorgeous!"

Encouraged, she started to undo her jeans, but he couldn't
seem to keep from touching her any longer. Closing the distance between them, he ran his knuckles down her bare arms
before lowering his mouth to hers.

His lips felt every bit as good as Savanna had hoped. So did his hands. They moved up her back as he parted her lips and found her tongue.

She wasn't sure if she was the one who moaned or he did, but when he cupped her breasts, her knees nearly gave out on her. "This feels completely new," she said. "As if I haven't been touched in years."

"You obviously haven't been touched in the right way," he said.

There was a reverence in how he treated her that made her feel valued, important. He gave her the impression he felt lucky to have this opportunity and respected her as an individual, another person with the right to make choices and decisions of her own. After they were married, Gordon had so often treated her as an object, one that existed solely to make *his* life easier. The stark difference between the two men bolstered her belief that Gordon *had* to be guilty of attacking those women, and that came as a relief. After the excuses he'd given her this morning, her confidence had begun to flag, and those terrible questions she tended to ask herself—*Am I the one at fault here? Could I or should I have done more?*—had started eating at her again.

She leaned back as Gavin's mouth moved down her neck. All the nerves below her stomach seemed to be drawing into a tight knot, creating a minibomb of energy that felt ready to explode. And he hadn't even taken off his clothes yet.

"Your skin is *so* soft," he said. "I've never touched anyone this soft."

When his beard tickled her breast, she almost laughed. She remembered wondering what kissing him would be like. Now she knew. She could definitely feel his facial hair—on her lips and on her body. But she liked it, liked *him*. The deliberate way he kissed her. The confident and yet sensual way he touched her. She couldn't regret inviting him over.

His mouth settled over one of her nipples and that proved the end of clear thought. Everything melted into sensation and instinct took over. As she rubbed her pelvis against him, he responded by squeezing her ass and finding her mouth again.

It took some self-restraint to break away. But before this went any further, she had to ask him a question. "Do you have birth control? Because I stopped taking the pill…"

Looking slightly dazed, he lifted his head. "I grabbed a couple of condoms when I went home."

"A *couple*?"

"Okay, three. Since tonight's all we have, I didn't want to be caught shorthanded."

"Sounds as if we're going to make the most of our time together."

He gave her a devilish grin. "We're *definitely* going to do that."

She liked the conviction in that statement, the license it gave her to cut loose and enjoy his body without reservation or restraint. Pulling the tie from his hair, she let her hands delve into the silky thickness, even buried her face in it. "Your hair smells nice," she said.

"You're easy to please," he joked. "It's time a man took better care of you."

"I can tell I'm in good hands now. I bet there aren't many men who know how to make love like you do." She could tell he was surprised by the generosity of the compliment, but she meant it. Maybe he could tell. Maybe that was why her words seemed to stoke the fire of his excitement, making it burn that much hotter and brighter. She loved the purposeful glint in his eyes as he started to undo her pants.

She dragged his mouth back to hers and kissed him deeply, hungrily and far more passionately than she'd ever kissed anyone else. She was letting loose, letting herself forget the concerns that had been weighing on her so heavily. "Just tasting and touching you. It's *so* good. Maybe it'll be enough," she told him.

"I hope not," he said with a hoarse laugh.

She laughed, too. "You're right. Forget I said that. When are you going to get rid of your clothes?"

"After the lights go off."

She could tell he was joking. "Funny," she said. "But the lights are staying on. It's my turn to see you."

He went back to her jeans instead. "I was hoping to take it slow, but—" his hand slid inside her panties, and she felt his fingers seek and find the place where she was most sensitive "—I'm not capable of it right now. I'm dying to have you. So to hell with slow. We'll go slow next time, okay?"

"Or the time after that," she said, her voice barely audible as he pressed a finger inside her. She caught her breath at the pleasure that simple act brought, but it was the raw desire on his face as he added a second finger that triggered an even more powerful response. She'd never felt such primal need. And the tautness of his body, the rigidity of every muscle, told her she wasn't alone. She could tell he was trying to be gentle instead of *completely* unleashing, and that built her excitement, too. The apparent difficulty of that struggle made her feel powerful in her femininity.

"Good thing you brought three condoms," she told him. "I think we're going to need them."

He didn't even crack a smile. He seemed to understand that she wasn't joking. "We don't have to stop at three. I can always go back for more," he said, and removed his hand long enough to yank off his shirt and pull her onto the bed.

Gavin felt guilty for what he was doing. He wasn't back with Heather, and he hadn't promised Savanna anything more than this one night. *She* was the one who'd made that stipulation. And yet he knew he was operating in a gray area, that he shouldn't be feeling what he was feeling toward his new neighbor when his old girlfriend could be pregnant with his child. His wanting someone else didn't seem fair to Heather, even though she'd obviously been sleeping with Scott the past two months.

Still, with all the uncertainty in his life right now, he was being foolish to complicate the situation. That was why he'd tried to talk himself into leaving Savanna's house before he could wind up in her bed. He just hadn't been able to follow through. And he couldn't entirely regret that decision, not when he finally entered her, not while he moved inside her. He loved the way she responded to his touch, the way she stared up at him and met each thrust with a look of wonder on her face, as if she was only now discovering how enjoyable sex could be, and how close it could make two people feel.

She deserved far more than she'd received from the man who'd been responsible for loving her so far. Not only had Gordon betrayed her in the most painful and humiliating way possible, he'd starved her of the nurturing all humans needed. Gavin hated him for that as much as the rest of it. Maybe *she* was confused because she wanted to believe the father of her children when he proclaimed his innocence, but Gavin had little doubt Gordon was indeed the rapist the police believed he was. The physical evidence was overwhelming. They'd tied him to one of the victims. He had a job that gave him the freedom to be out and about on his own. And they'd found zip ties, a knife and a mask in his locked shed! Even his extreme selfishness didn't speak well of him. How could the man who'd attacked those women be anyone else?

When Savanna's eyes drifted shut and her lips parted, Gavin knew she was close to climax. He was close himself, *too* close, which was why he'd been thinking about Gordon and anything else that might help him hold off. He didn't want to come before she could.

"That's it," she suddenly gasped. "Oh, God, that's good!"

Her words snapped his restraint, which had been tenuous to begin with. Gavin clutched the pillows on either side of her in an effort to give her a little more time. But when he felt her body jerk, he knew it was impossible. That familiar tightening had already started in his groin and was now bringing with it a cascade of exquisite pleasure. He wanted her to look up at him as he let himself go—to finish together—and the moment was made perfect when she did.

"That was the strongest climax I've ever had." She was sweaty and breathless but obviously happy, so he was surprised when, several minutes later, he heard her sniff quietly and felt her move to wipe her face. She even got up, turned off the light and went into the bathroom for a while, where he heard her blow her nose.

When she slid back into bed, he lay there, staring at the ceiling for several seconds, wondering if he should give her some privacy or try to console her. Something was wrong...

When she sniffed again, he rose up on one elbow. "Are you okay?"

"Yeah. That was great."

He could hear the false cheer in her voice. "Then why are you crying?"

She let her breath go on a long sigh.

"Savanna?"

"I don't know," she replied.

"Are you sorry you asked me to stay?"

"Are you kidding? No. It's just that...the tenderness you showed me has made me realize how stupid I've been. How naive."

He pulled his hair back so it wouldn't fall into her face. "You're talking about your marriage?"

"Yes. I should've left him years ago."

"You stayed because you were committed. You were trying to be a good person, a good mother and wife."

"I was oblivious. An idiot. I didn't even realize how badly my marriage was broken. I knew Gordon was difficult, of course. But I thought all marriages were probably a challenge. I tried to love him, despite so many things. Didn't expect or demand enough. That's on me."

"The fact that you didn't get what you needed is *his* fault," he said. "Some of the people in our lives—even the people closest to us—may not possess the compassion or concern they should." He was speaking from experience. That was what he told himself whenever he thought of that moment at the park when he'd first realized he'd been left behind. He hadn't done anything to deserve his stepmother driving away. And yet it was hard not to feel she'd rejected him because he was unworthy of the love he needed. The ironic thing was that even after his father chose his stepmother over him, the marriage didn't last. His father was now married to someone else, someone much nicer, not that Gavin was willing to have a relationship with either one of them.

"I've been under a lot of pressure, that's all." She was trying to minimize what she felt so that she didn't bring him down with her. He'd done the same thing, many times. And he'd seen the boys at the ranch act in a similar fashion.

"Do you have some lotion handy?" he asked.

"Lotion?" she repeated.

"Yeah."

"In the bathroom. Why?"

"Will you get it for me?"

When she did as he asked, he had her roll onto her stomach and used the cream to give her a massage.

"This feels amazing," she said, "but I shouldn't be letting you do it."

"Why not?"

"Because it's late, and you've already done so much for me. I'm your neighbor. It's not like you owe me anything."

"Relax. This isn't a chore. I like feeling your skin, your body. I'm doing it because I want to." And because he believed that touch, when used in the appropriate way, and with care and concern, had the power to heal. He'd seen his mother hold students who were so hardened, so tough, that they'd been sent to New Horizons as a last-ditch effort to help them avoid prison—and who, before long, ended up breaking down and sobbing in her arms. And he'd watched how she used every opportunity to reassure the troubled boys who attended school at the ranch by patting them on the back, giving their arm an affectionate squeeze, welcoming them with a warm hug. She always demonstrated love, and he'd seen how quickly it could make a difference. The love she'd given him had acted as a beacon that'd led him out of the storm that'd been his own childhood.

"Wouldn't you rather make love again?" she asked. "At least then there'd be something in it for you."

"Not right now."

"Because..."

She had a hard time allowing others to be the one to give, he decided. "Because this is more important," he said, and was relieved when she finally succumbed to his ministrations and eventually drifted off to sleep.

CHAPTER ELEVEN

"Mom, I had another accident."

Savanna opened her eyes to see Branson standing at the edge of her bed. Since she didn't have drapes on the window yet, it was easy to tell that the sun hadn't come up. The color of the light indicated it was close to dawn, though.

She allowed her eyelids to slide closed again. Just for a few seconds, she told herself. She'd been sleeping deeply, was loath to return to full consciousness.

"Mommy?"

Branson. Her son needed her. The distress in his voice finally pierced through her grogginess. Then she remembered *why* she felt so relaxed and fulfilled and, in a panic, flung out her arm to see what she might encounter on the other side of the bed. Was Gavin still with her? She hadn't meant to let him stay until morning, didn't want her son to see him lying next to her. But since they'd granted themselves only one night, she'd wanted to claim every minute. Not only was he the best lover she'd ever had, which wasn't saying much considering Gordon was her only other experience, he was also the best lover she could imagine.

Fortunately, her hand encountered nothing but bedding and

pillows. And, from what she could tell, he wasn't in the bathroom, either. There was no light, no noise. He must've gotten up and left while she was sleeping.

Thank goodness he'd been aware enough to do that…

Drawing a deep breath in an attempt to compensate for the adrenaline that'd jolted her into full wakefulness, she smiled at her son. "It's okay, honey. Did you wash off and change your clothes?"

"Not yet."

No doubt he was wondering why she wasn't getting up to help him. But she wasn't wearing any clothes, and she couldn't ask him to leave while she dressed. She didn't want him to know she was naked in the first place, since she generally didn't sleep that way. "Then you go wash up and change while I get you some fresh bedding, okay?"

He hesitated a little longer. "Why is this happening?" he whispered. "Even Alia doesn't pee the bed. And she's younger than me."

"Everything's going to be okay," she told him. "I'll be there in a second."

As soon as he went out, she pushed back the blankets and forced her body to obey her brain's commands. Her night with Gavin was over. Time to be a mother again.

With a small smile for how many times they'd woken up and made love, especially for how Gavin had encouraged her to ride him after he'd been on top for the two previous encounters, she shoved her hair out of her face and that beautiful memory to the back of her mind. She wanted to hang on to the good feelings he'd inspired for a little longer, but the afterglow of their night together disappeared when she found her son, changed into dry clothes, crying.

"Branson, what is it, honey?" she asked, pulling him into a hug. "I hope you're not crying over a few wet blankets."

"I am," he said, his voice muffled against the nightgown

she'd quickly pulled on. "I'm too old to pee the bed. But I don't know how to stop."

"You're just sleeping too deeply to get up and go to the bathroom." She hoped, by not making a big deal over it, she'd be able to help him through this rocky period. She'd been trying to take it in stride. Everything she'd read online suggested she not shame him, not turn it into a huge issue. "It could happen to anyone."

He pulled back. "Then why doesn't it happen to you or Alia?"

"It could, in the future," she told him.

"But I never used to do it!"

Not until his father had been arrested...

Savanna took his hands. "Sometimes things happen in life that make us feel bad. And even though we may tell ourselves we're okay, our bodies can show that we're upset."

"You're saying it's because of Daddy."

"That's what I think. Don't you?"

He didn't answer.

"When your father did...what he did, he hurt us all," she continued. "This is how your body is responding. I understand that wetting the bed is upsetting and embarrassing for you, but you won't do it forever. You'll stop when you feel safe and loved again. And you *will* feel safe and loved again. I'm right here, aren't I? I'm not going anywhere. I'll continue to take care of you as I always have."

With a sniff, he threw his arms around her waist and clung tightly.

She held him for several minutes, trying to comfort him by rubbing his back. Then she ruffled his hair. "Come on. Let's get your bed made. I'll lie down with you for a while, and we can talk about whatever you'd like. It's too early to get up."

He wiped his face. "Okay."

Savanna shook her head as she remade the bed. Lately it seemed as if she was always feeling some strong emotion. In the past twenty-four hours, she'd been angry, aroused, excited, happy, confused and in tears herself. "We're going to be okay," she told Branson as he crawled under the covers with her.

Once they were both comfortable and settled, she asked him what he wanted his room to look like. Then they talked about the new house, what needed to be done and how it had once belonged to someone in her family who'd died, which made it special. He said he loved the creek and all the space he had to play here in Silver Springs but was afraid to start at a new school.

Savanna reminded him that wouldn't happen until fall and that he'd be feeling much better about everything by then. She was going to help them finish up their current year herself. Fortunately, they'd always done well in their studies, were both at the top of the class. Even though she wasn't experienced with homeschooling, she didn't think having her take over for such a short period would hurt them in any way.

Branson drifted off to sleep just as the full brightness of the sun started to slant through the window. Savanna knew Alia would be up soon. Then Branson probably wouldn't be able to sleep any longer, either. But if she was quiet, Savanna thought she *might* have a few minutes of solitude to reflect on what had transpired last night. She'd felt so connected to Gavin. As a matter of fact, she'd felt closer to him than she had Gordon, at least for the past several years.

After slipping out of Branson's room, she made herself some coffee, pulled on a sweater to protect against the early-morning chill and carried her cup outside. She needed to buy some chairs for the porch, she decided. Right away. She could tell this was going to be one of her favorite places at the new house.

The sounds of birds chirping and squirrels scrabbling among the trees seemed to come from all around as she leaned on the banister. Cradling her cup in both hands, she stared toward the copse of trees that hid Gavin's house from her view. Had he left for work?

She felt bad for keeping him up so late, and yet it made her smile to remember how readily he'd shrugged off her concern when she mentioned it to him. "This is worth it," he'd said as she bit his neck and then his chest and helped herself to what she found much lower.

Her cell phone rang. She'd brought it with her so that she could call the contractor Gavin had recommended for the bridge. But she wasn't expecting anyone to call her, so she cringed as she pulled it from her pocket. She assumed it would be Dorothy again—or Gordon, since it was an hour later in Utah—but caller ID indicated it was someone from the Nephi Police Department.

Savanna wasn't sure that was much better. She cast another longing glance toward Gavin's house but knew even if he was home there'd be nothing he could do to relieve the anxiety knotting her stomach right now.

Knowing she had to face whatever it was, or she'd only get another call later, she hit Talk. "Hello?"

"Savanna, it's Detective Sullivan."

She managed to avoid an impolite groan. "What can I do for you, Detective?"

"I'm standing outside your place, but...it doesn't look like you live here anymore."

"If you're outside the Nephi house, I don't."

"You moved?"

"I live in California now."

Silence. Although he didn't say a word, she could feel his disapproval.

"Hello?"

"I wish you would've stayed," he said. "We might need you to testify at the trial, remember?"

"I'm hoping you *won't* need me. What's happened hasn't been easy on me or my kids."

"It hasn't been easy on Theresa Spinnaker, Meredith Caine

or Jeannie West, either," he said. "That's why we have to make sure we get a conviction, no matter how hard it is on *everyone*."

He'd had so little empathy for her. And yet she understood that he had to separate himself from his compassion in order to do his job. She also understood how he felt about the possibility of Gordon getting off. She was beginning to worry more and more about that herself. If her soon-to-be ex *didn't* go to prison, what would he do? Come out to California? Try to reconcile? "If it becomes important that I testify, I will. The DA can let me know."

"I'm glad you're willing to help."

"Is that why you called? Because you were concerned that I might've escaped the whole mess?"

When he hesitated, she knew he'd heard the bitterness in her voice. It was tough not to blame him, at least partially, for what she'd been through. He'd been so belligerent in the beginning. But he wouldn't even be involved in her life if not for Gordon. Gordon was clearly the one to blame. "I called because we need a favor."

"You mean beyond my testimony?"

"To be honest, I consider that your duty, not a favor to me. But we're still gathering evidence, building the case, so we're not quite to that part yet. What we need right now is for you to see what you can get out of Gordon about someone named Emma Ventnor."

Savanna gripped her phone tighter. "He won't tell me if he raped her. He's still claiming he hasn't raped anyone."

"It'll involve more than simply asking him about Emma. We'd like you to get him to say whatever he will about her. The calls from the county jail are recorded. We're hoping to get something on tape."

Squeezing her eyes closed, she pressed a fist to her forehead. "When was this woman raped?"

"She's been missing for over a year, Savanna. We think he might've killed her."

"No way. Gordon might be a rapist, but surely he isn't a *murderer!*"

"We don't know. That's why we need your help."

"I told you. He won't even admit what he did to the three victims you already know about. What makes you think he'll tell me anything about a fourth?"

"You'll have to rile him up. Get him angry. Push him to the point where he's not monitoring himself."

Great. Then maybe he'd complain to his mother, and Dorothy would harass and threaten her that much more. "This other woman can't be from Nephi. I would've heard about it if someone had gone missing."

"Emma wasn't a woman, Savanna. She was only sixteen. And you're right—she didn't live in Nephi. She lived in Bingham."

A chill ran down Savanna's spine. Almost everyone in Utah knew that the world's largest copper mine was located in Bingham. "By Kennecott."

"Yes. And Gordon was there, fixing a pump, the day she went missing."

CHAPTER TWELVE

"Heather came by."

Gavin had just accepted three small cookies and a carton of milk from Aiyana, who'd brought those items from the cafeteria. She stopped by his tiny office, which basically consisted of a desk he'd wedged into the maintenance building along with all of his tools and other supplies, quite often. Bringing him something to eat or drink was her way of continuing to care for him, and he knew it. She was the reason he'd been so hesitant to pack up and leave to pursue his music. He knew she depended on him; his loyalty wouldn't let him go. "When?" he asked.

"While you were gone, picking up that part for the lawn mower."

"You bumped into her on campus?"

She pulled the long black braid that ran down her back around to the front so she could fix the tie. "No, she came to the administration building."

"Why would she go there? She knows my office is on the other side of the ranch."

"I'm guessing that when she didn't find you here, she decided to stop in and say hello to me."

Gavin could no longer taste the cookie in his mouth. Heather was hoping that Aiyana would become her mother-in-law—and she was getting impatient because he hadn't contacted her since she'd given him the news. "Has she ever come to see you before?"

"No, but she's never been pregnant before. Maybe she was hoping to determine whether you'd told me."

After washing down that bite of cookie with a drink of milk, he set what was left of both on his desk. "Did you let on?"

She folded back the linen sleeves of her blouse. She almost always dressed colorfully, but today she wore tan pants with a white shirt and left all the color to her sandals, which had red, white and turquoise beads, and the large chunks of turquoise in her jewelry. "No, I played dumb. Asked how she was. Said you'd be back this afternoon."

"She didn't want to wait?"

"I'm sure she would have, had I encouraged her. But I made it sound like it could be a while." She studied him closer. "Should I have done something else?"

"No, definitely not." He stared down at his work boots as he remembered how he'd touched Savanna last night, how easy and natural it had felt. He'd *wanted* to be with her, hadn't had to talk himself into it…

His mother waved a hand under his face to get his attention. "You look completely dejected. What are you thinking?"

"I'm wondering what I'm going to do. I shouldn't have left Heather hanging. It's been two days since she told me about the baby. But every time I pick up the phone to call her, I put it down again. I mean…what do I tell her?"

"Why not tell her the truth?"

"That I don't know if I can love her?"

She winced but doggedly stuck with her original answer. "If it's true, what else can you do?"

"If I tell her that, she'll go back to Scott."

"Maybe she *should* go back to Scott."

"You're talking about a man who told me he'd never let my 'filthy' bastard grow up in his house. He's jealous and angry, and that's a dangerous combination, especially when there's a defenseless baby involved."

With a sigh, she sank into the fold-up chair across from his desk. "What about your next-door neighbor?"

"What about her?"

"Eli says she's pretty."

The image of Savanna taking off her shirt last night flashed through his mind. She was more than pretty; Gavin thought she was *gorgeous*. Sweet, too. Unassuming. Earnest. Underappreciated. But he did what he could to downplay the attraction. "She's not bad."

She arched her eyebrows. "He said that you two seem to really like each other."

Gavin thought about sharing what Savanna had recently been through but couldn't bring himself to do it. That would explain why he'd been trying so hard to help. It wasn't just that he found her attractive; she deserved a break. But he'd told Savanna he'd keep her secret. "She's just coming out of a relationship, isn't ready for another one. And what I've got going is hardly something I'd feel comfortable dragging anyone into." Which was why he felt bad for giving in to temptation last night...

"I hate that this has happened," she said. "You've been through so much in your life. You deserve the chance to be happy."

"Being a responsible parent comes first."

She rose to her feet and walked over to hug him. "Somehow I knew you were going to say that."

There was a woman at Gavin's house.

Savanna stiffened when she saw her standing on his stoop.

Hearing Savanna's footsteps crunch on the gravel road, the tall blonde turned and stiffened, too. "Who are *you*?" she asked, obviously startled to find someone else in an area with a normal population of one.

Savanna wanted to ask her the same. But she was the newcomer here. So she forced a smile. "I'm Savanna, Gavin's next-door neighbor."

"I didn't know he had a neighbor," she said.

"I haven't been here long. Moved in last Friday." Technically, she'd only arrived on Friday and moved in on Saturday, but that small detail didn't matter enough to even mention it.

"Oh." The woman didn't provide her name. She still seemed to be processing the surprise. "Does Gavin know you're here?"

"Yes. He was nice enough to help me move in. Are you his... sister or something?" She knew this woman *couldn't* be his sister. When he'd told her he had seven brothers, he would've mentioned if he had a sister, too. But she hoped her question would lead to some explanation as to who this person was and what role she played in Gavin's life. It was none of her business, even after last night, given the terms they'd agreed upon, but she couldn't help being curious, especially because Gavin's visitor looked about his age, which was also close to hers, of course.

"No. I'm..." She seemed to struggle to define the relationship. "I'm a good friend," she finished, as if she'd have to settle for that. "Do you have any idea where he is?"

"I'm guessing he's at work. He told me he works at New Horizons Boys Ranch."

"I went by there, but his mother told me he was out running errands. I thought maybe he stopped by here to get something or grab a bite to eat."

"Haven't seen him, but that doesn't mean anything. I probably wouldn't have seen *you* if I hadn't come out to get my mail." Her mailbox was clear down the street near the turnoff, which meant she had to walk past Gavin's house. "Have you tried calling or texting him?"

"No, but I will." She stepped off the stoop. "My name's Heather, by the way. Heather Fox."

Savanna met her in the middle of Gavin's yard to shake her hand. "Nice to meet you. I'm Savanna Gray."

It was easy to read the curiosity on Heather's face. "You're *so* pretty."

"Thank you. So are you."

Heather smiled but didn't seem completely believing of the compliment. "You're new in town, then? Where are you from?"

"Utah."

"And you're living in the old ranch house across the creek, the one that's been abandoned for so long?"

"Yeah. Scary prospect, right? But the house used to belong to my great-grandmother, so I can't wait to put it right."

"That's cool. Should be a fun project."

"An expensive one," she said with a rueful smile.

Heather hiked her purse up higher on her shoulder. "You aren't tackling that alone, are you? I mean, you came here with someone—a significant other?"

"No. It's just me and my two kids. They're at the house watching a Disney movie right now."

The smile disappeared from her face. "So...you're divorced?"

She'd known she would face this question, but she refused to volunteer too much information. "Essentially."

"All the single men in town will be excited to hear that."

"Oh, I'm not looking to meet anyone."

"Until you do, right?" She laughed again, but Savanna didn't get the impression she honestly found what she'd just said funny.

What constituted attraction? Gavin wondered as he sat at his desk after school let out. Heather was a nice person. He knew her well, knew she'd do her best to make him a good wife. And she loved him. She'd made that clear. So *why* couldn't he return her feelings? Why was he so much more interested in Savanna, a woman he'd only recently met and barely knew?

Had to be that Savanna was new in town, different, and if that was it, what he felt probably wouldn't last once the newness wore off. That was why he couldn't let his preoccupation with his new neighbor affect his long-term life plan. He'd never fallen head over heels in love or he probably would've found it much more difficult to remain friends with the women he dated. If he wasn't hurt, upset or jealous, why would he refuse to remain in contact?

Sure, there were a few who no longer stayed in touch with him—once they started dating someone else or got married usually—but he'd always been willing to settle for friendship if they were. That meant, even if Savanna *was* willing to move forward with a relationship, the same cycle of initial excitement fading to something that wasn't very intense at all would most likely happen with her, too. He had to be careful not to neglect Heather and his duty to his child, if it was his child, by reaching for something that wasn't real, anyway.

Light streamed in from outside as Jared Hawthorne poked his head into the room. "Hey, dude! What are you doing here?" he asked the moment he spotted Gavin. "Aren't you coming today?"

Usually, Gavin went over to the basketball courts after school and played a game or two with the students. He liked having fun with the boys, if he had time, and since the number of kids who waited at the outdoor courts grew from the beginning of the year to the end, he knew it was something a lot of them looked forward to each day. But, as Gavin had told those who'd already stopped by looking for him, he was too tired to run that hard this afternoon. He hadn't even fixed the lawn mower after driving to Santa Barbara to get the part. Although he'd handled some paperwork and stopped a leak under the sink in one of the bathrooms, he'd mostly been sitting and stewing—and yawning, since he'd gotten so little sleep. "Can't make it today, bud."

Jared's face fell. "*What?* Why?"

"Was up late last night."

"Doing what?"

Gavin bit back a smile. "Just some stuff I had to take care of. You guys go ahead without me."

He scowled. "But it's no fun if you're not there."

Gavin hated to disappoint them, but he knew he wouldn't last ten minutes. His heart simply wasn't committed to basketball today. "I'll try to make it tomorrow."

"O-kay," he said, drawing out the word in obvious disappointment.

As soon as the door shut, and Gavin was once again alone, he told himself to make the call he'd been dreading since Saturday. That Heather had stopped by New Horizons indicated she was getting impatient. And he couldn't blame her. It wasn't nice of him to keep stringing her along.

With a sigh for his reluctance, he steered his mind away from Savanna, since thinking about her made him *not* want to make this call, to Scott, since thinking about him did. Even before this happened with Heather, Gavin hadn't particularly liked Scott. And since he didn't feel Scott would be a good stepfather, he essentially had no choice.

Besides, what was the big deal? He and Heather had reconciled before. Why not give it another try? He couldn't hold back because of Savanna. She'd made it clear that she had a lot of healing to do, wasn't a viable option. Besides, he planned on leaving Silver Springs if his mother ever married Cal Buchanon, the rancher she'd been dating for quite some time. Once that happened, Gavin could move on knowing she was happy and well taken care of, wouldn't have to stay and look out for her as he felt obligated to do now. If he could make it work with Heather, he'd take her and their baby and move to Nashville. She'd talked about that before, insisted he'd make it huge in the music industry if only he gave it a concerted effort, so he knew she'd be happy with that decision.

"It's the right thing to do," he muttered, and called Heather while he had the willpower.

She answered on the first ring. "Hey."

Hearing the hope in her voice made him feel even guiltier for how self-indulgent he'd been last night. "How've you been?"

"Pretty good. You?"

Thanks to Savanna, he'd been *great*, at least for the hours he'd spent in her bed. But he knew Heather wouldn't be excited about that. "Fine. My mom said you stopped by today."

"Yeah. I took a sick day, couldn't face teaching, and wanted to see if you were ready to talk. I've been trying not to push you, but my parents keep asking me what I'm going to do."

"You've already told your parents?"

"Of course. I needed their support."

Knowing Sid and Vickie, he wasn't sure that was the kind of support *he* would've been looking for. He found them to be over-bearing in the extreme. But who was he to criticize how she'd handled the situation? There was no rule book for this type of thing. "Right. Of course they'd be concerned." He curved his hand into a fist. "Go ahead and tell them they don't have any-thing to worry about."

"What does that mean?" she asked.

"It means your child will have a father. I'm willing to try again." There. He'd said it. The words were out. The decision had been made.

"You *are*?"

He winced. Even her excitement and relief bugged him. He supposed it was because he felt cornered, and no one liked to be cornered, but that wasn't her fault. He was lucky she wanted him instead of Scott. At least that put *him* in the position of choosing. "Yes."

"So...would you like me to come over tonight? I could make

you dinner. You like my beet and goat cheese salad. And I've found a new recipe for pesto chicken I'm positive you'll love."

"Sounds great. Just…not tonight, okay? I'm still at the school, but I'm exhausted. I'm going straight to bed as soon as I get home."

"Should we get together tomorrow, then?"

"Sure. But…let's take it slow. I'd like to start over from the beginning."

"In what way?" She sounded confused.

"We'll date at first—nothing exclusive—to give us both time to acclimate to the recent changes. We have seven months. There's no rush."

"Oh. Right. Of course."

"That's okay, isn't it?"

"Sure it is." She didn't sound excited by the idea, but she sounded…tolerant. "I want you to be happy, too."

"Perfect. I'll call you tomorrow," he said, and hung up.

After another fifteen minutes spent staring off into space, Gavin finally rose to his feet. He should feel good, he told himself. He was making a worthy sacrifice. In a sense, it was the sacrifice his father had refused to make for him. He'd put his child first.

But if he didn't even want Heather to come over and make him dinner, how was he going to marry her?

CHAPTER THIRTEEN

A ding indicated Gavin had received a text. After parking in his drive, he checked his phone.

You son of a bitch!

Nice... There was no name attached to the number. That meant the sender wasn't in his address book. But he could guess the person's identity. Who is this? he wrote, just to be sure.

The response, when it came, didn't answer the question directly. It did, however, provide a strong clue. You're getting back with her? Really?

Scott.

If the baby's mine, I want to raise it, Gavin wrote.

We won't know that for seven months!

But he knew he'd take better care of Scott's baby than Scott would of his. After living with Aiyana and working at the ranch, he felt like a trained warrior when it came to defending the powerless. Anyway, even if he was wrong about Scott's parenting ability, he couldn't trust Scott well enough to take the chance. He had to stay involved in order to make sure his child had everything he or she needed. That was the reason he'd chosen to take Heather back—it would provide him with the most control over the child's life, even though it wasn't necessarily the path he *wanted* to take.

I'm sorry you're disappointed.

Bullshit! If you were sorry, you wouldn't do what you're doing. I saw the way you were looking at Heather when we were at the bar the other night. You wanted to make sure she still wanted you but only as some sort of ego trip. You don't love her, not when it comes down to it. You were just messing with her head, trying to screw things up for me.

That was such a load of crap. Gavin had been *glad* to see them out having fun. He'd thought Heather had finally gotten over him, that he no longer had to feel he was disappointing someone he cared about as a friend.

He didn't bother to respond, but Scott didn't wait for a reply. He added: You'd better watch out. If I get the chance, I'm going to kick your ass!

You've got my address. Gavin knew better than to provoke the dude, but he couldn't help it. He was spoiling for a fight right now himself. Just turning down the road that led to his house reminded him of his new neighbor and brought back, in exquisite detail, what it'd felt like to make love to her last night. He wanted to go back over there. That he couldn't made him angry. But he knew what would likely happen if he did, and it wouldn't be fair to sleep with someone else after he'd told Heather he was willing to start over with her.

When Heather's ex-boyfriend didn't continue the argument, Gavin got out. Maybe Scott's silence meant he was on his way. Gavin had been planning to go in, take off his clothes and crash—with the hope that the world would look better in the morning. But that exchange with Scott had shot him full of adrenaline, making sleep impossible. He decided he'd sit out on the porch, like he did most other nights, and work on his latest song, try to calm down and keep an eye out at the same time, but when he reached the stoop, he found a note tucked into his front door.

I made beef stew in my Crock-Pot today and got some crusty sourdough bread at the bakery in town. I even have some no-bake cookies Alia and Branson helped make for dessert. Not a bad meal for someone who doesn't have a stove or oven. Would you like to join us for dinner? If so, come on over. We'll wait until seven. —Savanna

"Shit," he muttered as he stared down at her delicate handwriting. Telling himself he'd be crazy to flirt with that kind of temptation, he crumpled the paper. He had to stay away from Savanna, or he could—*would*—wind up compromising his integrity. But he couldn't say no to dinner. Although he'd given her his number, she'd never called or texted him, so he didn't have hers. He couldn't get out of going there without walking over to tell her. And if he did that, he might as well eat. He didn't want her to think he was acting weird after last night when last night had nothing to do with what was going on in his life.

Besides, he was hungry, and this meant he wouldn't have to make something for himself.

"It's just dinner," he muttered. It wasn't as if she'd invited him back into her bed. They'd agreed that last night would be an isolated incident. Besides, it was early, so her kids would be up and interacting with them. Surely, Branson and Alia's presence would keep him from doing anything he shouldn't. Why sit here, angry and morose, waiting for Scott to arrive and make his night even worse?

He could always deal with Heather's former boyfriend later.

The absurdity of fighting at all hit him as he showered. But he knew he might not have much choice in the matter. He wouldn't allow Scott to push him around. If his childhood had taught him anything, it was how to deal with a physical threat. Scott seemed to believe that brute force could get him what he wanted, which proved that he was as big a fool as Gavin had first thought.

It was six-fifteen by the time Gavin was ready. He didn't see Scott's Camaro out front, though Scott had had plenty of time to drive over. Was he not coming?

Gavin checked his phone. There'd been no further word from him, either.

Hoping Heather's former boyfriend would just let it go, Gavin pulled his hair back. He wouldn't need his car keys, since he'd be walking over. But he was tempted to slip a condom in his wallet...

"*See?*" he said, disgusted that he'd even have the thought, and forced himself to leave without one.

He wasn't going to sleep with Savanna again.

Savanna had splurged while she was in town earlier and bought a new blouse as well as a nude-colored bra and panty set. She figured she owed herself something after so much scrubbing and cleaning and unpacking. It was the first thing she'd bought beyond absolute necessities since Gordon had gone to jail, and it felt like Christmas. She loved being able to make such a purchase without having to account for it later, after Gordon got home. It was especially exciting to wear her new clothes knowing that Gavin might be coming over. He made her feel *so* desirable. And that was a rush, especially after going so long feeling as though she was merely an afterthought to her husband.

Still, the house needed repairs. She had no business buying sexy underwear. But she wouldn't splurge again, and she *was* slowly improving their living situation. She'd removed all the junk and trash, knocked down the spiderwebs (the hardest job yet), cleaned out the closets and emptied at least half the boxes. In another day or two she'd have herself and her children completely moved in. Then she'd be able to tackle the list she'd been making of the things that needed to be repaired or replaced, get some bids and pull together a budget.

As she set the table, she kept glancing out the front window to see if Gavin was coming up her drive.

When she spotted him, her heart jumped into her throat. One night was never going to be enough, she realized. She supposed she'd known that when she bought the lingerie. But she wasn't willing to get into another serious relationship, wasn't ready to introduce another man into her children's lives. Anyone who felt relieved just to be able to buy a bra, a pair of panties and a shirt needed to retain her freedom for a while. But she and Gavin could continue to enjoy each other physically, if they wanted to. They lived close, had the privacy and were extremely attracted to each other. At least, he'd seemed every bit as interested in her body as she was in his...

It would depend on whether they'd be able to keep the physical side of things in perspective, she decided. That alone was a big question mark. But, in case they continued to see each other in that way, she was glad she hadn't thrown out her birth control pills. She could easily start taking them again.

The moment Gavin knocked, Branson jumped up from where he and Alia were sprawled out on the floor in front of the TV. "I'll get it!"

As he raced past, Savanna went back into the kitchen, where she could hear Gavin greet Branson and tease him a little at the door.

"Come on in. Dinner's almost ready," Branson told him. Then he squealed and began to laugh as Gavin came around the corner carrying him by his ankles.

Savanna's breath caught in her throat as she met Gavin's eyes. She'd been worried that seeing him might be awkward—part of the reason she'd taken a moment to collect herself while Branson got the door. What they'd shared had been so intimate, yet they didn't know each other that well.

She shouldn't have worried, she told herself. Gavin could make anyone feel comfortable.

He smiled as he put down her son. "Thanks for the invite."

The new bra and panty set she was wearing seemed to be burning her skin. "I'm glad you could come."

The way his gaze swept over her made her wonder if he was thinking about last night, too. If so, he didn't give any other indication. He gestured at the table. "What can I do to help?"

She pointed to a pitcher of lemonade. "If you could pour us all a drink, I'll ladle out the stew."

"You got it."

As he slipped past her, she was tempted to lean toward him. She craved contact.

Fortunately, Branson had stayed to tell Gavin about the black widow he'd found in the old woodpile, so that kept her from acting on the impulse.

Gavin told him he had to be careful around woodpiles, that snakes liked them, too. Then Alia called out to tell Branson that his favorite cartoon was coming on, and Branson hurried back to the living room. Savanna thought maybe Gavin would touch her—if only briefly on the elbow—or show some other sign of the familiarity they'd enjoyed, but he didn't. Although he was kind and polite, he seemed afraid to get too close to her.

"Is everything okay?" She eyed him curiously after she put the last bowl on the table.

"Fine." He spoke as if he was surprised by the question, but he avoided her gaze, suggesting there *was* something wrong, so she lowered her voice.

"You don't regret last night, do you?"

He scowled as he looked up at her. "Of course not. I loved last night."

"So did I," she admitted, but there was still something wrong. She could feel it.

She didn't get the chance to press him. She wasn't sure she would have, even if she'd had the chance. They'd agreed that last night would be what it was. She didn't have the right to expect anything. So, doing her best to maintain a smile, she served dinner.

Fortunately, the kids were excited about a snail they'd put in an old aquarium they'd found in the barn, so they kept up the conversation by talking about that. Savanna could feel Gavin's eyes on her occasionally, but whenever she looked back at him, he'd glance away. And as soon as they were finished with dinner, he said he was exhausted and heading home to bed.

Savanna couldn't blame him for being tired. They'd been up for much of the night. She was tired, too. But it was a good kind of tired, one that came with a sense of satisfaction. She hoped last night wouldn't prove to be the isolated encounter she'd insisted on, but Gavin was acting so remote she doubted anything would happen between them this evening.

What was he thinking?

She toyed with the idea of asking but lost her nerve. Last night, even before he touched her, she'd been sure of where she stood with him. Tonight…she was confused. Sometimes she *thought* she detected a hint of desire—especially when he'd first arrived. But if she searched his face to try to determine what he was feeling, he shuttered his eyes and feigned interest in the mundane.

"I'm sorry if you had a hard day," she said as she walked him out. The kids wanted to join them. They stuck to Gavin like glue. But she promised them another cookie if they'd go inside and let her have a few minutes to talk to their neighbor alone.

"I didn't have a hard day," he said. "Well, I did. But not for the reason you might think."

"You weren't too tired?"

"I didn't mind that."

"So…what happened?"

She got the impression he had something important to say, but then her phone went off. It was Detective Sullivan. He'd told her he'd check in one final time to be sure she was ready for Gordon's call, should it come tomorrow. He wanted to coach her on a few things—like how to get Gordon to say something he wouldn't have had any way of knowing unless he was involved in Emma Ventnor's disappearance.

She frowned as she stared down at caller ID, but she didn't hit the talk button. If she was going to do as Sullivan asked—purposely try to get Gordon to talk about the missing sixteen-year-old—she could wait to call him until after Gavin went home.

"Your mother-in-law again?" Gavin asked.

"Not this time," she said as she silenced the ringtone.

"I thought you only looked that troubled when she called." He offered her a smile she could tell was specifically engineered to cheer her up.

"It's the detective who searched my house in Nephi," she explained with a grimace.

"They need you to come back and testify?"

"When he called this morning, that was my guess, too. But this is about something else."

Concern registered on his face. "Don't tell me he thinks you know something you're not saying…"

"No. He knows I'm innocent of all that. At least, I think he does. The police are hoping to tie Gordon to another case."

"A rape?"

"Possibly more than that." She explained what the detective had told her.

Gavin ran a finger and thumb over his beard as he listened. "Wow."

"Right? I *really* hope he isn't responsible for this one. None of his other victims were so young. And he eventually let them go."

"Why would she be different?"

"That's the question, and what makes me think it has to have been someone else." Unless there'd been extenuating circumstances. Maybe he'd beaten her too severely, without truly intending to kill her. Or someone was coming, and he'd had to silence her quickly.

All kinds of gruesome thoughts had filtered through Savanna's mind...

"For you—and Alia and Branson—that would be a welcome break," Gavin said.

He sounded supportive but not convinced Emma's attacker was someone else. "So I should do what I can."

"*I'd* rather you didn't."

She leaned on the porch railing and gazed out at the tranquil night. "Why? Sullivan—the detective—insists it's my duty to help in whatever capacity I can."

"He's concerned about putting Gordon away for life. And while I'd like to see that happen, too, I'm more concerned about *you*. I'm guessing Gordon's a psychopath, since he seems capable of compartmentalizing to the point that you and the kids had no idea what he was doing. Provoking a man like that could be dangerous."

"Not as long as he's behind bars..."

"That's the problem. Even if he's found guilty, we have no idea what kind of sentence he'll get, or if something will happen later where he's released for good behavior, overcrowding, whatever. And his mother, who's his fiercest defender, is able to move around at will. What if she gets angry enough to come out here and start trouble?"

Savanna had been trying not to worry about that possibility. Dorothy was twenty-two years older. It seemed silly to fear being physically attacked by someone's mother. And yet... Dorothy was willing to go further than most people. She didn't have a lot of control or restraint. The night she'd shown up at their house in Nephi and started screaming and kicking the front door had been unsettling, if not downright frightening. Savanna had fully believed that Dorothy would attack her, given the chance.

Even if Savanna could overcome her, she didn't want her children to be subjected to another emotional episode like the last one. Watching the cops drag their grandmother off had been a difficult thing to see.

"She has a temper," she admitted. "You should hear some of the stories Gordon told me over the years. Sometimes I wonder if all the alcohol she's consumed has destroyed her brain."

"You have my number," Gavin said. "All you have to do is call me if you need anything. It doesn't matter what time. I'll come as soon as I can."

"Thank you." She felt a measure of relief. He seemed to care about her safety, so maybe last night *hadn't* destroyed their friendship, as she'd begun to fear. "With any luck I won't need to bother you."

"I'd rather you call, even if you're only frightened." His hand accidentally brushed hers, and the same spark she'd felt last night zipped through her, making her wish he'd mention the possibility of returning after the kids went to bed. But he didn't. Pulling his gaze away from her face, he thanked her for dinner and told her good-night.

"'Night," she murmured as he stepped off the porch.

Why didn't he tell her?

Shoving his hands in his pockets, Gavin put his head down as he walked home. He'd nearly mentioned Heather, would have done so if the detective hadn't interrupted. But after he heard everything Savanna was dealing with, he'd figured he could keep *his* problems to himself. She'd already let him know she wasn't a romantic option, so he didn't need to explain why he couldn't sleep with her again.

Or did he? Was he just using that as an excuse, holding out hope that something would change?

As soon as he crossed the creek and knew he was out of sight of her house, he kicked a rock down the road and cursed under his breath. The good news was that he didn't see Scott's Camaro in his drive. The bad news was that he saw Heather's Pathfinder—and found her sitting on his front step.

"What are you doing here?" he asked.

She stood as he crossed the lawn. "Scott called me earlier. He was *so* angry. I was afraid he might come over and start a fight, if not with me at my place, with you over here. I came to make sure he couldn't surprise you."

"It wouldn't have come as a surprise," Gavin said. "He texted me earlier, trying to start something."

"What'd he say?"

"Just a bunch of bullshit."

She hugged herself against the cool night air. "I'm sorry. He's not making things any easier."

"It's not your fault. You didn't plan this. How long have you been waiting?"

"At least thirty minutes. Where were you?"

He jerked his head toward Savanna's. "Next door."

Heather pressed her lips into a straight line.

He knew that look well. "Is something wrong?"

"Not if... I mean, you told me you were going home to bed."

"Heather, stop."

"I'm just wondering what you were doing there, that's all."

He considered mentioning dinner but didn't want to kindle her jealousy when he'd managed to back away from Savanna so successfully. It hadn't been easy, but he'd kept his hands to himself and he'd said almost nothing about last night. "Just helping out a little." Although that was stretching the truth a bit, he didn't have it in him to try to reassure her tonight.

"Savanna's pretty, don't you think?"

Recognizing that as the trap it was, he sidestepped the question. "You've met her?"

"I stopped by earlier, when I was looking for you. She was out getting her mail."

He pulled his house key from his pocket. Typically, he didn't bother to lock his doors, not if he was in the area. But he'd locked them tonight. He hadn't wanted to come home to find that Scott had trashed his belongings. "Why didn't you call me?" He held the door so she could precede him into the house. "Let me know you were waiting?"

"I *tried*," she replied.

He pulled out his phone to see why he hadn't been alerted and discovered that it'd run out of battery. He'd been so engrossed in fighting his attraction to Savanna he hadn't checked it since he'd left the house. "Oh. Sorry. It's dead."

"So what did you do for your gorgeous neighbor tonight?"

Gavin gave her a pointed look. It was her possessiveness that had broken them up the last time—because an ex-girlfriend had come to town and had wanted to see him. "Heather, please. Let's not start that again."

She lifted a hand. "I won't. I'm just a little insecure, considering our history and the situation I'm in right now." She looked close to tears when she slipped into his arms. "I guess I need a little TLC. It's been a rough week."

"I bet." He rubbed her back, trying to give her that TLC. If he was going to be her significant other, he had to fulfill her somehow—couldn't care only about the child. But when she took that as a sign that he might be amenable to more and turned her face to kiss him, he had to pull back.

"I'm sorry," he said. "I'm not ready."

CHAPTER FOURTEEN

After she'd returned Detective Sullivan's call, Savanna carried her laptop to the couch in the living room. She was exhausted and needed to sleep, but she also needed to prepare for the next time Gordon tried to reach her, which could easily be tomorrow morning. She hadn't heard from him or his mother today, which was a little odd given how often they'd tried to reach her in the preceding weeks. She assumed they were both angry over how she'd handled their last conversation. She doubted they'd let her go on her way that easily, however. They'd contact her again, and while Dorothy could do so whenever, Gordon had access to a phone only while he was out of his cell and in the day room, or general area, where the inmates spent most of their time.

Her stomach cramped as she typed the name "Emma Ventnor" into a search engine. Although she hated to put a face to that name, she thought a picture might tell her more than she knew. At the very least, the accompanying articles could provide information Detective Sullivan had not. The police had been so calculating with her in the past, revealing certain details while keeping others hidden, that she didn't trust them much more than Gordon. She understood the reason for the games they'd played with her, of course, but she also preferred to go into this phone call prepared, didn't want to help them tie Gordon to a murder if he wasn't responsible for it.

Several links populated the screen. She clicked on the first one and a picture of Emma appeared. The girl had been pretty, all right, with shiny dark hair and big brown eyes. Savanna could easily see her ex-husband being attracted to such a beauty, especially as she read more. Emma had been popular, a cheerleader and a straight-A student—the kind of girl Gordon would've longed to date in high school but who would've been out of his reach. He'd been pudgy back then, until he'd grown serious about wrestling. He'd also been such a troublemaker, which was why he'd been sent to an all-boys school for reformation.

"Heaven help me," she muttered as she scrolled through the article, which had been written shortly after Emma had gone missing.

Please, if you have information, contact the police. We'll do anything to get our daughter back. She's always been such a sweet, loving person.

That heartfelt plea from Emma's father made Savanna wince. She had a daughter, too. She couldn't imagine the pain involved in what Emma's family was going through. Surely, Gordon would not resort to *murder*, would not take a child away from her parents.

Emma's car had been found on the side of the road with a slight dent on one side. According to her parents, she'd been coming home from cheer practice when she went missing. The police speculated that whoever kidnapped her had hit her car, and she'd pulled over to exchange insurance information. No doubt she'd felt perfectly safe, since it was in the middle of the afternoon.

Savanna found the same article on her phone and texted the link to Gavin along with a note that said, This is the girl. She needed to talk to someone, especially him after what'd happened last night, but when she didn't hear back right away, she assumed he'd gone to bed.

After a final check on her kids, and a silent prayer that Branson could get through the night without another accident so he wouldn't feel so terrible in the morning, she told herself to be strong. She couldn't start leaning on Gavin. She couldn't lean on anyone.

She was just putting on her nightgown when she heard her phone ping. Although she feared it might be Dorothy, or even Detective Sullivan giving her some last-minute warning or instructions for tomorrow, it was Gavin.

Are you okay? he'd written.

Relieved that he'd responded, she sat on the bed. The way dinner had gone, she couldn't help but question what he was thinking and feeling. I'm fine. A little nervous about tomorrow, is all.

Want me to come over while you talk to Gordon?

Don't you have to work?

I could go in late. I have more sick days than I could ever take.

I'd rather not burden you with that. Just wanted you to see the girl. I wish I could say he'd never target someone like her, but I can't. She's beautiful, don't you think?

No question. But he had an even more beautiful wife waiting for him at home, so that doesn't explain it.

Reading that made her feel so much better. Somehow, intertwined with all the other emotions she'd been experiencing lately lurked the depressing thought that she hadn't been enough for the one man she'd tried to give everything.

Thank you for being so kind.

It's true. Are you sure you don't want me to come over tomorrow while you take that call? For moral support, if nothing else? I'd like to make sure that detective doesn't push you any more than he already has.

I shouldn't even have to talk to Sullivan tomorrow. He's set everything up. I'm supposed to text him if the call comes in, and that's it. He'll get the recording from whoever handles that sort of thing at the jail.

What if the call doesn't come in?

I wait until it does. Then I text him. But now that you've offered to help…

What can I do?

Because of what I might have to say to get Gordon upset, I'd rather not have the kids around to overhear the conversation. If you really wouldn't mind missing a little work, it would be nice if Branson and Alia could come to your place for that hour when he's most likely to call.

When do you think that will be?

I sent a text to his mother earlier, told her to have him call me at ten. I think he'll do that if he can. I've never requested a call before, so he should be curious if nothing else. Anyway, if I'm here alone, I'll be able to go after him the way the detective wants me to without having to watch my words and language.

Are you sure you want to do this, Savanna?

I don't see any way out of it. I have to help Emma's parents, if I can. And if I'm going to help, I might as well go all the way. Make it count.

The kids can certainly come here. I'll take them to the park in town to see the ducks and get ice cream.

You don't have to go to that much trouble. They'll be excited just to hang out with you. ☺

I'd rather make it fun so they'll want to come back.

He didn't understand that simply being around him was fun—for all of them. Thank you.

She hoped he'd continue the conversation. The more contact she had with him, the more contact she wanted. But he wrapped up the conversation with No problem. See you tomorrow.

"Who was that?"

As he put his phone back on the nightstand, Gavin glanced over at Heather, who was on the other side of the bed. When his screen had lit up, he'd waited a few minutes, hoping Heather would fall asleep. They'd been lying still for fifteen minutes or more—he deep in thought. But it was too much to hope for that she wouldn't notice his text exchange. That it was such a long one didn't help. He would've sent Heather home except she was now claiming to be afraid of Scott. If she was truly afraid, if Scott *had* threatened her as she claimed, he didn't want to put her in a bad situation, especially now that she was pregnant. And he couldn't give her his bed and sleep out on the couch, even though he would've preferred it. That would've offended her for sure, since they'd made love so many times in the past.

Hopefully, once he'd gone without sex for a while, he'd be

more interested in getting intimate with her again. It was just too soon, an awkward time, given everything that'd happened recently.

"It's no one," he said.

"Who would text you this late?"

"My mother. Eli. A gig. Any one of my friends. A lot of people. It's not *that* late. It's only ten."

"So *was* it Eli? Or someone else?"

"It was a friend."

"*Which* friend?"

He punched his pillow. "Heather, I'm exhausted. Can we go to sleep?"

She fell silent and remained that way for so long that Gavin finally began to drift off—only to be jerked back to consciousness when she said, "Something's wrong. It's different with you this time."

Stifling a frustrated groan, Gavin pretended not to hear her, and eventually she fell asleep. At least, he assumed she did. The next thing he knew the sun was peering through the blinds, and she was up and rushing to get home so she could shower and dress before she had to be at school to teach her fifth graders.

Gavin breathed a sigh of relief when Heather left with only a quick hug for him. Thank God she'd been in too much of a hurry to demand they talk—or suggest they do anything else. After last night, he realized how badly he needed some time to acclimate to the decision he'd made and to file away the feelings he had for Savanna. He thought it would be nice to let things calm down with Scott, too, before he and Heather were seen all over town together. They had months before the baby was born; he didn't see any reason they had to move fast.

He made a pot of coffee and a plate of fried eggs. Then he called his mother to let her know he wouldn't be in until noon and carried his guitar out on the porch. He wasn't quite finished with what he'd been writing recently, but lyrics for another song were beginning to take shape in his mind. He closed his eyes as he pictured Savanna smiling at him just after having removed her blouse and tried to capture the promise of that smile and the way it'd made everything inside him go a little crazy.

Two hours disappeared in what felt like two minutes, but he had a new song written by the time Branson and Alia came running down the road with Savanna walking more slowly behind them.

"Ready to go to the park?" Gavin called out.

"My mom gave me money to buy bread." Branson waved a few bills in his hand. "She said we might be able to feed the ducks!"

Gavin set his guitar aside. "You will be able to feed them. And I've already got a loaf of bread that's too stale to eat, so we're all set."

"Do they bite?" Alia, breathless from trying to keep up with her brother, sounded much less excited by the idea.

"Some of the geese can be a little aggressive if you rush them, but the ducks are usually tame." He winked at her. "Anyway, you have nothing to worry about because I'll be there to make sure nothing happens to you."

She gave him a sweet smile. "I like your hair," she said. "I wish mine was that long."

He laughed. If he was getting such envious compliments from little girls, he obviously needed an edgier look.

He shaded his eyes so that he could see Savanna despite the glare of the sun. She was wearing a pair of jeans with a T-shirt that made the most of her beautiful figure, but she looked tired and stressed as she approached. "How'd you sleep?" he asked.

"Not well," she replied. "Mostly tossed and turned. You?"

"I managed to do a little better than that."

"Good. I, uh—" she went slightly red in the face "—kept you pretty busy night before last, so I'm sure you needed the rest."

"I didn't mind losing sleep."

She flashed him a self-conscious grin. "Thanks for saying that. I came on so strong I've been afraid that maybe it was... *too* strong."

"No. You did nothing wrong, nothing I didn't like."

When their eyes met and held, he wondered what it was about this woman. She got to him on such a gut level. He couldn't help letting his gaze slide down to her mouth. He wanted to taste her again... "You could've used a good night's sleep yourself," he said.

"Tonight will be better, providing I get that call I'm expecting."

"What call?" Branson wrinkled his nose as he looked up at his mother.

"I'm dealing with some of the contractors who will be fixing our house this morning, remember?" she said, letting Gavin know that they weren't aware she might be speaking to their father.

Gavin tried to draw Branson's and Alia's attention. "Have you ever seen a guitar up close?"

"No." Branson crouched down to get a better look. "Can you play it?"

"I can," Gavin told him. "I play it all the time."

"Will you play it for us?"

Before he could answer, Alia added, "And sing for us, too?"

"Sure." Gavin slung his guitar over his shoulder. "What would you like to hear?"

They looked to their mother to answer for them. "I'm not sure what type of songs you do," Savanna said.

"I play folk rock, blues, soul, even a little pop rock."

"Is there a song you've been doing a lot lately?"

"I'll play one that's been going over pretty well at my shows. It's the only true country song I do, but I've thrown it into my set because some of the bars I play are out in farming communities, and they typically like country music."

"Sounds good to me."

He sang Keith Urban's "Blue Ain't Your Color" but, considering the lyrics, decided afterward that it probably wasn't the wisest choice. By the time he finished, he and Savanna were staring at each other with such naked longing he felt transfixed.

"You sing *good*!" Alia piped up, shattering the moment and reminding him that they weren't alone.

He cleared his throat as he put down his guitar. "Thanks. I plan on moving to Nashville soon."

Savanna's eyebrows shot up. "Nashville! *How* soon?"

He *had* to leave Silver Springs, he realized. Right away. Even if Aiyana wasn't ready to marry Cal. He'd been trying to wait, but his peace of mind was at stake. He could never be the kind of husband he wanted to be to Heather—the kind of husband he'd always envisioned himself as being—when he wanted Savanna instead. And that would impact the kind of father he was, too. So he had to get far away from her. "In the next couple of months," he replied.

That was fast to plan and execute a move, especially because he had to find a replacement for himself at New Horizons before he could leave town. Even still, as he remembered Savanna arching her back to meet his thrusts, her hands fisted in his hair and her mouth open and receptive beneath his, he wasn't convinced it would be fast enough. Two months would equal *sixty* nights he'd have to overcome the temptation to return to her bed...

"We'd better get over to the park," he told the kids, putting his guitar in the house and locking up before helping them into his truck.

CHAPTER FIFTEEN

Why hadn't Gavin mentioned that he was planning to move?

Savanna felt sucker punched. The news had come out of *nowhere*. Hadn't he just bought his house? Why would he purchase a property knowing that he'd be leaving the area in such a short time?

It didn't make sense. The Gavin who'd come to dinner last night and the Gavin she'd spoken to this morning were somehow different from the Gavin who'd built the makeshift bridge and spent the night in her bed. The old Gavin had been easygoing, unguarded, and made no secret of his interest in her. *This* Gavin seemed to be backing away in spite of that interest.

Was it the sex that'd changed him? Made him decide to leave town?

It was ridiculous to even speculate that could be the reason. He'd told her, in so many words, that he'd enjoyed being with her. And yet...it was that night that seemed to have changed *everything*.

Suddenly bereft—as if she was about to lose her only friend, since that was sort of the case—she stood in his yard, forcing herself to wave and smile while he drove off with her children.

Then she stared down at her phone. Without the brief flash of joy Gavin had brought into her life, she'd be left with nothing but work. The work involved in rebuilding the farmhouse. The work involved in rebuilding her family. The work involved in rebuilding herself. And amid all of that work she'd probably learn more and more about Gordon's crimes. She might even be called upon to do more of the same type of thing the detective had asked her to do today.

She was about to call Sullivan to tell him she couldn't get involved, after all. She wanted out. But the memory of Emma Ventnor's parents clinging to each other on that news clip she'd watched, begging for anyone with information to come forward, made her resist canceling. She wasn't doing it for Sullivan. She was doing it for them, for two people she wished she could help in any way possible.

She'd just started for home when her phone rang.

The call was coming from the county jail. Gordon. Here he was. Apparently, his mother had been able to pass along the message Savanna had asked her to.

Instead of finishing the walk home, Savanna returned to the shade of Gavin's porch, drew a steadying breath and answered. "Hello?"

After the usual rhetoric about the call being collect and recorded, she heard her former husband's voice.

"Savanna, thank you for taking my call." He sounded slightly surprised and yet relieved that she'd broken down.

She took the chair Gavin used when playing his guitar. "I only accepted because I read something that has me totally freaked out, Gordon. And I want to hear you say you didn't do it."

Leery now—she could feel it in the sudden tension between them—he paused before responding. "What are you talking about?"

"Another case."

"Oh, give me a break!" His emotions switched to irritation.

"The police are going to try to pin anything they can on me. But I'm innocent, like I've told you. Look at it practically if you don't believe me. There's no way one person could do everything they claim."

She wondered how many wives of other serial rapists or murderers had heard similar logic. "This isn't a rape."

"Then why'd you bring it up?"

"Because a girl, only sixteen, has been missing for almost a year."

"Emma Ventnor. I should've guessed. I don't want to talk about her."

He should've guessed? What did that signify? And why didn't he want to talk about her? Was he ashamed, guilt-ridden?

Savanna gripped the phone tighter. "Then you're aware of the case."

"Of course. She lived in Bingham, not far from Kennecott Copper. When she went missing, it was all over the news. But *I* didn't hurt her. They won't be able to pin her death on me."

"Death?" she echoed. "How do you know she's dead?"

"It's been a year since they found her car on the side of the road. Where do *you* think she is?"

"They haven't found her body."

"If it's been this long, they're not going to find it. She's probably out in the woods somewhere—or a lake—fully decomposed. Whoever got her was smart."

"Sounds like you admire him..."

"I'm so sick of the police it's hard *not* to start rooting for the bad guys."

"You're not one of those 'bad guys'?"

"How many times do I have to say it?"

"Sullivan is convinced you killed Emma."

"Why would you even listen to that bastard? He's treated you like shit from the beginning, and everyone knows *you* haven't done anything wrong."

She ignored the part about the way Sullivan had treated her, even though it was true. The police had not been her friend. Because she had a possible motivation for hiding the truth, they'd considered her less than trustworthy from the beginning, which had alienated her even more—and caused the community to react in much the same way. "Emma Ventnor was only sixteen."

"I told you, I'm not the one who kidnapped her!"

From what Savanna had read, there'd been no sign of a struggle. "You kept a rifle under the seat of your van." He was a good marksman, too, looked forward to deer hunting season all year. "You could easily have used that to convince her to get in with you."

"I drove to remote places late at night. I had to have some way to defend myself, just in case. If I remember right, once upon a time, you thought carrying that rifle was a good idea."

Because she'd believed him, believed almost anything he said. "Until that rape kit was found in our shed."

"Here we go again!"

She broke in before he could add anything more. "Have you seen the news clip of her parents, crying and pleading for her safe return? Can you imagine what it would be like to be in their shoes, Gordon? What if *we* were those parents? What if Alia was the one who'd been taken?"

"That's enough. I'm done with this topic."

"Even though I'm upset and need to talk about it?"

"I only have so long. There are other guys waiting to use this phone. And I'd rather hear about my own kids. How are they?"

She hadn't told him about Branson's bed-wetting. She knew how it would make him feel about his son. He'd assume their boy wasn't as strong or manly as he should be. "They're fine."

"And you? How's my wife?"

"We've been down this road," she said. "I'm *not* your wife, Gordon. Not anymore."

"That's what you say now. Sullivan has gotten inside your

head. But I won't be behind bars forever. I'm going to beat the charges. Then I'll be out and will be the kind of husband and father I should've been in the first place. I realize now that I wasn't attentive to you and the kids. I took you for granted. But I'll be better. I promise."

Squeezing her eyes closed, she let her head fall onto the back of the chair. "I don't want you to be better."

"It's too loud here. These assholes never know when to be quiet. What'd you say?"

It wasn't just what was happening on his end. She'd spoken softly, but she'd spoken the truth. Opening her eyes, she raised her voice. "I don't want you to be better. I don't want you at all."

Silence. She'd always been so careful not to upset him or hurt his feelings. There was no telling what would trigger one of his infamous mood swings. Her words had to have come as a shock. But Detective Sullivan had asked her to rile him up, and arousing his jealousy was the quickest way to go about it.

"I'll ignore that because you've been going through such a hard time."

It surprised her that he was hanging on to his temper for a change. She'd have to push a little harder. "It's not only that," she said. "I've met someone else."

That wasn't merely a line calculated to upset him. It was true, she realized. She *had* met someone, someone who made her crave his company and his touch. That changed everything, made her determined to fight for the same type of magic in the future. That Gavin was leaving was beside the point. She could never go back to Gordon after meeting Gavin.

"What are you talking about?" he asked. "I've only been behind bars for *two months*. And you've been bitching the whole time about how miserable you've been. Are you saying you've had a boyfriend all along? Is that why you moved to California? The two of you left together?"

She started to laugh. She didn't find what he'd said funny,

and yet there didn't seem to be a better way to respond, to cope. He'd always been so quick to accuse her of wanting someone else—and it had never been true, until now.

"You think it's funny?" he challenged.

Hearing that frightening edge to his voice, the one that used to make the hair stand up on the back of her neck, she sobered. "No. Only ironic. While you were out stalking and raping women, I was waiting faithfully for you at home, hoping you'd eventually get around to showing me some small scrap of attention. I didn't meet Gavin until I moved here."

"Which was when?"

"On Friday."

"Five days ago."

"Yes. But I've changed and learned so much in those five days, it seems much longer."

Although she could tell it was forced, Gordon barked out a laugh of his own. "Give me a break! You've barely met the guy, don't even know him. It's the stress of what we're going through that makes him look so good, and he's probably a big enough prick to take advantage of that."

"No." As she stared toward the Topatopa Mountains, she realized why Gavin sat out on his porch so often. There was a lot more foliage blocking her view; his was better. "I've never wanted a man like I want him," she admitted. "Doesn't matter that we just met. I'd sleep with him again if I could."

"Again?" he cried. "You selfish bitch! You'd better not be fucking other guys around Branson and Alia. They're still *my* kids. You can't shut me out that easily."

"What'd you do with Emma Ventnor's body?" she asked.

"Do you think I'm an idiot?" he spat.

"The least you can do is take responsibility for your actions and bring her parents the resolution they deserve."

His voice dropped to a menacing level. "You're making a

mistake, Savanna. I might be powerless right now, but I won't always be this way."

"I don't care," she said. "I'm *past* caring. I'm taking control of my life. I will come and go as I please. I will raise my children as I please. I will sleep with any man I please. And I will never have to put up with you or your mother again."

"Now you're really pissing me off…"

"So what are you going to do about it?" she asked. "Get out of jail and kill me like you did that poor girl? *Where'd you put her body, Gordon?*"

He didn't answer; he hung up.

Savanna had expected to be shaken, upset by the call. But she felt strangely empowered. She was done trying to keep his moods steady, keep him happy, keep her marriage intact. She'd been so upset when he'd broken everything apart, and yet she was quickly coming to realize that he'd done her a huge favor, at least in one way.

Again, she closed her eyes, simply feeling the wind on her face. *I'm free. I'm going to be okay. He's gone.*

After a few minutes, when she felt ready, she texted Sullivan. He called me. You can listen to the recording if you want. I did my best, but I didn't get a confession or any information that could help. Gordon was too smart for that.

She waited a bit longer to gather her thoughts and her strength. Then she called Gavin.

"Any word?" he said the moment he answered.

"Yes. He called. I just hung up with him."

Gavin's voice lowered, grew more serious. "How'd it go?"

"It was a total waste of time, as I feared it would be. Sullivan is crazy if he thinks Gordon will ever say anything to incriminate himself. He never tripped up when we were living and sleeping together. Why would he suddenly divulge important details over a *recorded* line now that we're apart?"

She heard Gavin sigh. "That's partly why I was so concerned

about Sullivan's request. *Trying* to piss off a guy like Gordon is reckless, especially when there was so little chance of success in the first place."

"*Somebody* has to do something," she said. And all of his other victims seemed to think she should've known and interceded a long time ago.

"You were thinking of Emma Ventnor's parents. That's why I didn't try harder to talk you out of it. Just in case it *would* help. So...how'd the call end? Did you manage to make him angry?"

She remembered telling Gordon that she'd slept with someone else and wanted to do it again. She couldn't repeat what she'd said to Gavin, but it was true. Whenever she thought of Gavin's hands on her body, she felt tingly and light-headed. "Definitely. But...where are the kids? They can't hear you right now, can they?"

"No. They're across the room, putting some change in a prize machine. They saw the sign flip to Open in the ice cream store as we rolled past and decided they wanted to stop here before feeding the ducks," he said with a laugh. "We were the first ones through the door."

"It was really nice of you to take them and make it so fun." She wished she could've gone with them. "I can't tell you how much I appreciate it."

"It's no big deal."

"It is. You're the first friend I've had in a long time. But you don't have to keep them away any longer. You can come back and go to work. You've got to be feeling some pressure."

"I'm not in a huge rush. I'll stay at the school a little later tonight, get caught up."

She stood and gripped the banister as she continued to stare at the mountains. "Are you *really* moving to Nashville?"

There was a slight pause. "If I want my music to go anywhere, I have to."

She let her head fall against the support beam. "Of course. I understand. You're very talented. I like your version of the song you sang better than Keith Urban's, and that's a huge compliment because I love the way he sings it, too."

"Thank you."

Hearing the smile in his voice, she couldn't help smiling herself. "Maybe, before you go, you'll make me a recording of it. As a goodbye present."

"I could do that."

"I'd like to have something to remember you by." Savanna heard her children's voices in the background as they returned to wherever Gavin was standing or sitting.

"Your mom's checking on you," he told them.

"Tell her we're having fun. She should've come," Savanna heard Branson say.

"Tell him I'll come next time," she said. "Hopefully, you'll give me that chance before you leave."

She thought he'd readily agree. What was an ice cream date? So it surprised her when he didn't commit. He just said they'd be home soon, that they were going to feed the ducks, and then he was gone.

Alia was overwhelmed and frightened by the ducks, especially when they began to congregate around Branson to get the food. She immediately lifted her arms for Gavin to hold her so that she could feel safe while she looked down at them, and he was happy to oblige. She had to be the cutest little girl he'd ever seen. Branson, on the other hand, loved every minute of being right in the midst of the flock. He fed them as much as Gavin would allow. Gavin didn't want to overdo it; he didn't know if it was possible to make ducks sick on bread, but he couldn't imagine it was healthy to overfeed anything. Then they played tag in the park among the trees until the kids were too exhausted to keep running.

"Can we get more ice cream?" Alia asked as Gavin put her down and started to guide them over to his truck.

"More?" Gavin echoed. "Already? What about lunch?"

"I don't care about lunch," she responded.

He pinched her soft, round cheek. "Sorry, Blondie. But the party's over. I have to get to work."

She grinned up at him and put her little hand in his. "I like you."

Branson didn't say anything, but he took Gavin's other hand.

Savanna's kids were good kids. Gavin hated that once they were old enough to understand exactly what Gordon had done, they'd have to live with the stigma of their father's crimes.

Gavin was just wondering if they'd ever have the desire to visit Gordon in prison when he heard his name and turned to see Scott, wearing overalls, a construction hat and boots, and carrying a soda and lunch sack, striding toward him. "What are *you* doing here?" he asked as he pushed the children behind him.

"I work across the street." He pointed to a building—a church—that'd just been framed. "Eat lunch in this park almost every day."

Gavin had known Scott did construction, but he'd never paid much attention when it came to his particular jobs. "Good for you." He started to turn away, but Scott kept talking.

"What are *you* doing here? That's a better question."

"We came to feed the ducks," Gavin replied.

Scott eyed Branson and Alia. "They relatives of yours?"

Gavin could feel Savanna's kids leaning around him to be able to see Scott. "They're my neighbor's kids. And they don't need to be a party to what's going on between us. So let's let whatever this is go for now and talk later."

Scott's eyes narrowed. "Wait a sec. You don't have any neighbors."

"I do now. They moved in last Saturday."

"And you're already *babysitting*?" he said with a demeaning laugh.

"This morning I am. Their mother needed a little help, so I stepped up. You have a problem with that?"

"Their mother..."

"That's what I said."

Scott crumpled his sack and soda can and tossed both into the garbage receptacle nearby. "What about their father?"

"He's no longer in the picture."

"Interesting..."

"Not particularly," Gavin responded with a shrug. "A lot of people are divorced these days."

Scott picked something out of his teeth. "That's not the interesting part. What I find interesting is that you're not at work. You're taking care of some woman's kids even though you got *my* girlfriend pregnant with your own."

Gavin twisted around to point his key fob at his truck. He was farther away than usual, but the lights flashed, telling him the button had worked. "Go get in," he said to Branson and Alia. "I'll be over in a minute."

Although they did as he asked, they kept looking back as if they were worried about what might happen to him. "You're really starting to piss me off, you know that?" he said to Scott. "Heather is no longer your girlfriend. I had no say in that. And I won't have you giving me shit every time you see me."

Scott spread his arms wide. "Oh, yeah? What are you going to do about it?"

Gavin shook his head. He wasn't going to get in a fight in front of Savanna's kids. "Heather told me you threatened to beat the shit out of her last night. She stayed at my place, was too afraid to go home."

"Oh, brother!" he said. "She knows I'd never hurt her."

Gavin stepped closer. "Did you threaten her?"

"I might have yelled a few things I shouldn't have. I'll admit that. But she's not upset that she's pregnant, like you think. She's *glad*, happy to finally have some way of forcing you back to her."

Their raised voices were attracting the attention of others in the park. Gavin didn't feel like having this argument in public. "Just leave her alone," he said, and stalked off to make sure Branson and Alia were buckled up.

CHAPTER SIXTEEN

Gavin didn't go in when he dropped off the kids at home. He pulled into the drive, told them to tell their mother he'd see her later and left. He hated how torn he felt in Savanna's presence, felt he'd be smarter to limit contact as much as possible. Besides, he had to get the football field mowed before school let out, since Track and Field used it.

By the time he arrived at New Horizons and got the riding lawn mower fixed, he barely had enough time to get it done before the bell rang. He generally developed new ideas for songs or thought about his music career while cutting the turf. Thanks to the contacts of a fellow performer he'd met at one of his gigs, he'd been able to record a couple of demos in a studio in LA, which he'd sent to Republic Records. He was hoping to interest the label in his first two songs, but he knew he probably wouldn't hear back. It seemed like the only way to sell a song these days was to move to Nashville, make connections, perform at the various bars, become a known entity and build from there. He'd read blog after blog stating the same thing—some from experienced and successful songwriters who'd lived in Nashville for years and were still busting their asses, hoping to attract a big label or a major artist.

Even if he relocated, he knew his chances were slim of attaining the kind of success he occasionally allowed himself to dream about, which was part of the reason he hadn't felt too bad about trying to hold out until Aiyana married Cal. He didn't want to leave his mother and the students at the ranch without his help and support only to have his career go nowhere, anyway.

Today, he didn't think about music, however. He thought about how difficult it was going to be to support Savanna while he was in town, even as a good friend and neighbor, while trying to fulfill Heather's needs at the same time.

Putting his foot on the brake, he shifted into Neutral, pulled out his phone and texted Eli. Do you think Mom will ever really marry Cal?

He pulled off his cap and wiped the sweat from his forehead while waiting for Eli's response. But at least the answer, when it came, was hopeful. I think they're getting darn close.

How much longer?

Is there any rush?

"Yes," he muttered in frustration. But that wasn't what he texted back. He wrote, Of course not, and shifted into Drive so he could finish cutting the football field. He didn't want to push Aiyana into Cal's arms. He just wanted to start preparing for his move so he wouldn't be tempted to spend his nights in Savanna's bed.

"What's wrong?"

At the sound of Eli's voice, Aiyana glanced up to see her oldest son standing in the doorway of her office. She'd been so deep in thought she hadn't even heard him approach. "Nothing."

He came in and closed the door. "Sorry, not buying that. I saw the look on your face when I walked up."

"I'm worried, I guess."

"About…"

"Gavin. I admire his sense of duty, the kind of man it makes him. But I fear, in this instance, his honor is leading him down the wrong path."

"You mean with Heather."

"That's exactly what I mean."

Elijah folded his long body into the chair on the other side of her desk. "You don't like her."

"Not a great deal."

He rocked back. "Whoa! You saying that is like someone else saying they hate her."

"Stop. I don't hate her."

"Do you believe she's trying to trap him?"

She nibbled at her bottom lip. That was a serious allegation. She didn't want to go that far for fear of misjudging Heather. "I have no idea, but I believe she's secretly elated to think she will finally have the man she's always wanted. She's gone after Gavin so many times. And he's tried to like her in return, given the relationship chance after chance. He just doesn't feel for her what he should feel, and I can't stand the thought that getting with her might make him unhappy."

"So what do we do?"

"Is it even our place to get involved? He's an adult. We have to let him live his life."

Eli rested his chin on his steepled fingers. "He just asked me when you were going to marry Cal."

She felt a fresh fissure of alarm. "He did? I wonder why he's never asked me that question."

"He doesn't want to push you."

"But…"

"I think he'd like to make sure you're taken care of, so that he can feel free to move on with his life."

"I didn't realize I was holding him back."

"You aren't. His love for you is. Now that Heather's pregnant, I bet he's planning to leave Silver Springs. To pursue his music."

"If he's having a baby, wouldn't he be smarter to stick around here, where he has family? Surely, he'll want us to be part of the child's life."

"I'm guessing he knows he won't be entirely happy with Heather, and this is how he's planning to compensate."

"You're essentially agreeing with me—at least when it comes to Heather."

"I am."

"So do we have a talk with him? Or would that be too intrusive? I've never wanted to be overly controlling."

Eli crossed his ankles. "He won't listen even if we do. But we could show him another possibility."

"What does that mean?"

"Gavin never misses Sunday dinner, right?"

Aiyana invited her sons for a meal nearly every Sunday, and those who lived close usually came. They felt comfortable bringing a friend or a date, too. Aiyana liked touching base with her boys, liked providing a big meal where they could talk and laugh and reconnect. She thought it was healthy for her youngest son to have that time with his older brothers, and for her college-age son to return when he felt like making the long drive from San Diego.

She remembered when Eli had brought Cora for the first time, how much she'd liked Cora and what their relationship had turned out to be since... "Of course not. It's the only time he gets home-cooking."

"So we can be reasonably confident he'll be there this Sunday."

"Not this Sunday. Cal's got something going in Idaho, a cattle purchase. He's asked me to fly up with him."

"Then next weekend."

"What does this have to do with anything?" she asked.

"Remember Savanna, that pretty neighbor I told you about? I say we make Sunday dinner a week after next a barbecue and swim party and invite her and her two children."

Aiyana wasn't convinced Eli had hit on the high-powered solution they needed. "Roger Nowitzke's coming that weekend. I've already invited *him* for dinner." She often included various alumni from the school, if they were in town, and she was anxious to see Roger again. He hadn't been back since he graduated twelve years earlier. Even the boys she hadn't adopted were sort of like her sons.

"He can be there, too. There's no reason he can't."

"But I've never even met Savanna. How can I invite her over?"

Eli jabbed a thumb into his chest. "I'll do it. Let's put the two of them together for a few hours of fun, see what happens. I'm telling you, there's something between them. I could feel it when I was around them."

"What about Heather and the baby?"

"If he doesn't love Heather, marrying her won't change anything. She may *think* she wants him, that she'll somehow make him love her. But odds are it'll end in divorce. That's what's troubling you, isn't it? The fact that it wouldn't be wise, or even healthy, to enter a marriage the way he feels? She deserves more, and so does he. For that matter, so does the baby."

Aiyana shook her head. "He'll never see it that way. He won't want to give up control over his child's life. He's taking his job as that baby's protector very seriously. *I* wouldn't want anything to happen to the child, either—his or anyone else's—and that ties my hands."

"Not completely. Even if he doesn't marry Heather, if the baby's his, we'll all stay involved."

"Providing Heather will let us!"

"She will."

"Gavin won't take that on faith."

"Then he'd better be good at resisting temptation," Eli said, and stood. "He came to work late today, right?"

"Around noon. Why?"

"He'll probably be staying late to finish up. You go talk to him, delay him if you have to, and I'll drive out to invite Savanna to the barbecue."

"I feel guilty for meddling," Aiyana admitted.

Eli turned back at the door. "We're not *meddling*. We're welcoming someone new into the community. There's nothing wrong with that."

He had a point. They were only having a barbecue.

Aiyana straightened the blotter on her desk. "How do we make sure he doesn't bring Heather?"

"We'll let him know we've invited Savanna. If he brings Heather knowing Savanna will be there, it'll mean he's completely committed and doesn't like Savanna as much as I thought. There's nothing we can do to save him at that point. But if he *doesn't* bring Heather..."

She lifted the bottle of water on her desk as if she was making a toast. "Here's hoping."

Once again, Savanna made dinner in her Crock-Pot. Sweet pork burritos were a family favorite. And she had plenty to share. But she wasn't sure whether or not to invite Gavin back. She'd been deliberating on that while breaking down the last of the boxes and finishing the cleaning. She didn't want to make him feel cornered or pressured, as though she was constantly approaching him, but she did want to provide a hot meal if that was something he'd enjoy.

When she heard a knock, she thought it could be him and decided to go ahead and invite him if it was. But when she swung the door wide, she saw Eli and not Gavin on her stoop. "Hi," she said in surprise.

Gavin's brother smiled. "Sorry to bother you…"

"No problem. It's not like I get many visitors. You and Gavin are the only two people I know so far." She glanced behind him but didn't see a vehicle—his or Gavin's.

"Gavin's not back from the ranch yet," Eli said, accurately reading the question in her mind. "He should be home soon. While I was waiting for him, I thought I'd walk over and invite you and the kids to a barbecue and swim party a week from this Sunday at New Horizons. My mother and I both live on the ranch, but my mother's place is larger, and she generally does the cooking for our family get-togethers, so we all go there."

Savanna hadn't expected this. "You're inviting me to eat with your family? Your mother and your wife and… Gavin?"

"Yes. As well as my youngest brother, who goes to New Horizons. Sometimes another of our brothers shows up, too. He goes to San Diego State and can make the drive in about three and a half hours, if traffic isn't bad."

"How nice of you."

"My mother would've asked Gavin to invite you, but I was with her when the subject came up, so I figured I'd do the honors, since I'm the first one here. It can be a challenge to acclimate to a new area, and we want you to feel welcome."

It wasn't easy for Savanna to get to know anyone, since she wasn't putting the kids in school until the fall, didn't have a job and didn't belong to a church. She felt like she could easily go undiscovered by the community until fall—a relief in one sense but probably not so good in another. Complete isolation had its own drawbacks.

"I hope you're free that day," he said.

"I am and I'd love to come." She'd made good progress moving in, was down to the outside cleanup, and she'd have that squared away by then. She still had plenty of work for contractors, but it would feel good to get out and be with other people—people who hadn't been part of her life with Gordon and had no preexisting ideas of who she was or should be. "What time?"

"Three? That'll give the kids a couple of hours to swim during the hottest part of the day."

"They'll be so excited. Thank you. And please thank your mother."

"I will. You can ride to the ranch with Gavin. Or you can drive yourself, if you prefer." He lifted his phone. "Would you like me to text you the address?"

"Sure." She gave him her number and watched as he typed the information.

"Cora and I will look forward to seeing you and the kids Sunday after next, then," he said, and sent it.

She smiled as he gave her a farewell nod and strode off.

"Who was that?" Alia asked as she and Branson came out of his bedroom, where they'd been putting together his train set.

"Gavin's brother."

"What'd he want?"

"To invite us to a swim party and barbecue a week from this Sunday. Doesn't that sound like fun?"

Alia's eyes widened. "He has a pool?"

"The party's at his mother's house. I'm guessing she does."

"Yay!" As her children began to dance around, Savanna couldn't help feeling some anticipation, too. She didn't have a decent swimsuit—couldn't remember the last time she'd needed one—so she'd have to check the shops in town, but even that felt exciting.

She was smiling as she went back to finish the last of what she hoped to get done before supper. And she was smiling when her phone buzzed, indicating she had a new message. Since she'd been hoping to hear from Gavin, to have the opportunity to invite him over, she looked down with some anticipation. But as soon as she saw the number on her screen, she felt her smile wilt. It was yet another text from Dorothy.

How dare you cheat on Gordon after all he's been through! As far as I'm concerned, that's it. I'm coming for you. You won't know exactly when, but I'm going to make you sorry. And that's a promise.

CHAPTER SEVENTEEN

Heather studied Scott, trying to gauge whether or not her ex-boyfriend was simply trying to upset her. After staying late at school with another teacher to get ready for a joint project they were planning to do between classes, she'd stopped by his place to pick up the last of her things.

"You're lying," she said as they glared at each other in the middle of his living room.

His smug expression undermined her confidence, despite the conviction with which she'd spoken. "You think so? Because I wasn't the only one at the park. Ask Johnny Coontz. He saw Gavin with those kids, too."

Johnny worked with Scott and often went to the same park to have lunch, so it made sense. But...

"It *couldn't* have been Gavin," she said. "He was at New Horizons all day." He'd called her when he was driving home and told her as much. She'd asked how his day had gone, and he'd indicated that it had been nothing out of the ordinary.

"I know who Gavin is!" Scott snapped, incredulous that she'd continue to deny what she'd heard. But he'd misinterpreted her reaction. It wasn't that she didn't believe what he said; it was that she didn't want it to be true. "I spoke to him," he added. "Saw him *and* the kids up close."

"So…what was he doing there?" And why hadn't he told her about babysitting when she'd asked him what his day had been like?

"I told you! He was helping his new neighbor." He arched his eyebrows to give his next statement more meaning. "A *divorcée* who just moved in. He tried to act like it wasn't anything. But that's what made me feel like it was. I saw him playing with that little boy and girl, got the impression they mattered to him."

Heather curled her fingernails into her palms. "Of course they matter to him. Gavin's good with kids. *All* kids," she clarified. But it was difficult not to allow her hand to go to her stomach. She felt nauseous. She'd fought so long and hard to win Gavin's love, and every time it seemed as though she was *finally* getting somewhere with him, he slipped through her fingertips again. She couldn't allow that to happen this time. She was carrying a child, for God's sake. She did *not* want to become a strapped and lonely single mother, another cliché. Without someone around to help, she'd hardly be able to leave the house. That wasn't the future she anticipated for herself.

"If it was completely innocent, why'd he act so weird?" Scott asked.

"For all I know, he didn't. Anyway, you can quit trying to scare me. It's not as though Gavin's up to anything. We're already back together."

Scott propped his hands on his hips as he loomed over her. "Does *he* know that?"

"Of course he does! He said as much," she insisted. But that wasn't *entirely* true. Gavin had said he was willing to try again. He'd also said he wanted to start from the beginning, and he wanted to take it slow. He specifically said they weren't exclusive. Not yet. Last night when she was over, he hadn't so much as kissed her. But she knew if she could only get him to quit looking beyond her, they'd be happy together. No one could love him more. He just had to give her the chance to prove it. "Anyway, I'm not going to stand here arguing with you. I've got to get my things."

Scott grabbed her arm as she started toward the laundry room. "Not so fast. I don't care what Gavin said. He acted like I'd caught him doing something he shouldn't."

She jerked out of his grasp. "Stop trying to cause trouble between us!"

"I don't need to cause trouble. Can't you see that trouble already exists? He doesn't want you, Heather," he said, stabbing a forefinger into her chest. "Not like I do. Why can't you see that?"

"Stay out of it." She knocked his hand away. "You don't know anything about Gavin, and I won't let you wreck this for me."

His jaw dropped. "*Wreck* it for you? You say that as if you set it all up so carefully."

"That's crazy!" she said. But it wasn't *entirely* crazy, and she feared the lack of conviction in her words made the truth all too apparent. She'd secretly gone off the pill almost three months ago, before Gavin had broken up with her. She'd known he'd marry her if only she could get pregnant. But they'd gotten into that stupid argument about his ex-girlfriend, and he'd broken up with her only a week after she'd stopped taking the pill. She'd had no recourse except to hope she was already carrying his baby—or would soon be carrying someone else's. She knew the possibility that the baby *might* be his would be enough to get him to give her one more chance. At least, that was what she'd told herself. Now that the baby was a reality, she was scared she might lose him regardless, especially now that his hot new neighbor had come onto the scene. "How dare you accuse me of something so heinous!" she cried, pouring a bit more effort into her acting.

"You're telling me you didn't?" Scott countered.

It felt as though he could suddenly see right through her, as though he'd figured it all out, and that made her uneasy. Always before, he'd been so eager to get with her he'd just kept trying—to replace Gavin in her heart, in her bed and in her future. "Of course I didn't!"

"You just want what you want, and you don't care who you tear apart in the process."

A trickle of guilt made her even more defensive. She'd known from early on that her relationship with Scott wouldn't last. There'd never been anyone for her except Gavin; there never would be. She'd only gone back to Scott because she'd needed to get pregnant, had to reach for this one final chance...

And now that she had that chance she wasn't going to let Scott or anyone else get in the way. "I'm sorry," she said. "I never meant to hurt you."

He grabbed her arm again. "Why don't you try saying that like you mean it?"

"I do mean it!" She'd told Gavin that Scott scared her, but that hadn't been the case until now. She'd merely been looking for an excuse to appear at Gavin's house, one he'd be particularly sympathetic to. Not that showing up there had improved the situation. She'd imagined their night together going so much better than it had.

"You're carrying my baby and you know it," Scott ground out. "Why are you pretending it might be Gavin's? Why are you making *him* believe it's his?"

"Because it could be." That was true, she told herself defiantly.

Scott's eyes widened until she could see white all around the brown irises. "Oh, my God! You're trying to trap him! And he's stupid enough to let you."

A red-hot rage shot through her. When she'd spoken to Gavin an hour or so ago, he'd indicated that he had some things to do and wouldn't be able to see her tonight. He'd said she should go to her parents if she felt threatened by Scott, which had set her insecurities ablaze. That wasn't like him. Normally, he'd do anything to make sure she was safe, not direct her to someone else. So Scott was prodding a sensitive spot. "Don't you dare say that! Either one of you could be the father. And Gavin's *not* stupid. Unlike you, he cares about kids, even if they don't belong to him."

"That's the thing!" Scott said. "You knew what he's been through, how it's made him sensitive to deprived children. That's what gave you the idea, isn't it? You didn't come back to me because you cared about me. You were using me to get Gavin back. And you didn't even think, or care, that if you *did* get pregnant with my child, and you managed to convince Gavin that it might be his, *I'd* be the one out in the cold."

"That's ridiculous," she said, but her voice was too high and breathy to make that statement as convincing as she needed it to be.

His lip curled. "You're pathetic. I hope you know that. And you should know something else. I'm going to do everything I can to screw this up for you. You won't get Gavin. He's going to figure out what you're up to, because I'm going to make sure of it."

"How nasty can you be? You don't know anything! It would be cruel to even get involved."

"You're the one who involved me."

She grabbed hold of his wrist. "Don't you dare say anything to Gavin…"

A malevolent smile curved his lips. "Watch me call him right now. By the time I hang up, he won't ever speak to you again."

Panic sliced through her as he pulled out his phone. The way Gavin had been acting, she wasn't nearly as certain of him as she wanted to be. She needed more time, couldn't let Scott ruin her future. Gavin was the best man she'd ever known; she wasn't going to lose him. "I won't let you take him from me!" she screamed.

"You're sick. Obsessed." He shook his head in apparent disgust as he started pressing buttons.

Galvanized by the fear rising inside her, she grabbed his phone before he could finish dialing and threw it against the wall. It shattered upon impact, and he slapped her so hard her head whipped back and her ears rang. But that wasn't enough. She saw the rage on his face, the fact that he'd pulled back to hit her again. She had to get out. She'd pushed him too far.

But he stood between her and the door...

Grabbing the closest lamp, she swung and hit him with it on the shoulder. She was hoping that would knock him down, give her enough time to get around him.

He didn't even stumble. "You bitch!" he cried. "You're dead now!"

She dropped the lamp and dashed for the door. But she didn't make it, just as she knew she wouldn't. He caught her by the hair and spun her around to face him, and the blow that came next rattled her teeth.

It was nearly nine by the time Gavin got home. He'd stayed extra late at the school, sorting through his desk, organizing his equipment, fixing a few things he'd been putting off in favor of more important repairs—essentially avoiding his personal life.

Fortunately, working late seemed to have done what he'd hoped it would. Heather's Pathfinder wasn't in his drive, and there wasn't another note on his door from Savanna. He wasn't so much excited about not hearing from his neighbor as he was relieved. He *wanted* to see her; he just knew he wouldn't be able to resist her again. Last night had been difficult enough.

The ringtone for his phone went off, signaling an incoming call.

He ignored it, didn't even check to see who it was. He planned to eat and then sit out on the porch with his guitar and work on perfecting the lyrics for the song he'd been writing the night Savanna came barreling past him in that moving van. He needed

to reclaim a bit of normalcy, find calm, peace. And after he finished playing? He was going to get some rest.

He made it through dinner before whoever was trying to
reach him called so many times he couldn't help checking, with
a measure of exasperation, to see who it was. He'd received five
calls from Heather, which came as no surprise. She was as obsessive as ever. But the last call had been from Eli, and that was
the one he returned. He couldn't make himself call Heather, or
even check her messages. He'd told her earlier that he wouldn't
be able to see her tonight, and he was determined to make her
respect what she'd been told.

"What's up?" he said when Eli answered.

"Just checking to see if you're still at the school. Cora's made
that strawberry cheesecake dessert you like. We thought maybe
you'd want to walk over."

"Too late. I'm home now. Maybe you can save me some for
tomorrow."

"I wouldn't count on it," he joked. "When did you get home?"

"A few minutes ago."

"Late night at work."

"Had a few things to do."

Eli laughed softly.

"What?" Gavin said.

"My poor little brother."

"Stop it."

"Fine. How's the music coming along?"

Gavin set his dishes in the sink. "I have a gig in Santa Barbara
tomorrow and Saturday. Same place as last week."

"We haven't been to one of your shows in a while. I'll check
with Cora, see if we're free."

"I'll text you the address, if you're serious."

"Send it to me. Are you going to Mom's a week from Sunday?"

As far as Gavin was concerned, that was a given. "I show up
every time she cooks, don't I? Why?"

"I invited Savanna and her kids over for a barbecue and swim party, so we're starting a little earlier than usual."

Gavin froze with his plate under the faucet. "You did *what?*"

"Mom wanted to welcome her to the area."

"Bullshit!"

"It's true!"

"No, it's not. Quit playing dumb. You know I'm not in a situation to pursue a relationship with Savanna, so why are you sabotaging my efforts to do the right thing?"

"Lighten up, bro. It's just a barbecue."

"Sure it is."

"Here's the thing. It is if you want it to be," he said, and hung up.

Gavin cursed as he stared down at his phone. Then, against all his plans and self-talk, he texted Savanna. How are you today?

Good. You? came her response.

He hadn't been good since she moved in. He'd been torn. Should he ask to meet with her tonight? Tell her about Heather? If she knew about the baby, maybe she'd help him maintain some distance.

But he didn't ask if he could come over. He wrote, Tired, instead.

I have some good leftovers. Is there any chance you're hungry?

He was hungry, all right. Just not for food. And that was going to become more and more of a problem. Already ate.

Your brother came over and invited me to a barbecue a week from Sunday. I hope you won't mind if we come.

Why would I mind?

I'm not sure. It just felt weird that he would invite me instead of you.

It was because his mother and brother were playing games. I would've invited you myself if I was home, he lied. I'll give you a ride.

No, considering the situation, I should drive.

She was probably right. It would look much less like a date that way. Okay. At least I'll get to see you there. God, he wanted to see her *now*. He scratched the back of his neck as he wrestled with himself—and ultimately won. Have a good night.

There was a long pause before she responded. But then she wrote, You, too.

With a curse, Gavin tossed his phone away from him. He finished his dishes, but he didn't go out on the porch. He knew he wouldn't be able to concentrate. He'd wind up heading across the creek.

When he heard yet another buzz—a text from Heather—he refused to read it, silenced his phone and went to bed.

Savanna's heart began to pound against her chest the moment she saw headlights shining through her front window. After that text she'd received from Dorothy, she'd been looking out the windows, checking for signs of trouble all day. She hadn't heard from her ex-mother-in-law since, but she feared it was because Dorothy was finished talking and planned to act on her words.

So...was this her? Who else could it be? It was close to midnight. No one from Silver Springs would be coming out to visit her so late—except maybe Gavin, and he'd just walk over.

She stared down at her phone, wondering if she should call her neighbor. He'd told her she could. But she didn't want to go running to him every time she had a problem, didn't want to be a pain in the butt.

Her other choice was the police. But Dorothy hadn't yet done anything for which she could complain, so that seemed like an extreme response.

She'd have to at least attempt to handle Dorothy herself...

After a quick check on her kids to make sure they were asleep, she closed Alia's door, hoping the noise, if there was significant noise, wouldn't wake her, and grabbed her son's baseball bat before closing his. She was determined to defend herself and her children, if necessary.

Whoever it was knocked on the door as Savanna finished pulling on a jacket and shoes. She put the bat against the wall behind the door, so she wouldn't appear ready for a fight, and peeked out. "What are you doing here?" she asked, feeling a little jolt of adrenaline when she saw Dorothy's lined visage in the dim glow of the porch light.

"You and I need to talk," she said.

Savanna wasn't about to let her in the house. But she couldn't grab the bat she'd put against the wall and take it outside with her, either. Doing something that aggressive, before it was even warranted, would only set Dorothy off and ensure this meeting went in that direction.

Still hoping to keep everything calm and civilized, Savanna stepped outside. "There's nothing left to talk about."

Dorothy hitched her heavy purse over her shoulder. "I'd like to do a lot more than talk, but you're not worth going to jail for. So if you'll give me a check, I'll leave."

"A check," Savanna echoed.

"Gordon needs a few things—like a better defense. And you've got the money to provide it."

Savanna pulled her jacket tighter. It wasn't cold, and yet she was chilled to the bone. "I can't take care of Gordon and the kids, too, Dorothy. Gordon's going to have to fend for himself."

"How? What can he do from behind bars? You got that big inheritance. He told me about it, and I'm not leaving until you give me some of that money. By rights, he should get half."

Still hoping not to wake the kids, Savanna lowered her voice. "Gordon raped three women. Since he's going to prison, he

won't be around to help support Branson and Alia. I consider
his half of *my* inheritance child support—what he owes me for
attacking those women and putting me in the position of having to raise our kids alone."

Dorothy's chin jutted out. "I keep telling you he didn't do it.
He'd be able to help you, be able to be a father, if you'd only
help him beat these bogus charges!"

"Are you sure they're bogus, Dorothy? Down deep in your
heart, haven't you ever asked yourself if it could be true?"

"No," she snapped without even considering the question.
"Unlike you, I love Gordon and have some loyalty to him. My
son would never hurt anyone. He's never hurt you or the kids,
has he?"

Although Savanna hadn't realized it at the time, he had hurt
her and the kids—with his extreme narcissism. He'd taken advantage of her, used her to keep his house clean and care for his
children while he was out doing God knows what. Essentially,
he'd turned her into an emotional slave, someone who had to
put up with his mercurial moods, someone who had to walk
on eggshells for fear of setting him off, someone who couldn't
expect any forbearance or nurturing in return. It was his selfishness as much as the hard evidence that caused her to doubt
him. "I don't want to argue with you," she said to Dorothy. "It's
late and I'm tired. I'm sorry you've made such a long drive, but
I can't give you any money."

Dorothy folded her arms. "Then I'm not leaving. I'll camp
right on this damn porch, if I have to."

Gordon's mother hadn't asked to see the kids, hadn't so much
as mentioned them. That made Savanna as heartsick as anything.
But Branson and Alia didn't need her. Indeed, they were better
off without her, which was why Savanna almost went back inside for her purse. How much would it take to get rid of Dorothy? Savanna didn't want Gordon's mother hanging around,

dragging all the negativity she'd had to deal with in Nephi to Silver Springs.

But Savanna knew she couldn't part with the money that a top-notch defense team would require. When Gordon was first arrested, she'd given Howard Detmer a twenty-thousand-dollar retainer and gotten only half of it back when she let him go two weeks later. "The kind of defense Gordon requires could cost hundreds of thousands of dollars, far more than I have. Even if I hired Detmer back, I wouldn't be able to keep him on for long. He'd run through what little I have in no time, and then how would I get by? How would I feed the kids?"

"Maybe you'd have to work, like I do!"

That statement kindled sufficient anger to help Savanna overcome the intimidation she'd always experienced around Dorothy, who was, like her son, so much more volatile than other people. "I've *always* worked, and I will do so again. But I'm not footing the bill for Gordon's defense. Throwing a big chunk of money at some fancy lawyer won't make any difference in the end, especially now that the police think Gordon is guilty of far more."

Dorothy had opened her mouth to continue arguing, but at this she hesitated. "What are you talking about?"

"Emma Ventnor. That's what I'm talking about. And who knows how many others."

Dorothy stumbled back, until she could help support herself with the porch railing. "Who's Emma?"

"She was a beautiful sixteen-year-old girl who went missing a year ago. Someone wrecked into her car right in the middle of a rainy afternoon. When she pulled over to exchange insurance information, she was kidnapped and hasn't been seen since."

Savanna expected Dorothy to respond with the usual heated denials. Her son could never have hurt anyone. He's innocent. The police are out to frame him just to put someone behind bars and escape the public scrutiny and pressure associated with not having a proper suspect. But those denials didn't come. Neither did the questions Savanna would've expected—first and fore-most, *why* would the police think Gordon had something to do with this girl's disappearance? They had to have *some* evidence or reason to believe he might be responsible, but Dorothy didn't so much as ask where Emma was from.

"What is it?" Savanna asked. "You look as though you've seen a ghost."

"Nothing. It's…nothing. I'm tired, that's all," she said, but she didn't stick around as she'd threatened to do. Without another word, she rushed back to her car, climbed in and drove off—so fast that Savanna nearly yelled to watch out for the bridge. Although the bridge was sturdy, it was still temporary and would be easy to miss in the dark. But yelling would be futile. Dorothy would never be able to hear her.

Once Savanna felt certain her ex-mother-in-law had cleared the creek, she started to relax, but even then she was confused. Her encounter with Dorothy had been so strange. Dorothy had driven all day in order to reach Silver Springs, had come because she was determined to get what she felt Gordon needed and deserved. Instead of standing her ground, however, she'd given up without a fight. That wasn't like her. Something had changed her mind.

Savanna didn't get much time to puzzle out what that could be, however. Only seconds later, just before she went inside, she heard a loud *boom*.

CHAPTER EIGHTEEN

The crash that reverberated through Gavin's house made him think someone had driven into his living room. Jolted awake, he pushed himself up and out of bed and hurried down the hall to find out what the heck was going on. Fortunately, the house seemed to be intact. But as soon as he opened the front door, he saw a white car, which had smashed into the back of his pickup, reverse before racing off with its front bumper dragging.

Throwing the door open wide, he dashed out, hoping to stop whomever it was. But the culprit raced down the gravel road, indifferent to all the bumps and potholes, and swerved onto the highway without so much as pausing to look for oncoming traffic.

Gavin thought he caught the first three digits of the license plate number, but he wasn't sure they were correct. Not only were there no streetlights where he lived, it was a very dark night and the cloud of dust churned up by the tires made such details hard to see. Besides, it'd happened so fast.

"What the hell!" he muttered as he walked over to inspect the damage.

Fortunately, his truck had been hit in the rear, which was

preferable to the engine. The impact had pressed the back right panel into the tire, which would rub when the axle turned, but it looked as though he might be able to pull the metal back far enough to make the vehicle drivable until he could get it repaired. That was the good news. But why was that crazy person on his street to begin with? Especially so late at night?

Was it Scott? That hadn't been a Camaro, but Scott could've been with someone else...

Because Savanna had just moved in, it didn't occur to him that whoever it was had been visiting her—until he heard footsteps running across the bridge.

"I'm *so* sorry," she said, coming up behind him. "I can't believe she did this!"

He turned to face her. *"She?"*

"That was Gordon's mom. She came all the way out here from Utah, arrived a few minutes ago. We argued on my porch, but not for long. Something suddenly came over her, and she jumped back into her car and took off."

"You don't know why."

She shook her head. "I thought it would be much more difficult to get rid of her. I'm still trying to figure out what happened."

It wasn't until that moment, when Savanna stepped up next to him, that he even thought about the fact that he hadn't taken the time to dress before dashing out of the house. He was standing outside in his underwear and no shoes. But he wasn't concerned for the sake of modesty. Savanna had seen him before. He wasn't completely naked, anyway.

Resting his hands on his hips, he frowned at the crushed metal. "Was she drunk?"

"I don't think so. To be honest, she sounded more lucid than usual."

"So what'd she come here for?"

"To get what she's wanted from the start—money for Gordon's defense."

He pulled his hair back. "What'd you tell her?"

"I refused to give her any. I thought I'd have a real fight on my hands. I had Branson's baseball bat hidden behind the door, in case I had to defend myself. That shows you what I was expecting. She'd sent me a text earlier saying she was going to make me sorry for abandoning Gordon, as if she was coming out, looking for revenge. So I was shocked when she left out of the blue and without getting too ugly."

Gavin scowled at her. "If she's been threatening you, and you thought she might act on those threats, why didn't you call me? Or at least let me know the moment she arrived?"

Looking a bit rattled, she hugged herself. "I didn't want to wake you. And it seems as if, I don't know, as if you don't really want to see me anymore. I want to give you your space, if that's true. Don't want to keep bothering you, especially for more favors."

That was why she'd asked if she could accept Eli's invitation to the barbecue. She thought he was trying to pull away, and he was, but not for the reasons she supposed.

"What's happening in my life has nothing to do with you," he said, but he realized almost as soon as he'd spoken those words that they weren't strictly true. He'd barely met her, and yet she'd made a huge impact on everything. He couldn't imagine himself being quite *this* reluctant to get back with Heather, to do the right thing by the child she carried, if he didn't have someone else he wanted more so close at hand.

"I came on too strong the other night. I'm sorry about that," she said. "My whole world is jumbled right now. I'm not thinking straight, not acting like I should. Most people get to know each other before...well, before that. Hitting you up so soon must've put you in an awkward position. Just because *I'm* flailing around like a drowning person doesn't mean I need to drag you down with me." She laughed, a short, self-deprecating chuckle. "Anyway, you've been great. Really. I hope you'll forgive me. I hate that I might've messed up our friendship."

"Savanna…"

She rubbed her arms as she gazed up at him. "What?"

He heard the uncertainty in her voice. "You haven't messed up anything."

Her eyebrows gathered. "But you just want to be platonic friends, right? I crossed the line? I mean… I thought you were into it, too, but… I've been thinking about how forward I was that night and feeling like an idiot."

"There's no need to feel like an idiot. I wanted you then. And I want you now." Taking her hands, he pulled her against him and lowered his head to kiss her.

She seemed startled when what started as a soft exploration of her mouth turned into an intense and hungry devouring. He knew it wasn't consistent with the subdued response he'd been giving her recently. But the desire that welled up was carrying him away like a tidal wave. He couldn't summon any resistance; he wanted her too badly. "You taste like honey," he told her. "And you feel— God, you feel like heaven."

He'd never had sex outside, but he'd lived in the country for only two months. He loved the privacy his new place gave him, because he didn't want to let her go. He knew his conscience would reassert itself if he broke away, even for a short time. Or she'd say she had to get back to her house or something.

Her fingers slipped into his hair, pulling out the tie that was falling out, anyway, and he heard her groan as he kissed her neck. "I don't have any birth control on me," he admitted, although that was probably obvious, since he had no way of hiding anything, including his raging hard-on.

"I went back on the pill after…after we were together," she said.

He lifted his head. "You did?"

"I hoped you'd be interested in more than one night."

"I *am* interested." He peeled off her sweater and lifted her T-shirt over her head before tossing both onto the grass nearby.

"I don't know how long it takes before it's effective, though," she said with some caution.

"Hopefully, it's already kicked in. I'll pull out, just in case."

"Okay, but...wouldn't you rather go in the house?"

He wouldn't. He wanted to feel her close around him *immediately*. Wanted to drive into her as if there wasn't any reason he couldn't have her. "No. I need you now," he said, and it was true. He needed her to help him forget what lay ahead...

She didn't seem opposed to that idea. When her hand slipped into his boxers and her fingers curled around him, he felt his knees go weak.

She was wearing a pair of high-waisted cutoffs. They showed off her legs, which he loved, but he wanted to see everything. He helped her shimmy out of them and removed the thong she wore underneath. Then, lifting her in his arms, he pressed her up against the door of his truck and buried himself inside her.

Wrapping her legs around his waist, she clung to him as he began to thrust. Making love while standing took strength. Soon, he was too breathless to kiss her with any skill, so he buried his face in her neck. And that was when everything besides her ceased to exist. All worries. All cares. Even the stars. Nothing could wrest his attention from the softness of her breasts, the scent of her skin, the warm wetness he loved most and the little sounds she occasionally made as he drove into her. He knew he wasn't being as gentle as he probably should, but he could feel her abandoning all restraint, and that encouraged him to do the same.

When he felt that sweet upwelling of pleasure, he didn't want to pull out. But he had no choice. With a curse for the self-mastery it required, he withdrew at the last second.

The whole thing hadn't lasted long, but it had been particularly momentous. They stared at each other for several seconds as if they were both surprised by the intensity of the experience and the connection they felt because of it.

"I should get back inside. Would you like to come over and spend the rest of the night?" she asked softly.

He got the impression she was testing him to see if he'd react as he had before—by distancing himself. And his heart sank as he watched her dress, because he had no choice. "I'm coming over to make sure Dorothy doesn't return and cause you any trouble. But..."

"But?" She paused to look up at him. Obviously, she'd heard the reservation in his voice.

He raked his fingers through his tangled hair. "Before I touch you again, I've got to tell you something."

"She's *pregnant*?" After the passionate encounter they'd just shared, Savanna didn't know how to react. She felt numb as she sat in her kitchen, staring across the table at Gavin, who'd gone back to his place to get dressed before showing up at her door.

The regret she saw in his body language helped a little, but it couldn't do much to soften the blow, because what he'd told her changed everything. She'd believed she wasn't ready for another relationship, and yet she'd done nothing except fantasize about her new neighbor ever since she met him. He made her feel good, and after Gordon had made her feel bad, for so long, that was a powerful thing. She'd even had the crazy thought that perhaps she'd been meant to come to Silver Springs, that maybe her father was acting as some sort of guardian angel, guiding her to a better man, someone with whom she could be truly happy.

Now that she'd heard about Heather, however, that just seemed silly...

"Yes," he said.

"And it could be *your* child."

"We broke up a little over two months ago, and I haven't been with her since, but…she's about that far along."

"When did you learn about it?"

A sheepish expression claimed his face. "Last Saturday. After I got home from my gig that night, she was waiting for me."

"So…before we slept together the first time."

He winced. "Yeah. I'm sorry about that. I should've said something sooner, but… I don't know. I didn't want to face it myself, didn't want to voice it because that would only make it more real."

"That's why you backed off so fast. Because of Heather."

"Because of the situation, yes."

She cradled a glass of water between both hands. "And…what were you thinking tonight?"

"I have no excuse for tonight. I knew I shouldn't touch you. I just couldn't help myself."

"I see." She cleared her throat in order to fill the silence, to give herself some time to think. "I saw Heather in front of your house when I went out to get my mail yesterday. She seemed quite curious about who I was, when I'd arrived and whether I was married."

"That last part doesn't surprise me," he said wryly. "She views any other single, attractive woman as a rival."

"Considering what we've done, I'm not sure we can fault her for that—"

"True," he broke in. "With you, she has reason. But that hasn't been the case in the past."

Savanna struggled to overcome the disappointment she felt. "Does she know that…that we…"

"No." He spoke immediately, saving her the trouble of trying to finish that sentence. "I haven't told her."

Savanna was relieved. She didn't want to have an instant enemy in Silver Springs. And yet… "Are you going to?" she asked.

"I haven't decided. We're not exclusive, if that's what you're wondering. It's not as if I've been cheating on her. But I will have to restrict my...*activities* at some point. And soon. I can't be sleeping with you if I'm trying to make something work with her. That wouldn't be fair to anybody."

"True." Savanna wanted to ask if he'd slept with Heather since sleeping with her, but she didn't feel she had the right. *She'd* been the one to stipulate that there were no expectations attached to their night together. Of course, they hadn't established any "rules" for what'd occurred between them at the truck. That had come out of nowhere. But she could see why he might approach a second encounter with the same understanding.

"This might be too intrusive of a question," she said. "If it is, you don't have to answer. But I can't help wondering..."

"What is it?" he asked.

She braced herself, in case she was about to get an answer that would sting. "Do you love her?"

He studied her for several seconds without answering.

She lifted a hand. "Never mind. Like I said, that was too intrusive."

"Savanna, if I loved her, I wouldn't be doing what I've done with you."

She couldn't help feeling some relief, even though she knew his lack of feeling would only make what he had planned that much harder for him. "So what you're doing...it's all for the baby."

"Entirely. Getting back with her, becoming a full-time parent, is the only way I can guarantee the baby will never be neglected or mistreated."

Savanna didn't know what to say. He was trying to do what he felt was right for a child, possibly *his* child. She couldn't argue with that. "Okay, I'll respect your decision, of course—and be careful to maintain the new boundaries you've set."

He looked as troubled as she felt. "I'm sorry."

"It's fine. What we feel—it's probably just sexual attraction, right? Infatuation? It can't be anything serious, not this soon or this fast. Maybe I can't keep my hands off you because I'm drunk on my newfound freedom. Or I'm trying to escape the harsh reality of my current situation. In any case, I'm in no position to make sound romantic decisions. This forces me to…to gain control of myself. Depending on how you look at it, it could be for the best." Except what she felt for Gavin felt a lot more authentic than what she'd felt for Gordon the past few years. That was the strange thing.

"I appreciate your understanding," he said.

"Of course. We can still be friends, though, I hope. We live so close it'd be a shame if that weren't true. My kids idolize you already. I'd hate to think I blew their chance to have you around now and then."

"We can certainly be friends. I'm staying the rest of the night—on the couch—just to make sure you're safe. And I'll be only a phone call away whenever you need me."

"I appreciate that. Truly. I'll support you in what you're trying to do, will hope it turns out for the best."

"Thank you."

"No problem. But… I should cancel out on the barbecue next week, right?" Her kids were looking forward to the party so much she hated the thought of telling them it wasn't going to work out, but if Gavin was planning to bring Heather, she wasn't sure she could stand to watch him with another woman no matter how many times she told herself she had no right to feel jealous.

"No, don't cancel. I think Branson and Alia will really enjoy it. You and I, we'll be fine. Friends, like you said."

"Okay." She hoped he was right.

His phone went off before he could say anything else.

"Aren't you going to get that?" she asked when he made no move to answer.

He grimaced. "I'd rather not."

"But it's so late. What if it's your mother? Or brother? Aren't you worried that it might be an emergency?"

"Not really."

The truth dawned on her. "You think it's Heather..."

He scrubbed a hand over his face. "I'm almost certain of it. I'll call her in the morning, deal with...with everything after I've had a bit more sleep."

His phone fell silent but pinged a moment later to indicate an incoming text. This time, probably because she was watching and he didn't want her to see him continue to ignore it, he pulled it out of his pocket and looked down at the screen. Then his jaw went slack.

"What is it?" A trickle of concern put her on edge. "Is everything okay?"

"Heather's in the hospital."

Pushing away from the table, Savanna came to her feet. "What happened?"

"She says Scott beat her up."

"The boyfriend she just broke up with."

"Yes. She told me he was acting threatening, but I never believed he'd go this far. I feel bad for ignoring her tonight. She's been trying to reach me since I got home from work." He typed a quick response before getting to his feet and shoving the phone back into his pocket. "I've got to go."

"To the hospital?"

"Yeah."

"But...how will you get there?"

He put a palm to his forehead, signifying he'd forgotten that Dorothy had hit his truck. "Right."

"You can take my car."

"Thanks. That'll be quicker and easier than trying to make mine drivable."

She got her keys out of her purse and handed them to him.

"If Dorothy comes back, make sure you call me—or the police, if you think they can get here sooner. I don't want anything else to happen tonight."

"Don't worry about us." She forced a reassuring smile, but her heart sank as she watched him go. She'd known him only a week; she shouldn't feel quite as terrible as she did. But he was different, special. Whoever got him would be lucky. And, given the baby, there was no way she could ever hope to compete with Heather.

CHAPTER NINETEEN

Heather wasn't nearly as bad off as she'd made it sound in the voice mails she'd left him. Gavin had had time to listen to those while driving to the hospital and felt worse with each one. He should've picked up earlier. "Wouldn't you know, the one time she wasn't just being obsessive, I decided to ignore her." That he'd been making love to Savanna while Heather was coping with such pain made everything even worse.

He was afraid Heather would have to stay in the hospital overnight, but they were just getting ready to release her when he arrived. Gavin passed the doctor as the doctor stepped out of the curtained cubical, so he heard the tail end of the conversation.

Heather had a fat lip. She'd told Gavin that in her text. But there didn't seem to be much other damage. Overall, she'd gotten lucky. The neighbor who lived in the other half of Scott's duplex had been home. He'd heard the fight break out, called the cops, and, since an officer had been right around the corner, help had arrived quickly.

"I'm sorry for what you've been through," Gavin said.

Her eyes filled with tears, so he walked over to pull her into his arms. "Are you going to be okay?" he asked, resting his chin on her head as she clung to him.

"Doesn't feel like it right now," she replied, her voice muffled by his shirt.

"Haven't they given you any painkillers?"

"They've given me some. The whole thing has just been such an upsetting ordeal."

"I bet." He stepped back as soon as he felt it would seem too obvious that he hadn't wanted to hold her in the first place. "But they're releasing you now? Is that what I heard? You can go home?"

She picked up an ice pack and held it to her face. "Yeah."

Thank God he'd finally looked at his phone. Her last text had said that she needed a ride. Her parents lived in the area, but he knew she'd be reluctant to call them with this problem. They were already upset about the unplanned pregnancy. "What happened with Scott? Why would you ever give him the opportunity to do something like this by going to his house?"

"I had to get my things!" she said, instantly defensive. "And *you* said you had to work late tonight, so it wasn't as if I could ask you to go with me."

He heard the blame in those words. She could've waited until he was available or asked a friend to go over with her, but he didn't point that out. Why get into an argument? She'd been through enough. "And? He wouldn't let you?"

"He kept trying to talk to me, kept telling me that you don't love me, so I'd get back with him. When I refused, he…he got super angry."

"Angry is one thing. But violent? How did it go that far? He's never hit you before, has he?"

"No, but…" Although she sighed to indicate she really didn't care to go into the details, he lifted his eyebrows to communicate the fact that he expected an answer. This was serious. He was going to meet up with Scott and make sure nothing like this ever happened again.

"When he started yelling, I decided to leave, even without my stuff. But he wouldn't let me go, and...and everything sort of escalated from there."

The thought of any man striking a woman made Gavin clench his jaw. But a pregnant woman? That was even worse. "Did he hit you with his fist?"

"I don't even remember."

"Bastard!"

Obviously mollified by his interest and concern, she sniffed. "He *is* a bastard. I can't believe I was ever with him."

Gavin couldn't wait to hold Scott responsible. "How many times did he hit you?"

"I don't remember that, either. I just remember the police coming and helping me get up off the floor."

The keys Gavin had pulled from his pocket cut into the palm of his hand, making him realize he was squeezing them too tight. "Did the doctor check to see if the baby's okay?" he asked, easing his grip.

"He didn't do an ultrasound, if that's what you mean. He told me I should get one in the next few weeks, when I go back to my ob-gyn. He checked the baby's heartbeat, though. Scott didn't hit me in the stomach or anywhere close. So the doctor doesn't think we have any reason to worry."

We. She was talking as though they were already together, already concerned parents.

"The baby's so tiny right now it's well protected," she added.

It was easier to focus on Scott and the anger Scott's actions provoked than to sift through the mixed feelings he had about having a child with Heather, so that was what he did. "I'm going to have to have a talk with Scott. I've tried not to let this situation turn into some kind of feud, but he has to understand that there are consequences to what he's done, has to know I won't tolerate anything like this ever happening again."

"Gavin, no," she said. "I don't want you to get involved. Please stay away from him. He's been arrested, so the police will take care of any consequences. I plan on pressing charges."

How much time would Scott get if she was going to be okay? Chances were it'd go on his rap sheet, and he'd have to pay Heather's medical bills and perform some community service.

That wasn't enough, not in Gavin's opinion. But Scott was in jail, at least for the time being, so Gavin couldn't do anything tonight. He needed to calm down.

"Where were you earlier?" she asked as they reached the automatic doors, which whooshed open to disgorge them into a quiet, moonless night. "Why didn't you answer my earlier calls and texts?"

He didn't see any reason to make her night worse by telling her he hadn't wanted to hear from her so he'd been ignoring her attempts to reach him, or that he'd been spending every minute he wasn't engaged in something that required his full concentration thinking of someone else. So he kept his answer vague. "I was so exhausted by the time I got home from work, I went to bed. I wouldn't have seen your last text, either, if someone hadn't run into my truck while it was parked in my drive. The crash is what woke me, right before you tried to call."

Her eyes widened. "Someone hit your truck? You just bought that last year!"

He shrugged. "Shit happens, I guess."

"But how'd something like that happen all the way out where *you* live?"

"I have a neighbor now."

"Savanna."

He didn't ask how she knew Savanna's name. He already knew they'd met. "Yeah. Her mother-in-law wrecked into it and then took off."

"You're kidding! A hit-and-run? But… Savanna will give you her contact information, won't she?"

"Of course. She feels terrible."

"Was her mother-in-law drunk or something?"

"Savanna doesn't know *what* got into her." Gavin used Savanna's key fob to unlock the doors of the car and opened the passenger side for Heather.

Heather blinked at the Fusion as though she was only now seeing it. Apparently, she'd been too intent on the conversation and letting him guide her through the lot to pay any attention to the vehicle they were approaching. "Whose car is *this*?"

"Savanna's."

"She let you take it?"

"You were in trouble. And my pickup wasn't drivable."

"It's that badly damaged?"

"I'm not sure. I might be able to pull the metal away from the back tire. This was just easier, since I was in a hurry."

"How nice of her to step up," she said, but Gavin heard the caution and displeasure in her voice. She didn't like Savanna, simply because she feared *he* might.

He wished he could tell her that she was silly to feel threatened. But he couldn't bring himself to play her that false, not when what'd happened outside less than an hour ago was so fresh in his mind. If he closed his eyes, he could still smell Savanna, still feel her smooth skin and taste her soft lips.

Savanna told herself to go to sleep. She needed the rest. She had kids, couldn't sleep late in the morning. But she couldn't seem to nod off. She kept thinking about the strange way Dorothy had acted on the porch, from the second she'd mentioned Emma Ventnor's name, what'd happened afterward at Gavin's truck, how quickly a few words between them had turned into so much more and whether Gavin was spending the rest of the night with Heather in the hospital.

Would he bring her home with him in the morning?

Savanna hated the thought that she might bump into Heather on a routine basis. She lived so close to Gavin, and they were so isolated, that it would feel as if she had a front row seat to Heather's advancing pregnancy. That she cringed whenever she imagined Heather's baby really did belong to Gavin wasn't fair, and she would be the first to admit it. She didn't have any claim on him. Maybe it would actually be easier once they moved to Nashville...

Fluffing her pillow, she rolled over and again tried to quiet her mind. But after spending another ten minutes tossing and turning, she leaned up on her elbow and grabbed her phone. She hadn't heard an alert but hoped maybe she'd missed that tell-tale ping. She'd tried to reach Dorothy at least ten times. Had Gordon's mother finally responded? She'd hit Gavin's truck, for crying out loud. Surely, she'd have to explain her behavior— and be held accountable for it—at some point.

Nothing. No calls or texts from anyone.

Where had Dorothy gone? And was she gone for good? Judging by the hastiness of her retreat, Savanna could only assume that she wouldn't be coming back. But the question was...*why*? She'd been so intent on forcing Savanna to give Gordon some money that she'd driven a whole day to reach Silver Springs...

Savanna replayed the scene in her mind yet again. Dorothy had recognized Emma's name, she decided. That *had* to be it. Nothing else that'd been said could've triggered such an abrupt reversal. So what did that mean? Had Dorothy simply freaked out to think her son might now be accused of murder on top of rape? Or had Gordon made some offhanded comment that led her to believe, for the first time, he might truly be the monster the police claimed? Had he mentioned Emma's name to her?

Savanna was about to set her phone down when a text came in from Gavin. She hadn't expected to hear from him again tonight, so she couldn't help feeling a strange sort of relief that he'd be in touch so soon.

We're back. Heather's going to be fine. From what I can tell, he only slapped her a couple of times. That's bad enough, of course, but you know what I mean. Is everything okay with you?

She was tempted to feign sleep. This late, he'd think nothing of it if she didn't respond, and she felt that would be easier than trying to step into her new role so quickly. After the passion they'd shared, what he'd revealed about Heather and his future plans had given her emotional whiplash. She hated the idea that he had this other woman with him, that Heather might be looking over his shoulder, reading his texts right now.

"You were the one who told him it was only sex!" She spoke aloud in an attempt to give her words greater efficacy. "It's not fair for you to get jealous!"

Problem was, she couldn't help what she felt. So she simply promised herself she'd never let her jealousy show. She'd back away from him with some grace and dignity, understand that he was in a difficult position and help him do what he felt he must.

Drawing a deep breath, she tamped down those negative emotions and tried to replace them with the friendship she'd offered him. I'm glad she's okay. That must've been frightening—and painful. I have an ice pack here. Unpacked it only yesterday, so I can find it quickly, if she needs it.

Thanks, but the doctor sent her home with one. She's all set.

Of course. Well, if there's anything I can do, let me know. I'm not leaving the house tomorrow, so you can keep the car if you need it to get to work. The contractor you recommended is starting on the bridge first thing, and I'm hoping to have him give me a bid on dealing with some dry rot around my windows and foundation. There's also a section of siding under Branson's window that needs to be replaced.

Don't have him do the dry rot repair. I can do that sort of thing and save you a lot of money.

Question was...*should* he? She was the one who'd asked if they could at least maintain a friendship, but she was afraid she'd always want to touch him in ways that were decidedly more than friendly. And she could easily guess how difficult it would be to spend any time with Gavin if he was seeing Heather. When they'd been talking, and she'd been trying to absorb the shock of his news, she'd been thinking of Branson and Alia and how badly she didn't want to lose him entirely.

You have enough to do with your work and your music. "And now your pregnant girlfriend," she muttered a little less generously, since she had the privacy to allow it. I've got this.

Just hold off. I'll take a look at it when I can.

Are you sure?

I'm sure. Any more word from Dorothy?

No. But I have her contact information for your insurance.

I'll get that from you tomorrow.

I can text it to you.

When he didn't respond, she resisted the urge to add anything else—although there was a lot she felt she *could* say. "God, tonight was good," or "I can't get you out of my mind," or "Is she staying over with you?" just for starters.

"He's a *friend*," she said, and set her phone aside.

★ ★ ★

Gavin let Heather stay over. She didn't want to be alone, and he felt too guilty about what'd happened to her not to oblige. If he hadn't been so busy avoiding her calls, maybe she wouldn't have gone to Scott's to get her things…

She wasn't planning to teach in the morning. She said she'd call in a sub. But they stopped by her place so she could grab a few things. Sadly, she was on painkillers, couldn't drive, so they'd have only one car between them, for the time being, and his was damaged.

He'd texted Savanna while Heather was in the bedroom. It was much easier to deal with Savanna when Heather wasn't questioning every move he made. He hated feeling as though he had to communicate with Savanna on the down low. But it was his own fault, he told himself, for crossing lines he shouldn't have crossed.

"All set?" He put his phone back in his pocket as Heather appeared with bags that looked heavy enough to support an extended stay.

"Yeah."

He took what she carried. "Let's go. I'm tired."

She slid into the middle of the seat and rested her head on his shoulder as he drove, but once they got home, and he carried in her bags and helped her get comfortable, he didn't go to bed with her. Preferring to wait until she was asleep, he picked up his guitar, went out on the porch and tinkered with a few of his songs. After such a terrible night, he expected her to go straight to sleep. But it was only a few minutes later that she came out to find him.

"I thought you were tired," she said.

He shrugged. "I'll be in soon. I'm just taking a few minutes to unwind."

She listened to him work on the song he'd started a few days ago. "I don't think I've ever heard that one before."

He changed chords to see if he liked that sound better. "It's new."

"I like it. It's...heartfelt, tender."

"Thanks," he mumbled, but he kept his attention on his guitar, since he'd been thinking about Savanna when he wrote it.

Heather listened a little longer. "Is something wrong?" she finally asked, breaking in again.

"With me? No."

"You seem...remote."

"I told you. I'm willing to start over, but I want to take it slow. It's not going to be like it was, maybe not for several months." If ever. Try as he might, he still wasn't sure he could force his heart...

"I understand. I'm willing to give you time. But still. I don't know. You seem more than remote, I guess. You seem troubled."

"Hearing about Scott got my adrenaline going." That was true at least. He *was* angry with Scott and planned to do something about it. But he was more upset by the fact that he had to let Savanna go. He wished, at a minimum, he could wait until the last possible moment, but he knew if he continued to see his neighbor he'd only undermine his ability to do right by his child.

Heather walked over and, resting her hands on his shoulders, dropped a kiss on his head. "I love you."

He wished he could say the same.

"She knows something." Savanna had called Detective Sullivan as soon as she'd fed Branson and Alia breakfast. While her kids were happily engaged in cleaning out an old kiddie pool they'd found in the detached garage, she looked on so they wouldn't get hurt but stood far enough away that they also wouldn't be privy to her conversation.

"That'd be good news if there was any way she'd talk to us," he said.

After explaining her encounter with Dorothy the night before, Savanna had expected a much more enthusiastic response. "Can't you *make* her talk?"

"Getting her to talk is one thing. Getting her to tell the truth is another."

"I understand. But I didn't believe you, either, not at first. Maybe you can convince *her*."

"If what we've found so far hasn't convinced her, I'm not sure it's possible. That's the problem. She knows about the items in the duffel bag, the DNA, all of it."

Savanna waved as Alia yelled for her to watch and squirted Branson with the hose. He squealed and began to chase her to get hold of the water so he could return the favor. "I'm telling you, hearing Emma Ventnor's name instantly changed her whole demeanor! She nearly stumbled off my porch. Then she crashed into my neighbor's truck and took off without even bothering to leave her insurance information."

After a long silence, he said, "Okay. I'll stop over to see her, try again."

"That's it?"

"What do you mean?"

"You need to do more!"

"Like what?"

"Get a search warrant and go through her place the way you did mine. She lives in Salt Lake. Gordon stayed over there on occasion, if he was too tired to finish the drive home or had to be at a mine that was closer to her place than ours the next morning. They were very close at the end." Closer than he'd been to his own wife—as Savanna had come to realize.

"It's not as easy as you might think to get a search warrant. Warrants have to be very specific. I have to name the part of the house I plan to search and what I'm looking for. I can't violate his mother's privacy by going on some kind of fishing expedition."

"I just told you—he stayed with her on occasion."

"I know. And she started acting strange when you mentioned

Emma's name last night. I heard you. I'm saying that might not be enough."

"Are you kidding me? He could've left his bloody clothes there, because he certainly never brought them home to me. I know you don't believe me about that—or haven't in the past—but it's true. Tell the judge you're searching his mother's house for Gordon's bloody clothes and possibly a pair of boots."

"I'll try, like I said. Have you heard from Gordon this morning?"

"No."

"Call me if you do."

She covered the phone to tell Branson that he'd served up enough revenge on his little sister, and they finally went back to cleaning out the pool. "He's not going to admit to having anything to do with Emma," she said when she removed her hand. "He knows those phone calls are recorded."

"Is there any chance you'd consider going to see him, then?"

She took a step back, even though he couldn't see her. "No, I can't do that. I don't want to see him. Besides, I live in California now, and I'd have no one to watch my kids while I was gone."

"We'd provide a licensed caregiver to stay with Branson and Alia, and we'd fly you in, so it wouldn't take that long. What's the flight time from LA to Salt Lake? An hour and a half? That's nothing."

She pinched the bridge of her nose between her thumb and forefinger. Would Gordon tell her anything even if they were sitting face-to-face? Probably not. Visits were probably monitored, too. "He doesn't trust me. He won't give anything away."

"You could convince him to trust you. You know him well, know what he'd most want to hear."

He'd want to hear that she'd take him back and that she'd give him the money she had for his defense. Desperate as he was, that would make him amenable to almost anything. It would be her best shot, at any rate. But telling him those lies, trying to trap him, was dangerous. If the DA wasn't able to get a conviction in the end, Gordon would go free. And if he could kill a poor, innocent stranger, a girl of only sixteen, what might he do to *her*?

Gordon's going to kill you when he gets out... Maybe Dorothy's text would prove more prophetic than she'd actually intended.

Savanna opened her mouth to refuse again, but her conscience stepped in. If every person who could help the police thought only of the danger involved, how many more evil people would be running around in society, continuing to harm innocent victims?

She had to be brave, had to do all she could. Didn't she?

Shit, she silently cursed. "I'll think about it," she said, and disconnected.

CHAPTER TWENTY

The next week seemed to last forever. Heather stayed over for most of that time, while she was healing, which was probably why every day proved a new challenge for Gavin. She claimed she was afraid to go home for fear Scott would confront her, but as angry as Gavin had been a week ago Wednesday, when he'd picked Heather up from the hospital, he didn't think Scott would continue to be a threat. Scott was already out on bail, so it wasn't as if he *couldn't* come by, but he had a court date in a few weeks, seemed to know and care that he was in a lot of trouble and wasn't acting like he would do anything to make matters worse. He'd texted her to say she could relax, that he wouldn't so much as approach her, and so far he'd kept that promise. Although she was at Gavin's from dinnertime on, which meant she had protection, Scott knew where she worked. He could easily have gone by her classroom after the final bell. She sat there alone for two hours, usually didn't leave until five. If she was truly afraid of him, she would've changed that pattern and asked someone to be with her then, too. That was what Gavin secretly thought, but he hadn't said anything. He didn't want to be wrong again and have her get hurt.

The last thing he'd expected was for Scott to approach *him*, so he was surprised when his mother called, interrupting his lunch on Friday to say that Scott was at the administration building. Although Gavin normally ate in the cafeteria with the students—it gave them another chance to socialize with an adult who cared about them, something they desperately needed—the past few days he hadn't been interested in talking to *anyone*, even the boys. He'd been eating in his small office, which was where he was today.

"Hello? You still there?" Aiyana asked when he didn't respond.

His first inclination was to ask what Scott wanted, but if his mother had to relay that question, it would only drag her back into his business. He preferred she not get involved, since she didn't seem entirely supportive of his current course of action. She refused to accept that he had to get back with Heather. "I'm in my office. Tell him how to find me, will you?"

It was her turn to hesitate. "Don't you think you should take this off campus?"

"I'm not going to start anything. And I doubt he'd choose this setting for a fight. He's already facing a court date."

She covered the phone. Gavin got the impression that Scott had overheard her and was trying to convince her that he wasn't looking for trouble, because she came back on the line and said, "I'm sending him over."

Ten minutes later, a knock sounded on his door.

Curious, as well as a little apprehensive, just in case, Gavin turned the knob and shoved the metal panel open with one shoulder. "Wow. It's bright out today," he said, squinting against the sudden intrusion of sunlight. "Come on in." He motioned to the only other chair he had, a cheap fold-up he kept on hand for the occasional visitor.

Scott stepped inside but didn't take the chair. He didn't even approach the desk. He kept his distance, probably to prove he hadn't come to fight. "I told myself I wasn't going to do this," he said. "You'll think it's just sour grapes, that you got the woman I want and now I'm jealous and vengeful—"

"You *have* been jealous and vengeful," Gavin broke in. "And what you did last week—"

He lifted a hand in the classic stop motion. "I know. I shouldn't have let her get to me. I can't explain what happened. I snapped, have never been so angry. But hitting her was stupid. She isn't worth the trouble she's bringing me."

"That's what you came to say?"

"No, I came to tell you the truth."

Gavin straightened the calendar on his desk. "And that is?"

"Heather got pregnant on purpose, Gavin."

Feeling his shoulders tense, he studied Scott closely. Was Scott still out to hurt Heather, just in a different way? Was that why he'd come? "How do you know?"

"By the way everything went down. She wanted you back, and she knew a baby would make all the difference."

"She couldn't have *known* that."

"She couldn't be positive. But she knows you well, knows how you feel about kids—what you do out here for so many orphans and boys who are in the system. And if it didn't go her way? She was confident that she had a worst-case scenario."

"Which was..."

He widened his eyes as if it should be obvious. "She knew I'd marry her even if you didn't."

Gavin sat on the corner of his desk. "And you drove all the way out here to tell me this because you're doing me a favor?"

When Scott chuckled without mirth, Gavin knew he'd heard the sarcasm. "No. I'm telling you because I'd hate to see her get away with it. But all I can do is warn you. What happens from here is up to you. I've told the police—her, too—that I won't bother her again, and I haven't. I won't bother you again, either."

He started to go, but Gavin stopped him. "You're washing your hands of the whole affair?"

"I am," he said when he turned back. "I'll pay the price for what I've done and then…that's it."

"What if the baby's yours?"

"I'll demand proof, of course. And if I get it, I'll pay child support, but only because the state will force me to. I no longer want anything to do with Heather or the baby."

And Gavin had thought the situation was bad when Scott still maintained an interest in Heather. Now, if the child *did* belong to Scott, and Gavin didn't marry her, the baby would have no father. "The child's not to blame," he pointed out.

"*I'm* not to blame, either. I was honest in my intentions all along. I loved Heather—I would've married her. But she wanted you, and she used me to get you. Now we're all in this terrible mess together. Sure, I was wrong to strike a woman. But what she did was worse. Think about it. A busted lip will heal in a few weeks, but she's screwed up all our lives, possibly for good," he said, and walked out.

The meeting with Scott hadn't drifted anywhere near violence, and yet Gavin felt as if he'd taken a strong right hook. Could Scott be telling the truth?

No. Heather would never do something so terrible. Gavin knew her. She'd been single-minded in her pursuit of him, and she was certainly using the situation to her advantage now that she was carrying a child, but she was a decent person, a kind person. The pregnancy was an accident, as she claimed.

But what if Scott was right? How would that change things?

For one, Gavin would be as angry as Scott was. Manipulating other people to such a degree was unconscionable, *especially* when it involved a baby.

He checked his watch to see what Heather would be doing. He wanted to talk to her, see what she had to say in response to

Scott's claims, but she'd be teaching right now. She had to take her lunch earlier than he did.

Anyway, he knew what she'd say. She'd say it wasn't true. Given the possible consequences of admitting to something like that, she'd almost *have* to. So what difference would it make to ask her?

She *couldn't* be that bad, he decided, and tried to finish his lunch. But he wasn't hungry anymore.

Gordon hadn't called Savanna since she'd mentioned Emma Ventnor. That, more than anything, made Savanna believe he was the one who'd kidnapped and possibly murdered the girl, which made her feel a greater sense of responsibility to grant Detective Sullivan's request to return to Utah and meet with her former husband. She didn't want to see Gordon, had been putting off making a final decision. But she knew in her heart that she'd most likely have to go. How would she live with herself knowing that Emma's parents were suffering and she'd done so little to help? Gordon had to be guilty. Otherwise, why would he back away the minute she mentioned Emma's name? He still didn't have the money for the high-powered attorney he felt he needed, and yet Dorothy had quit bothering her, too. Savanna had texted and called her ex-mother-in-law numerous times over the past week, but Dorothy hadn't picked up or responded, not until Savanna threatened to involve the police to make sure Gavin received remuneration for the damage to his truck. Then Dorothy had sent her insurance information, but that was it. No other comment. No pleas for money or threats that Savanna would be sorry if she didn't stand by Gordon.

Savanna had forwarded Dorothy's text to Gavin so he could get on with taking care of the financial arrangements. He was already moving forward with having his truck repaired; she'd seen the rental car he was driving. Now his insurance could get reimbursed. Although he'd thanked her, that was about the only

contact she'd had with him since the night they'd made love so
spontaneously outside under the stars—other than a few texts
where he'd been showing her various carpet remnants for the
living room and trying to schedule a day when he could come
over and take care of the dry rot repairs. They'd agreed on a
week from tomorrow, a Saturday when he'd be off work, but
she would see him in less than forty-eight hours if she attended
the barbecue at his mother's place. He insisted she should still
come, despite his current situation, but she wasn't convinced
either one of them would be comfortable. Would Heather be
there? Would Savanna have to see Heather and Gavin together?

Probably. Heather was staying with him. Savanna had seen
the Pathfinder parked in his drive. Sight of that vehicle made
her sick, because she knew what it meant.

Fortunately, she hadn't bumped into Heather in person since
learning of the baby. Savanna purposely went to the mailbox before Heather could get back from work. She didn't want to feel
obligated to wave and speak to Gavin's girlfriend. Just knowing she was there with him, and probably in his bed at night,
was bad enough.

Realizing that she'd once again allowed her mind to drift
back to her sexy neighbor, she sat down with her computer at
the kitchen table and forced herself to focus on searching the
classified ads for the Silver Springs area. She was tired of ordering out or making dinner in a slow cooker; she needed to find
a good deal on a stove so that she could at least fry eggs in the
mornings.

Although there wasn't anything nearby, she saw several options in LA. Problem was, she no longer had a vehicle with
which to transport such a large and heavy object. She'd been
hoping to use Gavin's truck, but, thanks to Dorothy, it was in
the shop.

She wondered if Eli would mind loaning her his. Borrowing
a vehicle was a lot to ask of someone she didn't know well, but

he'd been so friendly and helpful. And she had his number from when he'd texted the address for the barbecue.

She tried to make herself reach out to him but didn't have the nerve. And she couldn't think of a better alternative. It wasn't as if she could ask the seller to deliver to an address that was an hour and a half to two hours outside of LA. She doubted anyone would be willing to do that, not for a five-hundred-dollar stove.

She decided she'd just keep limping along without one and hope for a better opportunity later.

Because she'd decided to give up, for now, she was surprised when she received a text from Gavin as she was closing out of her browser so she could get dinner on for her kids.

How are you?

She bit her lip as she studied those words. It was difficult not hearing from him all week, always wondering what he was thinking and wanting him in spite of everything. But any contact only made the desire she felt more acute. Fine. You?

Hanging in. Any word from Gordon?

No. Nor Dorothy.

That's a good thing, isn't it? You want them to leave you alone.

I do, but it's weird. They both backed away, went completely silent, as soon as I mentioned Emma Ventnor.

She saw his name come up on caller ID as she was waiting for his next text. "Hello?"

"You think that means Gordon *did* have something to do with Emma's disappearance?" he asked.

The sound of Gavin's voice was far too welcome to her, which just went to show how infatuated she'd become. "I do." She told him about Sullivan's request to have her meet with Gordon in Utah.

"I don't know if that's a good idea, Savanna. Sounds like a long shot to me."

"They have to try everything. And they think I might have some pull with him."

"You don't?"

"That's the thing. I might. I have the money he wants, so he should at least talk to me. I'd say I have a small chance of getting *something* out of him."

"So what are you going to do?"

"I don't know yet."

"If you decide to go, when would you leave?"

She toyed with the hem of her shirt. "We haven't discussed that yet. I haven't even given the go-ahead. But I think I'm going to do it. I'll call Sullivan after we hang up."

"What about the kids? Would you take them with you?"

"Sullivan said he'd get a licensed caregiver to stay here with them while I'm gone. He claims it wouldn't be a long trip, a night and a day at most."

"I'll help keep an eye on Branson and Alia. Bring pizza for dinner. Make sure they're happy while you're gone."

"I'm thinking your girlfriend might have a problem with that."

He hesitated briefly. Then he said, "She isn't my girlfriend."

She was staying at his house every night... "Then what is she? Your *fiancée*?"

He sighed. "There's no label yet."

When she said nothing, he added, "I'm sorry for the position I've put you in. I feel bad about it. I hope you know that."

"Mom, when's dinner going to be ready?"

Savanna whipped around to find Branson poking his head into the kitchen. He and Alia had been playing a board game in the living room. "Soon," she told him.

"What are we having tonight?"

"Leftovers."

He wrinkled his nose. "Oh."

She covered the speaker on the phone. "I'll get a stove soon. Then things can get back to normal."

"That's what you keep saying, but...*when?*"

She couldn't mistake the complaint in her son's voice. "The first chance I get. I promise."

"Branson, are you coming?" Alia called.

"I beat her," he stated with a proud grin. "Now she's dying to play again."

He hurried off, leaving her to her conversation with Gavin. "I shouldn't come on Sunday," she said. "It'll only make things... weird, awkward."

"Are you kidding? Knowing you'll be there is the only thing getting me through the week."

In an attempt to siphon off some of the nervous energy pouring through her, she stood up and began to pace. "I'd rather not see you with Heather. I'm not...not ready for that."

"Heather won't be there. She leaves for Vegas first thing in the morning. Her older sister is throwing a big birthday bash there for the weekend."

"That's even more reason to back out."

"Don't," he said.

She pressed a palm to her forehead.

"Savanna?"

Cursing her lack of self-control, she dropped her hand. "Okay."

There was a long silence. She could tell he wanted to say more. She wanted to say a few things herself. But neither one of them spoke.

"Did James finish the bridge?" he asked at length, changing the subject to a topic filled with much less tension.

He was referring to his friend James Glenn, the contractor

he'd recommended she hire. Glenn had been working to re-place the temporary structure Gavin had created. "Said he'd be done tomorrow."

"I checked out his progress late last night. Thought it looked close, but it was hard to see in the dark."

"It's getting there. Thanks for putting me in touch with him. He's a nice man."

"I'm still looking for a piece of carpet you'll like. Is there any-thing else you need?"

"No. Don't worry about me. I'm not your problem."

"What about the stove you just mentioned to Branson? Or was it Alia? I know you need one. Have you found anything yet?"

"I have, but it's in LA, so I'll have to wait."

"Why?"

"Because I don't have any way to pick it up."

"I could borrow Eli's truck and get it for you in the morning."

"I can wait until a more convenient time. I don't want to put you out."

"If it's a good deal, don't miss it. Tell the seller I'll be there at ten."

"But driving to LA will take up your whole morning!"

"I don't mind," he said. "Text me the address when you have it. I'll get Eli's truck before I head home tonight. I'm about to leave the ranch now."

"You can't keep helping me, Gavin. You realize that."

"Helping you is all I *can* do," he said, and hung up.

CHAPTER TWENTY-ONE

Eli accompanied Gavin when he arrived at a quarter after twelve. Relieved that picking up the stove had come off without a hitch, Savanna made sure there wasn't anything obstructing their path so they could carry it in, and watched as they installed it. She was afraid a problem might arise when they hooked it up. She didn't want them to run into anything that would make the job harder, since they were already being so nice, but Gavin knew what he was doing. He'd brought plenty of tools, had even thought to stop and purchase a new corrugated connector, which she wouldn't have known to suggest.

Thanks to his knowledge and preparedness, everything went smoothly, and it didn't take long. They were done in twenty minutes.

"It'll be so nice to be able to bake again," she said as she tested the oven. "I can't thank you enough for going to all this trouble."

"Happy to help," Eli said.

Gavin didn't respond. He'd been quiet and focused all morning. Last night he'd sent her a short text to confirm he'd received the address where he was supposed to pick up the stove, and he'd texted her again this morning to let her know that they'd gotten off on time. But that was it. Since he'd arrived, he'd been busy with the stove. And now he was showing Branson and Alia what some of his tools were for, since they were curious.

"That was a big drive, definitely more than one neighbor should expect of another." Savanna knew Gavin could hear what she and Eli were saying, but he didn't contribute. Although he *could* have joined the conversation here and there, he seemed to prefer talking strictly to the kids.

"I wish I could've found a viable option that was closer," she added. "I owe you both, so if there's anything I can ever do for you, I hope you won't hesitate to ask me."

Eli waved off her words. "You don't owe us anything—although Gavin probably wouldn't complain if you made him dinner once in a while."

If Gavin heard his brother's suggestion on his behalf, he pretended he didn't.

Savanna cleared her throat. "Why don't I make you and your wife dinner sometime?"

"We'd like that," Eli replied. "Cora's looking forward to meeting you."

"She'll be at the barbecue tomorrow, won't she?"

"She will. She would've come today except she had to help a friend from high school decorate for her wedding."

Savanna set the glasses she'd used to give them a drink in the sink. "How'd you meet Cora?"

"She's a teacher at New Horizons."

Out of the corner of her eye, Savanna could see Gavin showing Branson how to hold a hammer and hit a nail. "So you work together."

"Yes. We're keeping it all in the family," he joked.

When Gavin put the hammer away, latched his toolbox and stood, Savanna shifted her gaze to the man she'd had difficulty *not* looking at ever since he and Eli had pulled into her drive. Just the sight of him made her chest tighten and her fingers itch to touch him. She'd never craved contact the way she craved contact with him, and it didn't matter how many times she told herself that she was being ridiculous, that she'd met him only two weeks ago, that she was acting like some kind of lovesick teenager. She couldn't seem to control her reaction. She felt how she felt. "Thank you," she told him.

Acknowledging her gratitude with a nod and a fatalistic smile, he started toward the door.

"Hey, Savanna's promised to make you dinner," Eli called after him, catching him before he could go out.

Savanna hadn't included Gavin in her invitation, but since Eli had just put her on the spot, she quickly agreed. "Yes, um, I will. Of course. If you and...and Heather would like to come when I have Eli and his wife over..."

Gavin raised his eyebrows to signify that he had no idea where she was going with such an invitation, and she let her words fade away. *She* didn't know where she was going with it, either. That was opposite to anything she'd ever really want to do. She was just trying to be polite so that Eli wouldn't find it odd that only he and his wife were invited.

"Or maybe I'll drop something off sometime," she finished lamely.

"You coming?" Gavin said to Eli. "We promised the boys at the ranch we'd play some ball today, and I'm sure they're getting tired of waiting for us. Then I've got a gig that's four hours away."

"I'll be right out," Eli said.

The screen door slammed shut but didn't stay closed. The kids followed Gavin outside while Eli hung back. "Don't mind him," he said, lowering his voice and gesturing toward Gavin's retreating back. "He's dealing with some personal problems that have nothing to do with you."

She drew a deep breath. "You mean the baby."

He stood taller. "He told you Heather's pregnant?"

She nodded.

He clicked his tongue. "Here's hoping he doesn't marry her."

"He's going to," she said, and she couldn't blame him. Part of her even admired him for trying to be such a stand-up guy.

"It would be just like him," Eli agreed with a frown.

The kids came back inside as Savanna watched Gavin and Eli drive off. Gavin hadn't touched her, hadn't even brushed against her, given her a sexy smile or tried to be alone with her since that night they'd made love under the stars. That brief flash of sexual activity was over, she told herself. Even if the attraction remained, they couldn't act on it. She needed to accept that.

She *did* accept it, she told herself.

And yet she was still taking her birth control.

That afternoon, Savanna drove the kids to town. The stove was installed. The bridge was finished so she could cross it with confidence. The broken windows Gavin had boarded up in the beginning had been replaced along with the back door. There was still a lot to do, but she was feeling good about the progress on the house. She'd even called Detective Sullivan and told him she'd be willing to come to Utah, if he felt it was truly necessary, and he'd said he'd see about making the arrangements.

After all of that, she felt as if she, Branson and Alia deserved a little family fun, and with Gavin's mother's barbecue and swim party tomorrow, she hoped to find a new swimsuit. She doubted Gavin would even look at her. He was being so careful not to say or do anything that could be construed as inappropriate for a man in his situation that everything had become odd and strained between them. Whenever she caught his eye, a troubled expression would descend on his face before he pulled his gaze away. She hated that.

Again, she considered backing out of the barbecue, but it was all her kids could talk about. She didn't want to disappoint them. And she was interested in meeting Aiyana. From what Savanna had been able to determine so far, Gavin's adoptive mother was someone worth meeting. While Savanna was in the dressing room trying on a pair of shorts, Branson told the salesclerk at the thrift shop that they were going to New Horizons for a swim party, and the clerk said that Aiyana was one of the nicest people in the world.

Savanna bought the shorts, since they were only four dollars. She bought a few things for her kids, too, and then they went out for ice cream. Branson wanted to show her where Gavin had taken them. They even stopped by the park and fed the ducks before visiting the only shop in town Savanna thought might sell swimsuits.

She found a gorgeous black bikini as soon as she walked through the door, but it was too expensive.

She put it back on the table, checked the other swimsuits and found that they were all beyond her budget. She was about to leave when she spotted the clearance rack. Since it was spring, she didn't expect to find any swimsuits on sale, but she checked, anyway, and was surprised to find a stunning one-piece in a nude color that looked like it might fit. The tag said there was a seam coming undone on one side, so it had been marked down, but she could easily fix that.

"How do you like it?" the salesclerk asked once she was in the dressing room and had had time to put it on.

Savanna smiled as she gazed at herself in the mirror.

"Is it pretty, Mommy?" Alia wanted to know. She and Branson waited just outside the fitting room.

Savanna wasn't sure she'd ever looked better. The suit was sexy without being overly revealing, and it suited her coloring and figure better than the black ever could. Best of all, it was half price.

"I think I'll take it," she said.

Gavin had never been in a worse mood. Somehow, against all odds, given what'd happened to him as a child, he'd managed to find peace in his life. He'd managed to hang on to that peace, for the most part, even after Heather had told him she was pregnant. There had certainly been a few bright spots, but those were due to Savanna. The more the news settled in, the more he had to face all the ways it would change his life, the more tense and irritable he became.

Thank God Heather was out of town for the weekend, he told himself as he drove to Bar None, the little honky-tonk in Soledad where he'd be playing tonight. Having her around all the time was part of the reason he was so wound up. The pressure to feel something he didn't and to deny other feelings he did have made it so he could hardly look at her, which only caused her to become more determined and clingy.

What Scott had come to tell him at New Horizons troubled Gavin, too—definitely contributed to his sour mood. He'd be lying if he pretended it didn't. Part of him wanted to disregard Scott's accusations, to give Heather the benefit of the doubt. He felt he owed her that much, simply by virtue of the months they'd been together over the previous three years. The other part of him was tempted to believe Scott because then he'd at least have *some* justification to walk away, to handle the situation the same way Scott was—with the promise of a child support check if the paternity test was positive.

But what about the baby? If it *was* his, he wanted to be a good father and sending a check every month wasn't enough. Heck, even if the baby wasn't his, it was *a* baby and would have all the same wants and needs he'd had when he'd been so painfully rejected. He should step up regardless.

"Shit." No matter how hard or how long he thought about the situation, there didn't seem to be a way out. He couldn't put his desires first, not if he wanted to feel good about himself. And yet he was having a difficult time simply hanging out with Heather, couldn't avoid feeling a bit of resentment, even though that didn't seem fair if the pregnancy *was* an accident.

He should be *glad* she wanted him. Otherwise, he could be put in the position of having to plead with her just to let him spend time with his child. He didn't care what the court set up. Without her cooperation, it would be a nightmare.

Then there was Savanna. She needed someone in her life right now, too; she was going through so much. He wanted to be there for her. But just the amount of time he spent thinking about her made him feel disloyal to Heather.

He was glad when he finally arrived in Soledad. The long car drive had given him entirely too much time to focus on his problems. He was looking forward to performing, to giving everything he had to the crowd and not feeling anything except the music. But when he approached the door, he found a sign posted that indicated the place was closed. There was no explanation, but it looked official, so he wondered if they'd lost their liquor license or something. And why hadn't anyone called him?

Shaking his head, Gavin pulled out his cell phone to find the email of the person who'd booked the job through his website. There was a phone number in that message for a Paul Timpson, but "Paul" didn't answer when Gavin tried him. He sent the guy a text, asking what was going on and received a brief explanation that they were having "management" problems between two partners.

Thanks for letting me drive four hours for nothing, he wrote back, and received an apology—something about how stressful and sudden everything had been. Gavin had received a fifty-percent deposit upon booking but should've received the other half of his money tonight, after the performance.

The guy promised he'd pay it, since it was his fault Gavin hadn't been notified, but Gavin knew chances were slim that money would ever come in.

Shoving his phone back into his pocket, he returned to his rental car and headed home.

★ ★ ★

Detective Sullivan called not long after eight that evening to tell Savanna she was scheduled for a Tuesday afternoon flight from Los Angeles. The male inmates of Juab County Jail could receive visitors only on Wednesdays. If she didn't get there *this* Wednesday, she'd have to wait until next week, which Sullivan didn't want to do. He told her a licensed caregiver would arrive Tuesday morning so she could spend some time with the woman and make sure she felt comfortable leaving her kids. After that, she'd fly out of LA and into Salt Lake on a direct flight, pick up a rental car and drive to Nephi. He'd meet her at the Safari Motel on Main Street, where she'd be staying, for a little coaching, and then she'd visit Gordon the following morning.

Sullivan had thought of everything, had made it as easy as possible, but the knowledge that she'd be returning to a place that held such a terrible stigma for her—and knowing that she'd have to face Gordon—made her anxious. She'd spent her entire married life making excuses for her husband's behavior (blaming it all on his past as he did) and trying to placate him and avoid arousing his temper. Now she'd not only have to face him, she'd have to *confront* him. Taking him on over the phone was one thing. She'd been so upset since she'd begun to believe he was guilty that she'd let loose a time or two. But those emotional eruptions had been natural outcroppings of her hurt and anger. They'd been *real*. Railing at him in person, *trying* to get him upset enough to incriminate himself in a case for which he hadn't even been charged, would be a different story.

Would her acting skills be up to the task?

She didn't see how they could be. She'd never been a good liar. And Gordon knew her so well. Part of her feared he already suspected that she was trying to help the police or he wouldn't have stopped calling since she brought up Emma Ventnor. She hadn't even received a letter from him since they last talked, and her mail had certainly had time to forward from her old address. It'd been over a week since his last call...

She'd mentioned her concerns to Detective Sullivan, but he said she was jumping at shadows. Sullivan believed Gordon was just playing it safe, that he thought he could get off for the rapes (he *had* acted confident when she'd spoken to him on the side of the road Sunday before last) but was afraid if he was ever connected to Emma Ventnor's disappearance he'd be looking at prison for the rest of his life, because he would be.

Savanna could see Gordon pulling back for those reasons, could see why he might not want her to bring up the subject again. But it was also possible his silence had nothing to do with Emma Ventnor. He could be angry that she'd "abandoned" him and gone so far as to file for divorce. Talking to her had to be upsetting, after all.

With a sigh, Savanna poured herself a glass of wine and sat staring at the burgundy-colored liquid. With the kids in bed, the house was quiet. Too quiet. If she wasn't obsessing over what she had to do next week, she was thinking about Gavin, which wasn't a whole lot easier. She hated how cautious and circumspect he was acting. It was almost as if he was afraid to get too close to her. And yet she couldn't help admiring him for making the welfare of an innocent child his top priority.

When she finished her wine, she poured herself another glass. She liked Silver Springs, but living in the country could get lonely. She'd had so little interaction with others since she came here. Just Gavin. And that had turned out to be *too* intense. She needed to make an effort to meet people, to get out more now that she was settled into her new place. The kids needed the opportunity to make friends, too, so that their lives could return to normal as much as possible.

Tomorrow they'd meet Gavin's family. She had to admit she was looking forward to that, to having a legitimate reason to be in his company again. But Savanna wasn't sure becoming so familiar with his world would prove to be a good thing. She was having a hard enough time putting her relationship with him into perspective.

Carrying her glass with her, she went out on the porch to get some fresh air. Nights were particularly beautiful in Silver Springs. She loved the smell of the valley. There was no exhaust, no stench coming from the family of ten's garbage cans next door, no nasty marijuana smoke drifting on the wind from somewhere up the block. The air was clean. And now that she was outside and not staring at four walls, the quiet seemed more enjoyable and less oppressive.

She listened for the gurgle of the creek and couldn't hear it, but she heard something else—a man singing.

Gavin. When she concentrated, she could recognize his voice even though she could barely hear him from where he was probably sitting, on his own porch.

What was he doing home? Why wasn't he at his gig?

Unable to resist the temptation, she walked down to the creek so she could make out the song he was singing. But she remained behind the trees, where she could listen and watch without interrupting or disturbing him. She felt a little like a stalker, since she wasn't making herself known, but she was too tired to battle the desire she felt whenever he was around. Since she'd learned about Heather's pregnancy, she couldn't even justify wanting him, and that added guilt to all her other emotions.

She needed to put a stop to what was happening in her head and her heart. And she would, she told herself. But tonight, she just wanted to enjoy the beauty of his voice, let it carry her away. What was the harm in that? She figured secretly listening couldn't be too damaging or creepy if she remained on her own property.

He sang the slow version of "Dancing on My Own," which she loved.

Gavin was *good*. Even better than she'd realized when she heard him before.

He sang the same song a few times—practicing, she supposed—but when she finished her wine, she pushed off from the tree she'd been leaning against to go in and check on her kids. She had enough going on without pining after a man she couldn't have. She needed to let Gavin go and focus on rebuilding her life. The nightmare that'd started with the investigation into Gordon's crimes wasn't going to end as a fairy tale. Gavin wasn't going to sweep her off her feet; he had his own problems to deal with.

Besides, the more she listened, the more she came to believe that he was doing the right thing marrying Heather and moving to where he could pursue his music. The world needed to hear him. And she needed to help find Emma Ventnor, or at least make sure Gordon was held accountable if he'd harmed her, get the farmhouse fixed up so she could sell it and pay her brother his half of their inheritance, money he would need to set up his practice once he got out of school, and continue to provide the love and stability her children needed.

And she needed to do all of that no matter how lost or lonely she felt herself.

CHAPTER TWENTY-TWO

Gavin had been up most of the night, wrestling with himself over whether to contact Savanna. He'd nearly walked over to her place a dozen times, would be lying if he said he hadn't thought of the fact that, with Heather out of town, he had the perfect opportunity to see her—and yes, maybe even spend the night in her bed. She lived right next door, which would make it so easy. No one would see his vehicle in front of her house; no one would have to know they'd been together if they decided to keep it a secret.

But he had to stop seeing Savanna at some point. And he refused to be reduced to the kind of man who was sneaking around. He'd only hurt both women by doing that. So he'd stuck it out on his own last night—only to be hit harder than he'd expected by the sight of Savanna at the barbecue and pool party the next day.

She'd never looked better. She'd arrived in a pair of white shorts, a pretty shirt with full sleeves and sandals. But the kids had insisted she go swimming with them almost the moment she walked into the backyard, so those clothes had come off. Now she was wearing a nude-colored swimsuit that had nothing but strings connecting the front to the back, leaving four inches of her sides bare. A whole piece, it wasn't as revealing as a lot of swimwear, and yet the sight of her in that suit had made his mouth go dry. With her dark auburn hair falling loose and curly, and polish that matched her hair on her fingernails and toenails—even a similar shade of lipstick—he couldn't get over how golden she looked *everywhere*.

He wasn't the only one having a difficult time keeping his eyes off her. Roger Nowitzke, the New Horizons grad who'd come back to visit Aiyana for the weekend, and someone Gavin typically liked, was making no secret of his attraction. He hadn't left Savanna's side. For the past twenty minutes, he'd been sitting on the lounge beside her, talking and laughing and doing everything he could to be charming while she watched her kids swim.

"You okay, little brother?"

Gavin glanced up to see that Eli's wife, Cora, had walked over to the grill where he was flipping burgers. He was so miserable he hadn't even noticed her approach. Today, everyone other than Savanna seemed almost invisible to him. They were just dark, murky shapes that hovered on the edge of his consciousness. "Yeah, I'm fine." Trying to act more like his regular self, he added, "These are almost done."

She put her arm around his shoulders. "You're such a good guy. Eli and I—and Aiyana—we all want you to be happy. I hope you know that."

"I *am* happy," he lied.

She didn't seem to believe him, but she acted hesitant to argue. They were in the middle of a party; it wasn't the time.

With a sympathetic squeeze and a smile, she walked over to where Eli was talking to Cal. Aiyana had invited her own boyfriend and Dawson and Sadie Reed, as well as their son, Jayden, and Dawson's sister, who had special needs and whom Dawson and Sadie cared for. Dawson was another alumnus of New Horizons. He'd settled in Silver Springs but knew Roger, too. Then there was Gavin's youngest brother, Bentley, who was still in high school, and Liam, who was going to college in San Diego. Liam had made the drive to Silver Springs despite the fact that he'd miss two classes tomorrow before he could get back.

Gavin was just stacking the burgers on a plate so that they could eat when Eli came over.

"Roger really seems to like your girl."

Gavin scowled at him. "She's not my girl."

"She could be," he said with a wink, and took the plate of burgers over to the table.

Gavin sat as far from Savanna as possible. He knew he wouldn't be good at conversation today. He was too twisted up inside, too consumed with jealousy. He had to let her meet and enjoy other people, had no claim on her, but watching her with Roger wasn't easy.

Unable to finish his meal, he went inside and started cleaning up the kitchen so that his mother wouldn't have to do it later. When he heard a creak behind him, he assumed it would be Aiyana. At various points since he'd arrived, he'd caught her watching him with a worried expression.

But it was Savanna.

"You're already doing dishes?" she asked. "The party only started an hour ago."

He shrugged. "My mom works too hard. Figured I'd get this done before she could even think about it."

"Even though you're missing the fun?"

"I have to leave soon, anyway." He wasn't sure why he'd said that. He had nothing in particular he *had* to do. He just hoped to escape having to watch someone else move in on what he wanted. "But you and the kids can stay as long as you like and swim. You don't have to leave because I am." If she was enjoying Roger's attention—and she seemed to be—Gavin was sure Roger would stay as long as she did...

When he spoke over his shoulder, didn't even turn to talk

to her, she hesitated in the doorway. "Is everything okay? I feel like maybe you're upset or something."

"I'm not upset. I'm fine. I hope you're having a good time."

"I am. Thank you."

Silence fell on the heels of that polite response. Then she said, "If you don't want to talk to me, would you mind telling me where the bathroom is?"

He ignored the first part of what she'd said. Now wasn't the time to get into it. "I just heard someone go into the bathroom down the hall, so you might want to use the one at the top of the stairs." He showed her where the stairs were and, since he stayed to watch her go up, saw her cast him an uncertain glance as she reached the top.

He went back to doing the dishes, but ultimately, the hurt behind her words—*If you don't want to talk to me*—got the better of him. He couldn't resist the opportunity to see her for a few minutes alone, if only to apologize for his surly behavior. It didn't matter what he was going through. He was her only friend in Silver Springs so far. He needed to treat her better than he was. So after he heard Dawson leave the bathroom on the main floor and go outside, he went upstairs and waited until she came out.

She stopped the moment she saw him, and he opened his mouth to tell her he was sorry for behaving like a jealous ass. But then he saw the tears glistening in her eyes. "What's wrong?" he asked. "Is it Gordon?"

"Gordon?" she echoed.

"Has something happened?"

"Other than the fact that I have to fly to Utah on Tuesday and visit him on Wednesday morning, no. I'm not looking forward to that, but I had been looking forward to this."

"I'm sorry," he said.

"You tell me we're friends but you won't even look at me," she responded.

"Because I'm struggling! I need to keep our relationship

within certain boundaries, but I can't seem to do it. I'm trying—God knows I'm trying. But, for a change, friendship isn't
enough for me. I want you so badly it makes me frustrated and
angry that I can't have you." He gripped her by the upper arms.
He'd merely wanted to get her to look at him, *really* look at him
and believe him, but touching her turned out to be a mistake,
because the next thing he knew, they weren't talking anymore.
He'd ducked his head and found her lips, was communicating
in a way that felt far more natural when it came to her.

They couldn't be seen from the front door, but if someone
climbed the stairs, they'd be right in plain sight. Despite the
sudden deluge of testosterone and the relief of getting what he
really wanted, that thought dimly occurred to Gavin. He tugged
her into his old bedroom, but that was a mistake, too, because
he couldn't resist pulling down the top of her swimsuit so he
could touch and taste her breasts.

"*This* is why I can't even look at you," he muttered as his
mouth moved over her soft skin. "This is what I want to do
when I see you."

She lifted his head as though she'd stop him, take on the voice
of his conscience. She looked unsure of what they were doing,
maybe even a little frightened by the sudden intensity. They
were at a barbecue with his family and her kids, after all. But
once she saw his face, she must've changed her mind, because
she guided his mouth back to hers and kissed him every bit as
hungrily as he'd been kissing her.

"Mom? *Mo-om?*"

Branson was wandering through the house, calling for her.
The last thing Savanna wanted was to be interrupted. She had
Gavin's hands and mouth on her again, was feeling all the wonderful things he could make her feel. When she was with him,
there was such a sense of belonging, of having come home,
which was strange considering she'd never known anyone like

him in the past. The past ten days, she'd missed him more than she cared to admit. She wanted to stay right where she was, get even closer to him, and with a bed so close at hand, they'd been heading in that direction.

It was disappointing not to get what they both craved, but her son's voice finally cut through the sexual frenzy, reminding her of her responsibility as a mother and that she was a guest in Aiyana's house.

"That's Branson," she gasped, and felt everything come to a stop as Gavin pulled back, looking as overcome and disheveled as she knew she must. She'd removed the tie from his hair almost the moment he'd started kissing her so that she could bury her fingers in the thick mass of it, and she'd pulled off his T-shirt, which lay, probably stretched out at the neck, somewhere on the floor at their feet.

"Mom?" Branson called again.

She and Gavin were both breathing hard as they stared at each other. She swallowed, hoping to steady her voice before she responded. But Gavin put a finger to her lips to indicate silence. Evidently, he'd heard something she'd missed—someone else coming into the house—because a second later, she could hear Eli telling Branson to come back outside, that he'd watch him and Alia while they swam.

"We can't get in the water until we check with our mom," Branson insisted.

Savanna had made it clear that they weren't to go near the pool if she wasn't around. She would've been proud of him for his obedience, except his determination to find her put her in the awkward position of having to come out of an upstairs bedroom with her hair mussed, her face flushed and her heart racing. She was already trying to right her swimsuit, and Gavin was doing what he could to help.

"She must still be in the bathroom," Eli said. "Let's give her a minute, okay?"

"Eli's got it," Gavin whispered, attempting to calm her.

Sure enough, that seemed to be the case. "There are Popsicles in the fridge," she heard Eli say. "I'll get one for you and your sister, and by the time you eat that, you'll be able to ask your mom if you can go swimming again."

"Okay!" Branson seemed pleased by that solution, which made Savanna breathe a bit easier.

They heard some rustling below. Then the door slammed.

Eli and Branson had gone out.

"I have to get down there," she said, and since she had her swimsuit tied again, Gavin opened the bedroom door for her.

Savanna found Eli sitting with her kids in the barbecue area, both of whom had red lips from the dye in their cherry Popsicles.

"There you are!" Branson cried when he saw her. "I was look-ing all over for you. Where'd you go?"

"To the bathroom." She hoped the party would just move on, that no one else would remark on her prolonged absence or look closely enough to see how ruffled she was, and that seemed to happen. But Gavin never came out. She realized later, when she was helping to clean up and had a legitimate excuse to go back inside, that he must've left shortly after their encounter, because the dishes had only piled up from the point where she'd interrupted him.

She was just walking back to get more of the leftover food, which Aiyana was covering and putting in the fridge, when she caught Eli studying her with an appraising look. She gave him a tentative smile, and he smiled back when he realized that she'd noticed his attention.

"Thanks for inviting me to the party," she told him. She was carrying the last of the food but had curved around the pool to get close enough to speak to him. "I had a lot of fun. So did the kids."

He bent to retrieve a floating raft from the water. "I'm glad," he said as he let the air out of it. "I'm sorry Gavin had to leave so early."

She cleared her throat. "Maybe he had a few things he had to get done."

"Maybe," he responded, but the way he was grinning when he said it gave her the impression he found something about Gavin's sudden departure more amusing than it should've been.

Gavin sat on the couch, facing Heather. She'd returned from Vegas sooner than she'd originally planned, hadn't wanted to leave Silver Springs in the first place. And he knew he was the reason. She could sense that he wasn't in the emotional space she wanted or needed him to occupy and that scared her. With a baby coming, he could see why. It worried him, too, but he was beginning to realize that he couldn't get back with her. Not right now. He wasn't feeling what he should be feeling, and he couldn't live a lie.

"So what are you saying?" she asked, her voice trembling.

She'd texted him while he was at the barbecue to see where he was. That was part of the reason he'd left early. He hated feeling as though simply attending that barbecue made him somehow less than loyal. His encounter with Savanna in his old bedroom had simply underscored the fact that he needed to let Heather know he was struggling, so it wouldn't come as a nasty surprise later.

"I *care* about you," he said. "I'll do everything I can to support you during the pregnancy and after. I want what's best for you and the baby, whether the baby's mine or not." He kept emphasizing that he wouldn't abandon her, but it didn't seem to help. She looked stricken.

The tears he'd anticipated, given the pitch of her voice and how rapidly she was blinking, began to roll down her cheeks. "But you can't *love* me..."

"I'm not saying I *can't*." He didn't want to make her feel there was anything wrong with her. There wasn't. But he had to be honest. "It's just… I've met someone else."

"Your new neighbor."

He tucked his hair behind his ears. After Savanna had taken the tie out of it, he hadn't bothered to pull it back again. "Yes."

"But you don't even know her."

"I'm getting to know her."

"She's only been here two weeks!"

"What does that matter? I'm attracted to her, and I can't seem to change that."

She laughed humorlessly. "I can't believe this. When I ran into her that day while she was getting her mail, she told me she wasn't interested in meeting anyone."

"She wasn't. I can vouch for that. The attraction has taken us both by surprise."

Heather's expression hardened as she lifted her chin. "*Attraction?* Have you already slept with her?"

Gavin didn't answer. He didn't consider the details of his physical involvement with Savanna to be any of Heather's business. But he wasn't going to deny that his relationship with Savanna had gone that far. He was trying to be as up front as possible. In his mind, that was the only decent way to be.

"Oh, my God!" She covered her face as if the truth was just too terrible. "I'm going to have your baby in seven months, and you're fucking someone else!"

He felt terrible, knew she was in an untenable position and hated that he couldn't solve the problem so no one would be hurt. "It's not like that. There's no guarantee we'll wind up together. The relationship could fizzle in a few weeks or months, so please, don't overreact."

Her voice climbed even higher. "*Overreact?* I'm pregnant! That means I'll have a baby in a few months. *Your* baby."

Or Scott's baby… That was what made this thing so difficult. "What I have going with Savanna is completely new—unexplained and uncategorized—which is why I haven't said anything until now. It could turn out to be nothing."

"Or you could wind up marrying her instead of me. What you have going with her has to be *something*, or we wouldn't be having this conversation."

He lifted his hands to indicate he didn't know what more to say, because he didn't. He felt sick that there didn't seem to be a solution he could live with. He didn't *want* to let Heather down, didn't want to let his child down, either. That more than anything. And yet it felt wrong to quash that special thing he and Savanna seemed to have when they were together. He'd never felt anything like it before.

"You slept with her this weekend, while I was gone, didn't you?"

"If I did, I did. Don't try to call it cheating, because you know we're not committed to each other right now."

"That's a yes," she said, ignoring everything else. "That's what's causing this. If I hadn't gone to my sister's stupid birthday party, it never would've happened."

"I didn't sleep with her while you were gone. You were right to go to your sister's party. It didn't cost you anything."

"But you saw Savanna..."

"It's not as though I took her out behind your back! I helped her get a stove, and I saw her and her kids today at my mother's barbecue."

Heather's eyes narrowed. "And how'd she get invited to that?"

She obviously thought she had him there, but he hadn't invited Savanna. Eli had done it, not that Gavin was going to get that specific. "You know my mother. She learned I had a new neighbor and wanted to make her feel welcome."

"I knew I shouldn't have left."

"This would've happened regardless."

She wrung her hands. "But you said *we* were going to try again."

He *had* tried, as hard as he could, but maybe something would change... "There's still hope. Who knows what the future holds."

"We're having a baby together. I think I deserve something a little more certain than that."

"The pregnancy came out of nowhere, and not while we were together. That changes things."

"It doesn't have to."

Gavin blinked in surprise. "What are you talking about? You were dating someone else. You don't even know which one of us is the father. Anyway, like I said, I can't say if my relationship with Savanna will go anywhere." After what Gordon had done, Savanna might not be able to trust again, not so soon. But Gavin wanted—*needed*—the chance to pursue what he felt. He'd been denied the close relationships most children had when they were young, so feeling as he did when he was around Savanna meant even more to him. What if he'd finally found what Eli had with Cora?

He'd begun to doubt that would ever happen for him.

"You want to be with her, even though *I'm* the one who's having your baby..."

He almost said, *You can't even tell me it's mine!* but he'd already made that point, and she was only reacting to the hurt she felt. He couldn't let himself get as emotional as she was or this would go even worse. "I want to be fair to both of you," he reiterated.

"How can you be unfair to *her*? You don't owe her anything!"

"She's new here, could use a friend."

"There are plenty of men in town who'd be happy to befriend her."

"Heather..."

She stood. "And if I go back to Scott?"

He recalled Scott's parting words the day he'd come to Gavin's house—*I don't want your filthy bastard growing up in my house*—and felt his muscles tighten. Was he essentially abandoning his child to the fate of having a bad stepparent? Someone who was unkind or unloving—like what he'd known growing up? Scott claimed he wouldn't take Heather back, but that could have been said in the heat of the moment. Scott had always been there for her before.

Gavin couldn't help wondering if he should've persevered, even though it was becoming so clear that he'd fail in the end. "Is that what you're going to do?"

"Maybe I will!"

He caught her by the wrist. "Please don't do anything rash, okay? If we play this by ear, take each day as it comes, maybe things will work out for us. I'm not ruling that out. I just... I wish we could be friends, for the moment, and see if more grows from that."

"You mean you want me to be patient and wait around while you decide if you'd rather have the pretty redhead next door!"

He raised his voice for the first time, simply because she didn't seem to be listening. "I don't know what's going to happen with Savanna!"

"And yet you want her more than you want your own child."

"I need the time and space to figure out how I really feel."

"You're no better than Scott or anyone else!" She tried to hit him, but he caught her hand before she could land the blow.

"Heather—"

"I've been such a fool," she said on a sob. "You don't deserve the love I've offered you. All you've ever done is break my heart."

He tried to stop her from leaving. She needed to calm down before she got behind the wheel, but she wouldn't listen. She stormed out and nearly hit the fence with her SUV as she tore out of his drive.

"So much for trying to be honest," he muttered, and let himself drop back on the couch.

CHAPTER TWENTY-THREE

Savanna had spotted Heather's Pathfinder sitting in Gavin's drive almost the first moment she turned down the narrow road that led to both their houses. As she drove past, she'd told herself to ignore it, that she shouldn't have expected anything less, but the sight made her feel so low that when her brother called, she didn't answer. She wasn't sure she had the mental energy to pull off a conversation with Reese, not without him figuring out that something was wrong. And she was tired of constantly putting him in the position of having to encourage and console her. She wanted to return to her usual role as the big sister, and she felt confident she would've been on that path again at last if she hadn't gotten involved with Gavin.

What made her sleep with someone she'd just met? She had *one* neighbor. Just one. And she'd *had* to take him to bed.

Even worse, she'd liked being with him, and now she couldn't quit thinking of that night and the one where they'd made love up against his truck. If Branson hadn't come into the house when he did today at the barbecue, she might've found herself with yet another memory like that—this one at Aiyana's, no less!

"You're screwed up, or there's more to that rebound business than you've ever cared to believe," she told herself. But when she'd first slept with Gavin, she hadn't thought she was truly getting involved with him. She'd thought it would be an isolated event, a temporary escape. One night of companionship. One night of forgetting.

Why couldn't either one of them seem to leave it at that?

Reese's call transferred to her voice mail, but once she sent Branson to shower in the hall bathroom and Alia to shower in the master bath, she carried her phone out on the porch to listen to his message.

"Hey, finals are over and I managed to do okay. I'm one step closer to becoming Dr. Pearce. This is such a long process. Anyway, call me, will you? We need to catch up."

He'd been so busy with school and the new girl he'd been dating that she'd hardly heard from him since she moved to Silver Springs. He'd texted her a few times to check in, but she hadn't called him nearly as often as before. She got the impression he thought she was going to be okay now that she was out of Nephi, that she was forging ahead with her life. And that was mostly true. He didn't need to know the rest. She hadn't wanted to disturb him if he was under pressure, or say anything that might let him know she was actually creating problems in this new place.

After summoning the mental wherewithal, she returned his call.

"There you are," he said when he picked up.

"Sorry, I was at a swim party earlier and was trying to get the kids in the shower so they can wash the chlorine out of their hair."

"A swim party, huh? You must be making friends."

She would like to believe that Eli, Cora, Aiyana and Roger were now her friends, not to mention the others she'd met. They'd all been so nice. But they were still just acquaintances. Gavin was her only friend, and she wasn't even sure she could call him that. People didn't typically dream about making love with their friends, did they?

"Yeah, things are going well," she said, which wasn't a *complete* lie. The house was coming together. Thanks to what Gavin had done, and what James Glenn had accomplished, she now had all basic appliances, a sturdy new bridge over the creek, patches in the Sheetrock where bullets had created holes and several new lighting fixtures. She was shopping for new carpet, believed she'd soon find something she could afford. And she had more improvements scheduled in the next couple of weeks, including the dry rot repair Gavin had said he'd do next Saturday. On top of all that, Branson hadn't wet the bed for several days, so he seemed to be doing better. It was only the possibility that Gordon had murdered Emma Ventnor, and that Savanna somehow needed to get that information out of him—and her love life, of course—that were giving her problems right now.

"Glad to hear it."

"You coming out?" she asked.

"I can't. Not right away. I have such a small window before classes start up again, and work is crazy. We're short on bartenders, so I'm putting in a lot more hours than I'd like to be. Once they hire someone else, I'll be able to fly over for a few days, though. Shouldn't be too much longer."

"No problem. I'd rather have the house further along, anyway, so you can see what it's going to look like."

"What's left to do?"

"A fairly long list. I need to put on a new roof, for one, but we'll be getting to the cosmetic stuff soon. That's when it'll get fun."

"Do you have enough money?"

She'd have to get a job in a few months. No way could she take a year off as she'd hoped. Everything cost far more than she'd budgeted. But the kids would be in school by the time she had to find work, so she wouldn't need to hire a babysitter, except for maybe a couple of hours after school, so that was good. "For now."

"And you're comfortable living out in the country?"

Thanks to Gavin, she was. She loved having him so close. Maybe she'd screwed up when she slept with him, but she figured she shouldn't be *too* hard on herself. He had a way with women, a magnetism that wasn't necessarily apparent at first glance but grabbed hold soon after. Besides, she'd needed someone, and he'd been there for her. The move would've been *so* much harder without him. "Yeah. I'm happy here, glad I came," she said, which reminded her that she'd soon be traveling back to Nephi, so they talked about Emma Ventnor and what she hoped to accomplish when she visited Gordon.

Reese didn't like what Sullivan had asked her to do any more than Gavin did, but she told her brother the same thing she'd told her neighbor: she didn't feel as though she had any choice, not if there was any chance of recovering Emma, or even her body.

"You don't *really* believe Gordon will screw up and say anything, do you?" Reese said. "He's not stupid."

"He's *definitely* not stupid, but he should be feeling a measure of panic, which might make him reveal something he wouldn't under normal circumstances. At least, that's the logic. Sullivan thinks if I get him angry he won't be watching what's coming out of his mouth."

"I'm not convinced such a small potential for success will be worth causing him to turn his hatred on you."

"He *could* screw up," she insisted. "Who knows? He's out of his element, must be feeling some panic."

"About whether or not he'll be going to prison?"

"That, too. But he's a bit antisocial to begin with. Doesn't like being around people—hates a crowd, especially. Being crammed into such a small space with so many other men has to be a daily struggle for him. Think of the lack of privacy. He can't even go to the bathroom without feeling as though he's on display."

"You're assuming the stress of his situation will make the difference."

"I'm not assuming. I'm *hoping.*"

"That's not very likely."

"I know," she said. But what else could she do?

Gavin didn't go to Savanna's that night. He wanted to talk to her, felt as though he *needed* to talk to her, since he'd disappeared from the barbecue after that highly charged encounter in his old bedroom without even saying goodbye. She had to be wondering at his inconsistent behavior. But he had to gain some perspective on the situation first, had to make sure he hadn't made a drastic mistake telling Heather he wasn't ready to try again. He didn't want to swing back and forth between the two like a wrecking ball. But duty warred so perfectly with desire that he felt torn in half. When duty got the better of him, he feared he'd never be able to live with himself for making the choice he'd made with Heather. When desire got the best of him, he believed he'd never really had a choice.

In an effort to quiet his mind, he played the guitar for a couple of hours, but even that didn't have the soothing effect it normally did. *I don't want your filthy bastard growing up in my house...* He kept hearing those words over and over in his head.

Was Heather at Scott's right now, trying to make up with him? And would he let her? It was entirely possible that he'd just been talking when he came out to New Horizons...

Gavin feared he'd abandoned his child in all the ways that counted most—done the one thing he'd promised himself he would never do, and he couldn't seem to get past it. Finally, he called Eli to see if his brother would meet him in town for a drink.

It was a Sunday night, and they both had to work in the morning. Gavin thought Eli would most likely decline, but he didn't. He agreed to meet up in fifteen minutes, which was about as long as it would take Gavin to get to town.

"You okay?" Eli asked, coming up behind him at the Blue Suede Shoe.

Gavin was standing over the old-time jukebox, silently cursing the poor selection of songs. The bar featured live bands on the weekends, some of which were pretty good. Gavin had played here quite a few times. But there was no live music on Sundays. On Sundays and all the rest of the week, there was only the jukebox, with its sparse collection of country songs or Top 40 from a decade ago. He felt they should at least have more classic rock. "I've been better."

"Did you get a drink?"

"Bought us both a whiskey when I came in. Bartender's pouring them."

"Great. So what's going on?"

Gavin shot him a look. "What do you think's going on?"

Clapping an arm around his shoulders, Eli guided him to a booth, where they both took a seat. They could've sat almost anywhere; the place was empty except for a few diehards who played billiards in one corner.

"I like Savanna," Eli said, jumping in without preamble. "If you have to choose between them, I say you choose her."

"Two whiskeys!" the bartender called out.

Grateful for the reprieve, even though *he* was the one who'd called this meeting, Gavin got up to retrieve their drinks.

Once he returned, Eli took his glass but didn't seem overly interested in drinking what was in it. "Not only is Savanna beautiful, she seems nice," he said, trying to open the discussion again.

Gavin wasn't nearly as ambivalent about the alcohol as his brother. He welcomed the burn of the whiskey as it traveled down his throat.

"Are you going to talk to me?" Eli asked, finally growing impatient. "Or are we just going to drink?"

"We're just going to drink." Sheer escape. No more mental torment. That sounded good to Gavin. "Do you think Cora will pick us up?"

Eli shot him a look. "I didn't drag my ass out of the house tonight to get smashed, leave my vehicle here and wake up with a hangover tomorrow. I did it for *you*. Tell me what's going on."

Gavin couldn't decide if he was willing to go into it, after all. He was suddenly loath to even think about Heather and the baby and what he'd done at the barbecue, but he felt bad for dragging Eli out of the house, so he made himself explain what'd happened with Heather, and once he got going it wasn't as difficult as it seemed it would be to continue talking.

"You're being too hard on yourself," Eli said when he finished. "Ease up, okay? Wait and see what happens."

"What if she goes back to Scott and together they try to make it difficult for me to spend time with my own child?"

"If you think she'd ever make it difficult for you to see your child—that she won't care more about the child than getting revenge on you—she's no one you want to marry, anyway."

Gavin turned his drink around and around on the scarred old table. "She's so sure we belong together, and that I'm making a mistake, she'll do what she can to punish me, make me regret my decision."

"Gavin, you were relieved when she seemed happy with Scott, remember? That right there tells you all you need to know. That has nothing to do with Savanna. But since Savanna has come into your life, we should probably talk about her, too. There's something between you. I can feel it. Even Mom and Cora noticed it—the way your eyes kept going back to each other at the barbecue today. Mom said she's never seen you so excited about someone." He took a sip of his drink at last. "I'm going out on a limb here, but I doubt you could make it work with Heather, baby or no."

Gavin agreed, or he wouldn't have done what he'd done. "But

if I don't get back with her, I'll have so little control. How will I protect my child?"

"You'll do everything you can to ensure you get proper visitation, even if it means going to court. And you'll keep a close eye on the situation to be sure the child's treated kindly. There are a lot of couples who aren't together, and their children are fine. It doesn't have to go the way it did with you. I say wait and see if she's carrying your baby before you worry too much about that, okay?"

"So I should give what I feel for Savanna a chance."

"Definitely. Get to know her, see what happens."

"In spite of the fact that another woman might be pregnant with my child?"

"Life is messy. If she cares about you, she'll understand how it happened and that you want to be a good father. She'll support you in doing the right thing."

"What about what she's been through recently?"

"What about it? Can you think of a time when she might need you more?"

No, he couldn't. And Gavin wanted to be there for her. *Her* kids mattered, too. If Gordon went to prison, they wouldn't have a father, not even one who could take them on weekends. Why should they be any less of a consideration than the baby Heather was carrying, even if it was his? Every child mattered. "Okay. Here's hoping she hasn't decided she never wants to see me again," he said, and stood.

Eli gestured at what remained of their drinks. "Wait. We haven't finished our whiskey."

"I don't feel like drinking anymore. We both have to work tomorrow," Gavin said, and Eli started to laugh.

After she hung up with Reese, even after she'd put the kids to bed and had a shower herself, Savanna wouldn't let herself go out of the house, not even to stand on the porch and enjoy the stars. She knew she wouldn't look at the sky for long. She'd head down to the creek to see if Heather was still at Gavin's, and what would be the point of finding out? Why continue to torture herself? He'd told her he was getting back with his former girlfriend. She needed to accept that, despite the confusing encounter they'd had at the barbecue earlier. Those few seconds of unbridled passion had flared up out of nowhere—and then nothing. The way he'd behaved, both before and after, suggested he hadn't changed his mind about the future. She needed to accept that Heather was going to be around a lot—at least until they moved to Nashville—and quit cringing every time she thought of running into them together.

The next day when she drove past his place on her way to the grocery store, she told herself not to even glance over, but she couldn't help it.

The Pathfinder wasn't there. Neither was Gavin's rental car, which he was still driving because he didn't yet have his truck back from the collision repair place. But the absence of both vehicles didn't tell her anything. This time of day, they'd both be at work.

"She'll be there again tonight," she muttered as she came to a stop in front of the mailboxes.

"Did you say something?" Branson asked.

Savanna looked over at her son. He rode in the passenger seat, while Alia sat in back, since she was smaller and it was safer there. "Me? No. Nothing important, anyway."

"It's my turn to get the mail!" Alia called out. Branson had done it yesterday, so Savanna gave her daughter the key.

It took Alia longer than Branson. She had to stand on her tiptoes, and the lock wasn't always easy for her small hands to manage. But she enjoyed the challenge, so Savanna didn't mind the wait.

"We got three letters and a magazine," Alia announced as she climbed in the car.

"I hope the letters aren't all bills," Savanna joked.

Branson reached back to take the mail and glanced through it. He handed Savanna the magazine, then a notice from the power company and a solicitation for a new credit card.

"What's that one?" Savanna asked when he held the last envelope for several seconds.

"It's a letter from Daddy," he replied softly.

She could tell her son missed his father.

Branson was a good reader for third going on fourth grade, but she didn't dare let him attempt to read what Gordon had sent, whether he missed him or not. She had no idea whether Gordon would be sending his love or villainizing her for leaving him.

Fortunately, Branson didn't ask to open it. Pretending he didn't care what Gordon might have to say, he handed off that letter, too. "I wish he'd just leave us alone," he grumbled.

Savanna wished the same, except, if she hoped to get any information on Emma Ventnor, she needed to keep up a relationship with him. That he'd sent a letter came as a bit of a relief, since he hadn't called in so long. She hoped it might give her a better idea of what to expect when she paid him a visit in two days.

She put his letter in her purse for later, when she wasn't around the kids, and was about to shift into Drive when her phone beeped. Since she was already stopped, she took a moment to look at the text.

Can I bring you and the kids dinner tonight?

It was from Gavin.

Savanna felt her heart pound as she stared down at his message. She wanted to see him in the worst way, but she knew it wouldn't be wise. She was complicating her life when it was already complicated enough.

And where will Heather be? she wrote. I know I was the one who insisted on remaining friends. I wanted to hang on to some small part of you at least. But it's getting too confusing for me. You're such a great guy, and I appreciate all you've done for us, but at this point in my life I don't have the emotional resilience to deal with the ups and downs. The kids and I will be okay now. You're free to do what you feel you should with Heather, and I wish you both nothing but happiness. Honestly. You deserve it. Thanks for helping us get a solid start here. And please know, especially for when you leave, I'll always remember you fondly.

She stared down at that text for a long time without sending it, so long that Alia and Branson grew impatient.

"Mom, come on!" Alia said.

"What are you doing? Aren't we going to go to the store?" Branson added.

"Yeah. We're going." After briefly closing her eyes, Savanna forced herself to hit Send, even though it felt like she was running her heart through a shredder, and dropped her cell in her purse. She hoped what she'd done would finally release her from the constant preoccupation she had with Gavin. She had to do *something*; he was all she could think about.

But as the day progressed and she got no response, sending that text only made her feel worse.

CHAPTER TWENTY-FOUR

Gavin walked to Savanna's door and, three different times, turned away without ringing the bell. He had no idea if his involvement in her life would turn out to be a positive thing, and he didn't want it to be a negative. If they wound up in a serious relationship, he could easily imagine Heather being unkind whenever she and Savanna bumped into each other. And if Heather would soon be the mother of his child, they'd bump into each other on a regular basis.

It could get difficult; he had to acknowledge that.

He also had to acknowledge that he wasn't simply choosing between two women. There was more at stake than that. If he didn't get back with Heather, there was a possibility that he wouldn't be able to move to Nashville. He *couldn't* leave if he had a child here in Silver Springs. He'd owe it to that child to stick around and help raise him or her.

Bottom line, he and Savanna were both in such complicated situations. He couldn't imagine a relationship between them would work—and yet he felt something that was hopeful and promising enough to make him risk his best chance for a successful music career.

That, more than anything, told him he might as well ring the bell, see if she'd refuse to have any more to do with him, or if he could change her mind.

She answered wearing those cutoffs he'd taken off before, the ones that showed her legs to perfection. She had her hair down, too, which he also liked. But he was determined not to focus on the physical. He needed to slow things down, make sure they weren't letting sexual attraction cloud more rational thinking. The sexual attraction had been so instantaneous and strong...

Instead of acting excited to see him, she bit her lip, so he quickly lifted the bottle of wine he'd carried over. "It would be rude to turn away a neighbor who's bringing you a peace offering."

"And I wouldn't want to be rude." Although she spoke those words with a slight smile, she sobered almost immediately. "But I'd better not invite you in. The kids are in bed."

Still hoping to get her to soften, he winked at her. "That's okay. I wasn't going to offer them any."

She laughed in spite of her general reluctance to be welcoming. "I meant they wouldn't be around to make sure you and I didn't...you know, do anything you might have to explain to Heather later."

"You mean like yesterday."

"Yes, like yesterday." She raked her fingers through her thick, curly hair. "What was that, anyway?"

"I was a jealous ass yesterday. Seeing Roger chat you up and follow you around drove me nuts. I'm sorry."

"Roger was only being nice!"

Gavin gave her a knowing look. "He was being more than nice."

"Even if he was, it doesn't matter. I'm not interested in him."

"You're sure?"

"Without question! Do you think I'd make out with you upstairs if I had even the slightest attraction to him?"

"Jealousy isn't always logical or trusting. But I'm glad to hear you're not that into him, because what happened when you came out of the bathroom was totally honest."

"Honest," she echoed.

"Yes. Real. Spontaneous."

"And yet you walked out without even saying goodbye."

"Heather was texting me to let me know she was back, and I wanted to talk to her."

She propped one shoulder against the doorjamb. "Did you tell her?"

"I didn't bring that up specifically, no. But I did let her know that things have gotten physical between you and me in the past, and I'd like the opportunity to explore what I feel for you."

Her eyes widened in apparent surprise. "What about the baby? And moving to Nashville?"

"If the baby's mine, I'll have to stay in Silver Springs."

"And that's okay? You love music. And you're so good at it. I wouldn't want to be the one holding you back."

"You wouldn't be holding me back. I'll do what I can from here and possibly LA. Granted, that doesn't put me in the best position for success. There are far more opportunities in Nashville these days, despite what others might think of LA. But if I have a child, I won't move away from him or her."

"If you married Heather, you could have both," she pointed out.

"I've considered that. But then there's you, and there's no getting away from the fact that you hold some magic for me."

Another smile threatened, but she seemed to fight it off. "As much as I like hearing that, I don't know if I can let you make such a choice."

"Because..."

"I want you to have what will make you the happiest."

The sincerity in her voice destroyed any doubt he had left about breaking off with Heather. *This* was the type of woman he wanted. "How do you know that won't be getting together with you?"

She stepped outside and closed the door. "Think about it, Gavin. I don't have a lot to offer. I have two kids who are great, but they are struggling, especially Branson. Since his father went to jail, he's been wetting the bed. I thought it had stopped, but he had another accident last night, so I'll probably have to figure out a way to afford therapy for him. Beyond that, I'm not officially divorced. So if Gordon doesn't go to prison, I might not be able to finalize the paperwork, at least for some time. He could sue me for custody of Branson and Alia, demand visitation even if he doesn't get custody, balk at paying child support and generally make me—and anyone who's attached to me—miserable. It's not even as though I have many possessions or money to make life easier, only this broken-down house that I'm trying to fix up and barely enough savings to carry me until fall, at which point I'll be searching for a job. Why would you ever want to get involved with me?"

"There's a lot that's broken in your life right now."

"Exactly."

"Well, I happen to be really good at fixing things," he said.

She laughed. "But don't you think we're up against too much? Why would you ever be willing to jump into such a mess?"

He stepped closer so he could cup her cheek with his free hand. "Because I think I could love you like I've never loved anyone else."

He'd told himself he wouldn't kiss her tonight, that they'd just talk and get to know each other better. But the way she looked at him, with an endearing yet modest expression, he couldn't help himself. As his hand slid to the back of her head, he lowered his mouth to hers—and was soon lost.

Savanna let her eyes slide closed as she gave herself over to the taste of Gavin's lips. They'd kissed before, and those kisses had all been good, but this one was filled with a fragile promise—the promise of something new and untried—and while that made succumbing to Gavin feel far more risky, it also made the contact more meaningful.

"I love that you're different," she told him when he lifted his head.

He smiled as he looked down at her. "In what way?"

She could tell he'd heard those words before but was curious to hear her specific take. "You're so emotionally honest and unafraid. You're willing to bare your heart and actually *feel* something regardless of the risk. I admire your courage."

"It's hard not to feel something for you." He bent his head to kiss her again, but she stopped him.

"Except... I wasn't exaggerating about what we're up against, Gavin. Before you commit yourself to getting any more involved with me, maybe you should come in and hear the latest."

He seemed concerned. So was she. Her world was threatening to fall apart again—and he'd shown up right in the middle of the latest crisis. "Something's changed?"

She nodded. "And not for the better."

Savanna had cleaned off the other chairs in her living room— everything was now unpacked—so there were plenty of places to sit. When Gavin took the couch, she perched on the edge of the chair across from him, too upset and nervous to sit back.

"What's happened?" he asked.

"A couple of things. First, I heard from Gordon today." She held up the letter she'd left on the coffee table, which she'd been reading and rereading when Gavin had rung her doorbell.

"What does he have to say?"

"I'll let you read it, if you want, but it says that he's shocked and heartbroken that I would be disloyal enough to believe he could rape those women. That he's innocent and will soon be getting out, and then I'll be sorry that I didn't stand by him." She let her breath go in a sigh. "That's the gist of it."

Gavin's eyebrows drew together. "Sorry in what way?"

"He doesn't specify. Just blames me for breaking up our family, which he claims didn't need to happen if only I'd had a little faith and remained true to him."

"But...that's the type of stuff he's been saying all along, isn't it?"

"For the most part. It's when you take this letter and couple it with what Detective Sullivan just told me on the phone that it all gets worrisome."

"What'd Sullivan have to say?"

The panic she'd felt when that call first came in welled up again. "He told me that the DA is thinking about dropping the charges."

Gavin came to his feet. *"What?"*

"I know." She stood, too. "I can't believe it myself. I've been over here pacing another hole in this old carpet, wondering what I'm going to do."

"Why would the district attorney ever even *think* about dropping the charges?"

"Remember the victim—Theresa Spinnaker—whose blood was found in our van?"

"Yes..."

"She's admitted to having accepted a ride from him."

"So?"

"So the district attorney feels the DNA evidence is no longer what it needs to be. Proving Theresa was in Gordon's van doesn't mean what it did when she was swearing up and down that she'd never met Gordon before the attack, and he was saying the same."

"But it was her *blood*."

"They don't seem to care about that, since it was found in such small quantities. They said taking that to court might actually backfire because the defense would argue that it was negligible, that if she'd *really* been hurt as badly as the pictures prove she was hurt, there would be a lot more blood than a few tiny droplets."

"What about the items in that duffel bag?"

"Bad news there, too. The lab came back with the results of all the DNA testing. There's no genetic material on any of those items."

"*None?* Isn't that a little odd in and of itself? If Gordon handled those things—the knife, in particular—they should've found *his* DNA at least. *No* DNA indicates he must've cleaned it."

"I asked Sullivan the same thing. He said they needed at least one item from that duffel bag to establish a firm connection to one or more of the victims, and it didn't happen. Instead of being the strong forensic evidence we all expected, the rape kit is now as circumstantial as everything else, and circumstantial evidence isn't what they need to get a conviction."

"You've got to be kidding me," Gavin said.

She wiped her palms on her cutoffs as she'd been doing all evening. "I wish I was."

"They don't have anything else on him?"

"Meredith Caine swears she recognizes his voice from the attack, but human memory is notoriously unreliable. She can't ID him visually, since he was wearing a mask, and the DA won't go with voice recognition alone."

"If the charges are dropped, he gets out, goes free, can do whatever he wants."

She said nothing.

"This is terrible," he said.

"That's why he went silent after I mentioned Emma Ventnor. He knows he probably won't need a defense, and he doesn't want to make the mistake of saying anything that could get him in trouble on an entirely different case. No doubt he's told Dorothy to leave me alone, too. He only sent me that letter because he couldn't help letting me know I shouldn't have sided against him, that he'll soon be back in the power seat."

"And he could think a letter through, make sure it was safe."

"Yes."

"Wow." Gavin rested his hands on his lean hips.

Savanna frowned. "See what I mean?"

"Does Sullivan still want you to go to Utah?"

"I was supposed to leave tomorrow morning but just put it off by a week."

"What for?"

"If I'm only going to have one shot at this, I need more time to prepare. I'm thinking I should send a letter or two, establish a more positive dialogue with Gordon. Maybe even put some money on his books. I'll have the strongest hand to play if I make him feel as though I'm interested in staying together."

Gavin didn't look as though he particularly liked the idea. "What will that do?"

"It'll make him feel he has something to lose if he can't convince me that he had nothing to do with Emma Ventnor's disappearance."

"But you've already asked him about Emma."

"I'm going to say the police have some new evidence tying him to the case. That just when I believed he was innocent, of everything, they came to me with...something. I can't decide what."

"You're going to bluff."

"Absolutely. If the police *don't* come up with new evidence, everything will rest on my visit to the jail. I *have* to get him to say something incriminating."

"Now that he thinks he's getting out, it'll be even harder. But at least he won't find it strange that you're suddenly coming to visit. I was worried that would work against you." Gavin took the letter and read through it. "This opens you up to reconciliation, so when you write him back and give him some money, he might buy it," he added when he was done.

"I believe he raped those women, Gavin. I believe he'll hurt others, if he can. Since I didn't stick by his side, he might even hurt me."

Gavin tossed the letter on the coffee table and sat back down. "You'll have to use everything you know about him, exploit his tiniest weakness. You realize that? It won't be easy. What happens if doubts creep in?"

"And what if I do my best and it still doesn't work?" That was what *really* frightened her. "What if he gets out in a few weeks? He'll come here. I know he will. He might even try to take the kids."

Gavin rubbed his face with both hands. "Shit."

"I'm sorry," she said. "I told you I'm not in a good situation."

He got up and walked over so he could pull her into his arms. It felt wonderful just to be that close to him again. She'd been so upset all evening, so scared of what might happen. She'd escaped Nephi, thought she'd escaped the whole situation—for the most part. Now everything had been turned on its head. How could all the evidence that'd been so compelling be too weak to get the job done?

Would Gordon show up at her door in a few short weeks?

He would if he had the chance. And what would that do to Branson and Alia?

"Don't worry." Gavin gave her a soft kiss on the neck. "We've got seven days. We'll figure it out."

She pulled back to look him in the face. "Are you sure you don't want to run for the hills? I wouldn't blame you."

"I'm not going anywhere."

She rested her cheek against his chest. "Please tell me they won't let him out."

"Somehow, we'll make sure of it," he said, but she knew he was only trying to comfort her. He had no way of keeping that promise.

It was all on her.

CHAPTER TWENTY-FIVE

Heather wrung her hands as she paced back and forth in her living room. After what Gavin had said yesterday, she'd barely made it through school today. She hadn't felt like teaching, had almost called in sick again, or left after lunch. She would have, except the principal and other teachers were beginning to complain about her lack of commitment. She feared she'd put her job in jeopardy if she didn't stay until the usual time, and she couldn't allow any more of her life to fall apart. The people she worked with didn't understand that she had serious problems. Her whole future stood in the balance. She'd thought Gavin might reconsider what he'd said yesterday and call or text, ask her not to go back to Scott, as she'd threatened. But she hadn't heard from him. Why? She knew what kind of father he hoped to be. They'd talked about it before. And, as far as he was concerned, she was carrying *his* child.

Her pregnancy should've made all the difference, should've brought them together again.

So why hadn't he called? Was he spending time with his new neighbor? Did he like Savanna that much?

He had to, or he wouldn't be letting things stand as they were...

That thought caused the worst kind of panic Heather had ever experienced. How could it be that just when she'd decided to quit messing around and *make* him step up and commit, Savanna Whoever She Was moved into town? And not just into town, right next to Gavin?

"It's sheer bad luck, bad timing...a bad joke." How was she going to gain control of the situation again?

Her phone dinged, indicating she had an incoming text.

Please let it be Gavin, she prayed. But it wasn't Gavin; it was Scott. She'd been texting him, telling him that she was sorry for everything she'd put him through, acting as sweet as she possibly could. She hadn't indicated she wanted to get back together. She'd stopped short of that for two reasons. If she came off too desperate, Scott would hold all the power, which wouldn't bode well in the end. And she didn't really want to get back with him, not if there was any chance Gavin would reconsider. Still, she had to extinguish Scott's anger, in case she needed him later. She was beginning to fear she'd wind up a single mother, and that fear only grew worse when she read Scott's text. Fuck off.

The panic churning in her gut burned until she thought she might scream. *Don't do it. Don't freak out. Everything will be okay.* She didn't need Scott. Who did he think he was? Somehow, Gavin would come around. He'd said he wasn't ruling her out. He was just hoping to explore the attraction he felt to his neighbor, and why not? He deserved to have a little fun before they settled down. Gavin hadn't been with anyone since she got with Scott. Chances were it wouldn't go anywhere. He was meant to be with her; she'd known it for years.

She still had his baby, which was a powerful bargaining chip. If it really was his baby...

"God, help me." The child *had* to be Gavin's. If it was Scott's, her life would be far worse. Scott could be so vengeful. Unless she forced the issue, he wouldn't even pay her child support.

Her phone went off again; her mother was calling.

She silenced the ringtone. She couldn't deal with her parents, not on top of everything else. Ever since they learned she was pregnant, they'd been hounding her about what she was going to do.

Another text came in. No surprise—it was from her mother. Apparently, Vickie refused to be denied.

Why won't you pick up? You're not fooling me. You have that phone in your hand 24/7.

With a sigh, Heather forced herself to call back. Vickie would only be more difficult to deal with if she put it off. She shouldn't have told her parents about the baby, but she'd been trying to put as much pressure on Gavin as she could, and she thought making the announcement official would finally convince him to get serious about their future together.

"Sorry, Mom," she said when Vickie answered. "I was in the bathroom."

"How are you feeling?"

"I'm fine," she lied. "Just tired. Had a hard day at school."

"What was hard about school?"

Showing up was hard, especially when she wanted to be anywhere else. "Teaching isn't as easy as it seems."

Ignoring that, her mother launched into what *she* considered important these days. "Have you talked to Gavin?"

Heather winced. "Not today. Why?"

"Why do you think? We're wondering when we should schedule the wedding. We need to pick a date before you start to show, and the church is getting booked up."

"I realize that you're feeling some pressure." What did she think Heather was feeling? "But we're...we're thinking of getting married *after* the baby's born."

"What?" her mother squawked. "Why?"

"Gavin says there's no reason to rush and... I agree." She hated that she'd said the last two words so softly, but she'd always found it difficult to stand up to the gale-force wind that was her mother's will.

"What are you talking about? There's *every* reason to rush. Do you want your child to be born a *bastard?* Doesn't Gavin care whether his child carries his name?"

She'd thought he did. But he'd broken things off instead of setting a date. "He's not particularly religious, Mom."

"But *you* are, and so are we. He should have some respect for our beliefs."

She was far less religious than her mother believed. She just couldn't admit that, either. "Mom, *please.* Don't start. My life is difficult enough right now. We have to give him some time to adjust. I was with *Scott* the past two months. Gavin's the type that...that's responsible and kind, but he needs...he needs to come to terms with the sudden change and the shock."

There was a slight pause. Then she said, with more suspicion than Heather cared to hear, "Are you *sure* it isn't Scott's baby?"

The tears that'd been burning behind Heather's eyes for most of the day welled up. It *could* be Gavin's child. She'd gone off birth control a week before they broke up. But she couldn't admit that. It was, however, part of the reason she'd freaked out when his ex-girlfriend came to town and wanted to spend some time with him. She'd felt she might already be pregnant and they should be beyond that. "We'd better hope not," she said simply.

"What does that mean?" her mother demanded.

"It's over between Scott and me. When...when I went back to Gavin, that was it."

"Gavin's the one you love, anyway. You've chased him for years. And you said he was going to marry you. That's true, isn't it?"

"Of course," she said. But he hadn't called her since he told her he wanted to see someone else. And he didn't call her for the rest of the week. By the time the weekend came and she had to check his website to see where he'd be performing instead of hearing it from him, she knew she had to do something—or she'd lose him for good.

Gavin had enjoyed the week. Every day when he came home from work, he joined Savanna, Branson and Alia for dinner, but he didn't spend the night. Savanna didn't want to make her children feel as though their father had already been replaced, and since Heather was pregnant, possibly with his child, Gavin felt he had to be more restrained and cautious than they'd been with such a whirlwind start. As difficult as it was, not sleeping with Savanna gave him the chance to be sure he was interested in her for the right reasons, that he wasn't simply avoiding the situation with Heather. So they'd eat and play games with the kids while Branson and Alia were awake, and then they'd stay up talking until Gavin could finally convince himself to head home and go to bed—alone.

The crazy thing was, he looked forward to seeing Savanna each day like he'd never looked forward to seeing anyone else. Going without sex didn't change anything, except make him want it that much more. He wasn't sure how much longer they'd be able to hold out, but abstaining felt decent, right, considering the circumstances, so they were trying. In any case, they had plenty to distract them, since they also spent a great deal of time after the kids went to bed brainstorming her upcoming trip to Nephi.

Twice Gavin stood over Savanna's shoulder, providing input and advice as she wrote Gordon. She also added a hundred dollars to Gordon's "books" so he could buy more products at the commissary. Even if he didn't need anything, he could trade items for better shoes, a newer jumpsuit, physical protection or other favors, which would make his stay in jail more comfortable. Those with money fared much better on the inside than those without.

Gavin could tell Savanna hated pretending she had *any* interest in her former partner. She couldn't help wondering if she was sacrificing her integrity by deceiving him. At times, Gavin felt the same reluctance she did. But Allison March, the detective from the Emma Ventnor investigation, had reached out to encourage them. March said that not only was Gordon working nearby the day Emma went missing, he had no verifiable alibi—wasn't at the mine—when it happened. He claimed he was getting lunch but couldn't remember where he ate, and she hadn't been able to find video footage of him or his vehicle at any of the fast-food restaurants or gas stations in the area.

"I can't wait until it's all over," Savanna said as Gavin drove them both to his gig at a bar called Limelight in Santa Barbara on Friday night. They'd dropped the kids off at his mother's house, since Aiyana had offered to babysit.

Gavin reached over to take Savanna's hand. "Won't be too much longer now."

"What if we're mistaken?" She turned to him with a worried expression. "What if Gordon's innocent, like he claims? I would hate to wrong someone so terribly, especially him. I'm not in love with him anymore, haven't been for a long time, but he *is* the father of my children. Hurting him means hurting them. And even if there wasn't that connection, I don't want to make his life any worse than it has to be. I don't want to make *anyone's* life worse than it has to be."

"Because *you* have a conscience," Gavin said. "From what the detectives are telling us, Gordon does not."

"Do they know?" she asked.

"I can't say they do with any certainty," he replied. "But we're only trying to make sure he wasn't involved in Emma's disappearance. You won't be able to get information he doesn't have, so if he didn't do it, he's safe."

"That's what I keep telling myself. But he's been claiming all along that the police are out to get him, and there have been plenty of examples of that type of thing happening to other people in the past. I'm scared that, when it comes right down to it, I'm doing this for the wrong reasons."

He pressed the brake as he came up on a slower-moving vehicle. He finally had his truck back. It'd been repaired and Dorothy's insurance had paid the bill, but Dorothy had maintained the strange silence that had started the night she so briefly showed up in Silver Springs, which continued to be both a relief and a curiosity to Savanna. "How could you be doing it for the wrong reasons?"

"Keeping him in jail serves my own purposes now. *Our* purposes, if we continue seeing each other. I'm happier than I've ever been, would rather he not be free to bother me, which I know he will if he has the chance."

"You were going to Nephi even before we started officially seeing each other, weren't you?"

"Yes. I keep telling myself that, too. It'd just be so much easier for us if he remained behind bars. That makes me feel guilty for doing what I can to keep him there."

"If he's been attacking women, he deserves to be locked up. You believe he attacked the three victims he's being charged with raping, don't you?"

"I do. And yet... I can't be one hundred percent. That bothers me."

He gave her hand a squeeze. "At the end of the day, you have to be able to live with yourself, Savanna. So play it by ear when you're with him. Weigh what the police have found against what you know of him and his character, what he says and what you think of his current behavior. That's all you can do, right? Make an educated guess."

"The stakes are so high. I hate to base everything on a guess. But you're right—that's all I can do."

"If he gets out, we'll deal with it as best we can."

She offered him a smile. "Thanks for understanding."

They fell silent, listening to the playlist on Gavin's phone, which he'd plugged into his stereo system. But even after several minutes, Savanna seemed pensive, so Gavin turned the music low.

"Are you going to be okay tonight? Maybe, with all the stress you're under, you would rather have stayed at home." He'd wanted her to come with him, so he'd made the arrangements with his mother and hadn't really probed whether she felt up for a night out. Maybe he'd assumed too much and she hadn't spoken up because she didn't want to disappoint him...

"I'm looking forward to seeing you perform," she insisted. "It isn't that. It's Gordon, like we've been talking about."

"But we've been dealing with Gordon all week, and you haven't seemed quite *this* troubled."

"It's getting closer to Tuesday." Her chest lifted and fell as she sighed. "But you're right. That isn't everything."

He punched the gas pedal to get around the vehicle in front of them. "So what else is going on?"

"I hate standing in the way of you getting back with Heather if it means you won't be able to be the father you've always wanted to be."

"Don't worry about that," he said. "That's my problem."

"It's my problem, too," she argued. "We might be able to ignore the situation right now, but what will happen once the baby arrives? Will you be miserable? Regret getting with me?"

"No."

"But you won't be able to move to Nashville. Are you sure I'm worth such a sacrifice?"

He lifted her hand to his mouth so he could kiss her knuckles. "I'm more sure of it every day."

"That's what you say now. But what if you begin to resent me for what I've cost you? I've never met anyone like you, Gavin. I

don't want to take more than I have a right to take, don't want
to rob you of anything when you've been so kind and gener-
ous with me."

He'd been expecting this subject to come up eventually.
They'd been so focused on the more immediate problem of
Gordon that they'd barely spoken of Heather. To top it off, Savanna didn't know much about his background and how that
might impact his response to the situation. He'd glossed over the
painful details, given her the sanitized version he reserved for
new acquaintances. But it would have an impact, make things
more difficult for him, and she deserved to understand why.

They should talk about all of that. They had at least an hour
yet to drive, so they had time. But just remembering made him
sick, and he had to perform tonight. "You're not taking anything from me I don't want to give," he said, and let go of her
hand so he could turn the music back up.

The bar was crowded when they arrived. Savanna knew Gavin
was a good singer, but she hadn't realized that he'd already developed somewhat of a following. She couldn't help feeling a
sense of pride in his ability and accomplishments as she watched
him set up onstage. She'd been telling the truth on the drive
over. She was concerned about the situation with Heather and
how he might feel about his choices later. But it was difficult
to let that or anything else bring her down once she got swept
up in the excitement and anticipation of those around her. She
was with the man she wanted to be with. That made her happy
right there, even if it wouldn't last.

Gavin had made sure she had a front row seat and turned
every once in a while to acknowledge her. He'd grin and she'd
grin back, and then she'd try to tell herself that somehow they'd
overcome everything they were up against. She'd never met
anyone like him, anyone who remained so peaceful and calm
and measured in his reactions. That brought peace and calm

into her life, too. She was falling in love—the head over heels variety that made her feel dizzy and breathless and too warm every time she thought of him—which was why she was worried. She'd just been through a shocking ordeal, and it wasn't over yet. She couldn't imagine coping with a painful breakup on top of everything else.

But the moment Gavin started his set, she was able to forget her fears and simply enjoy the performance. Like so many of the other women there, she was mesmerized by his voice, the convincing emotion he put into each song and his personal charisma.

She was having such a great time that when she went to the bathroom an hour later, she wasn't even thinking about Gordon or Heather or any of the potential pitfalls she and Gavin faced. She was looking forward to hurrying back to her seat, ordering another drink and listening to some more songs when someone grabbed hold of her upper arm.

She turned and found Heather, dressed in what looked like a sheer black bra and miniskirt, pushing to get past the last two people separating them in the narrow, crowded hallway. "Heather!" she cried. "What are you doing here?"

"What am *I* doing here? I could ask you the same," she retorted. "What kind of person tries to move in on another woman's man when that woman is expecting a baby?"

Several of those who were jostling to get into the bathroom whipped their heads around to see who was talking. "Whoa!" Savanna heard one woman say to her friend. "There's gonna be a fight in here tonight!"

Hoping to avoid any more of a scene, Savanna lowered her voice. "I haven't done anything to 'steal' your man. I'm sorry for your situation. It must be frightening. But Gavin hasn't been with you since I've known him. I couldn't take what you no longer had."

"You're kidding yourself if you really believe that. You're the only thing standing between us. He'd marry me if not for you.

Do you really want to be responsible for his child going without a father?"

"He'll be there for his child—without a doubt."

"It's not the same, and you know it."

Conscious of the stares of those around them, Savanna cleared her throat. "Heather, don't start something. This isn't between us. This is between you and Gavin. You need to talk to him."

"No, I need to talk to *you*." She seemed oblivious to the attention she was drawing. "You're the clueless one. Do you even know anything about him? Do you know what his childhood was like? How badly he hates his father for allowing his stepmother to abandon him when he was only six? That's right," she added, smirking when she accurately read Savanna's surprise. "She left him at a park. The authorities eventually brought him home, but the next week she beat him so badly social services got involved and took him away. After that, he went into foster care and lived with a weird family who didn't give him any love."

Savanna's heart broke for Gavin. "That's tragic."

"So tragic that if you think his past isn't going to come into play once I have this baby, you're sadly mistaken. He'll change his mind, decide to be the kind of hands-on father he's always promised himself he would be. Do you understand? Then you'll only be in the way."

Savanna might've argued. Gavin seemed to know his own mind. She didn't feel she had to make decisions for him. But he hadn't revealed any of that about his stepmother or his foster situation. As a matter of fact, he'd made his childhood sound only a trifle more difficult than most everyone else's. He hadn't "gotten along" with his stepmother so he'd "acted out" and been sent to New Horizons. That was how he'd presented it to her. Aiyana had adopted him because he'd been so much happier there with her.

But being abandoned put what he'd experienced on a whole new level. He had to bear deep scars, just as Gordon did. Savanna didn't think Gavin would ever react the same way, by physically harming others, but if Gavin carried that much pain, it could manifest itself at any time and change all kinds of things.

"Why didn't he tell me?" She was mostly speaking to herself, but Heather was only too happy to supply the answer.

"Why would he? The only people he tells are the ones he trusts. *That's* how you can determine how he really feels about you. What he has with you? It won't last."

Suddenly struggling to draw a full breath in the overheated, overcrowded, cologne-and perfume-drenched hallway, Savanna broke Heather's hold on her arm. "Get out of my face." Because she didn't want to get trapped in the bathroom with Gavin's ex, she jumped out of line. But she couldn't bring herself to go back into the main area, where Gavin was performing. She wished she could leave, but she didn't have a car and was an hour from home, so she simply went outside, where she could breathe more freely.

Fortunately, Heather didn't follow her. She seemed to be satisfied to have upset her.

"Damn it," Savanna muttered. It *was* too soon to get involved with someone. For all she knew, Gordon would get out of jail and raise hell—or Heather would have the baby and draw Gavin back via guilt, obligation, the desire to be a good father or all three.

CHAPTER TWENTY-SIX

When Savanna didn't return to her seat, Gavin grew worried about her. He took a break earlier than usual in his set so he could look for her and finally found her sitting on a bench out front. "What are you doing *here?*" he asked.

She glanced up. "Aren't you supposed to be singing?"

"I'm on break." He sat down next to her. "Don't you like the show?"

She sent him a sideways glance. "I did until a few minutes ago."

"What does that mean?" He looked truly confused.

"Why didn't you tell me?"

His stomach muscles tightened at the accusation and hurt in her voice. "About..."

"Your stepmother. Did she *really* abandon you at a park?"

Only a few hours ago, when they were driving to the bar, she'd been completely unaware. "Who told you?"

"You haven't seen Heather tonight?"

He stiffened. "No..."

"She's here. Or maybe she left. I haven't been keeping an eye on the door. I've been trying to think, to decide if I'm racing toward a brick wall by falling in love with you."

Gavin couldn't help looking around in case he could spot his ex-girlfriend. Small clumps of people stood outside to talk or smoke, but she didn't seem to be among them. That she'd shown up at his gig and upset Savanna made him angry, and yet he wasn't all that surprised. He was more surprised that he hadn't heard from her the past several days. He'd texted her on Wednesday to see how she was feeling and to tell her he'd be willing to go to her doctor appointments with her, if she needed the company, but she hadn't responded. He suspected she was purposely holding out, hoping he'd stop over. He probably would have, to prove he'd be supportive even if they weren't together, but he'd been loath to walk into an emotional ambush, and he was pretty sure that was what she had waiting for him.

"Savanna, I would've told you eventually," he said. "But I don't discuss my past often. I try not to let what happened impact the present."

"How could a past like that *not* impact the present?" she asked.

"My life is different now. Thanks to Aiyana and Eli and most of my other brothers, I'm whole and happy. I refuse to let what I went through as a child damage my ability to find peace and joy in my existence."

"Is that a decision you—or anyone else—can make?"

"It's more of a process than a decision," he admitted. "But I've been wrestling with my demons for years, and I believe I'm winning the battle."

"Heather told me that you'll go back to her once she has the baby. That you won't be able to do anything else. And the more I get to know you, the more I understand who you are, I could see you making that decision. So... I'm not sure I can come out of this in one piece, no matter how supportive I am of your relationship with the baby."

"I already tried to start over with Heather for the sake of the baby, remember? But it didn't go anywhere, couldn't even get off the ground, because it was too late."

"In what way?" she asked. "The baby isn't even born yet."

He stared at her for several seconds. He'd been asking himself that same question over and over. Why hadn't he been able to fulfill the duty he felt? And he always came back to the same answer. "I'd met you and was already falling in love."

Her lips parted and her eyes widened. "That fast?"

"I think it happened the day I met you and you told me you were going to become a lesbian," he said with a laugh. "So what do you think? We're both going through some crazy shit. But if I hand over my heart, will you be willing to trust me with yours?"

She broke into a slightly begrudging smile. "I guess I've been sitting out here for nothing, because I don't really have any choice."

"You *do* have a choice."

"No, because I'm already in love with you."

The tension and anxiety inside him instantly eased. "I've made the right decision, Savanna. You're a beautiful person, nothing like my stepmother was. That's what will make the difference. If Heather is carrying my baby, we'll both be good to him or her."

"Of course we will," she said.

He loved her earnestness, her transparency, her lack of guile. Those were the things that set her apart from everyone else, he decided, including Heather.

He pulled his phone from his pocket and let her watch as he typed a message. I'm sorry, Heather. I won't be coming back to you. Ever. If the baby's mine, I'll do everything I can to support him or her and to be kind and sensitive to you as my child's mother. But I'm in love with Savanna, and I think you need to know it.

Savanna looked up at him in surprise. "Are you really going to send that?"

He hit the button. "It's done. Now I have to get back and

finish playing. Come in with me and quit worrying. Somehow, we'll beat the odds," he said, and hoped to God he was right as he led her inside.

The blowback from that text to Heather turned out to be pretty severe. Gavin glanced through several hateful replies as soon as he finished performing.

I'm never going to let you see this baby! You have screwed yourself for good!

I'm going to marry Scott, and we're going to move away. You'll have no idea where we went.

I'll never forgive you for this, you selfish bastard!

There were other messages, too, but they didn't make as much sense. He began to suspect she'd been drinking, which was, of course, not good for someone in her condition.

Where are you? he texted back.

Wouldn't you like to know.

He had to make sure she wasn't a danger to herself or anyone else.

Don't do anything you might regret later, he wrote. Whether you try to make things difficult for me or not, I'm sorry if I've hurt you. That was never my intent.

Fuck you, came her response.

He scratched his neck while trying to decide what to do. Did you drive here?

No answer.

Heather? You need to call a cab.

I don't need a cab. I found a club with far better entertainment and will be going home with a handsome lawyer who's just dying to get in my pants.

"What is it?"

Startled by the interruption, Gavin turned to see Savanna coming up behind him. She'd been talking to some of the people who'd been sitting near her table while he packed up. "Nothing, why?"

"You seem upset."

He nearly shoved his phone into his pocket. He didn't want her to have to deal with every little problem that came his way, especially if that problem involved Heather. But he knew she'd eventually ask him if Heather had responded, that he'd have to tell her, so he lifted his phone to let her see for herself. "Heather's freaking out."

She scrolled through the messages before handing his phone back. "What are you going to do?"

"She's an adult. There's nothing I can do." Fearing he'd face the same frustration, only tenfold, once the baby was born, he prayed the child wasn't his. "Let's get out of here."

After they drove in silence for a few minutes, Savanna reached over to touch his arm. "Are you okay?"

"Yeah. We knew it wouldn't be easy."

"She might settle down once she adjusts to the idea that she's not going to get you back."

"It's possible."

She seemed surprised when he didn't turn in the direction they'd come. "Where are we going?"

"To the ocean."

"What for?"

"I thought it might be nice to walk on the beach and talk."

"About Heather? Or Gordon?"

"Neither," he said. "I'd rather you hear about my childhood from me over anyone else."

She rested her head on his shoulder. "I'm ready."

★ ★ ★

When Gavin parked in a small neighborhood somewhere south of Santa Barbara and guided her down a narrow road that ended in a set of wooden stairs leading to the beach, Savanna couldn't help feeling some trepidation about what she was about to learn. Heather had alluded to a past that was far more tragic than Savanna had expected. Savanna hated the idea that Gavin had suffered, but she was encouraged he was willing to trust her enough to tell her what happened. Having that level of intimacy and understanding would be important if they were to build the kind of relationship that could endure what lay ahead.

The wind whipped at their hair, carrying the briny scent of the sea—a scent that took her back to her childhood in Long Beach. She'd missed the coast far more than she'd realized, felt so happy to be in this place, especially while holding Gavin's hand.

They were alone as they ambled along the damp sand at the edge of the surf, listening to the powerful and awe-inspiring roar of the waves rising up and crashing against rocks and land not far away. They had only a full moon to provide light, so they couldn't tell if the dark spots on the beach were rocks, seaweed or crabs—unless the crabs scuttled away to get out from underfoot—but Savanna wasn't uneasy. She felt more calm and confident than she had in a long while. Gavin had told her he was falling in love with her, and she was falling in love with him, too. Maybe their feelings were new and untried, but she believed they'd grow instead of diminish. Despite all the things working against them, whenever she was with him, it felt right.

"Are you sure you're ready to talk about the past?" she asked. "I'd like to understand what you went through, but it doesn't have to be tonight. Tonight's already been rough."

He led her up the beach a bit, where they didn't have to worry about getting hit by the spray, and pulled her down next to him in the soft sand, which still radiated some heat from earlier in the day. "There's not a lot to tell," he said. "My stepmother was the problem, but I blame my father for not stepping in."

Savanna crossed her legs and listened attentively as he told her about his real mother dying when he was two and his stepmother coming into his life at four. He couldn't remember much of what happened when Diana first married his father, but he definitely remembered the details of the day a year later when he came out of the restroom at the public park to find his stepmother gone. He also remembered how terrified he'd been when a policeman took him home, knowing, as Gavin did, that she wouldn't be happy to see him. He said the beating he took a few days later was for "making a mess," but he'd always known it had nothing to do with the toys he'd left on the floor. She'd exploded because she didn't want him there.

Savanna removed her shoes and dug her toes in the sand. "Do you think you'll ever want your father back in your life?"

He hesitated as if that wasn't an easy question to answer. "He's called me a few times," he said at length.

"And? What'd he say?"

"Not much. I hang up as soon as he identifies himself."

"Why do you think he's reaching out?"

Gavin leaned back, resting the bulk of his weight on his hands as he stared off, across the water. "To apologize. At least, that's how he starts the conversation. But he's far too late for that. I'm not interested."

She listened to several more waves wash up on the beach, marked the foaming surf as coming closer to them, which told her the tide was rising. "What about the foster family who took you in? Do you have any contact with them?"

"No."

"Why not?"

"They were so fanatical. We never connected."

"Fanatical in what way?"

"They belonged to this religious cult where just about everything was a sin."

She listened to how difficult he'd found it to fit in with a family who looked at every joy in life as a temptation to be conquered, how, in an attempt to find others he could identify with, he'd eventually fallen in with the wrong crowd at school despite his foster parents' disapproval—or maybe because of it—and started ditching classes and getting into fights. Pretty soon, he was such an embarrassment to his foster family that the money they received to care for him wasn't enough incentive to allow "Satan" a place in their home. So they gave him back to the state, at which point he'd been sent to New Horizons.

"Did your foster family have any other kids?"

"They thought they couldn't have children. Maybe that's why they decided to foster. But then they wound up having biological twin girls, nine years younger than me."

"How'd they turn out?"

"I only lived with them for seven years, so the girls weren't that old when they sent me away. They were indoctrinated young, though. I'm guessing they turned out just like their parents."

"You don't know?"

"I haven't been in touch since I once again became a ward of the state."

Savanna thought it was heartbreaking that none of the people from his early years had tried to stay in contact. "It's amazing that you've turned out to be such a great person. How'd you overcome all of the rejection and grief?"

Not once had she heard him use his background as an excuse the way Gordon had so many times...

"Aiyana," he said simply. "I owe her a lot."

"She was able to heal what was broken inside you."

"The love she offered me did that."

"How could anyone *not* love you?" she asked.

He leaned forward to push the hair out of her face. They'd been so careful not to get physical since that crazy encounter against his truck, had been trying desperately to slow things down so they could be sure they weren't making a mistake. There were too many beleaguered hearts to take into consideration—hers and her kids', Gavin's, even Heather's. But they'd moved beyond hesitancy and fear to a sense of surety and commitment. "You're the one I've been waiting for."

As his lips touched hers, Savanna thought maybe the past few months had all been worth it if they'd been leading to this magical moment. "I'm so glad I found you," she murmured when he lifted his head, and she felt Gavin press her back onto the sand as he slid his hand up under her dress.

The wind rippled through Gavin's open shirt as he drove into Savanna. He'd never felt so wild and free, so *victorious*. He wasn't sure why that particular word would come to mind, but he couldn't think of a better way to describe the exhilaration he was feeling. His soul seemed to be soaring over the beach, the ocean, the whole earth. He didn't have the answers for the myriad problems they'd likely face. He was aware of all the challenges that could come. But he'd answered the biggest question of all, finally understood the fierceness of Eli's love for Cora. Maybe that was the victory. He'd found that same rare, once-in-a-lifetime love, knew who he wanted to share the rest of his life with.

He couldn't make out Savanna's expression. His body blocked the moonlight, casting her face in shadow. But he could feel her beneath him, could hear her breathing escalate as the pleasure built. Demonstrating what they were feeling physically came as a natural conclusion to the evening, but they'd held off touching each other for so long that it also provided a much-needed release.

"You're still on the pill, right?" he muttered as soon as he felt her shudder her climax beneath him. He was free to let go, but he wanted to come inside her and stay inside her for as long as possible.

She responded by tightening her legs around his hips so that he *couldn't* pull out, and that was all it took to throw him over the edge. He groaned as that familiar wave of ecstasy started in his groin and sent a wave of goose bumps throughout his body.

After some time, he dropped beside her. "Any chance you'll reconsider going to Nephi?"

She started righting her clothes, and he did, too. It was unlikely anyone would come strolling down the beach at this hour, but it was a possibility. "What do you mean?" she asked.

"I don't want to do anything to draw Gordon's attention back to you. Why provoke him?"

"Because of Emma, remember?"

"I feel bad for that girl. I do. But she's probably dead, Savanna." He knew that was an entirely practical approach—probably a selfish one, too. But Savanna was the person he most wanted to keep safe. "*You're* what matters to me."

She smoothed the hair from his face. The tie had fallen out while they were making love. "If I don't get something else on him, something more than the police have now, he could get out of jail, Gavin. Going to Utah and getting him to implicate himself is the best way to protect against that."

He rolled onto his back and let his breath go in a long exhale as he stared up at the sky.

"I *have* to do it," she added, and he didn't say anything because he knew it was true.

CHAPTER TWENTY-SEVEN

Savanna was embarrassed when they returned to pick up her kids. It was nearly four-thirty in the morning, and the bar had closed at two. But Aiyana didn't seem to mind having her sleep interrupted at such an ungodly hour. She seemed as pleasant as ever when, wearing a robe, she let them in. "Did you have a nice time?"

"It was wonderful," Savanna said.

"I'm glad." Gavin's mother came off as sincere, and yet there was something about her smile that seemed to suggest she knew Savanna hadn't been referring strictly to the show. Had she spoken with too much enthusiasm? Was her hair mussed despite the number of times she'd combed her fingers through it?

Savanna cleared her throat. "I hope the kids were good for you."

"They were wonderful."

Gavin was busy carrying a sleeping Branson to the truck. Branson had been afraid he'd wet the bed, but Gavin gave her a quick shake of his head to signal that he hadn't. Thank goodness. Savanna had been worried for him, hadn't wanted him to be embarrassed. "Thank you for watching them," she told Aiyana. "I can't tell you how much we appreciate it." She realized she'd spoken as if she and Gavin were a couple and quickly corrected herself. "How much *I* appreciate it."

"It was an excellent opportunity to get to know them better." Aiyana touched her arm. "Maybe you and I can go to lunch one day so that I can get to know you better, too."

"I'd like that."

After Gavin returned from depositing Branson in the truck, he offered his thanks and dropped a kiss on Aiyana's cheek before scooping up Alia.

"Your mother knows what we did on the beach tonight," Savanna said as they were pulling away.

He didn't seem overly concerned, but he did seem curious. "Why do you say that?"

After mumbling a few words, enough to show they were aware they'd been picked up, Branson and Alia had gone back to sleep.

"I don't know..." She pictured the knowing expression on Aiyana's face. "That's the impression she gave me."

"Does it upset you that she might think we've been intimate?"

"Considering the situation with Heather, it makes me self-conscious."

"She didn't seem upset..."

"No. I'd say she was amused. That's the strange thing."

He started to laugh. "Then I was right."

"About..."

"She never liked Heather."

Savanna loosened the chest restrainer on her seat belt so that it wouldn't choke her. "Why not?"

"She's never admitted it, so I don't know."

Savanna frowned as they rolled under the arch at the entrance to the ranch. "What if she doesn't like *me*? She means so much to you."

"We have plenty of things to worry about, but that isn't one of them. I can tell that she likes you already."

"She seems to *really* like Cora," she mused.

"She does. And for good reason. I'll have to tell you that story sometime." He reached over to take her hand. "But not tonight. Tonight has been eventful enough. For now, let's just take my mother's behavior as a good sign."

The following morning, Aiyana felt like she was walking on air as she made herself some breakfast and sat down to call Eli. "Hey, I know you hear from me enough during the week," she said as she stirred a splash of cream into her coffee. "So I try not to bother you too much on the weekend. But I wanted to tell you something."

"Cora and I don't mind hearing from you whenever. You know that. But what's going on?"

The bougainvillea blooming on the trellis beyond the window caught her eye. She stared out at it while she talked. "I think you were right about Savanna."

"In what way?"

"She might be the one thing that could save Gavin from making a drastic mistake."

"You mean marrying a woman he doesn't love."

She set her spoon on her saucer. "Exactly."

"Why do you say that? Has something changed? Is he seeing her?"

"He must be. Last night, I babysat so that he could take her to his performance in Santa Barbara."

"How nice of you."

"I enjoyed it. But this is the thing—they got back *very* late, long after the bar had to have closed, so I'm guessing they made good use of the time."

Eli chuckled. "Another good sign."

She added sugar to her coffee. "So I'm relieved on *two* counts."

"You were afraid he wouldn't be happy with Heather. I know that was number one. What's the other thing?"

"I thought I might be the type of jealous mother where no woman is good enough."

"I remember. But you're in the clear?"

She considered how sweet, calm and grateful Savanna was. "Completely. I'm excited about this girl."

"You don't know her all that well..."

"*I* don't, but *Gavin's* happier when she's around. That's all I needed, the sense that he's following his heart."

"There's still the situation with Heather. If she's carrying Gavin's baby, you're going to want to be a big part of the child's life, and having him get with Savanna won't make that any easier."

"I'll do everything I can to love and support any child he has—except encourage him to marry a woman he doesn't love. He and Heather tried to make it work several times. To me, that's enough."

"I agree with you. That's why I wanted to put him and Savanna together to see what would happen. But don't get your hopes up too high. There's no guarantee he'll wind up with her long-term."

"I'm not so sure about that." She smiled before taking a sip of her coffee. "I feel like this is the one."

"What makes you say that?"

There was a satisfying click as she set her cup on its saucer. "There's just something different about the way he looks at her."

"If he marries Savanna *and* Heather has his child, you could get three grandchildren almost at once."

Aiyana lifted her cup again. She could think of worse things. "I'll take as many grandkids as I can get."

Gavin spent the weekend with Savanna, working on her house. The dry rot was more extensive than he'd first realized, but he enjoyed tearing off the old, ruined boards and replacing them. Savanna was always around to offer something to eat, put on some music or hand him a hammer, and the kids loved to help. Especially Branson. He followed Gavin almost everywhere. Even if Gavin climbed a ladder, Branson would stand at the base for however long, playing with the tools in Gavin's toolbox. He seemed so happy that it took Gavin by surprise when, finished affixing a new piece of trim to an exterior window, he happened to look down and saw Branson staring off toward the barn with a melancholy expression on his face.

"Somethin' wrong?" Gavin asked.

Once Branson realized Gavin was paying attention, his expression cleared. "No."

Gavin tossed his hammer into his toolbox. "You looked sad there for a minute."

Branson shaded his eyes as he looked up. "Do you know my dad?"

Gavin glanced around to see if Savanna was nearby. If Branson was going to talk about Gordon, he preferred Savanna guide the conversation, but she'd already taken Alia in the house to start dinner. "No, I've never met him. Why?"

"He doesn't like tattoos."

"He's mentioned that?"

"Yeah."

"He must not have any, then."

"He doesn't. He doesn't like boys to have long hair, either."

"Did he tell you why?"

"He said boys who want to look like girls are stupid."

"What do *you* think?"

"I don't think you can tell if they're stupid just from their hair."

Gavin laughed. "I'd have to agree with you there. Hair is a personal preference, right? People should be able to wear their hair however they want. As far as I'm concerned, tattoos are the same. They might tell you a little about what someone likes, but they don't tell you whether they're smart or dumb—or good or bad, for that matter."

"Yeah. I think that, too," he said. "I'm going to get a tattoo when I turn eighteen."

"Of what?"

"Maybe it'll be a picture of Spider-Man," he said. "And if my dad doesn't like it, I don't care. I don't like what he's done, either."

Gavin crouched down so they could be on the same level. "I know what's happened to you has been rough, bud. I had some bad stuff happen to me, too, when I was close to your age."

"You did?"

"Yeah. Have you ever heard the story *Hansel and Gretel?*"

He nodded solemnly.

"I had a mean stepmother like that one."

"Did she send you into the forest?"

"No. She left me at the park and drove away."

"And she didn't come back?"

"No."

His eyes widened. "Where did you sleep?"

"The police came and took me home, but she didn't want me, so they took me away again."

Branson seemed stunned. "To *jail?*"

"To an orphanage. That's where kids go when they don't have parents, right?"

"What happened to your dad?"

"He was afraid she'd leave him, so he did nothing."

"He didn't come get you?"

"No. After a while, I went to live with a foster family. Do you know what a foster family is?"

He shook his head.

"It's a family that lets you live with them for a while."

"How long?"

"I was there seven years, until I turned fourteen."

"Were they nice?"

"Definitely not. They didn't like anything about me, didn't want me around, either."

The way Branson's eyebrows knitted together revealed his concern. "So what did you do?"

"Eventually, I was sent to New Horizons, the school where I work. Did you know it's for boys who are having trouble? That the students at New Horizons actually live there?"

"No. Did you like it?"

Gavin grinned. "I did. Very much. I still do, even though I'm grown now and don't have to live there anymore. That's where I met the mom I have now, and you know how great she is."

"She told me you're her son."

"In all the ways that matter, I am, right?"

He took a few minutes to consider that. "I guess," he said at length. "But do you ever see your dad?"

"I don't. I probably could. But I'd rather not. I've decided I'm happier without him being in my life."

"You don't want to see him?"

"No. He isn't a man I can admire. You may feel yours has some good traits, and that's okay. When you get older, you can go visit him, if you like. Don't feel like anyone is trying to take that away from you. You have to listen to what your heart is telling you and follow that." Gavin pressed his fingers against the boy's chest to emphasize his point. "Your heart is your compass in life. I just want you to know that things have gotten much better for me since all of that happened. And they will get better for you, too." Figuring that was about as deep as he should get with an eight-year-old, Gavin turned to repack his toolbox and was nearly bowled over when Branson suddenly embraced him.

Gavin chuckled as he regained his balance and hugged Savanna's son in return. "What's this for?"

"I'm going to be just like you when I grow up," he mumbled into Gavin's shirt.

Gavin was still rubbing the boy's back when Savanna came around the corner. She'd been calling them for dinner, but when she saw what was taking place, she stopped and waited at the corner of the house. "You're going to be just fine," Gavin told Branson, and a second later, when Branson raced off to go in for dinner, Gavin told Savanna the same thing. "He's going to be just fine."

The day Savanna was scheduled to go to Utah, she was already awake when the alarm went off on Gavin's phone. So the kids wouldn't have any clue that he'd started staying over, he'd been getting up and going home in the very early morning, and, so far, it'd worked. They figured it would work until Branson wet the bed and got up in the middle of the night, but fortunately, that hadn't happened in the past few days. The more Gavin was around, the better Branson seemed to do. Gavin seemed to have a calming, stabilizing influence on all of them.

He was good for a lot of other things, too. The house was looking so much better. They had a running joke between them that she'd probably dump him once all the repairs were done, but she couldn't imagine her future without him. That was why she'd had so much trouble sleeping, knowing that the day of reckoning—the day of her visit to Nephi—had arrived.

"Are you going home?" Savanna whispered.

When he realized she was awake, he paused. "Did my alarm disturb you?"

"No." She'd been tossing and turning all night. She was surprised she hadn't disturbed *him.*

"You're nervous?"

"Yeah."

"I don't blame you. Should I buy a plane ticket and go with you?"

They'd already agreed that he'd take some time off work to drive her to LA. She'd tried to talk him out of it, said she could leave her car at the airport so she'd also have a way to get home, but he was insisting on taking her *and* picking her up. "Going all the way to Utah won't be necessary," she said. "I have to go to the jail alone, and that's the hard part. As crowded as flights are these days, you probably wouldn't even be able to get on the same plane. I'd rather you be here to check in on Branson and Alia, anyway. I think they'll feel more comfortable knowing you're close by."

He rolled her beneath him, propping himself up with his elbows. "I'm happy to hang out with them all I can, but I hate sending you off alone."

"I'll get through it." She smiled as though it wasn't that big of a deal, but she hadn't seen Gordon for two months. Her opinion of him had changed radically in that period. She'd accepted that he was a serial rapist, maybe even a murderer. And since he'd been arrested, she'd served him with divorce papers, refused to pay for his defense, taken the kids out of school and moved to California. She couldn't imagine he was feeling good toward her, couldn't help fearing how the conversation would go. He could get overly emotional, maybe even ugly; he had a temper like his mother's. Even if that didn't happen, the whole thing could be a waste of time and effort. Chances were better the charges would be dropped than she'd be able to garner some shred of evidence to support the theory that he was the one who kidnapped, and likely killed, Emma Ventnor.

They heard a noise in the hall and froze. One of the kids was up. Savanna assumed she'd hear Branson at her door. Gavin obviously anticipated the same thing, because he went into her bathroom, where he wouldn't be seen, just in case. But they heard a toilet flush and then, after a few seconds, a few creaks and house noises and not much else.

Gavin walked back into the room. "I think he went to bed."

"That he went to the bathroom is a good sign."

"Have you alerted the babysitter that he might need help in the night?"

"I have. She said it won't be a problem. And I doubt it will be. He's only had one accident in the past ten days."

"Still, with you gone... Would you rather I stay over than her?"

"I would. But things were different between us when I let Sullivan make the arrangements. At this point, I say we leave everything as it is and simply get through the next two days as best we can."

"Okay. Just don't worry. Everything's going to work out."

She was trying to be optimistic, but she knew how slim the chances really were. Allison March had directed Savanna to tell Gordon that the police had tire track evidence. They didn't. But she was supposed to say that although what they initially found at the crime scene a year ago had been too faint, they'd figured out a way to do some computer enhancements and would soon be able to check that tread against the tires on the van.

March wanted to see what kind of reaction that would bring. So did Savanna. She just didn't feel as if that was much to go in there with.

"He won't give himself away," she'd insisted when Detective March had called to do some roleplaying with her before bed last night. "He won't suddenly admit that he had something to do with Emma Ventnor's disappearance."

"He doesn't have to," March insisted. "Just get him to give you some kind of story, explain what he did that day, why it couldn't be him. The more details he offers, the better. If those details differ from the story he's already given us, that's something right there. We'll do our fact checking, hopefully catch him in a few lies that we can probe further. He might accidentally say something he'd rather not. I've had perpetrators subconsciously lead me right where they didn't want me to go, especially if they're scared. I'm hoping that's what'll happen here."

Savanna hoped the same thing. But if Gordon could deny DNA evidence, like he did back when they thought finding Theresa Spinnaker's blood in his van would really mean something, she doubted a bluff about tire track impressions would have the power to rattle him.

CHAPTER TWENTY-EIGHT

Savanna had never been inside a jail. She'd seen the sheriff's office where the jail was located on occasion, but not often. Although it was only eight minutes from the heart of Nephi, she rarely had reason to drive that far south. There was a Mormon church out that way and some gravel pits, but everything of any importance, at least to her, lay to the north, in the Provo/Orem or Salt Lake area. After Gordon was arrested, she almost could've ignored the fact that he was so close, except for the shock and all the publicity, of course.

Her palms were sweating on the steering wheel as she pulled into the parking lot. Somehow, Detective Sullivan had made a mistake thinking that visiting hours were in the morning. As it turned out, she couldn't see Gordon until seven in the evening, so they'd had to make several adjustments, like renting her motel room for another night, having the caregiver for her children stay over again and asking Gavin to pick her up on Thursday instead of Wednesday.

Savanna wasn't sure how Sullivan had blown it like that. He said *he* wasn't sure, either, except he didn't have to go to the jail during visiting hours and had just briefly glanced at the website. But arriving so early had given her far too much time to think. Because she hadn't wanted to be seen, hadn't wanted to bump into anyone she knew and be recognized, she'd stayed inside, waiting and worrying while the TV played program after program.

Now she was jittery because she'd been too nervous to go out and eat but had gone too long without food. The last thing she'd had was the free breakfast offered by the motel. She'd ducked into the dining area just before mealtime ended and grabbed a waffle, some yogurt and an apple, which she'd carried back to her room.

"This will only last fifteen minutes," she promised herself.

As she turned off her engine, she rehearsed, once again, everything Detective Sullivan had told her in their little coaching session last night. *Just get him talking. Get him to commit to a sequence of events. Express some doubt. Provoke him into trying to reassure or convince you. With any luck, he'll offer some kind of proof that he could not have been involved.*

They were hoping he'd trip himself up, of course. That they would be able to disprove whatever he said and catch him in his own words. But if it went the other way, and he *could* prove he wasn't responsible in the Emma Ventnor case, where would that leave Savanna? Sullivan hadn't been able to find any new evidence on the three rapes. Barring a miracle, the DA would drop the charges, and soon. They'd been stalling, hoping her visit might make all the difference. If it didn't, Gordon would go free.

She shuddered at the thought. *God help me.*

Her phone signaled an incoming text as she got out. You've got this.

Gavin. She'd spoken to him several times since she'd left. He always tried to reassure her.

There now. Going in. Wish me luck. She'd spent part of the time waiting in the motel room reading up on what to expect when visiting an inmate, but the Juab County Jail was such a small facility—capable of housing only fifty or so inmates—that she didn't have to put her purse and other personal belongings in a locker, go through a metal detector or suffer an invasive pat-down. She merely waited in line behind ten other people, filled out a visitation form, provided her ID and allowed her purse to be searched. After that, she was admitted into a non-secure area to wait her turn.

Problem was, the jail had only two visitation rooms, and each visitation could last as long as twenty minutes. *Just what I need—another hour and forty minutes to wait...*

She stared up at a television mounted on the wall. There was no sound, just subtitles, but it was all she had to help pass the time. She didn't care to talk to the others who were waiting to get in. She was far too nervous for small talk.

Fortunately, some of those who went ahead of her didn't take up all of their allotted time. It was only an hour before she was taken back to a small cubicle where she'd be allowed to speak with Gordon, when he arrived, via telephone while separated by a piece of Plexiglas.

Her heart began to pound as she sat down. She could feel each distinct thump in her throat. Not only was she frightened by what he'd done—what she now saw him to be—she was terrified of what he might do when he was released.

Savanna tried to even out her breathing, to settle down. She needed to be able to think straight. But the longer she waited, the more anxious she became. Where was he?

For a few seconds, she thought he might be refusing her visit. The way they'd gotten along, on the whole, over the past several months, even before he'd been arrested, she could understand why he might. But then she saw him, wearing the standard orange jumpsuit issued to all county inmates.

He looked like he'd lost some weight. He'd definitely lost a lot of color. Or maybe it was the lights that hummed overhead that made him look so washed-out. They seemed to cast every-thing in a bluish tint.

He didn't smile when their eyes met. He stared at her for sev-eral seconds. Then he sat down and picked up the phone.

Savanna claimed the handset on her side of the glass. "You don't seem happy to see me," she said.

"You haven't been supportive since I've been in here."

"I put some money on your commissary account. That's not supportive?"

"I've been in jail for two months, Savanna. What else have you done, except make everything worse?"

She gripped the phone tighter. After the letters she'd sent, she'd thought he might be more conciliatory, more hopeful of putting their marriage back together. Now she knew that was not the case, she had to prepare herself for a combative twenty minutes. That changed things, gave her even less leverage. "The past two months have been pretty crummy for me, too."

"Until you fell into the sweet, loving arms of *Gavin Turner*, right?"

Savanna froze. "That was nothing," she lied.

"You fucked him. I wouldn't call that nothing."

She loved Gavin, which was far more significant. But even if she were willing to divulge that, Gordon wouldn't understand because he had no idea what true love meant, didn't seem to possess the capacity for love.

She couldn't let on, regardless. There was too much riding on this meeting. "A onetime thing."

He leaned toward the glass. "Are you sure? My mother said you live on the same street. It's just the two of you out in the middle of nowhere. That provides a hell of a lot of opportunity."

When she'd mentioned Gavin, Savanna had been saying what-ever she could to get a rise out of Gordon, as she'd been in-structed to do. But it had been a mistake brought on by nerves and emotion to mention his name, and that mistake had been compounded when her mother-in-law wrecked into Gavin's truck, thus becoming familiar not only with his first name but his last and where he lived. "Are we really going to do this?" she asked. "Make this about how *I've* wronged *you?*"

"What have I ever done?" he said, but then he smiled as if he found that to be quite the clever joke.

His reaction was so out of sync with what the situation called for that Savanna could only gape at him. He wasn't distraught that he'd harmed innocent people, or upset by what he'd been through or even relieved that he'd be getting out. He considered this a game, of sorts, was not only proud of what he'd done but that he was going to get away with it. He thought he'd outsmarted everyone. That the game was almost over.

It was her job to keep it in play, or he *would* get away with everything.

She curled the fingernails of her free hand into her palm. "So are you going to sign the divorce papers?"

"Aha! Now we get to the *real* reason you've finally shown up."

That wasn't the reason, but she could understand why he'd find it much more believable than the reconciliation she'd tried to establish in those letters. "You thought I'd simply wait until you got around to it?"

"What's the rush?"

"I'd rather not have a rapist in my life. That's the rush."

He started laughing. "You deserve to be raped yourself, or worse."

"You think it's funny to talk like that?"

"It's funny to imagine it. It's also funny to think you believed a few letters making nice and a hundred dollars on my commissary account were going to make me forget everything else."

"What reason do you have to hang on to me, Gordon? You obviously don't love me."

She thought he'd at least mention the kids, but he didn't. "It's not about love. It's about money."

"We were barely able to pay our bills every month. The only money I have is what's left of my inheritance."

"So? I deserve a big chunk of that."

"How do you figure?" she asked.

"For years I made more than you did, which means I contributed more."

"That isn't true! I took care of the house and kids. You never lifted a finger to help. What kind of a dollar amount should we attach to all the child-rearing, cooking and cleaning I did while you were out attacking women?"

"I'm not attaching *any* dollar amount to it, and neither will the judge."

She sat back and folded her arms. "I see."

"You see what?"

"You still think you're getting out."

At last, that smug expression slid from his face. "I *am* getting out. You're kidding yourself if you don't believe it. My attorney told me yesterday that the DA has no evidence left, none that will result in a conviction. He'd be a fool to proceed. I'm surprised he hasn't already dropped the charges."

Savanna was the reason the DA hadn't acted yet, and she knew it. "They might not have the evidence they need on the three rapes, but they're getting what they need on Emma Ventnor."

He gave her a speculative look. "What are you talking about?"

"They have tire impression evidence."

"No, they don't. If they had that, I'd have heard about it by now. Emma went missing a year ago."

"And they found a tire track on the side of the road, but it was too faint. The pictures they took didn't show the ridge detail they needed. But some guy has figured out how to do enhancements on the computer and build a 3-D model from there. They're having him help, will be testing the enhanced impression against the tires on your van in a few weeks."

His eyes narrowed. "Good for them. Won't change anything. I had nothing to do with the Emma Ventnor case."

"You weren't at work when she went missing."

"I was getting a bite to eat."

"Where?"

That cocky smile reappeared. "Hell if I know. *All* the details from that day are fuzzy."

"What happened, Gordon? Was she screaming, fighting? You couldn't subdue her even with your super athletic and tricky wrestling holds? You had to kill her?"

She was taunting him, knew how quickly he could get incensed from gibes of that sort.

"I wouldn't make fun of those holds, if I were you," he gritted out. "I could choke you out in a matter of seconds."

"Is that what you did to her? Choked her out? Why did you pick her as one of your victims? Did you see her coming out of the school and start to follow her? Spot her in traffic and decide to wreck into her car to get her to pull over?"

"You're an idiot," he said. "If I wrecked into her car, there would've been damage on my van, right? Did you ever see any damage?"

The warning in his voice let her know she was going too far—that she was making an enemy for life. Gordon wasn't the forgiving sort. But Savanna didn't dare back off. This was the moment. She had to pull out all the stops, do everything she could. "Bumpers don't always show damage, Gordon. That van was like a tank."

"You don't know what you're talking about," he said, and stood.

Savanna's nails bit deeper into her palm. "Where are you going?"

"Back to my cell. I'd rather be sitting there, dreaming of taking off your clothes and—" he ran a hand over his neck "—

doing what I like to do in bed than see you sitting here, doing everything you can to help the police."

He meant he'd rather be in his cell, dreaming of choking her. She understood the allusion, but he could easily claim he meant something else, so that did nothing to help the case against him. He hadn't stated it such that the recording would shock or appall a jury. Even that brief touch to the neck, so meaningful a gesture to her, could be construed as though he just happened to be touching his neck.

Savanna was still hanging on to the phone when he hung up on his side and walked away.

Shit. She'd blown it, gotten nothing.

Gavin had been waiting to hear from Savanna for nearly four hours. He'd texted her and tried to call. He'd even checked in with Detectives March and Sullivan. They hadn't heard anything, either. Sullivan said that not long after visiting hours, he'd driven by and didn't see her car in the lot. He indicated it wasn't at the motel, either.

Gavin didn't hear back from Savanna until ten-thirty, which was eleven-thirty Utah time. *"Are you okay?"* he asked. Branson and Alia were in bed and the babysitter was watching TV, so he'd returned to his house for the night. He'd been sitting in his living room, watching the basketball playoff game he'd recorded earlier, pausing every so often to check his phone and try to reach her.

"I think so."

She didn't sound okay. She sounded rattled, upset. "Are you sure?"

"I'm fine," she insisted.

He'd been lying down. Sitting up, he muted the television. "What happened? Why didn't you call me right away?"

"I had my phone turned off."

"While you were doing what?"

"Nothing. Driving."

"*Where?*"

"Aimlessly."

He let his breath go in a sigh. "It must not have gone well."

"It didn't," she admitted, and he listened without comment as she repeated the conversation she'd had with Gordon.

"Damn," he said when she was done.

"That's putting it mildly."

"So where are you now?" he asked.

"Driving aimlessly soon turned into a dedicated effort to reach Salt Lake as soon as possible. I couldn't bear to stay another night in Nephi. I was going to catch the first flight out, come home right away instead of waiting until morning."

"But..."

"But by the time I got here, it was too late. The last flight left at ten."

"Does that mean you're going to stay over in Salt Lake and catch your scheduled flight in the morning?"

"No. I need to get something later."

He'd been so sure she'd say yes that he'd turned the game back on. "Wait, no?" He silenced the TV again. "Why would you need a *later* flight? I thought you were in a hurry to get out of there."

"I was. I am. But I can't face that Gordon will be getting out, know he'll make our lives a living hell. I have to do something."

"Like what?"

"He said if he wrecked into Emma Ventnor's car there'd be damage on the van, right?"

"March told us it was a small enough dent that there might not be. That sort of thing happens all the time. That's why she felt safe going with the fake tire track evidence."

"I know, but the tire impression stuff didn't seem to worry him, either."

"So maybe he's innocent."

"I don't think so."

"You seem more certain now than you've been recently."

"I vacillate. But when I saw him, I got the creepiest feeling. He *did* rape those women. It was almost as if he wanted me to know it—that he didn't care enough to hide it from me anymore, since he felt he was no longer in danger of going to prison, and he knows I'm not interested in patching up our marriage. Someone who's been wrongly accused wouldn't act that way."

"That concern goes well beyond us."

"I know. But while I've been sitting here—"

"Where?"

"In the airport."

"If all the planes to California have left, why are you still there?"

"I've been thinking, trying to figure out what to do."

"There's nothing more you can do."

"There might be. Certain things have occurred to me. When Dorothy came to my house after Gordon was arrested, and I had to call the cops to have them take her away, there was some damage on the front right panel of her car. I didn't think anything of it, because her car is a piece of junk, anyway, and the damage had been there for a while, but now I'm beginning to wonder how long ago that accident occurred."

Gavin scooted forward. "You're thinking Gordon might've been driving *her* car when he kidnapped Emma Ventnor?"

"It's a possibility. He stayed with her every once in a while. Stands to reason if his van broke down—and it did give him some trouble last year, although I can't recall the exact dates— he might have borrowed her car for the day."

"Maybe the police need to take a look at it, see if they can find any paint transfer that might prove it was the one that collided with Emma's."

"Except she wrecked into you when she came out here, remember?"

He fell back. "That's right. Damn it. We can't catch a break."

"What if she did that on purpose, Gavin?"

"Hit my truck?"

"Yeah. It wasn't until I mentioned Emma Ventnor that she started to act strange, remember? Before that, she was determined to start a fight with me. After, she backed away and took off. I'm wondering if she was remembering Gordon coming home a year earlier with some story about how he accidentally hit something with her car."

"And by crashing it into my truck, she was able to report it and have it repaired."

"Maybe she hasn't had it repaired. It's very possible she hasn't had the money to pay the deductible. But hitting you helps, right? Now she has a legitimate excuse for the damage, should anyone ask, and chances are no one will be able to say exactly what that panel looked like before."

"That gives me chills."

"Me, too. I have to go over there, see if it's fixed. If it's not, I'll take some pictures and send them to Sullivan and March, in case there is *something* remaining from Emma's car. I asked Sullivan to search Dorothy's house once already, told him that Gordon stayed there on occasion and could easily have hidden trophies or other evidence in her garage or basement, and he said he couldn't get a judge to sign off on the warrant. Maybe this will change things."

"Whoa, wait. Don't go over there alone."

"Dorothy's twenty-two years older than I am."

Gavin had heard enough about Gordon's mother to believe she was also a little unstable. "That doesn't mean she isn't dangerous. She could…hit you with something or who knows what."

"I'll only take a peek in her garage. She won't even know I'm there."

"Savanna…"

"I have to do *something*, Gavin. What we tried didn't work.

That means, in a very short time, a very dangerous man will be dumped back into society. Gordon's release feels so imminent that I'm more afraid of seeing that happen than I am of facing down Dorothy."

Gavin hated the thought of her being up there on her own. "I should've come with you."

"I've got this. Don't worry. Her garage isn't even attached to the house. I'll slip in tonight while she's sleeping, use the flashlight on my phone to check the car, take all the pics I might need and get out."

"Then why can't you catch your flight in the morning?"

There was a slight pause before she said, "Oh, that."

Gavin felt a fresh wave of concern. "Yes, that. You're making me nervous. What do you have planned?"

"I'm also going to take a look through the house once she leaves for work. She freaked out when I brought up Emma Ventnor's name. I have to figure out why."

CHAPTER TWENTY-NINE

It was nearly two in the morning when Savanna walked down the alley that led to the detached garage of Dorothy's rental house. She wore black jeans, a black top and a black beanie she'd bought at a twenty-four-hour Walmart. The goal was to blend in, go unnoticed, but no one else was out. The neighborhood remained quiet and dark, with only a sliver of moon grinning above the treetops.

Off in the distance, a dog barked. Savanna wasn't sure what she'd do if she happened to set off a dog who was much closer...

There was nothing she could do, she decided, except take the pictures and get out before Dorothy and the neighbors reacted to the noise.

Fortunately, she didn't encounter a dog. She reached the small one-car garage without incident, and she didn't have any trouble getting into it, as she'd feared she might. Dorothy hadn't even bothered to lower the door. Or maybe it was broken. The house and garage Dorothy rented were built in the 1930s, and nothing under her stewardship was in particularly good shape. That was one of the things Gordon had always complained about. He'd often called his mother a slob and recounted stomach-turning incidents of foraging among pots and pans filled with food that'd been left out for days in order to get enough to eat as a child.

Savanna wasn't looking forward to searching the house, partially for that reason. But she was going to do what she could while she was here. Gordon's taunting smile had made a lasting impression. She thought of that, pictured it, whenever fear threatened to stop her. She *had* to make sure he didn't get away with what he'd done. He believed she was powerless, had mistaken her inherent kindness for weakness. But she'd show him she had far more grit and determination than he'd ever given her credit for.

At least, she hoped she'd be able to show him that. It would depend on what she found here tonight, and tomorrow when she returned to look through Dorothy's house.

Once she stepped inside the garage, Savanna used the flashlight on her phone to walk around and inspect Dorothy's Toyota Celica. Sure enough, evidence of the accident with Gavin's truck was still there. Dorothy or someone else had pulled off the front bumper—or it had fallen off—but the damage was mostly to the right front panel, where Savanna would expect to see it if that same car had been used to hit Emma Ventnor's car.

"Did you hit Gavin's truck on purpose, Dorothy?" Savanna whispered. "And, if you did, did you do enough to camouflage that earlier accident?"

Savanna prayed she hadn't. This could be the only hope of justice for Meredith Caine, Theresa Spinnaker, Jeannie West, Emma Ventnor and who could say how many others.

Savanna's heart raced as she took several pictures. She was tempted to send them to Sullivan right away. But she wasn't sure they'd make a difference, and she held off in case he tried to stop her. She didn't want him to know what she was doing until she'd also searched the house.

Since Gordon could have stuck something above the rafters or in one of the old, warped cupboards along the right side, she decided to stay and search the garage instead of waiting until tomorrow for that, too. She knew she might not have a better opportunity. The opening faced the neighbor's backyard, and that neighbor could have kids or animals who would be out during the day. The longer she stayed, the more she ran the risk that the neighbor might get up to go to the bathroom and see her light bouncing around. To avoid that, she checked the garage door situation, found there was no electric opener attached and she could close it manually.

Apparently, it wasn't broken. Dorothy had just been too lazy or unconcerned to lower it the last time she'd driven her car, probably because she didn't have anything to protect. There were no bikes or tools in her garage or anything like that. Even her car wasn't worth much.

Once Savanna had the privacy to use her flashlight without fear that it might be spotted, she pulled on the gloves she'd also purchased at Walmart and looked through the car.

She found nothing unusual. Cigarette butts and smashed cigarette cartons, empty coffee cups, food wrappers. There was a letter from Gordon on the floorboards of the passenger seat that Savanna took a few minutes to read, but it didn't give away anything important. Gordon would know better than that, since all prison mail was monitored. He was merely telling his mother that he needed more money, that his cellmate was a "dick," that his defense was "shit" and would never work, that Savanna would come around eventually, to keep working on her (Savanna had to roll her eyes at that) and not to talk to the police at all or they'd take something she said and "make it into something it wasn't."

When she finished the letter, Savanna sat back in the bucket seat and tried to think. She had pictures of the accident, but what if they didn't show anything? What if the collision with Gavin had indeed obliterated the evidence of what had come before? She needed to find something that connected him to one of the victims he couldn't explain away, like his bloody clothes. Where would he have hidden them?

Not in the garage, she decided. If Dorothy was so complacent that she didn't close the door, anyone could gain access to the things in here. Her house would be a safer bet. But it was so small. Savanna couldn't imagine Gordon being stupid enough to hide anything under his bed or anywhere else his mother might easily run across it...

The basement was a strong possibility, though. Basically a dank, dark hole in the ground, lit by a single bulb dangling from the ceiling, it had to be filled with all kinds of spiders, but Savanna knew Dorothy kept some storage down there—Christmas decorations and such—because she'd seen it, had helped carry up boxes on occasion. The basement wasn't a pleasant place to go, however, so other than grabbing something from that small pile, *if* she decided to decorate, Dorothy wouldn't stay down there long. Savanna couldn't imagine she'd ever bother to check the creepy perimeter, especially in one particular section, an area maybe eight feet by eight feet, where there wasn't even room to stand up all the way...

If Gordon had hidden anything at Dorothy's, he'd hide it there, Savanna decided. He'd feel it was safe in such a spot. He'd also have fairly easy access to it, which could be important to him if it was a trophy or something else he prized due to the memories attached.

That sounded plausible, but she could be looking for something that didn't even exist. Maybe he didn't take trophies. And maybe he'd washed his bloody clothes while his mother was at work and worn them again, or burned them in her fireplace.

Savanna closed her eyes. She was an amateur, and she was searching for a needle in a haystack. Was she being foolhardy for even trying?

Her phone vibrated in her hand.

She turned it over to see that Gavin had texted her. You're scaring the shit out of me. Are you out yet? How'd it go?

She sent him the pictures. Then she searched the rest of the garage. It was filled with nothing but junk, stacks of old newspapers and magazines and worthless items Dorothy had collected from yard sales.

I'm out now. She sent that text to Gavin as she hurried down the alley and around the next block to where she'd left her rental car.

Did you find anything?

Nothing. Just the damage on her car. She must not have had the money for the deductible, like I said.

That may be our saving grace.

We can hope.

Are you really going back in the morning?

She got into her rental car and locked the door. I know it seems hopeless. But I have to try.

How will you know when she's gone?

I'll drive down the alley and look for her Celica. She leaves the garage door open, so it's easy to tell when she's home.

You need to get some sleep, Savanna. I know you've been too anxious to get much rest lately.

It'll be another short night, she wrote. But I can't let Gordon get away with what he's done, not without a fight. I owe it to his victims. I owe it to my children. And I owe it to myself.

Please be careful.

She returned to the hotel she'd rented before going to Walmart. It was right next to the airport, so it wasn't a far drive from downtown Salt Lake, where Dorothy lived. Savanna was exhausted, physically and emotionally, and yet she couldn't seem to unwind.

She took a hot bath before climbing into bed, where she finally drifted off. But then she dreamed of getting trapped in Dorothy's basement, of being unable to breathe, of Gordon coming down holding that knife the police found in his duffel bag, of waking up to find that she was covered in blood.

When she finally gasped awake, she interrupted a nightmare where spiders were crawling all over her bruised and battered body.

Gavin was at work when Detective Sullivan called him.

"What's going on? Have you heard from Savanna?" he asked without preamble.

Gavin had been trying to fix the boiler in one of the dormitories. Dropping the screwdriver he held, he sat up. "She's heading home today, as expected."

"Where'd she go last night?"

"She drove to Salt Lake, couldn't bear to stay in Nephi any longer."

"She could've called me. Or Detective March. We've tried to reach her several times."

"Maybe she thought it was pointless to tell you what you already know. She couldn't get anything out of Gordon. Surely, you've listened to the recordings of her visit by now."

"Of course. Still, we thought she'd check in, follow up."

"She's probably upset. This can't be easy for her. You realize that."

"Of course I realize it. But how hard would it be for her to give one of us a quick call?"

"She's been through a lot. Just leave her alone," he said. "She'll contact you if and when she's ready."

"You two are seeing each other, right?" he asked before Gavin could hang up. "You're romantically involved?"

Gavin didn't have time for this guy's nosiness, couldn't imagine how his relationship with Savanna figured into anything. "What business is that of yours?"

"None," he admitted. "But if Gordon gets out of jail, you might want to keep an eye out," he said, and hung up.

Gavin cursed as he shoved his phone back into his pocket. Savanna had asked him not to tell the detectives what she was up to, so he was keeping his mouth shut.

But he knew he'd never forgive himself if something happened to her as a result...

Although Dorothy was gone, Savanna couldn't be sure Gordon's mother was at her job. Normally, Dorothy worked full-time. Had to in order to survive. But that could've changed. Maybe she'd been fired. Or she'd quit. She'd been far more stable in recent years than ever before, but Savanna supposed anything was possible. She could only hope that wherever Dorothy had gone, she'd stay away long enough for Savanna to get in and out of the house.

It was a hot day for mid-May. Savanna could feel sweat rolling down her back as she approached Dorothy's house from the rear.

Dorothy's car was gone, but three small children were playing in the fenced yard of the neighbor closest to her garage. There was also a pit bull at the house kitty-corner to Dorothy's off the alley. But neither the kids nor the dog paid Savanna any mind. She told herself to walk confidently, as if she belonged in the area and had every right to be doing what she was doing, and that seemed to work. She arrived at the door leading into Dorothy's tiny laundry room without incident.

The door was locked, but Dorothy had always left a key out

for Gordon so he could get in if he ever stopped by when she wasn't there. Savanna had been with Gordon once when he used it. She was relying on that key to get her in, but when she checked under the rock where Dorothy typically kept it, there wasn't anything there.

"Shoot," she murmured, and began to circle the house to see if she couldn't find another way in.

She checked the front door. It was locked, too, but the weather was warm enough that Savanna found several windows open. One was in the bathroom, too small to squeeze through. Another was in the living room, where she could be seen by any car that drove by. The last was in Dorothy's bedroom, which looked out on the neighbor's side yard. Savanna didn't have a lot of cover there, should that neighbor come around the corner doing yard work or whatever, but it was her best option.

Putting on her gloves, so that she wouldn't leave any fingerprints, she tried to remove the screen and couldn't. Finally, in desperation, she took out the pocketknife she'd bought when she got her clothes and other supplies and cut the edges.

She bent the screen back, forced the window up higher and managed to wiggle through the small hole, although she fell on the dresser and knocked off the lamp.

Fortunately, the lamp didn't break. Savanna recovered as quickly as she could and righted everything before beginning a quick and dirty search of every drawer, closet, nook or cranny in Dorothy's house.

Before too long, she realized she was lucky the house was so messy. Thanks to the garbage, discarded clothes and worthless knickknacks that were strewn everywhere, Dorothy would be much less likely to notice that she'd had a visitor—although she would wonder about the cut screen, if she saw it. Savanna wasn't sure what to do about that. She thought she might use the duct tape she'd seen out in the garage to tape it shut on the outside.

With Dorothy's lack of attention to detail, and the messy house in general, she might never notice.

Savanna searched every room before approaching the door leading to the basement. She'd been hoping to find something that would make going down there unnecessary. But other than confirming that Dorothy was indeed one of the filthiest house-keepers she'd ever seen, and that her mother-in-law still had alcohol in her cupboards, Savanna had come up with nothing, other than a few more letters from Gordon. The accusations contained in some of those letters were simply ridiculous. He claimed that Savanna had wasted his money on furniture and clothes and frivolous purchases or they would've had more sav-ings, that it was her idea to take out a second mortgage on the house, that she'd colluded with the police to get him out of her life so she wouldn't have to share her inheritance. Those letters upset her, but no one else would care about them. They cer-tainly wouldn't keep him in jail.

She had to keep looking. And that meant…the basement.

She checked the time on her phone. She'd been at Dorothy's for over an hour already. She'd been working as fast as possible, but leaving everything as she found it took time, and the more time she spent in this house, the more anxious she became. She was dying to get out. If she didn't leave right away, she'd miss her flight. That meant a sizable fee—this time, one she'd have to pick up herself—another reschedule, alerting Gavin and trying to figure out what to do with the kids until she could get back.

Those concerns were almost enough to make her give up. But she knew she'd have to answer—to herself, if no one else—for not doing more while she had the chance.

Think of Emma Ventnor, and Meredith Caine, who felt you should've done more. Well, now you're doing it.

She had to force the door. As old as it was, it'd been repainted so many times it no longer fit the opening properly. But she got it unstuck with a reverberated *wham-am-am-am* and flipped the switch at the top of the stairs.

One bulb couldn't illuminate the darkest reaches of the damp and musty basement, couldn't reach around the corners to reveal what might be shoved or buried there, couldn't ease all of Savanna's misgivings. So she used the flashlight on her phone, too.

Taking a deep breath, she started down.

The stairs creaked beneath her weight and the smell that greeted her turned her stomach. It was far worse than she remembered—bad enough to make her fear she might find more than she'd bargained for. Could Emma Ventnor's *body* be down here? Other killers had buried their victims under their houses. John Wayne Gacy had done that with at least twenty-five people, if she remembered right. She'd seen a documentary on him. She'd also heard a news report years ago about an old lady in Sacramento who buried several of her boarders in her backyard and continued to collect their social security checks.

Savanna felt weak and shaky by the time she reached the bottom. Finding a body would be a *good* thing, she told herself. That would *prove* Gordon was responsible for Emma's death. But she didn't want to uncover something that gruesome, still wanted to believe that Emma was alive.

Stopping in the middle of the basement, she turned in a tight circle, training her light on everything around her. She'd already found Dorothy's storage pile. It was in disarray, like all of Dorothy's things. Savanna wasn't going to waste her time going through that now. She feared she'd wasted too much time trying to find something upstairs.

When nothing struck her as odd or out of place, she examined the floor instead of the walls, thinking she might find evidence of the dirt having been disturbed. She saw nothing that would lead her to believe a body or anything else had been buried down here—except that sickening stench. She wished she could tell Sullivan about it, that it would get him out here with a whole team of forensics specialists. On TV, she'd seen police search the ground with some type of penetrating radar, but would reporting the smell be enough?

She had only one chance. She had to get more while she was here.

"Emma, are you down here?" Thinking of the girl as being alive and needing her help made it possible for her to swallow her revulsion and press on, into that small area where she had to stoop over because the ceiling was so low.

There the stench was far worse. She'd never smelled a decomposing body, so she couldn't be certain, but this smell had to be similar. Was it Emma?

Her hand shook as she used her flashlight to go over the ground inch by inch. She should've brought a bigger flashlight, but she hadn't wanted to carry a lot of things. She'd felt she might need to be nimble, and she'd proved that when she'd had to climb through the window. But in this small room, she couldn't see anything that fell outside the six-inch diameter of her little flashlight, and that terrified her. A spider could drop on her at any moment, or she could accidentally step on a human hand jutting out of the ground—

Quit freaking yourself out, she admonished. *There are policemen and forensics people who have to do this all the time.* But the second her light hit the rotting carcass she'd smelled, she screamed and bumped her head as she jumped back, dropping her phone.

"Shit, shit, shit," she muttered as she went to her knees. She had to get her phone, couldn't leave it there and run. But once her hand landed on the hard plastic rectangle, she forced herself to take another look at what she'd found and realized it wasn't a human body. It was a dead rodent, caught in a mousetrap. That was what had caused the smell.

She gripped the wall for support. She was glad she hadn't called Sullivan to claim there was a dead body in Dorothy's basement. She could only imagine how embarrassed she would be, not to mention the police, if they believed her and acted on that information.

I'm an idiot, she texted to Gavin.

What's going on?

There's nothing here. We're totally screwed. Gordon's getting out of jail.

At least you tried, Savanna. You did all you could. Now let someone else take any risks that need to be taken. I'm tired of worrying about you. ☺

I'm leaving, she wrote back. I can't stay another second in this creepy basement. There's a dead rat down here.

Gross.

With a frown for her failure, and all it would mean for her and her children, Gordon's prior victims and any future ones, she did a final sweep with her flashlight. There was no need to get caught here on top of everything else, she decided, and was just turning to go when she spotted a mound that didn't look entirely natural. Someone could be buried *there*...

Surely she was wrong again. That pile of rubble was probably where the rats were nesting. If Dorothy wanted to get rid of them, she should also get rid of that, Savanna thought. And then she began to wonder why Dorothy hadn't. There wasn't any debris anywhere else...

Just to be thorough, she found a piece of wood lying nearby and used it to poke through the cast-off Sheetrock, wood chunks, dirt and rocks. *It's nothing*, she told herself, but before she tossed that piece of wood aside, she struck something that felt different—bigger, more solid, less yielding to her probe.

What is that?

She held her flashlight closer. It wasn't a body, but it wasn't simply more debris, either. It was a deep blue backpack.

Why would Dorothy, a woman who never camped and hadn't been to school in decades, have a backpack? And why would it be buried over here in the corner, where it was very unlikely to be seen?

Savanna kept looking over her shoulder as, trying not to breathe for the stench of that rat, she crept closer. She didn't want to touch anything down here, but she was curious enough to make herself unzip the top of the backpack. And she was glad she did.

It contained three high school textbooks and several small notebooks filled with assignments. The name on those assignments was Emma Ventnor.

CHAPTER THIRTY

"What do I do?" Savanna's hand shook as she held her phone. She was still standing in Dorothy's basement, staring at what she'd discovered. But she didn't know whether she should leave the backpack where it was or take it with her. She was afraid that if she carried it off, it wouldn't be admissible in court. She wasn't familiar with the rules of evidence, but she knew, especially after this find, that it was imperative Gordon never go free. They had to do everything right.

Detective Sullivan didn't respond immediately. She got the impression he was thinking. She'd told him everything, sent him the pictures of the car as well as several shots of the backpack and what she'd found inside.

"Can you think a little faster?" she asked when she felt like she couldn't wait another second. "My heart's about to pound out of my chest. I'm breathing in decomposed rat and could be standing on Emma's grave. If her backpack is here, her body might be, too. I don't want to discover that."

"I'm sorry. I've been studying the pictures you sent. Because the department paid for you to come to Utah, a defense lawyer would argue that you were working with us when you entered Dorothy's home."

"That's not good, right?"

"Not for our side. It means the evidence would likely be suppressed. There are a few exceptions to the rules for illegally obtained evidence, but given how you got into the house, I doubt any of those would apply."

Savanna was afraid she might throw up. Closing her eyes, she swallowed hard. "But if I leave the backpack here, will you be able to obtain a search warrant before she gets rid of it?"

"She's not going to get rid of it."

"How can you be sure? I'm shocked she hasn't gotten rid of it before now."

"Anything she throws away is no longer protected by privacy laws. And as far as she knows, we've been watching her closely. Leaving it in the basement means she can retain control of it, make sure it doesn't fall into anyone else's hands. It might've remained there indefinitely if not for you."

"It might be even simpler than that. Maybe she doesn't want to touch it. Maybe she found it there and decided to leave it where it was rather than get involved enough to actually dispose of it. Then she could pretend that what it means is none of her business, that she doesn't have the responsibility to turn in her own son."

"Could be true. If she touches it and we can prove she did, she could be implicated in covering up Gordon's crimes. As things stand now, she could claim she had no idea it was in her basement."

"But she *does* know. That's why she freaked out when I mentioned Emma's name that night at my place in Silver Springs." Someone had to have set the rattraps in the basement. While doing that, Dorothy had probably stumbled across Emma's backpack and then recognized the name when she heard it—not from the news reports, since those had, for the most part, happened a year ago, but from seeing the name on Emma's schoolwork, just as Savanna had. Perhaps she hadn't been certain what it signified at first, which was why she'd left it where it was. But then Savanna had told her what'd happened to Emma Ventnor, and she'd realized where that backpack had come from and the role the accident had played in a young girl's kidnapping. So she'd done what she could to cover the damage on her car—since there'd be no way to prove she'd crashed into Gavin's truck to destroy evidence. She'd also removed her hide-a-key from outside. She wasn't concerned with theft, wasn't careful in general. Why else would she bother?

"But you said you need probable cause to get a search warrant," she said. "Without this backpack, we don't have anything we didn't have before."

"Yes, we do. Thanks to you, we have the Celica."

Unable to tolerate the stench any longer, Savanna zipped the backpack and edged away, to where she could stand at her full height. She was reluctant to go any farther, though. She hated to leave what she'd found because of what it meant. Gordon was guilty. He knew where Emma was, whether she was alive. How could she walk away and leave such proof behind?

And yet the detective was telling her she had to do exactly that.

"You think the Celica's enough?" She needed more reassurance after all she'd done.

"You told me Gavin's truck is blue, didn't you?"

"It is…"

"Well, when I magnify the close-up you took of the damage on Dorothy's car, I think I see a few tiny bits of white."

"Emma's car was white."

"Yes."

"So…you *think* you see that or you *do*?"

"There's no way to be certain. But the fact that it could be there, and you say the car was damaged about the time Emma went missing, might be enough to make an impact on the judge."

"Who will, hopefully, sign off on the search warrant."

"Yes."

"But I took those pictures in Dorothy's garage. Wouldn't they be considered illegally obtained, too?"

"You said the garage door was open. That means anyone could go in there. But just to be sure, we'll handle it a different way. I know where Dorothy works. I'll go over there and take pictures of the car myself. With any luck, we could be searching her house tomorrow."

"That means I can leave."

"Yes, get out of there while you can," he said, but just before Savanna disconnected and started for the stairs, she heard movement coming from upstairs.

"Oh, my God. She's back," she whispered, and disconnected.

Gavin was eating in his office. Although he still battled a certain amount of guilt for not getting back with Heather whenever he thought about the baby, he was so much happier after making the decision to pursue a relationship with Savanna. Since he'd started seeing her, he'd been joining his mother and brother in the cafeteria for lunch with the students, as usual, but he was too stressed to interact with anyone else today. He was waiting for Savanna to let him know she'd gotten out of Dorothy's house and was on her way to the airport, and couldn't understand why he hadn't heard from her. Was she still on the phone with Sullivan?

He hesitated to keep calling and texting her, just in case. It'd been thirty minutes; they had to be deeply embroiled. But he needed to hear from her.

A knock sounded at the door, interrupting his vigil.

Setting his phone aside, he got up to answer it.

Aiyana stood there, dressed in a colorful skirt and purple

blouse, her black hair hanging straight and long instead of in its characteristic braid. "You're not having lunch with us?" she asked.

"Not today."

"Is everything okay?"

"Of course," he replied, but she gave him that look that let him know she wasn't buying it, and he sighed.

"I'm concerned about Savanna."

"Why would you be concerned? You told me she flew to Utah for a couple of days to deal with some business regarding her ex-husband. Don't tell me he's abusive or something else that would put her in danger..."

He stretched his neck to ease the tension knotting his muscles. "It's...complicated."

She lifted her eyebrows. "What's going on?"

Gavin knew, considering what his relationship with Savanna had become, that he could tell his family about Gordon. It wasn't as if Savanna expected that to remain a secret indefinitely. He just hadn't done it yet. They'd both been too focused on getting through her trip to Utah. "Are you sure you have time for such a long story?"

"I'll make time," she replied.

He beckoned her inside. "Then have a seat."

Savanna hadn't closed the door to the basement. She hadn't been able to bring herself to do that, not with how difficult it'd been to open in the first place. She was afraid she'd get stuck down there, hadn't wanted to feel as though she was cutting herself off from her only avenue of retreat. But the instant Dorothy saw that door hanging wide at the top of the stairs, she'd know something was up. It'd been closed tighter than a drum when Savanna arrived. Not to mention the light was on.

Savanna covered her mouth as she listened to the footfalls above her. The window in Dorothy's bedroom could also give her away. It was open wider than it had been before, and the screen was bent back. Good thing she'd taken the time to leave everything else as it had been. Otherwise, she'd have *no* hope of going undiscovered.

Why wasn't Dorothy at work? Had she gotten sick? Was she home for the day? Or had she just returned to get something she'd forgotten—or maybe lunch?

Regardless, the entrance to the basement was too centrally located for her to miss that giveaway door. Chances were she would've seen it already, except her phone had gone off almost as soon as she arrived at the house. Savanna could hear her talking from what sounded like the living room.

As soon as she came through to the kitchen, it would all be over...

Although her first inclination was to hide, Savanna forced herself to climb the noisy stairs. She could only rely on that phone conversation to keep Dorothy preoccupied. Savanna *had* to get to that door, had to close it, or who could say what would happen. At a minimum, the backpack evidence would be spoiled. Dorothy would try to get rid of it, and without Emma's schoolwork, Gordon would very likely go free. Savanna had little confidence in the "bits of white" Sullivan claimed to see in the Celica pictures, since she hadn't seen any of that herself. She had a feeling he was stretching the truth in order to get a search warrant.

"I told you, I have nothing to say to you... No, you need to leave me alone... That's ridiculous! You can't force me to testify against my own son!"

Dorothy was talking to Sullivan, Savanna realized. As soon as they'd hung up, he'd called Dorothy, was purposely hassling her in an attempt to create a diversion.

Savanna quickly weighed the chances of sneaking out the back. Would she make it?

She didn't see much hope. The house was too small. Dorothy would hear her or see her, especially if she had any trouble with the lock on the back door. And she could tell the conversation wasn't going to last but a few more seconds. Dorothy was adamant about not talking to the police. All Savanna could do was remain in the basement, pull the door closed, turn off the light and pray Dorothy wasn't home for the day. Otherwise, Savanna would have quite a wait before she could get out of the house.

The door didn't want to close all the way, not without a great deal of pressure, and Savanna didn't dare pull it that hard.

She closed it as well as she could without making a lot of noise and waited.

Sure enough, Dorothy hung up almost immediately. "Bastard," she muttered as she came into the kitchen.

Since Dorothy was right on the other side of the basement door, Savanna could hear her rummaging around in the drawers and cupboards and possibly the fridge.

"You won't get anything out of me," Dorothy added as if she was still talking to Sullivan.

Taking measured breaths to control her fear, Savanna clung to the knob of the basement door, in case Dorothy spotted that irregularity and tried to open it. Holding it wouldn't keep her from being discovered, but it might save her from being shoved down the stairs. She wasn't in the best position to protect herself should Dorothy get physical.

Don't look this way. Finish what you're doing and go.

Dorothy's phone rang again. "You can't harass me like this," she told the caller, which made Savanna guess that it was, once again, Sullivan, trying to help.

"No, I won't meet you for coffee... What? I've never shoplifted in my life! I don't care what you've got on video. That has to be someone else."

There was a long pause while she was, presumably, listening to Sullivan make a case for meeting him.

"I'm telling you that wasn't me."

They argued a bit more. Finally, Sullivan must've prevailed, because after she hung up, Dorothy swore a blue streak and went out the front.

Savanna listened carefully to see if Dorothy might return. She couldn't hear any evidence of that, but she forced herself to wait five minutes before charging out of the basement. To close the door tightly behind her, she had to use her shoulder like a battering ram, but as soon as she accomplished that, she let herself out the back, retrieved the duct tape from the garage and fixed the screen on Dorothy's bedroom window so that the damage could not be seen from inside the house.

Once she finally reached her rental car, she sent a text to Sullivan. Thank you. I'm out.

Great. I'll let Dorothy know that it won't be necessary for her to drive down to meet me, after all.

Savanna couldn't help chuckling at what he'd written. You told her you had her on video, shoplifting?

Yeah. But now that I've taken a closer look, I can see it isn't her. ☺

"She's okay?" Aiyana asked.

Gavin glanced up from the text that had interrupted their conversation. "Yes. Thank God. She's on her way to the airport."

"What took her so long to let you know?"

"She hasn't said." What happened? he wrote to Savanna.

I'll have to tell you when I get home. I'd rather not do it over the phone.

Is everything okay?

With any luck, everything will be better than okay. I'll let you know what time to pick me up as soon as I make the arrangements for my new flight. I can't wait to see you. XOXO

I'll be waiting.

He drew a deep breath as he set his phone aside. "Sounds like whatever happened was good," he told his mother.

It took Sullivan until Friday to get the search warrant. Waiting for that to come through, and waiting for what the search of Dorothy's house would reveal, made Savanna almost as nervous as when she'd been snooping around that house herself—and nearly been caught. She kept thinking that maybe Dorothy had realized someone had been in her house, that she'd seen the tape on the screen and disposed of Emma's backpack, so they'd wind up with nothing to tie Gordon to Emma's disappearance, after all.

But that didn't turn out to be the case. When Gavin was at work, and Branson and Alia were playing in the kiddie pool they liked so much, Savanna received the call from Sullivan that she'd been waiting for.

She answered on the first ring. "Tell me you found what you needed."

"We have the backpack," he said.

"What about... What about any remains?"

"No. Nothing like that."

That last part wasn't good news, but Savanna's relief was still so profound it almost robbed her of strength. She'd been thrown into what felt like an alternate reality ever since Gordon had first become a suspect in those rape cases. It'd been only a few months, but it seemed like years. So much had changed. And now the worst was over. Gordon wouldn't be able to hurt her or anyone else again. His lawyer, the public defender in whom he placed so little trust, would have a hard time explaining how Emma Ventnor's backpack wound up in Dorothy Gray's basement. So even if the backpack didn't contain any DNA evidence—which, of course, they hoped it did—Gordon would be charged with Emma's abduction if not her murder. "He won't be able to get past this," she said.

"No," Sullivan confirmed. "Detective March stayed up all night viewing the same video footage she'd been over before, when she was looking for the wrong vehicle. This time, she found two different shots of Dorothy's car—before it was damaged on the front. Between the backpack, Gordon's lack of an alibi, proof of an accident and his proximity to where Emma was taken, we'll have a good case."

"What about the white paint on the Celica? Will that help?"

"If it's there. We'll get everything we can, make sure he goes away for a long, long time. But the backpack is insurmountable. From the beginning, he's claimed that he's never seen Emma Ventnor before in his life, never heard of her except on the news. This proves otherwise. And now that we could charge his mother with obstruction of justice for wrecking into Gavin's truck to cover up the previous damage on her vehicle, and hiding Emma's backpack in her basement, we might finally get some cooperation from her. Depending on what she knows, it's even possible we'll recover Emma's body."

"Then you believe Emma's dead."

"Don't you?"

Savanna hated to admit it, but where else could the girl be?

"At least, because of you, Gordon won't be able to hurt anyone else," he said.

It was the first time Sullivan had ever attempted to make her feel better about anything. "Whoa! Are *you* trying to console *me*?"

There was a brief silence. Then he said, "I owe you an apology, Savanna. You're not the type of woman I thought you were in the beginning. I didn't treat you right."

"I understand why. Cops can get a bit jaded, I guess."

"Sadly, that's true. I still feel bad, but... I can't believe you were ever married to a man like Gordon."

She backed up so the kids wouldn't get her wet with all their splashing and running with the hose. "I almost can't believe it myself. I'm glad that's no longer the case. I'm much happier now."

"I hope you stay that way."

"Thank you," she said, and disconnected so that she could call and give Gavin the good news.

EPILOGUE

Eight months later...

Gavin had his hand at the small of Savanna's back as the hostess guided them through Costantini's, the nicest restaurant in Silver Springs. They'd left Branson and Alia with Aiyana so that they could have a night out together, and he'd made reservations for the outdoor patio, with its bubbling fountain and myriad blooming plants.

"I love this place," Savanna murmured.

"I know. That's why we're here," he teased. It was also the perfect place to celebrate all the wonderful things that'd happened. Last week, a hiker had found Emma Ventnor's remains in a gulley, covered with brush, only twenty minutes outside of Nephi. Now that the police could prove Emma was dead, Gordon would be charged with first-degree murder in addition to kidnapping, and probably be sentenced to life. After months and months of preparation, his trial was coming up soon. But Savanna wouldn't be required to testify. She was glad for that and glad they hadn't heard from him or his mother since her visit. Gordon hadn't even written to the kids.

"Considering all this, you must have something to tell me," Savanna said after they were seated and the waitress had delivered their water.

"I do," he admitted.

Although it was subtle, he could see the slight tensing that resulted from his announcement. "Does it have to do with Heather's baby?"

"It does." Now that Heather's baby had been born, they'd been waiting for the results of the paternity test.

She reached out to grab his hand as if she needed it for support. "Tell me."

"Little Bella Marie belongs to Scott."

Her jaw dropped as she let go of him to press her hand to her chest. "You're kidding…"

"No. It was conclusive."

She briefly closed her eyes. "I would've done everything I could to support you in that relationship. I hope you know that. But I'm not going to lie. This will be easier."

He laughed. "It'll be easier for me, too. Heather was so bitter throughout the pregnancy."

"She must feel like a fool now, poor thing."

"If she did what Scott emphatically claims, she got herself into what she's facing and doesn't deserve any sympathy."

"What do *you* think?" she asked. "Did Heather *try* to get pregnant?"

"I'd hate to believe she did. But I have to acknowledge the possibility. I'm just glad it didn't work, that my heart wouldn't let me take that wrong turn."

"Me, too," she said. "But I worry for the baby. Scott's still so angry. I don't see him being much of a father."

"Frankly, I don't, either. I feel bad about that, too. But I'm hoping little Bella will steal his heart."

"Children have a tendency to do that," she said.

"Your children have stolen my heart, haven't they?"

"You've also stolen theirs," she said with a laugh. "They worship you. So...are we going to sell our houses and move to Nashville?"

"You'd be willing?"

"Of course. You're so gifted. If moving to Nashville is what it takes, I say we pack up tonight."

He brought her hand to his mouth so he could kiss the back of it. "But it's so nice here. Your house is looking awesome, thanks to me," he added with a grin. "The kids are in school and happy—I can't remember the last time Branson wet the bed. Everyone is doing so well."

"We'll do well in Nashville, too," she insisted. "You and your aspirations are important. You deserve to have what you want."

He smiled at her.

"What?" she said.

"I want to stay. As far as I'm concerned, we're right where we belong."

Her eyes widened. "What about your music career?"

"I'll do what I can with it from here, see where it goes. But I'm not one of those people who has to achieve success in the entertainment industry at all costs. I'm happy in a bone-deep way. Especially now that I have you and the kids. How many people can say that?"

"Not many," she agreed thoughtfully.

"There's just one more thing I really need..."

"What's that?" she asked.

He pulled out the engagement ring he'd been carrying around in his pocket all day and got down on one knee. "Will you marry me?"

* * * * *